SAINT ELSPETH

WICK WELKER

ALSO BY WICK WELKER

Needle Work

Medora

The Medora Wars

Refraction

Dark Law Series

Dark Theory

Saint Elspeth

By Wick Welker

Published by Wick Welker

PO Box 7235 Rochester, MN 55903

Cover art by Damonza

To Mom and Dad. Thank you for giving me the gift of loving books.

SAINT ELSPETH

ONE

"ELSPETH, they wouldn't come here to just do nothing," Clive said, rubbing my belly. When the visitors appeared, strung in the sky like pinecones along a branch, I was still pregnant. My baby kicked a fitful stir as if reserving center-stage seats for the tableau in the heavens. I was going to name him Gabriel. The biblical happenings outside our window seemed fitting for the birth of my angel.

And angels were what we would need.

They descended from the heavens—irregularly shaped ovoids like oversized zeppelins, but they lacked the metallic sheen that science fiction primed us to expect. With a fuzzy border silhouetted against the sky, they were covered in an organic rind like peach skin. Aflame from atmospheric friction, everyone thought they would incinerate—smoldering to raining ash, never to reveal why they'd come. But after the pods lit in celestial conflagration, they glazed with a hardened shell like pottery fresh from the kiln. When they landed—having cleaved into thousands of clusters across the globe—we thought they'd open. Whether the pods

1

revealed intergalactic paratroopers or pacifist monks was anyone's guess, but certainly they would hatch.

But then nothing happened.

Millions of streaming videos appeared as a still frame—the bulbous pods of varying size motionless for days... and then for weeks... and then for months. From pundits to the religiously fervent, speculation wheeled around the news cycle. The visitors were from God, the demons were from hell—the invaders were proof that neither existed. Day after day, it would seem the pods were happy to take root and leave us all alone in blissful quiescence.

"So, why did they come?" I asked Clive, feeling his hand on my belly.

"They're either waiting for something or..."

"Or what?" I asked.

"They're afraid of something."

"Elspeth—I mean, Doctor Darrow?"

I flinch and push an IV needle too far under the skin of a patient who yelps and slaps my hand away. "Please don't sneak up like that," I tell my medical student, Ward, as I tape off the blown vein in the patient's hand. "What is it?"

"It's the new patient from Nevada. He looks bad." Ward adjusts his glasses, one of the lenses with a crack down the middle.

"You can't find another pair of glasses?" I ask.

"I riffled through a box at the wharf last week. All the lenses are too weak."

"Prasad should be getting a new salvage shipment soon that you can rummage through. What's wrong with the new patient?"

"I don't know, but he doesn't look good."

"I'm sorry for the blown IV," I tell the patient with a displeased scowl on his face. "I'll be back soon."

I move past patient beds, Ward in tow. Using old-world hospitals stopped making sense long ago. The enormous buildings and segregated rooms were impossible to manage with no maintenance staff and a skeletonized nursing crew. When San Francisco was re-colonized almost twenty years ago, transforming the entire east wing of city hall into our hospital made the most practical sense. We put a clinic near the lobby, and all patients without air-borne infections into the spacious catacombs of the basement. The air remained cool on hot days, and it was more efficient to heat one ward of patients rather than individual rooms. The fact that it was one of few major buildings in Neo SF whose plumbing hadn't corroded was also a bonus.

"Does the patient have a fever?" I ask Ward.

"Yes. Are you worried?"

"I'm never not."

We find the man in a gurney. The metal struts of the bed have eroded through the original mattress, requiring reinforcement with hay and threadbare wool. The patient is motionless, a wreath of sweat soaking the sheets. His belly protrudes from a shriveled body like he's in the third trimester. Jaundiced skin and blood-stained lips tell me part of the story. The fever, high heart rate, and low blood pressure tell me the rest.

"Why didn't you tell me about this patient sooner?" I ask Ward, biting back my annoyance.

"You were too busy arguing with Mayor Hutch."

"I wasn't too busy for this man."

"What's wrong with him?" he asks.

"What do *you* think is wrong with him?"

Ward squints at the patient as if trying to discern a fly on the horizon. He taps his fingers along a clipboard, studying the patient's vitals the nurse had recorded in pencil. "He's yellow."

"Your diagnosis is that he's yellow?"

Ward's arms tremble as he crosses them. I've never been certain about training him. An odd young man, really—squirreling away to his apartment across the city hall plaza every night where he lives alone. Jumping from one foster home to the next, your entire childhood isn't exactly conducive to good mental health. I have no idea why he volunteered to become my medical student and otherwise would have chosen someone else had a single other person stepped forward.

Ward chews his lip, stalling.

I point to the patient. "The patient is jaundiced. Now look at his abdomen. What's going on?"

"It's big."

"Why would a man with yellow skin have a belly that looks like that? Look closer at the skin," I say, pointing at a series of serpentine and engorged veins flanking the patient's belly button. "Do you remember what those are called?"

"No," he says, dropping his eyes in shame.

"You should be studying this. Like Medusa's hair of snakes, the patient's veins bulge from the backflow of a liver that has scarred down. The scarring of the liver causes failure in key metabolic and excretion pathways. Lactate rises, making the blood more acidic—are you listening?"

He watches my lips as if hearing a foreign language. "Yes. So, what do we do?"

I sigh deeply. It's a question whose only answer is tragedy. Twenty years ago, a doctor would've ordered a battery of blood tests, tapped fluid from his belly with a needle, started broad-spectrum antibiotics, transfused blood, and put him on a liver trans-

4

plant list. Now, there is no blood bank, no chemistry lab—no surgeons to put in a new liver.

Ward notices my brooding and asks, "What *can* we do?"

"It has been a long time since I've treated someone with such advanced liver cirrhosis," I whisper only to Ward. "Most do not survive long enough to even come into our little hospital. He must've contracted viral hepatitis or a drinking problem within the last couple of years—his symptoms only manifesting now." I look back at the patient, his sunken gaze pinned on us before retching up a spoonful of blood.

"Help me, please," the man says, lips quivering beneath beads of sweat.

I move toward the patient's bed. I want to take his hand. I want to tell him everything will be alright. But I can't do it, not only because it would be a lie, but because I don't have the emotional fortitude to break my heart over and over again for every dying patient that comes to my door. "Give him fluid and antibiotics," I tell Ward, stepping back from the bed.

"What kind?"

"Vancomycin and meropenem."

Ward falls silent.

"What?" I ask.

"We only have one vial of meropenem powder left. Five years expired."

"We've run out of that, too? When was the last time you did inventory?"

"Last week," he says with a grimace.

"Why didn't you tell me about the shortage? Mix up the antibiotics and give it. If he vomits blood, come and get me immediately. We may have to place a breathing tube."

"Okay." His eyes roll to the ceiling.

"And yes, that would mean you have to be on hand ventilation duty for six-hour shifts at a time. We only have so many nurses, and only one respiratory therapist, to take turns." I walk away.

"Where can I find you?"

"West wing. I'll be having a chat with our mayor."

When I arrive at his office, Mayor Jack Hutch is at the tail end of a conversation with several men I recognize from his scouting parties. Seated around a glossy table with the seal of the State of California burned across the top, the men wear grim expressions. The mayor's wicker hat sits upside down on the table as he wipes his brow and nods as if considering the men's words. They cut their hushed conversation when I knock on the door frame. Hutch puts his hat back on as if it conceals the truncated conversation and says, "Doctor Darrow, what can I do for you right at this moment?"

"I'd like to talk about supplies."

The crow's feet around his eyes wrinkle with his confusion. "What supplies?"

"For the hospital." The men from the scouting party share a furtive glance—Reece, the mayor's twenty-year-old son with enough red hair to call a mane, in particular.

"I think that can wait," Mayor Hutch says with a dismissive wave.

"I think not. I have a patient who will die of sepsis if I don't have more antibiotics soon. We need various medications—could use more IV kits, saline, chest tubes, other surgical supplies—"

The mayor puts up his hand and then motions to the men. "Boys, let's table this discussion. I need these things to marinate in my mind till this afternoon. I can also oblige our good doctor here and put her concerns at ease."

6

The men vacate as I take a seat, a strange unease in their silence. "What was your meeting about?" I ask Hutch.

"Nothing."

"Didn't seem like nothing."

He locks his gaze with mine. "Elspeth, what can I do for you?"

"We need medical supplies. It's been two years since I took a scavenging party, and I'd like to lead another one soon. This week, if we can."

"I can't devote men and gasoline to that right now."

"I'll go alone. I can kayak."

"And who will run your hospital?" he asks.

"It's *our* hospital—the colony's." I bristle, preparing to renew dormant arguments with the man.

"Who will run our hospital while you're gone off to—"

"San Jose."

His face darkens.

"I've long since cleaned out usable supplies from Oakland and Berkley. North in Marin was the first to be scavenged—don't think I'll find much there."

"You can't go to San Jose."

I cross my arms. "Do you know Mavis Ulrich? She's a patient in the east wing right now."

"You know I don't."

"She's an engineer with a staph infection of her leg where rebar ripped through her calf during her travels here. I think the infection has spread to her bloodstream. I've started antibiotics, which have helped, but I only have enough to treat her for another two days. We need more or we could lose an engineer, someone who can do a lot of good for the colony."

He breaks eye contact with me, absorbing the information.

"I have another patient—a farmer from Utah. He traveled west after the sandstorms cleaned out his colony there and left the ground inhospitable. He's ready to revamp our rooftop farming program but is laid up with a heart failure exacerbation. I'm almost out of diuretics. That's all he needs to get out of bed and start working—"

"I get it."

"Then I will set out tomorrow for San Jose."

"You can't go to San Jose," he repeats, impatience rising in his voice.

"Why not?"

"The meeting, just now—with Reece and the other scouts. They just came up from the south end of the Bay..."

"And?"

The mayor narrows his eyes. "They saw one."

"They saw one *what*?"

"A Hilaman."

"Bullshit. Not one of those scouts has ever seen one in their lives. I'm almost old enough to be their grandmother and I've never seen one."

"We believe they've had a colony around Monterey since before the wars," he says.

"And you think they're migrating?"

"Yes."

The thought does spill a thimble full of panic in me, which I extinguish. "No one knows why the Hilamen came in the first place."

"Don't be naive. Never mattered why the Hila came—only mattered what happened when they showed up and broke the damn world."

We share silence for a moment—knowing we are two of a minority of people in our colony old enough to remember when the Hilamen were in the sky. Windows of the past open in my mind. My husband, Clive, holding my chin in his hand, saying words I don't want to remember before leaving me to fight wars he knew nothing about. For twenty years, I wanted to find a Hila and ask them a single question: *why did you come?*

"They aren't responsible for what the world did to itself," I say, trying to convince myself more than Hutch.

The mayor refuses my gaze, too tired to delve into a decade-old argument about a world that no longer exists. "The Hilamen are migrating north—they're probably running out of resources—"

"What resources? We don't even know what they eat, what they farm, their social units, if they're nomadic—"

"Elspeth."

"What?"

"You're not going to San Jose."

Minutes later, I find Ward standing at the foot of the bed of our patient who is spitting globs of blood into a handkerchief. The man's chest heaves deeply—neck muscles drawn tight like ropes on a ship's mast to aid with every breath. His head swings pendulously around the neck—eyes twisting wildly trying to focus, grasping to understand the world through a dying body.

"He's delirious," I tell Ward. "The toxic metabolites that the liver can't process are going to his brain, confusing him. He doesn't know where he is anymore."

"Do you think we gave antibiotics in time?" Ward asks.

"He has other problems—"

And then it's like someone pulls a drain plug at the back of the man's throat. Blood flows from his mouth, cascades over his chin, and runs down his chest in layers of clot and stomach sediment. The man heaves, and with each retching, brings a new deluge of blood.

"Airway equipment!" I yell. "He's going to aspirate all that blood. Go!" I call for Nurse Max who gasps as he enters the room. "Max, go and get three bags of saline. Hook them up and open them free flowing to the patient. He's losing a lot of blood and needs volume replacement." I would call for a blood transfusion, but there is no blood bank—there are no blood donors. I move to the head of the bed and try to put an oxygen mask over the patient's mouth but he fights me off. Once Max returns with the saline, he holds the patient's arms down while I force air into his mouth. I worry about how much oxygen is left in the tank, how many tanks we have left, and where we will get more for other patients. I suppress past arguments I had with Mayor Hutch about refurbishing an oxygen condenser. "Someone go and get Tara from respiratory."

Ward returns with a backpack I'd packed for airway emergencies. "Take out a laryngoscope and an endotracheal tube," I tell him. "Draw up a paralytic." But Ward just stands there, frozen, and drops the backpack at his feet. "Ward, do it!"

His voice quivers. "I can't."

With panicked breath, I take the bag from him and rip it open, spilling its contents all over the ground. Armed with a breathing tube and a dull metal blade, I return to the head of the bed. "Max, give the paralytic." The nurse sifts through the vials of medications and finds the brightly labeled, red-top vial and reconstitutes the powder. The patient vomits more blood, filling the oxygen mask. I dump the mask of the blood and bring it once again to the patient's mouth. Another cough, another mouthful of blood. Through the chaos, I think that I shouldn't be here—standing with a breathing tube in hand. No, I wasn't supposed to do any of this.

I was once a nerdy pathologist who didn't have to talk to people.

I looked at thinly sliced tissue specimens under a microscope and called surgeons to tell them if they had clean cancer margins. I stained pancreatic tissue with dyes, lighting up a spectrum of biochemical processes to expose cancer cells. I did autopsies and post-mortem diagnosis and got off at five p.m. to have dinner with Clive on our couch while he rubbed my belly and talked about what kind of car we'd get our baby when he turned sixteen. I wasn't supposed to be the only doctor in post-apocalyptic San Francisco trying to save a man's life who no longer had any business being alive.

The paralyzing medication is in—the man's body collapses in the gurney. I'd only intubated a few hundred patients—only having read about the technique in medical textbooks. I open the man's jaw and advance the intubating blade, which illuminates the man's throat like a miner in a coal shaft.

There is nothing but blood.

I suction but can't keep up with the bleeding. Advancing the breathing tube through the blood would be a blind guess—would it go into the trachea or the esophagus? And if I do get it into his airway, then what? I only have so much oxygen to offer the man. And even if I have an infinite supply of oxygen, there are limited antibiotics, no blood transfusion, no way to stop the bleeding. And even if I have an unlimited supply of these resources, I'm still ignoring the dreaded fact that I have no new liver for him.

"Doctor Darrow, what's wrong?" Max asks, noticing my hesitation.

"Nothing." I close the man's mouth, bring my shaking fingers to the patient's carotid artery and feel a pulse snaking through the vessel. His heartbeat rages against the hypoxic blood in his body—and then tapers. Then ceases.

"5:03 p.m.," I say to Ward's confusion. "Time of death."

TWO

THE NEXT DAY, I sneeze while doing inventory in the dusty basement. When we first re-colonized San Francisco twenty years prior, I'd had metal shelving brought into the east wing basement and stocked with the salvage we'd taken from area hospitals. I'd arranged neat rows with appropriate labels—surgical supplies, airway instruments, intravenous access, central line kits, and wound care. We also made a new pharmacy in the library, placing pills and infusions where dusty books were once shelved. It had taken a full year to be fully organized and stocked. Since then, I performed yearly inventory and made note of deficits and would then commission a salvage team from the mayor. This was a task I'd taken on mostly by myself with aid from the nurses. One month prior, I showed Ward the inventory, took a cursory stock, and told him to complete the rest. Not only has Ward left the task incomplete...

But some supplies have nearly halved.

The day shift nurses chat while sipping coffee. "Max, what happened?" I ask.

He takes the tin cup from his lip. "Many things. You'll need to specify."

"The supply room. I don't remember using so much stuff last month. What happened to it all?"

He shares a look with the rest of the nurses. "I knew we should've checked with you first."

"Checked with me about what?"

"Didn't I tell you that we should've checked with Doctor Darrow first?" Max says to the rest of the nurses.

"Checked with me *about what?*" I say, temper flaring.

"Mayor's son, Reece, was here last week. Said he had orders from the mayor to get supplies for scouting crews."

I stamp my foot. "Reece came to the east wing and no one told me?"

The nurses divert their eyes and scatter. Max begins his apologies—that it was a busy day and that I was operating on someone's appendix.

"I get it," I tell him, remembering the child's appendix that had ruptured, seeding infection all over his abdomen. It had taken me fifteen appendectomies to get through the operation without a complication. It would have taken an experienced surgeon fifteen minutes, but for me, four hours, even after studying water-stained textbooks for months. "I'll take care of it." The last group of people in the colony that I ever want to upset is the nursing staff. Without them, there is no hospital.

"Would you like to round on our patients?" he asks.

"Where's my medical student? He was supposed to help me with inventory."

"Haven't seen him."

"Let's just get started," I say after Nadine, our one and only pharmacist, joins us with a cup of coffee in hand. Her disheveled hair and baggy eyes look exactly how I feel. We start at Mavis

Ulrich, an engineer with a staph infection of her calf. I remove the packing from the wound, exposing fresh pus that pools within the margins of the ruptured skin. As I express the infected tissue from the wound, the woman howls with pain and writhes in bed, grasping at bed sheets. She cries wildly about men with guns hunting her in alleyways.

"Probably delirium from the bacteria spreading to the bloodstream," I say. "Max, bring me some irrigation." A kidney-shaped basin with a fresh bottle of distilled water is handed to me, which I use to flush the wound. After two liters of irrigating, I see red streaks questing beyond the wound, infiltrating the healthy tissue above.

"What?" Max asks as I remain motionless.

"Flesh-eating bacteria. Nadine, how much longer can we treat her infection with antibiotics?"

The pharmacist looks at her clipboard. "This is her last day to receive antibiotics." Years ago, we decided that each patient with a bacterial infection would get a maximum allotment of treatment regardless of inventory supply—seven days. If they don't improve, we stop treatment to conserve antibiotics for other patients that could potentially fare better.

"Max, book this patient in the OR in an hour. I'll have to clean the wound or she'll die." I ask Nadine, "Sedatives and analgesia?"

"Yeah," she says with the enthusiasm of my absent medical student.

Our next patient is a fifteen-year-old boy named Jonas, who suffered a gunshot wound to the thigh a week prior. The boy had been exploring Golden Gate Park—outside the secured walls of the colony. He was shot and robbed by raiders and crawled his way back to the gates of Neo SF. Like most other patients in the east wing, he has a bloodstream infection.

I ask Nadine, "How many days of antibiotics does he have allotted?"

The pharmacist grimaces when she looks at the clipboard. "This is also his last day."

"Looks like he's almost cleared the infection."

"Maybe. Want to extend antibiotic therapy to make sure?"

"Do you even have enough antibiotic supply to do that?"

"We have enough left for three more days of treatment. That is all that remains in the pharmacy for all patients currently."

The pause between the three of us says everything. I can extend treatment for the boy—an unskilled person who can either push a plow or hold a rifle. Or I can extend treatment for the fifty-something engineer who is lying right next to him and actively dying—a person who could potentially bring electricity to the entire colony. The gap in expertise between the aging old-worlders and the young of the new world is astronomical.

"Dammit, we really need another salvage expedition," I say, clenching my fist. "But the mayor won't consent."

Max scoffs. "Doesn't mean you can't just go on your own."

"True..." I say, looking at the ceiling, crunching numbers in my head about how many days of travel would be ahead of me to San Jose, what supplies I would need, and how much I could haul back on my own.

"What should we do right now?" Nadine asks.

"Stop antibiotics for the boy. Hopefully, he has cleared the infection enough."

I look at Max—the man is grimacing as he extends his back. I ask him, "Still got those pins and needles running down your legs?"

"Getting worse," he says. "How's that hip of yours?"

"About as good as your back," I answer.

"We're too old to be running this place," Max says.

"No argument here."

We visit the newcomer from Utah—a farmer who showed up at Neo SF gates with ankles the size of an elephant's. The man's lungs were so full of congested water from his failing heart that he passed out when we rushed him to the east wing. I'd given him a dose of a loop diuretic to help him pee off the fluid.

"Good morning, Mr. Musala, how are you feeling?" I ask the man while pushing my finger into his shins. My index finger sinks one-third of the way into his puffy flesh. Better than yesterday.

"Much better, Doctor," he says with a low flow of oxygen running in his nose.

"I think we can get you off that oxygen today and out of bed."

The man hesitates.

"I think you're ready. I'd like to hold off on giving you more diuretics." I look at Nadine, who nods her approval.

"Why?" he asks.

"I'm going to be honest. We don't have a lot. I'd like to conserve the medication."

"I will contribute to Neo San Francisco," the patient says. "I will help build. I came to the city once as a little boy—walked along the wharf with my mother. The sky was so pink. I smelled fried dough and all that seafood. All around me were only happy people. Smiling and laughing and running. There were street shows and clapping. It was always a fond memory, but now, after everything, I know that it is the happiest memory of my life. LA and San Diego want to be the new capital, but no, I choose Mayor Hutch and this great city."

"Things have changed since then," I say.

"It is still a great city. You are bringing it back," he said to the rest of the staff, "all of you are helping make it shine again. I will help. I will farm your lands and bring produce to your people. You save your diuretics, Doctor, save them for people who can't get out of bed." The man then throws off his sheets, swings his feet to the floor, and stands.

After stabilizing himself on wobbly knees, I ask him, "Did you see anything in your travels here?"

He takes my hand for support and says, "There is nothing between here and Utah. No colonies. Only radiation, sand, and starvation."

"Did you see anything else?"

"Do you mean... the Hilamen?" he asks.

"Yes."

"Never. They have left us. Gone back to where they came from," he spits. "Took their hellfire and left us to rot, they did. But not here—not in this great city. We will start our nation once more within the walls of this colony. The people of the west are hearing the clarion radio signal of Mayor Hutch. This place can be the new White House." He raises his hands to the ceiling as in a grand gesture to the future he envisages. "Your name, Doctor Darrow, will be a legend amongst our re-founding fathers. And mothers." He adds the last part with a wink.

I let go of his hand. "Take it easy for a few days, Mr. Musala. We'll have plenty of work for you soon enough."

We finish our rounds on the remaining twelve patients in the wards. Most are improving and can potentially leave the east wing in a few days.

"Me and Nadine are ready for you in the operating theater," Nurse Patience informs me.

"Good. We'll be ready to go in fifteen," I tell her as I round the corner out of the wards.

"Where are you off to?" Max asks.

"Going to go and find our medical student."

· · ·

Neo San Francisco is much smaller than the original city limits—a mostly landlocked settlement within the peninsula of the original metropolis. I was among the first of the re-settlers arriving after a five-year incubation in government bomb shelters that had been dug beneath the Sierra Nevada mountains. There were only a few hundred of us who returned. Others went to help resettle the few cities that had been left unscathed from bombings, mostly in California. Many decided to wander their own paths in the post-war world. We had no idea how many cities still stood but there were at least fifteen major cities that had been recolonized with whom we still communicate via radio.

When we returned to San Francisco, city hall was claimed as the new center of the colony. We cleared the government building of new vegetation and all the dust and detritus associated with a city that emergently evacuated amidst fears of imminent nuclear attacks. The Civic Center plaza was then cleared, and Neo SF's first inhabitants settled into the surrounding buildings of the plaza. Resettling was quite simple as the city had never actually suffered any bombings or destruction of any kind.

We just walked in and tidied up the place.

As Neo SF's population grew, so did its attraction to the lawless. Bandits, marauders, and raiders began descending into the settlement, culminating in a bloody skirmish after two years of infarctions. The first mayor commissioned the erection of barriers to protect our budding colony—semi-truck trailers stacked across all open city blocks, thus encircling the settlement in its protective arms. As the colony grew, so did the barrier. Van Ness, the street just west of city hall, formed the backbone on which Neo SF would expand—east, toward the old financial district. We grew along Market Street to the south in a wedge shape as the protected city blocks expanded to accommodate growth, including portions of the wharf. Ever since Mayor

Hutch was elected eight years ago, he broadcasted the same message over the radio—any survivors should come to San Francisco.

It was allegedly in San Francisco that we would rebuild a nation. But also in Los Angeles, according to LA Mayor Carmichael. But also in San Diego, according to Mayor Gustavson down there. All of the current mayors completely ignored the charter that prohibited any colony from declaring itself the capital of California, or even worse, of a Neo United States.

And so, like a crown jewel within an urban jungle, Neo SF slowly grew within a womb of metal and gunfire. Survivors trickled in, and with them, disease and injury came along as companions to humanity. The harbingers of the middle ages had returned as infectious diseases—tuberculosis, malaria, typhoid, neurosyphilis, and the plague. Yet, modern disease had left its mark in the forms of HIV, viral hepatitis, and ever-mutating influenza and coronaviruses. I was a modern-trained doctor thrust back to the dark ages of medicine—no vaccines, no immunotherapy, and a dwindling supply of modern-day, ever-expiring antibiotic powder.

Back before the wars when I was a pathologist, San Francisco had one physician for every one thousand people in the city. Neo SF had grown to more than fifteen thousand. There was only one physician for all those people.

Doctor Elspeth Darrow.

My hip groans as I descend the city hall stairs, looking out over the plaza where groups of denizens congregate around ovens, grills, merchant kiosks, and miniaturized water distilleries that look like large glass swans. The plaza was deemed a communal space where one could either sell wares or share the common cooking implements by donating a small measure of one's game. Chanting, singing, dancing, and festivals were celebrated at the Civic Plaza.

After crossing the plaza and entering an apartment deeply redolent of mildew, I climb the stairs and arrive at a door painted in a myriad of colors—a frame of red wrapped around a smaller frame of blue, which, in turn, frames a yet more vibrant and smaller frame and so forth until it shrinks away in the middle of the door, creating a vertiginous effect on the viewer.

I knock. After no answer, I knock again with an impatient thud. "Ward?" The door creaks open, an eye peering from within. "Why haven't you come to the east wing? Are you ill?"

He opens the door a bit more and shakes his head, brown curls tossing about. "I'm not sick."

"You are needed."

He breathes deeply to stifle a sob I hear at the edge of his voice. "I don't think I can come anymore."

"Can I come in to talk about it with you?" I ask.

I walk in as he turns his back and disappears into the bathroom. Waiting at the Bay windows while the boy composes himself, I notice a painting resting on an easel. Vibrant colored oils have been layered on the canvas—thick, with multiple applications. There are swirls and eddies flowing along the canvas in a seaside abstraction—the sun, an amorphous bleed into the horizon with reds and oranges. At the foot of the easel, stacks of art history books lay—several open as if referenced in an artistic fugue state. Paintbrushes and tubes of paint litter the floor along a canister of paint thinner.

Ward sits on a chair with the wicker long since blown out, simply resting his legs over the wood frame. His high cheekbones and narrow face meet mine with a look of dread.

"You want to quit?" I ask.

"I shouldn't have volunteered to be your student in the first place. If that's quitting... then—"

"You want to quit?"

"Yes," he finally says. "I want to quit."

"Why did you volunteer to be my medical student?"

"Hard to say."

I bristle. "I can't wait here all day. Just tell me why."

"The other men—the mayor's son, Reece, the garrison boys, the scouts—they make fun of me."

"So, you wanted to treat patients because the boys make fun of you?"

Frazzled, he gestures with his hands instead of explaining, and then asks, "You knew my mother?"

"I delivered you."

"You were there when she died?"

"She died in my arms." I take a deep breath, trying to stave off the memory.

He swallows, his face turning pale. "Would she be embarrassed to have a skinny son—can't hunt, can't shoot, can't protect anyone because he's scared shitless all the time?"

"You want to be a doctor because it's some sort of trade-off for not being as manly as the others?"

"Sounds incredibly stupid when you say it like that."

"That's because it *is* incredibly stupid. Doesn't matter how I say it."

"But I can't even be a doctor. You saw me yesterday when that man was bleeding all over the place. I froze—couldn't move. I got in the way and I'm only hurting people. I study but nothing sticks. I hardly know what you're talking about when we round on patients."

I can't argue. The boy has absolutely no aptitude whatsoever and I'm inclined to agree with him and be on my way. But I'm tired and I don't want to waste the last six months of teaching him. Plus, I just want someone else to work instead of me so much. I motion to his painting and say, "Not bad."

He dismisses the compliment with a flick of the wrist. "I do them all the time. Got a stack in the bedroom."

I just look at him.

"What?" he asks.

"Where are you getting all the art supplies? I haven't seen this stuff for sale down at the wharf."

He freezes. "I..."

"Don't lie to me."

"Outside the colony. Old, abandoned art shops," he says.

"How do you get out without the guards seeing you?"

"It's not a fortress. There are ways over the barriers—and under."

"If a raider saw you, they wouldn't think twice about shooting and robbing you. In that order," I say.

Terrific tears begin to swell. "Yeah? So?"

"Ward, you risked your life... to *paint*." I gesture to the painting.

"I know, it's stupid."

"Doesn't seem like something someone who is scared shitless all the time would do."

His back stiffens as he considers my words.

I leave the Bay windows and open the front door. "We have surgery in thirty minutes. If we don't operate, our patient will die."

THREE

CLIVE PUT his cheek to my belly with his knees on the tarmac while I stood and watched a military transport plane take off. During a break in the noise, he got to his feet and took my hands in his. "It's so strange how things can be," he said, unnatural, like he was borrowing words from a movie.

"I'm never going to see you again," I said and then sobbed into the crook of my elbow. He waited and slid his hands up my arms and pulled me into an embrace, his face stubble grating along my cheek. His breathing in my ear matched the cadence of my sobbing and we hung there for an eternity, ready to be cast into bronze statues of lost love.

"You don't know that," he finally said.

"I do. This moment right now is the end of you and me."

"I'll come back to you and our boy."

"So you can watch him grow up playing in nuclear fallout? The world is over."

"Then we'll start a new world."

"I hate the Hilamen. I hate that they came," I said.

"They're here for a reason. Living beings don't travel across space for nothing."

"I know why they came," I said as plane engines revved around us. "To take you away from me."

———

I haven't slept in years.

Like an airborne kite tethered to the earth, my mind doesn't let go of consciousness. Worry has taken root in my brainstem—the primordial anxiety that arose sometime in the lizard era of human evolution has fully resurrected in me. My past haunts me and my present taunts me. I like to think that the daily human tragedy at the east wing of the city hall hospital rolls off my back. But I know that ever since the Hila came and knocked down their doomsday dominoes, I've been worn down like corn flour ground under a pestle ever since.

I can no longer sleep because of the worry, but it's no longer a worry for the present which is already sealed—the story already written. Nor do I worry about my tragic past that the Hila came and stole from me. No, I worry for the world that comes after the relics of pre-war people are finally swept from the earth. I worry that we're on the cusp of reverse human evolution where clinical trials are replaced by witch trials. I fear I am a mere residue on glass—an airbrushed silhouette of a grasping hand reaching from the walls of ancient caves.

We had one chance at civilization.

I'm uncertain we deserve another.

"Patience, more saline," I say after returning from Ward's apartment, the beep of Mavis Ulrich's vitals echoing through the oper-

24

ating room. The nurse dumps distilled saline into a basin that rests beside the patient's leg. "Nadine," I ask the pharmacist who stands at the head of the bed. "How's she doing up there? Is she over-sedated?"

"A little, yes," Tara, our only respiratory therapist, answers for Nadine who bristles a bit. "I'm keeping her airway open with a nasal trumpet. I'll mask her if she goes apneic."

"Good. Ward," I say, grabbing the medical student's hand. "Take the scalpel in one hand and open the skin like I just showed you."

His hand shakes as he reaches for the scalpel. The trembling intensifies as he cuts upward through the skin until the scalpel falls from his grasp. "Again," I tell him. With ginger movements, he makes small nicks in the skin while Mavis, despite sedation, still groans and pulls away. "I'll inject more lidocaine along the path." I puncture the skin with a syringe and deposit more local anesthetic. I tell Patience to hold the leg firmly while Ward continues advancing the blade—but he's too timid. I take the blade from him and fit the bevel under the edge of the skin and open the deeper layer of connective tissue, exposing the muscle. Ward dry-heaves as I bluntly reflect the skin backward, allowing more access to the deeper muscles of the thigh.

"You see?" I say, pointing to the muscle. What were once deep, cherry-colored tissues have mottled into a dusky shade—eroding holes are scattered along the tissue plane. "This is muscle necrosis. The bacteria finds an infection point where the skin has been damaged and then seeds to the muscle. Once there, it spreads along the muscle plane at incredible speeds. The bacteria can eat away at the muscle within hours and patients can lose their limbs. And it doesn't matter how many antibiotics we throw at them—an infection like this must be surgically removed from the tissues." I look at Ward, who is now standing straight up, face pale. "Do you need to vomit?"

He nods.

"Go, but come right back," I say.

He bolts from the operating room—ripping off the surgical mask and gown. After five minutes, I tell Patience to go and find him. He returns but without surgical attire. "It doesn't matter how repulsed and unequipped you feel," I tell him. "This infection is still here—still eating away at this woman's leg. Reality doesn't give a damn that you feel sick. She will die unless we act. You showed up for this operation, so I'm going to teach you everything I know about doing this. This will be one of the most common diseases that will confront you in your career. You need to know every single word I teach you. Do you understand?"

He swallows. "Yes."

"Good. Now, please, scrub back into surgery."

Mavis Ulrich survives the operation only after we'd surgically resected half a calf muscle. I tell Nadine to continue to treat her with broad-spectrum antibiotics despite our limited protocol and shortage. I'd taken the woman to surgery, and I'd be damned before wasting that effort on an engineer simply because we stopped treating the infection. Once we finished rounding in the east wing, bright red hair flashes in the corner of my eye—Reece. Beside him, his father, Mayor Hutch, stands with a performative frown.

"Mr. Mayor, to what do I owe this privilege?" I ask.

"Doctor Darrow. A word," he says, removing his wicker hat and holding it over his rotund belly.

"I have several for you as well," I bite back at him. "Come to my office." I direct the men to sit while I lean back in my chair, tufts of old-world cotton peeking through the torn upholstery. "Why did you steal medical supplies?" I ask, my anger boiling just beneath the question.

The two men are shocked for a moment until the realization sets in. "We didn't *steal* anything," Reece says with a pugnacious pucker across his face.

"Over half of our wound care and surgical supplies were taken without my knowledge or permission," I say.

Reece opens his mouth to retort, but the mayor squeezes his arm. "My apologies for not going through the proper channels when we acquisitioned the supplies for our scouts."

"I need to know everything that happens in this hospital. Lives depend on information."

Mayor Hutch nods in eager agreement. "It was an oversight by my son. I told him to come and quickly get supplies—and expressly instructed him to inform you of the need for our scouts in the field." He then looks at Reece, who nods in submission like a trained animal.

"Why do your scouts need those supplies?" I ask while trying to figure out which parts of the mayor's account are fiction.

Hutch waves his hand. "Only precautions. I've set up new watchtowers south of the city—along the Bay. I wanted them equipped with emergency medical supplies in case of injury."

"And do any of your scouts know how to use these supplies?"

"Yes."

"Who?"

Hutch crosses his arms. "Several have basic emergency wound care training."

"Trained by whom? I wasn't involved," I say.

"You may be the only physician in the colony now, but you're not the only one who is medically trained. We have old-world paramedics, police, firefighters—all people with a background in basic life support."

"And why aren't they working in the east wing with me?" I ask.

"I—Elspeth, I didn't come here to talk about this."

"I know. *I'm* talking about this."

He sighs. "I met with my council last night and we would like some changes in policy here in the east wing hospital."

I lean back in my chair. "A council that happened without my invitation? Please, go on."

"We understand there are certain protocols in place here that ration treatment for patients. Correct?"

"There is a hard stop when treating with antibiotics. We give any person seven days. If they don't improve, we withdraw to conserve the medications for others who may do better."

"Except treatment can be extended with your written permission?" He licks his lips like he's waiting to pounce with his point.

"Correct," I say.

"Like you did for the engineer," he says, flipping through some papers on his clipboard. "A Mavis Ulrich?"

"I see you've been busy interrogating my staff."

"Hardly an interrogation. Simply fact-finding," Reece interrupts. "It is in this colony's interest what goes on in the east wing of our city hall."

I look at Hutch. "I can give you weekly reports at the council —I'd, of course, have to be invited first."

The mayor looks out the window appearing exasperated at having to deal with me. "Doctor Darrow, did you withdraw antibiotics for a fifteen-year-old boy?"

"Yes."

"Why?"

I clear my throat. "He finished a seven-day course of antibiotics and improved enough that I felt confident to stop the antibiotics and reserve them."

Reece butts in and says, "And you don't think that is too much authority for one woman? Shouldn't more people be involved in that decision-making?"

I ignore the young man again. "Mayor Hutch, I'm grateful you've taken such an active interest in the east wing lately. I'd like to remind you that I petitioned you just days ago for a salvage team to San Jose to replenish our medical supplies and pharmacy —a petition that was outright rejected. I'd also like to remind you that this rationing may not be necessary if we made salvage trips a routine."

Reece stands, his face the picture of disgust. "And you think more supplies would've helped you save my *mother*?"

This time, Hutch does nothing to pacify the outburst from his son. I'd wondered for years if the mayor had blamed me for her death. Now, I no longer wonder. "Jack, I'm sorry for what happened to Grace, truly. Her death couldn't have been prevented. She had metastatic breast cancer—there was nothing to be done."

"Of course," Hutch finally says, his face flooding with something resembling diplomacy. "Reece, sit down." His son reluctantly takes a seat. "The council would like you to extend treatment for any young men fifteen years or older."

"And why?" I ask.

"We need men." He thumps his plump fist on the table.

"And you think a fifteen-year-old is a man?"

"As of right now, yes."

"Do you also need engineers?" I ask.

"We need men, Elspeth."

"So you can do what? Build an army?"

"Reserves. We must be prepared."

"Prepared for what?" I ask. "Have you spoken with that farmer from Utah? He said he hasn't seen a Hilaman in over ten years—didn't see anything on his way over to California."

Hutch nods. "I spoke to him, yes."

"And?"

"We believe they are out there."

"And what if they are?"

The two stand, having delivered their message. Hutch rests his hand on my desk as if intentionally drawing my eye to the golden wedding band of his dead wife. "There are more threats to this colony than just the Hilamen."

I narrow my eyes on him. "I will treat and triage as I see fit as a physician. I will continue to use my best judgment."

Reece glowers at me. "And why didn't you take the boy to surgery?"

"Because he had a different type of infection that wouldn't have responded to surgery."

"How do you know?" Reece asks.

I turn to his father. "Reece, like those born post-war, doesn't understand the scientific method and how truth can be revealed through study." Then I address Reece. "I know because I'm a doctor. That is why you should leave these decisions up to me."

Reece scoffs. "Like your little medical student, Ward?"

I stand, my ancient chair squealing in protest as it oscillates in the heated silence. "Mayor. I'm going to lead a scavenging party to San Jose. Once we have more supplies, we can lessen the rationing and treat all patients more broadly."

"My decision was final when we spoke the other day. We are not prepared to venture into potential enemy territory. San Jose is becoming politically dangerous as well."

"And if I leave there myself without permission?"

He moves to the door and turns the handle. "You'd abandon your post, forfeiting your position here."

"I'd retake it upon my return," I say.

"Not if I've already filled it." He leaves, the warning hanging in the air.

The next day, after rounds in the east wing, I hear a voice call after me down the hall. "Doctor Darrow." I turn and see Mavis Ulrich, wiry frame leaning on a can with a leathery face puckered at me like I'd just stomped on her toe. The patient has apparently arisen from her septic cocoon of delirium and is pissed about it. "I understand you're responsible for this." She pivots one leg at the hip, turning to show the calf that has been surgically scooped from below the knee. "Why did you do this to me?"

"You had a serious bacterial infection in that leg," I explain. "The only way to treat it is to remove the infected muscle."

"And did I consent you to do this to me?"

"You were delirious and not medically competent, so I made the decision for you. Plus, you'd be dead now."

"Still feel like I should've had a say in the matter."

"Where are you visiting from?"

She doesn't respond at first, only glances out the window, wrinkled concern circling her face. "San Diego."

"What kind of engineer are you?"

"Electrical. Material. Chemical."

"All of that?" I ask.

"I was trained in materials but learned much more on my own in Neo San Diego. When's the last time you heard from down south?" she asks.

"I'm not privy to updated info but we get traders all the time. I can get you in touch with our Comms people at the radio tower if you need to contact someone there."

"I don't have anyone there," she says this as if bragging about it. Her eyes finally turn to meet mine.

And then I recognize what's in those glassy orbs—trauma. "What happened? Are there Hila down there?"

A mirthless laugh escapes her lips like air from a flat tire. "No, no, no. The Hilamen are non-existent. Some believe they live up in the hills near San Diego, but that's bullshit."

"Then what was it?"

"Men being men. Ideas hatched from paranoia turn into rumors. Rumors turn into reality. Reality turns into surreality like that—" She slaps fist to palm. "And then human beings turn into animals." She slouches, already exhausted.

"What's happening in San Diego?" I ask.

"Mayor Gustavson is happening down there."

"What has he been doing?"

"Turning the colony into his own little dictatorship. Propaganda about San Diego superiority, bolstering his paramilitary group—the usual. I heard your transmissions," she says, a slight curl to the edge of her mouth. "Something about rebuilding, bringing back what we once were..."

"Yes?"

"What we once *were*? People are the same *now* as they were *then*."

"So, why did you come here?"

"You think I want to be here? I tore open my leg on some rebar trying to head north."

"What's up north for you?" I ask.

"Nothing. And that's the point. You can save whatever idea you have kicking around in your smart little brain that I'm going to help your colony out. I have no interest in being your engineer or anyone else's."

"So, what what're you going to do now?"

She turns from me and looks out the window. "Anything besides living in a colony."

Nurse Max grabs my elbow during my latest attempt to flee the east wing for a lunch break. "You're needed," he says, breathing hot on my ear.

We sweep through the halls of the east wing and see nurses congregating around a patient's room. It's Jonas' room—the fifteen-year-old with the bloodstream infection from a gunshot wound. I elbow my way in and see a trail of people spiraling outward from the bed. A line of nurses take turns pumping on the boy's chest. His limbs flail—head swinging like a pendulum on his slackened neck.

"Ward!" I yell. "Where is the medical student?" My only answer is the grunts from Patience as she pumps on the boy's chest. I find Ward in the corner of the room, eyes fixed on the dying boy through the crack in his glasses. "Ward, get to the foot of the bed and run this code!" But he's too timid as he shuffles through the nurses. "Hurry up!"

He looks at me.

"Lead the code blue," I yell at him. "Ensure high-quality chest compressions. Have them attach pads to the patient's chest. Do rhythm and pulse checks. Delegate tasks."

He continues to stare at me like a frightened deer.

"We've gone over this many times."

"I..." He withdraws to the wall.

"Doctor Darrow!" Max yells at me, fatigue in his voice. "We need some guidance over here!"

"Tara!" I yell to the respiratory therapist. "Get to the head of the bed and put in a breathing tube." At the two-minute mark, I yell for the compressions to stop. I feel along the boy's groin for a pulse. Nothing. I look at Tara who has her two fingers on the carotid. She shakes her head. I yell for chest compressions once more. "Epinephrine!" I bark at Nadine. The woman returns with several ampules of the medication and slams it in the IV. On the next pulse check, I feel it—like a butterfly, the femoral artery is flapping its wings.

Nurse Patience, sheathed in sweat, hovers her interwoven hands over the patient's chest, ready to start pounding. "Stop chest compressions," I say. "We have a pulse back. I want epinephrine and norepinephrine in the room and started on a drip. I need labs, basic metabolic, coags—just all of it. Chest X-ray—"

"Broken," Max says.

"EKG—"

"Also broken," he says.

"Jes—why doesn't anyone tell me about all this? Ward?" I ask, looking around for the medical student and discovering he has wedged himself into the corner of the room. "Ward. Come. Here."

He obeys but with shame painted on his pale face.

"You need to perform a neurological exam on the patient," I tell him. "He's at high risk for anoxic brain injury after being in a low-flow state to the brain from cardiac arrest."

"Okay," he says, returning to the patient's bed. He opens the patient's eyelids, floating a light over the eyes and then presses a ruler down the throat prompting a gag reflex.

"Doctor Darrow," Nadine says to me. "We can start another course of antibiotics for him. It will only be two days. And then we're out."

"Do it," I say, watching Ward make his way to the kneecaps,

hammering away on the tendons there to elicit a reflex. Once he's finished, he returns to me. "What's your assessment?" I ask.

"He seems to be neurologically intact," he says, something akin to confidence in his voice.

"Good. That means it was a good resuscitation—"

"Doctor Darrow!" Max yells, his two fingers on the patient's carotid. "Lost the pulse again!"

The room becomes a riot once more of flailing limbs and sweaty nurses. We get back on the chest, pumping the heart. Tara gets up top with a ventilator bag, pumping the lungs. Patience slams in one vial of epinephrine after another. We do a pulse check—nothing. After two minutes of chest compressions, we do another pulse check—nothing. Ward has scurried off once more as I yell and point and demand and sigh. Through the crowd, a flare of red hair emerges—red hair? No one on my staff has red hair—

Reece.

"What are you *doing* here?" I ask as he elbows his way toward me.

"I'm here under orders of Mayor Hutch." Reece stands like a bouncer outside a bar.

My cheeks flush with raw anger. "I *do not* have time for you right now. This child is dying."

"I am here *because* of this child—this man."

"Another amp of epi!" I yell.

"We're out," Nadine says.

"Go and get some more then."

"Doctor Darrow, we're *out*. That depleted our emergency reserves."

"That boy must live," Reece says. "At the order of the mayor. You must provide full treatment to the best of your abilities."

I stomp my foot. "What do you think I'm trying to do right now?"

"Okay then," he says, setting his jaw.

I'd like the boy escorted from the room, but I realize it may benefit the hospital for the mayor's son to actually see our struggle. We continue for another ten minutes. Chest compressions, pulse check, compressions, pulse check—the patient does not respond.

"Stop," I say, waving a hand in surrender. "Stop. We're done."

Max is on the chest, pumping the boy's now-broken ribs. He looks at me, I nod, and he lets up, the boy slumping back in bed.

"No," Reece says, breaking the silence. "*No.*"

"There's nothing else to do," I tell him, wiping sweat from my brow.

"Keep. Going," he demands.

The entire room looks at Reece and then back to me.

"You need to leave now," I tell him, my anger turning cold with impatience.

"I'm not leaving until you save that patient. We need him—"

And then I slap him. By the instant red mark on his cheek, I can tell it hurt him. But it felt tremendous for me.

"You—you—" he says, spittle flying, his outrage not fully ripened.

"Leave," I tell him. "I have a hospital to run." I strip gloves off my hands and leave the room.

FOUR

I KEEP nothing of the old world in my one-bedroom apartment. I call it an apartment, but it's really just an old office one floor above the east wing. Whenever I leave the patient wards, ascending a single flight of stairs to my bedroom, I never really go home because I have no home—the arrival of the Hila stole my home. For almost twenty years, I've been eternally on call, available at any moment to be awoken and summoned to the bedside of an unstable patient to then watch them die while we pretend our actions will save them.

My quarters are clean, with no personal effects because I have no person. I am a ghost in my body, moving tendon against bone until it gives out one day during patient rounds. I lay in bed, knowing that the only word to describe my hospital is adorable. A child's attempt to preserve the modern age.

As I sleep, the last image I want to see floats in my mind. The mayor's son, Reece, staring back at me from across my desk. His face is a crucible of arrogance and fear with something ancient emerging within his bones—into the colony's soul. Something narrow and dark. Something that does not ask questions and only speaks one language.

The next day, Ward appears at an east wing classroom, bag over his shoulder, prepared for one of my medical lectures that he's grown so fond of complaining about. I'm surprised to see him. After he'd receded to the corner of a dying patient's room, I thought he had given up again. Instead of the typical droop to his face, there is a faint smirk there. "What?" I ask.

"I didn't see Reece last night at communal dinner. No one did," he says, unable to contain the glee.

"So what?"

"Someone put him in his place."

"Don't get too excited. It was stupid what I did. There will be consequences. Believe me. Boys like him don't let things like that go. I imagine we'll see the mayor here in the east wing sometime this morning." He continues smiling at me with adulation in his eyes. I have a feeling that if I hadn't slapped his schoolyard bully, Ward wouldn't have even shown up this morning. I sigh, growing tired of his fickleness. "Listen to me," I say, changing my tone.

"What?"

"I'll be leaving tomorrow for a salvaging expedition."

He squints with confusion. "I thought Hutch said you couldn't go."

"I'm going anyway. We need supplies."

His face floods with fear. "What will I do when you're gone?"

"Just listen to the nurses. I'll only be gone two days."

"Will you be safe on your own?"

"It doesn't matter. Patients will die without supplies. I have to go." I pick up a piece of chalk. "Doesn't mean you're getting out of lecture, though. Have a seat."

Ward squeezes into the desk, placing a decrepit textbook on the tabletop. He flips through the crusty pages as if it's an arcane tome he's just discovered in ancient catacombs.

"Did you do the reading?" I ask.

"A little."

"What can you tell me about metabolic acidosis?"

He slumps, already defeated.

I cross my arms. "You didn't do the reading."

"I did. I just didn't understand anything."

"I'll show you." I flip open the pages, pointing to diagrams of cellular proteins and flowcharts of enzymatic processes full of molecular structures. I explain the biochemistry of cellular metabolism—glycolysis, cori cycle, gluconeogenesis, and the Krebs cycle. I teach how these processes relate to septic shock when the body has a dysregulated response to infection.

"How do you know all this stuff?" he asks.

"I was taught. Just like I'm trying to teach you."

"No. How was any of this stuff figured out? Don't all these things happen in the body smaller than anyone can see?"

"It took years and many minds using many instruments to learn all of these things," I say.

"But how did those people know to even start looking? How did they know to even build instruments to look at something that they didn't even know was there?"

"People before them figured out some of the science, and they picked it up."

"And what about the people before them? How did they know?"

I pause, trying to get to the root of his question. "Little by little, each human mind adds to the story of knowledge. Someone toils their whole lives trying to figure something out. They figure out maybe a millimeter of the problem, and the next generation takes it from there. Everyone is like one link in the chain of scientific knowledge."

"This is before the Hilamen came?"

"Yes," I say.

"So, where is the end of the chain now? Did it break when they showed up?" he asks, eyebrows angled with interest.

I place my palm on his notebook. "It's here," I say. I tap on my temple. "It's here." I tap on his temple. "It's going to be there."

He swallows. "Just us?"

"For now, at least. Every other student I try to train drops out. Death can be too much for them. They go into farming or trading or join the militia. There are still old-worlders around but they won't be forever. This textbook is not going to last forever either. You need to learn." I start back up teaching about how to recognize when a patient is going into shock. And then I see him wipe tears from his eyes.

"This is hard," he says.

"Yes, it is."

"Not just what you're teaching me but using this knowledge on a real human being. How do you take all this and throw it at the human body? It didn't help Jonas yesterday. He's dead now."

"People will die," I say. "They always will."

"Then what's the point of all this? What's the point of remembering what's in that thick book?"

"All this," I say, drumming my fingers along the book cover, "might do nothing. In all likelihood, it probably will be pointless for most patients that you see."

"But?"

"But what if you do help one person recover? Or what if you do extend someone's life so they can go on one last walk down the wharf? We can offer a little more of the most valuable thing in existence—moments of being human."

"How can you know who will get better?" he asks.

"You can't. And that's why you keep trying for everyone."

"So, you just keep trying to save people, having no idea if you're doing any good?"

I blink at him a moment and then say, "Yes."

"That's so stupid."

"Maybe it is."

He scoots back in his chair. "Seems like there's more good that you can do in the colony. Build walls as we grow, keep out raiders, go on patrols—defend the colony."

"How do you know those are good things?"

"Because it's protecting us from known danger. Protecting us from the Hilamen."

I click my tongue. "What do you think San Francisco was like before they came? It was full of people. A lot of people. Just this peninsula had about one million people in it. What do you think happened to them?"

"They died."

"Who do you think killed them?"

He shrugs. "The Hilamen."

I close my eyes for a moment. Clive's stubbled cheek flashes through my mind, reminding me that the Hila brought nothing but misery with their arrival. "Perhaps indirectly. But did you know there has never been an observed attack from them?"

"Then what happened?"

"We were so afraid of the dangers of our enemies from the sky that we became afraid of ourselves."

"So, we attacked ourselves?" he asks.

"Yes. Every nation had Hila pods inside their borders. Some nations let the pods live, other nations bombed their own pods and started to bomb nations that wouldn't get rid of the pods within their borders."

"Why?"

"They were afraid," I say.

"I'd be afraid, too."

"It's okay to be afraid. It's not okay to bomb away your fears, especially if they are imagined. That's how we're stuck in this situation where I'm trying to teach a single person an entire field of medicine. But here we are. Now, open your book and stop blaming our problems on the Hila," I say the last part more to myself than to Ward.

Later that day, I see Mayor Hutch standing near the front desk of the east wing, wicker hat in hand. I'm near certain I'll lose my position in the hospital for striking his son. I may even lose the hospital entirely.

"You have a new patient," Patience tells me from behind.

But I don't hear her, I only see Hutch walking my way. He sees me and begins a march down the hallway past the patient wards.

"Doctor Darrow," Patience says again.

"What?" I don't take my eyes off Hutch, whose gaze is locked on mine.

"A young woman is here to see you—" Patience says.

"Doctor Darrow," Hutch says with zero warmth. "A word."

"She's here now?" I ask Patience.

"She's waiting in the clinic rooms."

"I'm available right now. Please let all other visitors know that I'm currently with a patient." I turn my back to Hutch.

"Gladly," Patience says, crossing her arms over her chest as I walk away. I'm grateful Patience is a large woman. A strong woman. A woman that not even the mayor of Neo SF can get past.

I knock on the patient's door before a quiet voice says, "Come in." A young woman is seated on the patient table, naked shame cast across her face. "Priscilla," I say. "I haven't seen you in at least a year."

"It's been a bit, Doctor Darrow. I'm sorry that I haven't come to the east wing to visit." She shifts uncomfortably in her seat.

"Are you still interested in—"

"Training with you? No, no, not after what happened."

"None of that was your fault. It was no one's fault," I try to reassure her.

"I remember you saying that, yeah." There's an annoyed edge in her voice. She chews her lip nervously.

"How have you been?"

She twists her face. "I gave the patient the medication. Me. It was me who did it."

"That's true, but—"

"Ten seconds later, the patient was swelling up and her breathing..." A haunted vacancy sweeps her face. "That sound of squeaking air coming from her throat—"

"Giving the expired medication was the only option we had. The patient would've died anyway. Her reaction was a calculated risk, of which the patient was informed. It wasn't your fault."

Priscilla waves her hand as if casting away the memory. "It's fine. It's fine. Really. It was sign enough for me that all of this," she twirls her finger in the air, "is not for me." She nods as if retroactively affirming her decision.

"You're here as a patient then?"

"Yes."

I clasp my hands in my lap. "What can I do for you?"

"I've been sick."

"In what way?"

"I missed my period."

"Uh-huh," I say. "When was it last?"

"Sixteen weeks ago."

"So, you're not sick. You're pregnant."

Her face floods red. "I think so—"

We stop. There's a commotion outside the room. I suspect it's Mayor Hutch wanting to speak with me about how I slapped his son and embarrassed him in front of the entire east wing.

"Don't worry about that," I tell her. "What else?"

"What else? There's nothing *else*. I'm pregnant!"

"We'll need to do a pregnancy test first to confirm."

She looks at the floor, nodding. "And then what?"

"We'll do routine prenatal checkups. Probably once a month for now. I have newly compounded vitamins that you'll need to start taking today. We still have a doppler machine that works but no ultrasound. If you have any bleeding at all, you need to come and see me at once—doesn't matter what time of day."

She cuffs tears from her eyes. "Have you been pregnant before?"

"I have," I say, fighting back the memories bubbling in me.

"What's it like to deliver the baby?"

"Well... I'm actually not quite sure."

She appears perplexed and then nods in understanding. "I see. But you've helped deliver, right? I heard it hurts. A lot."

"It does," I say. "But I can place an epidural when you go into labor. It will help with the pain quite a bit." I don't tell her that I've only placed about fifty epidurals in my post-apocalyptic medical career. Most women these days don't trust me enough to even deliver their babies, let alone go poking about their spines. One death of a mother and a medical complication becomes a rumor, which becomes folklore that the old witch doctor at the east wing will kill your woman with old-world medicine. The majority of Neo SF births are at home.

"Is it dangerous? Giving birth?"

"Yes..."

"What can happen?" she asks with more earnestness.

"Many things."

"Have you lost any mothers?"

A baby boy wriggled through the surgical wound of his mother's abdomen. I swiveled the head, unraveling the noose of an umbilical cord that made the C-section an emergent surgery in the first place. The baby was freed, umbilical cord cut. I felt the uterus—it was enormous. Boggy like a sponge, it wept blood down my arms. I pressed my fist inside the uterus, extracting as much fragmented placenta as I could to aid the natural clamping of the muscle. Nothing. More blood. I yelled at Nadine to give all the medications—everything we had available to constrict the uterus. Nothing. I snaked a plastic hose in and inflated a balloon against the hemorrhaging lining of the cavity. For a moment, I thought it was over—that the bleeding had stopped. But then blood oozed around the balloon and kept flooding down my arms. I knew that the only thing left to save her was something that I'd never done before. I widened my surgical margins, exposing the abdominal space. Feeling around the outside of the uterus, I placed clamps on what I thought were the uterine arteries. Clamp here. Clamp there. Clamps everywhere.

The bleeding stopped.

I completely removed the uterus—a total hysterectomy. But I discovered I'd clamped the wrong things—what I thought were arteries were ligaments. I had widely exposed arteries dumping blood into her abdomen—garden hoses open at full blast. I didn't say anything. I didn't move. I just watched her skin turn bone-white against the crimson sheets wreathing her corpse—the baby now orphaned.

Days later, Nurse Patience rocked the baby in her arms, saying that she had named him Ward.

"Yes," I answer Priscilla. "I've lost some mothers. May I ask who the father is? He'll need education as well."

"He doesn't know yet."

"I won't tell him. Or anyone."

"Do you know the mayor's son?"

Against all odds, I successfully stifle a snort. "I'm familiar."

After a little more perinatal education, I exit the room with Priscilla and find Mayor Hutch standing there, arms crossed. Anger turns to befuddlement as his eyes cross from me to Priscilla. The nonplussed pause on his face tells me he is aware of Priscilla's relationship with his son. I can almost see the electrons zig-zagging across the circuitry of his brain as he connects the dots—some he knows are real, some he wishes are hypothetical. Priscilla dips her head, sidesteps the mayor, and beelines it for the exit.

"Mayor Hutch," I say. "To what do I owe this inappropriate intrusion into patient care?"

"I—" he glances at Priscilla, whose brunette ponytail whips in the doorway as she escapes.

"Yes?"

"Why was *she* here?" he asks.

"You know I can't tell you that. The fact that you even saw that she was here is a harsh violation of patient confidentiality."

He sticks that wicker hat on his head and bites his lips in contemplation. "Of course, yes."

"Why are you here?"

Change overcomes his face—a melting softness. "I wanted to apologize on behalf of my son."

"For intruding on patient care while a boy was dying the other day?"

"Yes."

"Somewhat similar to coming back here and intruding on my patient right now?"

"I—" He looks back at the empty doorway.

"You felt it was necessary to violate the integrity of this hospital by busting into here, overstepping my nursing staff just to apologize for your son's behavior by exhibiting that same behavior?"

"Yes," is the answer he decides on.

"You're not angry that I struck Reece?"

He winces. "Was it the best way of going about the situation?"

"I asked him to leave. He didn't. So, I slapped him and he left. It worked."

"He can be overzealous at times."

"That's one way of putting it."

He's suddenly in a hurry like he's left a burner going unattended.

"Do you need to be going?" I ask.

"I do." He leaves, exiting through the same door as Priscilla, and raises his hand to his brow, searching the plaza.

FIVE

I SLEPT ONLY an hour the first night in the underground bunker. My back ached from positioning the baby to my left all night. Acid reflux raged in my throat, stealing my appetite as I got in line for breakfast the next morning, but I shoveled eggs and oatmeal onto the tin plate. I quickly learned that bunker people are muted people. Conversation is lacking when, just the day before, you're hurried onto a helicopter and corralled into boxes of concrete and steel thousands of feet below the Sierra Nevada mountains. Word of the first nuclear strikes since 1945 graced our stressed-out brains as we descended rock and earth the night before. The sky had been pregnant with alien invaders only two months before the world of men decided to turn against themselves. The powder keg of brinkmanship and geopolitical opportunists had finally been lit while Clive was still out there somewhere.

An older gentleman I did not know sat across from me, chewing and staring. "Hello," I said, trying to make it less weird.

"Did that on purpose?" He motioned to my belly with his fork.

"Yes." I brought my palm to my abdomen and rubbed.

"I know I'm being rude. I just don't see the point of niceties anymore." He munched on a granola bar, crumbs littering his beard. "I know you're wondering why they let an old man down here to be pickled and preserved for the future generations."

"I wasn't wondering that. You have just as much right to be here as anyone else."

"I'm done. People of my age are wax Neanderthals looking at you from behind the glass at a history museum. You're eating breakfast with a ghost." He chuckled but he wasn't really laughing.

"So, why did you volunteer to come down here?"

He tapped his temple. "They wanted me. I'm a man who orchestrates. Been doing it for a long time. Nations rose and fell because of shadow men like me moving levers and cranking gears."

"And those are valuable skills once we re-settle neo colonies?"

He stopped chewing and brought his hands together. "Any time two people get together and imagine what things will be like, politics are born. The same factors that have led to bombs dropping above our heads right now will still be present when this bunker hatches, like a virus preserved beneath the arctic tundra of our thick skulls. You can engineer and sanitize all you want, but the virus will lay dormant in the spinal cord of humanity. All it takes are certain conditions—stressors, happenstance, someone with the right words at the right time—and that virus seeds along the nerves and—" He slapped an open palm on the metal tabletop, which resonated like a drum. "A rash breaks out overnight."

I crossed my arms. "So, what are you going to do about it?"

"They want me to set things up so it doesn't fall apart again."

"You don't sound optimistic."

He spoke between bites of bacon. "Oh, I'm not. Not at all. You can't socially engineer your way out of the human condition. I just thought I'd take the free ticket to an underground bunker while hell lets loose above." He stood, crumbs falling to the floor. "Why are you here? I mean, besides," he waved his hands over my belly, "repopulation."

"I'm a doctor."

"Not the answer I was looking for. The father isn't down here?"

"No." I breathed deeply. "He was called into active duty."

The man bowed his head as if attending a wake.

"They have a spot reserved for him here when he returns," I said, mostly to reassure myself.

"That's good." He looked up at the ceiling like he was trying to do math in his head.

"Not that it's any of your business, but yes, we conceived just before the visitors came. I'll emerge from here with an infant son and I'll be ready to help out at the re-settled hospital."

He made a frame with his fingers and peered at me through it.

"What are you doing?"

"Making a mental snapshot," he said, a single eye looking at me through the rectangle of his fingers. "Elspeth Darrow—doctor, mother, hope for the future," he said it like he was trying to sell a car.

"How do you know my name?"

"I know everyone's name. Along with everyone's personality profile and psyche assessments. That's why I'm here."

The day after Priscilla's visit with me, Mayor Hutch approves my salvaging expedition to San Jose.

"I've been apprised of my son's fiancée's situation," he tells me outside the east wing doors above the plaza.

I raise my eyebrows. "Fiancée?"

"Reece proposed last night after finding out."

"Congratulations, Mayor."

"You'll be able to find supplies in San Jose? Supplies for a safe pregnancy and delivery?"

"I hope so." I glance over his shoulder at the Civic Center Plaza. "Your scouts report that the area is clear?"

"We believe so, yes. But we've met some resistance down there with scouting groups from other colonies, so it's been some time since a full survey of the area. There may be increased flooding, so be careful."

"What kind of resistance are you all meeting down there?"

"Nothing much. Just be quick about it." He clears his throat. "I'm sorry, by the way."

I nod, not entirely sure for which of his recent trespasses he's apologizing. Ward exits his building across the plaza and stops short with a skittish sidestep as a group of bicyclists towing wagons ride past him.

Hutch eyes his approach. "Are you sure about him?"

"Not at all. He would've never been accepted to medical school."

"I mean, for the salvaging expedition. Are you sure he should come?"

"Part of new-world medicine is knowing how to salvage supplies. I need to teach him. Unless you have any other medical students around?"

He narrows his eyes on Ward. "I only ask that you watch him

closely. That boy never quite developed properly—suppose it can't be blamed being an orphan. Raised house by house—nobody could keep him longer than a few years or months at a time. Something's not right with that one."

"Anything else, Mayor?"

He places the tips of his fingers delicately together. "Yes. You've led quite a few salvaging expeditions over the years."

"Several dozen. All over the Bay Area."

"Would you let Reece take the lead on this one?"

"How old is he now?"

"Twenty. You'll, of course, truly be in charge. And you'll watch him—make sure he's making the right decisions. Just as you need to train Ward, I also need to train Reece how to lead a group of men."

I wave my hand in dismissal. "It's fine. Reece can lead the expedition."

"Thank you," he says with what looks like genuine relief that he doesn't have to start another argument with me.

Ward finds us, a backpack over one shoulder and a squawking ferret in one hand.

Hutch shares a furtive glance with me.

"Ward," I say. "We'll be gone several days—maybe a week. Are these all the supplies you have?"

"I—uh," he inspects his clothing as if realizing his lackluster preparation. "I wasn't—what else do I need?"

"Do you eat, drink, and sleep every day?" I ask.

"I do."

"Then you need to be prepared to do those three things every day with everything on your back."

"And fight," the mayor says, raising two fists. "You must be prepared to fight every day that you're out there."

"Mayor Hutch, thank you for commissioning the expedition. We'll see you back in the colony in a few days," I say.

Hutch reluctantly takes the cue to leave the two of us alone.

"And that?" I point to the rather long ferret in Ward's hand.

"Jericho."

"Why are you bringing an animal?"

"I found him almost dead by the garbage two weeks ago. Didn't have anyone. Been taking care of him at my place. I can't leave him behind or he'll die."

"You think it'll be safer on a salvage expedition?" I ask.

"Better than him trapped in my apartment the whole time."

"Don't make it a problem. Come on. Let's find you some gear."

Between the city blocks along the west side of Van Ness, walls of shipping containers loom over us, built three-high like castle walls. Men with automatic rifles stand as sentinels atop the improvised ramparts, watching beyond the borders of the colony. The alleys running perpendicular are choked out by the thousands of arms of ferns, stitched together with whips of ivy vines. The smell of damp earth tickles my nose from the late-night rainfall. Maturing trees have grown in the last ten years, looming proudly beside eroding concrete teething with rebar. Most building facades stare back at us with toothless brick faces, slowly imploding inward from structural decay. With careful footing, we move over spewed brick innards that form walls for wild flowers pushing through the soil.

"Wait, where are we going?" Ward asks.

"Embarcadero. And then the wharf to meet the salvage party."

"Easiest way from Civic Plaza is straight shot down Market along the colony border. Why are we heading north? We're almost at Geary. Doesn't make sense." His ferret chirps as if in agreement. I don't answer him for a long time. When he finally understands that I'm annoyed, he asks, "You're mad at me?"

"Just exhausted."

"Are you exhausted in general or exhausted because of me?"

"Both. Your lack of preparation has me doubting your judgment."

"I don't really have to go," he says like he has some sort of leverage over me.

He instantly shrinks at my glare. "You don't have to do anything you don't want to do. Head home if you want," I say but then hear his footsteps behind me as I keep moving.

We move through the Tenderloin, where several city blocks were cleared of rubble and sowed with various vegetables, tilled by the early morning workers. They eye us with despondency as we pass through—some former patients give me a polite wave. The inhabited buildings have mostly been gutted and remodeled with reclaimed furniture or flooring from luxury apartments that had not suffered water damage from the abandoned water system of the city after the mass evacuation. Glass windows are nowhere to be found—canvas tarps or repurposed shutters hang in their place.

Trickling stream beds guide our path as we pass through Union Square. Along the edge of the plaza, a few women calm a group of sheep behind their barbed pen, agitated at our approach. A line of cows stand idle, chewing carelessly as they are milked. Multilevel box gardens fill most of the plaza. Built four high and ten deep, staggered rows of thousands of plants bask in the dawn light as men and women tinker with an irrigation system that waters the plants in chaotic streams. A single obelisk still stands proud in the center of the square with the oxidized statue of a woman brandishing a wreath and trident to the world. Whatever old-world significance the statue has is lost on me as we pass underfoot.

"Which street is this?" Ward asks as we leave Union Square, following under a thick canopy of cypress and pines crowding the top of apartment buildings, reaching through crumbled rooftops.

"Grant," I say.

"How do you know? There are no street signs." He squints. "Anywhere."

"I used to live along here." I arch my neck, inspecting the crumbling roof cornices.

His brow furrows. "When? This is not very close to the hospital."

"Before."

"*Before*, before?"

"Yes."

"Were you a doctor then, too?"

"Yes. But a different kind," I say.

"There are different kinds?"

"All things you see me do at the east wing—no one doctor did all those things in the old world. Different doctors specialized in different fields."

"And what were you?"

"A pathologist."

His eyes bug out at the word.

"I studied diseases at the cellular level. Like with a microscope," I explain.

"Microscope," he repeats, fitting the new word in his mouth. "So, when did you figure out how to do everything else?"

"I don't know how to do everything else. I can do a little in a lot of different fields. After everything happened and the evacuees returned to make Neo SF, I was suddenly the only doctor after several died in the bunkers beneath the mountains and others left the colony. I read books and watched old videos on how to do procedures. Come on. We're almost there."

We move gingerly through small stream beds lined with tall grasses that come up to our thighs. The ground is spongy beneath our feet—a fine bed of plant and soil has covered where asphalt once reigned. Large mounds of grass line the street—the metal shells of ancient cars and vans transformed into wild garden beds. Some vestiges of an old-world city still reach through—a tattered banner hanging from a street lamp with faded colors advertising a parade, a street light leaning through tree bark that hugs the metal casing. We pass a rusted-out gas station, its carport station draped in ivy and moss like it has grown a head of hair. A tiny wheel spoke reaches through an old car window, covered in ivy—the wheel of a baby stroller.

Ward passes underneath a stone gateway, its multiple roofs have collapsed, leaning awkwardly against the stone pillars. The green tile of the roof still clings in some spots but is mostly cracked with mold and grasses sprouting through.

"Dragon's Gate," I say.

"What?"

"That's what this was called. Where you're walking through."

We start up the steep incline and pass by old-world shops. Beyond dashed showcase windows rests a graveyard of statues. Corroded by air and time, figures of monkeys on benches, women reaching toward the heavens, or wild dragons loom within the shops. Now cloaked in leaves, the statues look like a garden with hedged figures standing silently within the darkness of the abandoned buildings. The moss has reached their lips as if silencing their messages from the old world.

"What was this place?" Ward points. "Some sort of memorial?"

"It was a shop. For tourists. Nothing more. They claimed for years they were going out of business. Now they actually have.

Used to be hundreds of pigeons that ran around here. Now it's too wild even for them."

We round the top of the hill to the intersection of Pine and discover a street that has become a forested ravine. After two decades, repeated rainstorms washed earth over the cobblestones and asphalt, creating a fresh topsoil for seedlings to take root. Storm after storm carved through the neo forest bed and then deep past the asphalt layer and into the earth. The ravine is buried to the east where a building of black glass collapsed a few years back, covering several city blocks in fractured flooring, piping, dust, and other raw building viscera.

"Whoa," Ward says, inspecting the destruction. "I don't remember that thing collapsing. Guess I haven't been to this part of the colony."

"Too busy gallivanting *outside* the colony? Collecting art supplies?" I say with raised eyebrows. "The big earthquake five years back brought it down. A few others, too."

"I remember that. Were a lot of people killed?"

"Some. Those foolish enough not to follow the colony rules. You don't live where a huge building can fall on you. Come on, this way." I lead him west, up Pine.

"But we're heading to the Embarcadero, opposite way."

"Quick detour."

I lead him only a few doors up the hill to a metal gate that's been knocked from its hinges and now rests innocently at a tilt from the brick walls of the building. I step through and follow a concrete corridor to a blind parking lot. With the entirety of the parking lot surrounded by tall buildings, only a square of sunlight reaches the ground here where a single square of tall grass has broken the asphalt apart and thrives. I remove several stripped car hoods that lean against a covered parking spot and slip through into a small courtyard where a statue of Mary greets us with cracked eyes and crumbled lips. I shake off the ghoulish gaze that rests on us as I open another door to a stairwell. Our breath echoes as we climb the stairs. "It's an old catholic school," I finally tell Ward. "Ecole Notre Dame des Victoires."

Jericho, his ferret, looks wide-eyed at the stairwell. Ward peers at the mold that has caked its way up the length of the stairwell and sniffs. The air is deeply redolent of mildew. "Is the building sound?"

"It'll stay up. It was retrofitted to withstand earthquakes. Just another level. Keep moving."

We arrive at the third level, a dark hallway before us with shafts of sunlight peeking through flanking classrooms where mold and moisture reign. The carpet underfoot has rotted into a moist fuzz. The walls have spontaneously shed their sheetrock exposing piping alongside dormant electrical conduits. Despite a carpet of moss that coats one wall, curled paper is still tacked there, fragile as a flower petal. Across the papers are the faintest drawings from a world before destruction—a child's dreams unsullied, frozen in crayon and craft paper.

I shiver through the dank hallway and sidestep a hole in the floorboards exposing a classroom beneath. At the end of the hallway is a closed door with a locked bolt. "Looks like we're not going any further—" Ward says but stops as he hears the jingle of keys in my hand. I unlock the bolt and then the doorknob. The door creaks as agitated dust and fungal spores rise in the air. I shine my flashlight and gesture him in.

He eyes rows of boxes, containers, vials... "Medical supplies?" he asks.

"Yes."

He looks up and down the shelving. "You've got syringes, masks, saline bags, gauze, breathing tube equipment, basins—some surgical hardware, too." He looks at me. "This isn't part of our normal inventory."

"No."

"Then what's it doing way out here?"

"You are now only the second person who knows that this supply is here."

"Why?"

"I keep this here as a backup," I say. "Anything could happen to the east wing—fire, flooding, looting. Also, the supplies Reece took recently—that's not the first time the mayor has acquired supplies from the hospital. No one else can know about this, understand? These supplies must be kept safe. If I ever tell you I need these supplies, now you know where they are."

"We ran out of antibiotics. Do you have extra here?"

"We don't hoard anything here that is needed directly in the east wing. There aren't any medications here. We really need to go on this salvaging expedition. I just wanted to show you exactly where this is."

"What's all this other stuff?" he asks, pointing to a shelf behind the door. He picks up a small, woven baggie with *My First Rosary* stitched on the front. The beads rattle in his fingers as he removes it from the pouch.

"Left from before." I take the rosary and put it back in the pouch. "Time to get going. When we come back from salvaging, we'll leave some of the reclaimed supplies here before Hutch can get his hands on them."

We leave the way we came, except I take a hard right in the dim hallway and follow a new corridor to a dead end. I stand in the doorway of a classroom. There are still a few windows intact, covered in moss and dirt, scattering flits of sunlight across the room. The tables and chairs are clustered in groups, molded books still lined up in neat stacks as if awaiting an incoming group of children. At some time, a water line ruptured in the ceiling, breaking through the tile and spilling sewage over the teacher's desk.

Ward wrinkles his nose. "What do you keep in *here?*"

"Stolen dreams." I turn from the classroom, regretting I stepped into the room.

SIX

TOWERING monoliths of glass and steel scatter sunlight in my eyes. The view of the buildings from our journey down Clay Street offers the dazzling seduction of a thriving metropolis. As we near, the fractured decay of their facades shatters the illusion. The now-leaning towers of ancient corporatism loom like the corpses of mythical giants—a legend of old-world gods, part of the apocrypha of a once-powerful tribe.

As the forested street levels, an overgrown park glows green as the morning sunlight burns through the passing fog. Flocks of blue herons, sparrows, and wood ducks fuss and preen beside a sunken lake that now occupies two city blocks of park. The Embarcadero building towers above us, its hundreds of windows long gone—cracks meandering the length of the edifice. The Embarcadero plaza beneath has become the de facto market of the entire colony. A sore spot for the founding mayor—he gave into the colony who wanted the market closer to the wharfs for close proximity for the morning seafood haul from the fishing boats. Safety be damned if the Embarcadero came crashing down some future morning.

Skirting between the building and the lake, the market and wharf burst into view. Men and women busy themselves along the Embarcadero, dressed in overalls with tools clanging along their belts in tune with hoes and shovels pinging in their carts. It's mostly foot traffic from the Union Square vegetable gardens bringing in daily produce to barter. Several old minivans, now gutted of their engine block, ramble along the crumbling concrete street, horses towing them along their rusted rims. Planks of wood lay across the bare chassis, layered with straw and topped with crates of eggs. Others make their way along toward the water, fishing lines bobbing above their heads. There is a silence to the morning crowd, most greetings only a head nod as they appear eager to get to the day's work.

What was once an ice rink has been fashioned into a pen for livestock. Most of the north side of the Neo SF, the old Marina District, is dedicated to animal husbandry where sheep and cattle are raised and brought to the market for either butchery or sale. The Embarcadero plaza is where the market resides—shops and kiosks full of hand-stitched clothing, shop tool supplies, along with a myriad of street food assortments sold from immobile food trucks. Gas-powered generators chug along the periphery as we weave through the foot traffic.

We cross the plaza market and wait at Embarcadero Street while a wagon stuffed with cabbage heads rides along, pulled by a row of bicyclists. The Embarcadero is one of the few functional roads in all of Neo SF that is equipped for vehicles. It's kept clear of invasive plant life and serves as the only major north-south trade route of Neo SF, connecting the various industries throughout the colony. Clearing the road of detritus was one of the first major projects when Neo SF was re-founded nearly twenty years prior.

The clocktower of Ferry Plaza looms over us, bright and clean. We pass under the arches of the Ferry Building and find dozens more shops, many firearms and ammunition, which are traded freely in the colony. There are other products available—cutlery, wiring, copper piping, repurposed furniture, wood-carved board games, and even some old-world sports equipment refurbished or patched together with duct tape or wood glue. There is a line of shops selling moisturizers and perfumes made from colony lavender fields and soybean oil. One of the most popular markets is the spice shops, where denizens from all over the colony offer up wares and goods for a few precious grams of smoked paprika or cardamom—or whatever else may be available that week.

There are a fair number of men who have gone about the business of selling tonics made of a proprietary blend of balsamic oil and bullshit. They'd appealed to me a few years back for my endorsement. After my blunt refusal, a businessman named Jackie Handover found success just the same with flashy marketing and vague promises of health. It was no coincidence I'd had an uptick in rashes and gastric distress in the east wing hospital after he introduced a proprietary cure-all elixir.

After ignoring the sales pitches of the shopkeepers, we arrive at an outdoor outfitter shop. I'd curried enough favor with a shopkeeper, Prasad, to get most of Ward's gear for free as I'd treated him and his sons on more than one occasion in the east wing. Prasad hands over the gear with the agreement that I would bring him as many car batteries as I could reasonably haul back.

"Where are you heading anyway?" Prasad asks.

"San Jose," I say.

"Hmm." His black mustache twitches.

"What's wrong with San Jose?"

"I hear there is flooding. Have you been lately?"

"No. Hutch says the same but that it should be safe for salvage at least."

"Could be. Just be careful," he says.

"Have you heard of other conflicts down there?"

"What kind of conflict?"

"Anything. Hutch seemed to suggest men from other colonies sniffing around."

He crosses his arms. "Shouldn't be a reason to be afraid. Trading and salvaging territories between the colonies has been amicable, at least lately."

"Anywhere else in the Bay Area you'd recommend we go?" I ask.

"No. Things are picked clean pretty good now. Going to have to start sending crews further and further soon," he says, chasing worry from his face. "Just hope it's not too close to fallout zones."

I click my tongue. "I'm afraid salvage may be a dying business soon. It mostly is for us at the east wing."

"I hope you're wrong but I'm starting to see the writing on the wall. It's getting harder and harder to compete with some other businesses." He nods down the line of shops, indicating a store bustling with commotion.

"Harlo and Sons? What about them?"

"Getting lots of new products outside our normal trade routes. They have some sort of pipeline with a refurbishing plant in Neo LA. I could never get the kind of firearms they're selling. They're going to put me out of business." He looks out the window with worry settling over his bushy eyebrows. We share anxious silence while Ward riffles through a tray of ball bearings, spilling them onto the floor. "I'll get that," Prasad says, lifting an apron over his head. "Safe travels, Doc. Try to find some car batteries for me, yes?"

. . .

Ward trudges in front of me along the wharf as a stiff wind chills me. He moves awkwardly with a thirty-pound backpack full of traveling gear. Built like a praying mantis, his gait waddles as he adjusts to new shoes whose soles have been repurposed with rubber reclaimed from old car tires. The boy had been wearing flip flops earlier, fashioned from milk carton plastic and twisty ties. Jericho is perched on his shoulder, gazing at the foot traffic with fear in its eyes.

Pier 3 is where most fishing boats dock and bring in their haul. It is one of three piers along the entire wharf that has undergone any sort of renovation. We find Reece with a crew of two other young men aboard a twenty-five-foot pontoon boat, organizing the deck gear. Reece stands at the bow, pointing and shouting orders. I know them all—delivered every single one of them.

"Doctor Darrow," Reece says as we approach, his shoulders abruptly stiffen.

"Good morning, Reece. Thank you for heading our expedition."

He gives a curt nod and says, "It's my pleasure," with nothing more than the utmost professionalism. I can only assume his father had a long talk with him about how to treat Doctor Darrow with kid gloves.

"My medical student, Ward, will be joining us," I say.

Ward stands at the dock, arms crossed over his chest with hands in armpits, staring at the boys. His ferret is stuffed in the top of his back, also gazing at the activity. The tableau results in immediate laughter from the boys on the pontoon. Reece notices the daggers in my eyes and shushes his crew. "Welcome aboard," he tells us. "We're just finishing our checklist and will be able to embark soon."

"Reece, I couldn't help but notice there were more automatic rifles than human beings on the boat. What do you plan on running into out there?" I ask.

"We don't know. And that's the point. There have been Hilamen sightings recently."

"By whom?"

"Zeke Plinth and his scouts."

"And what do they see?"

His eyes narrow. "Movement."

"*Movement?*"

"Unusual movement, yes," he says with conspiracy.

"You're bringing that much firepower for possible movement?"

He examines my person. "Do you not carry protection?"

I lift the front of my poncho, exposing a Glock in my waist belt. "I have enough to scare off a raider. You're more likely to shoot yourselves with those weapons than anything of actual danger."

He stiffens at the insult. "Me and my men are fully trained."

"Indeed," I say, tapping one of the rifles with my foot that is resting unattended on the deck.

"Geddes!" Reece yells, pointing at the rifle. "Pick up your weapon."

Geddes, clearly embarrassed, reaches for the rifle and then accidentally kicks it away from himself, sending it sputtering across the deck and into the water. We all stand there, motionless for a moment, wondering if it had really just happened.

"I do feel safer now, thank you," I say.

Mouth agape, Geddes turns to Reece. "I—"

"You fu—" He brings his fingers to the bridge of his nose.

Another young man, Sabion, saddles up beside Geddes and strokes an enormous red beard that hangs down to his chest. He crosses his arms over his chest, showcasing legible biceps, and feigns like he's investigating what has happened to the rifle. "Geddes, did you lose something? Where'd your piece go, guy?"

Geddes, already humiliated, sets his jaw and glares at Sabion. "Just don't."

"Do you have any idea where we got that rifle?" Reece asks Geddes. "That's a new rifle. *New*. Not refurbished. That's Neo LA-grade artillery."

"I know, I know. I just flushed a priceless weapon down the drain," Geddes says.

"No, you didn't. When we get back, you're diving down there and retrieving it."

Ward finally steps on the pontoon, interrupting the public display of humiliation and offering the needed distraction for Geddes to slink to the stern and act like he is packing away gear that is already clearly stowed.

Sabion laughs as Ward sets down his bag with a huff and takes a seat on the edge of the boat. "Finally, we can launch the expedition, guys," Sabion says, gesturing to Ward. "Our field medic has arrived!"

I glare at Reece, who responds in kind. "Sabion!" he yells. "Stop dicking around and get ready to go."

Sabion slaps Ward on the shoulder with much more than just jocular force and says, "Just kidding. Nice to have you aboard. Get you some hair on that chest, buddy." Ward sulks, dipping his shoe into the water.

I find a corner on the pontoon to set my pack and inspect the supplies the boys have brought, mentally tabulating how long the journey will take and times it by a factor of the crew size. "Reece, how long will it take us to get to San Jose?" I ask.

"At thirty miles, traveling by water, it should take no longer than eight hours to sail there, assuming good winds. We'll arrive by around eighteen hundred this evening."

"We have enough food for the return journey as well?"

He nods. "Made sure of it. We'll camp tonight in San Jose, spend one day on the salvage operation, and leave the next morning."

"So, we have exactly enough for that journey?"

"No more, no less."

I squint my eyes at him. "And if we're delayed?"

"Why would we be delayed?"

"If we could answer that, then we'd never have to carry along backup supplies."

"Have you been delayed before?"

I click my tongue. "Every time. Every expedition."

An hour later, the boys return from the market with more supplies—mostly dehydrated vegetables and dried meat. Sabion makes his feelings known about having to go shopping again while Geddes silently stows supplies and ties them down. It's already mid-morning when we disembark. We shove off by pure manpower—Sabion and Geddes at the stern, standing with long paddles while Reece and Ward paddle at the bow. The Bay waters lap along the boat, calm and steady as I leave Neo SF with four teenage boys, one ferret, and enough firepower to storm a castle.

As the Bay Bridge approaches, Geddes unfurls the sail. The boat has been retrofitted with a mast, combining the open deck space of a pontoon with the wind power of a sailboat. With his neck craned, Geddes gazes proudly as the patchwork mainsail snaps in the wind and goes taut. The boat lurches beneath my feet as he and Sabion deploy the jib while Reece unnecessarily shouts out commands. Sabion takes the boon with what he likely believes to be stoic heroism. Meanwhile, Ward moves from one side of the deck to another to appear as if he is doing anything at all.

We pass beneath the bridge and see the blockade of concrete dividers, placed two stories high, blocking any unregulated traffic into the colony. It is manned at all times as the only entrance to Neo SF from the east bay. Ward waves to the men on the bridge in vain as if they're as excited for his first water voyage as he is. We go unnoticed, gliding underneath Yerba Buena Island, slinking away on our port side.

"Is the Bay safe?" Ward asks me.

"Nothing is safe," I say.

"Do raiders come out to rob on the waters?"

"They used to. Back when gasoline was more abundant, the Bay was full of motorboats of dangerous men with weapons who'd shoot at anything they came across. Ten years ago, we never would have made this journey by water. Now, sea warfare lacks speed since it's mostly human-powered. The energy to pillage watercraft is just too costly for those outside the colony. They spend their efforts on the roads between colonies now."

"How many people live outside the colonies, do you think?" Ward asks.

"At least a few hundred thousand along western America. There are factions everywhere. They fight and die and then fight more. It's been years since any of them have been organized enough to be a threat to SF in the Bay area."

Already, I'm exhausted from not only the morning travels to the wharf but the inane arguing and pubescent one-upmanship of the crew, arguing over maps and navigation. The waves are gentle, though, bathing the sides of the pontoon in delicate splashes, rocking me as I close my eyes. My mind spins like a disk, wondering and calculating—fretting over supplies yet accepting something akin to futility. The sun peeks through clouds, shushing my thoughts.

I sink my eyes under my hat and sleep.

SEVEN

"THANK YOU, EVERYONE, FOR JOINING," said Evangeline Yun, the de facto bunker president. She shuffled papers and looked out over her reading glass at the semi-circle of tables that crested the auditorium. "We're joined today by agriculture." She motioned to a group, "Engineering, social, safety, science, medical, and economy." Each group turned on their mic one at a time, giving updates about research, speculations about the future and outright conjecture about when it would be safe to let the bunker hatch and unleash our technocratic do-goodery all over the post-apocalyptic wasteland. Evangeline turned to my table and said, "Medical?"

Doctor Halbrough, bespectacled and gray, cleared his throat. "Typical numbers of inpatient and urgent care. No increase in communicable diseases. Vaccines are up to date in the entire bunker population. Thank you." He sat down next to me.

"Report from above?" Evangeline asked the Comms staff.

A uniformed man leaned forward into the microphone and

said, "Nothing we can report," which prompted annoyed grunts from all.

"News from the southern California bunkers, then?" Evangeline asked him.

The Comm man looked at the old man who ate lunch with me a few weeks prior, now busying himself with a game of solitaire on a folding table. The old man shook his head at Comms and resumed his game. "Nothing we can report," Comms said.

Visibly disappointed, debate and discourse ensued about drafting the first colony constitution once Neo San Francisco was resettled. The typical concerns about balancing a free market economy against wealth concentration were hashed over alongside the fact that the means by which democracies were subverted were supplied by the very rights and freedoms guaranteed by said democracy. The debate was old hat at that point, and I was already getting bored and hungry as I felt my baby kick.

After the meeting, the old man walked beside me down a hallway. "If it isn't Doctor Darrow, hope for the future."

"Why won't you share information from above?" I asked.

"Doctor Halbrough has metastatic cancer," he said. "He will die in a few weeks."

"What? That can't be. He would have told me."

"You will take over medical."

I shook my head. "But there's also Doctor Abdi. She has ten years more experience than me."

He shook his finger at me. "No. It will be you. San Francisco remains untouched as is all of California. The nuclear threat to this region of the country is now waning."

"How do you know that?"

He ignored my question. "You will probably be the physician who sets up a hospital in the San Francisco colony. I recommend you set it up at city hall."

"I can't do that. There are others better qualified. I don't know how to build and run a hospital. I'm just a pathologist."

"It's going to be you. Training doesn't matter here. This is about personality. You'll figure out the rest." He walked away from me but I grabbed his shoulder.

I searched his face for understanding but found it inscrutable. "What's going on above? What's going to happen when all the bunkers hatch?"

"Schismogenesis."

"What?" I sighed. "Why is everything a riddle with you?"

"As soon as there are divisions between people, whether those are tribe, race, gender, or literal concrete walls, a feedback loop is set up that creates a never-ending pattern of distinction. One tribe maintains a behavior, even if irrational, if only to distinguish themselves from the other tribe. This is schismogenesis. The fact that there are several bunkers in California, and from those bunkers new colonies will resettle, means that there is guaranteed division, strife, and eventual war until cultural consolidation and homogeneity takes over again and the cycle repeats itself. It doesn't matter how much your committee debates about a constitutional charter. Whatever you draft will have little bearing on what's going to happen when the bunkers hatch. All it takes is one person at an opportune time to shatter whatever constitution you come up with. The entire point of these committees and meetings is just to keep the eggheads occupied so you don't drive everyone crazy down here with your insufferable intellect. The feedback loop is already set in motion—the cycle will begin again. The bunkers will be born into conflict."

"And how do the Hila play into all of this?"

He shrugs. "Haven't heard from them."

"They *still* haven't done anything?"

"They're still up there, but they're not playing our game."

73

"What are they doing here?" I asked.

"Your guess is as good as mine. I only understand the minds of men."

I awaken on the pontoon deck from a painfully short-lived nap with a ferret sniffing in my hair.

"Jericho!" Ward yells, stomping toward the animal who scurries across the deck.

"That rat is going overboard if you can't get it under control," Reece warns. "Never would've let you on my ship if I knew you had that thing."

"He doesn't hurt anything," Ward says, scooping up the ferret before placing him in his pack.

Sabion crosses burly arms over his chest, a scowl curling his mouth. "Does the rat help out in your hospital? Fetch rusty needles and expired pills?" Reece joins in as he and Sabion delve further into the imagined escapades of Jericho, the would-be ferret nurse who stumbles through one misadventure to the next at the bumbling east wing hospital. Geddes rolls his eyes at the two while Reece studies me, calculating my response to their mockery. When he finds I'm inscrutable as stone, he shouts inane orders to the crew. The day is late as the sun slants into the horizon.

"What's the plan?" I ask Reece. "Getting late in the day. Think we're going to make it tonight?" I look to the south, knowing the answer.

"Yes. I've timed it out perfectly. We'll arrive at the south bay in four hours. Plenty of time to still set up camp." The winds pick up my hair as the waves churn. A head of clouds grumbles over the Bay with an approaching squall. The sails snap in the turbulent wind as the crew looks to him. "Keep the heading," Reece says. I hear fat droplets ping off our supplies as the crew hastily covers them with tarps. Reece peers through binoculars into the storm front as if directing its course through sheer anxiety.

Sabion wears an expression of unrelenting doubt and superiority. "Sure thing, Cap," he says.

"Reece," I say. "I don't think that storm will break."

"We have a schedule to keep," he answers.

"We won't arrive on time if our boat is at the bottom of the Bay. We need to dock."

And so, we head right into the storm front. I'm quickly soaked as sheets of rain are upon us as the boat rocks wildly in the gale. We are yelling over the wind, squinting through a sudden torrential downfall. Geddes clamors at the tiller, wrenching it portside, prompting the boat to lean starboard toward the west bay.

"What are you doing!" Reece yells at Geddes, who continues to grip the tiller, glaring at Reece.

"We need to moor," Geddes says. I can almost see the tiny gears turn in Reece's mind—calculating the benefit of reprimanding a subordinate versus the risk of his leadership becoming subverted.

"We dock," Reece says through chattering teeth as if it was his independent decision.

The storm stays with us right up to the point that we see land. It is only dumb luck that we are able to moor at a beach and not a rock shelf, which would have shredded the pontoon hull. Reece barks out commands, ordering us all to stay while he and Sabion brandish their weapons and set out to conquer the untamed beachhead. Ward looks at me, asking permission from me to disembark or something. I nod and follow the boys through the sand, gripping my Glock underneath my poncho. Hulking creatures loom from the fog just up from the beach. As we near, we discover they are the ivied remains of a swing-set. A jungle-gym dome has metamorphosed into a thicket of buckthorn and enormously wreathed nests of seabirds. We find shelter underneath an old park barbeque area, the roof appearing intact despite the prodigious plant-life thriving above.

"This'll do," Reece says. "We'll set camp here—take shifts throughout the night guarding the boat. We'll have to wait out the storm till tomorrow."

I lean my weight on the metal support beams and peer up at the ceiling. A gnarled mass of roots has woven into the roof. The structure seems sound enough, and I've certainly sheltered under worse conditions. I set my pack down, already wet and tired and only a few hours into the expedition.

"Where are we?" Ward asks.

"Probably near San Mateo," I say.

"How do you know that?" Reece asks.

"Because we never passed under the San Mateo bridge. I think I see it there." I gesture toward the water, where the darkened struts of the bridge can be seen through the fog. "Once the storm is clear, it should only be a few hours to the south end of the Bay."

"We'll leave first thing in the morning," Reece says.

"Sounds fine," I say, closing my eyes, wondering about the patients in the east wing, knowing that some may die because of the delay.

Reece doles out more tasks, sending Sabion to scout the area. Cradling his weapon, Sabion grins through his red beard and heads off into the thicket, and I count myself lucky to be rid of him. After Geddes and Ward bring the rest of the cargo to camp, Reece then tasks Geddes with setting up camp—fire, tents, and cookware. Sitting at a decrepit picnic table, Reece eyes Geddes as the boy works, unpacking implements for starting the fire. There is a weird silence as Geddes hacks wood while Reece bores holes in him with his glare. Ward offers to help chop wood.

"No," Reece says. "I want Geddes to start the fire."

"I can cook, too," Ward offers.

Reece just shakes his head at him. "Let Geddes work."

"Well, what can I help with?" Ward asks.

"Your help is not needed. You are the medical apprentice. You take commands from Doctor Darrow for whatever she needs. That is the command structure."

Clearly hurt, Ward disappears back at the boat somewhere. "Don't go far," I tell him. I suppose I should go and console the boy, but my hip hurts, and sitting in the dirt here is the most pleasant thing that has happened to me all day.

Geddes gets some sort of freeze-dried stew going, vegetable vapor wafting through camp. As the sunlight darkens, Sabion returns to camp declaring the surrounding area safe. After Geddes dishes out the stew, Ward slinks back to camp. He lets Jericho lap up a bit of stew from his bowl as the other boys watch with pleased disgust as if filing away yet another reason that Ward is strange enough to justify their unfettered mockery. As we chew in silence, Reece is the last to take a bowl, but he doesn't eat. He and Geddes are involved in some sort of silent standoff, both frozen and gazing at one another.

"Boys—men," I say. "What's going on?"

"He's mad," Geddes says. "Mad that it was me who forced us to dock."

"Is that true?" I ask Reece.

Reece says nothing.

Sabion approaches the fire and gestures to Reece. "Our fearless leader doesn't have the balls to say it."

"Say what?" I ask.

77

Sabion's red beard frames a delighted smirk. "That he was shown up by the guy who used to be bedding his girl, Priscilla."

Reece stands, fists clenched. "This coming from the guy who's never even been with a girl? Why is that exactly?"

Sabion answers by throwing a fist and then Reece is on the ground. Sabion stands over him, rubbing his hand from the impact on Reece's jaw. Before I can say anything, Reece is on his feet, fists cocked, a bloodlust delight in his eyes. They exchange a few blows despite my protest and may as well be bucking horns and kicking up dust with charging hooves. Reece wipes his lip, swelling with blood, and waits for Sabion to come in for another blow.

But Sabion only smiles once more. "Makes it even worse, doesn't it, Reece?"

Confused, Reece asks, "What makes it worse?"

"You know." His eyes dance to Geddes. "Rubs salt in the wound. Thinking about Priscilla and him being together. Your girl and a straight-up n—"

He says a word.

A word that I haven't heard in a long time. A word resurrected from the dust as violent as bullets but as brittle as glass. A word that now has me in between them with a fiery glare that makes Sabion shrink before the old wrinkly woman who is suddenly very pissed off.

"*Where* did you hear that word?" I hiss.

For the first time, Sabion is speechless.

"Where did you learn that word?" I ask again.

But then the arrogance returns with his casual shrug. "Dunno," Sabion says. "What difference does it make? I'm just joking around anyway." He returns to his seat and loudly slurps on his stew as if the whole scuffle never happened.

They all return to their meals, more scared of me than

anything else. Geddes is verifiably perplexed. "Jokes are words and words are ideas," I say. "And ideas become actions. If a word can get you to think that some people are different from you, they easily become something else. Do you understand me?"

Sabion avoids eye contact, but Geddes speaks up. "And what *is* that word? What Sabion called me."

"It was a word used to separate people who look like you from people who look like him."

Geddes nods in understanding. "My dad told me a little of what it was like in the old world. He's mostly quiet about it, but he's told me. There was money—not bartering. Dollars and coins. There were lots and lots of mayors like Hutch but spread everywhere and who ruled lots of cities and people. He told me that you couldn't just get up and go hunting or scavenging to get food for your family. But that there were rules."

"There were many more rules then," I say. "Both spoken and unspoken. Rules that used words that made everyone feel okay with something that was very wrong. When you start hearing words that separate one people from another, you will know that there is a new sheriff in town—a new boss has taken over and wants you to think that group is different."

"I said I was just joking," Sabion repeats. There is actually something close to contrition in his voice. "Let's just drop it. Eat."

I stand and place my bowl on a log. "You can have mine. Lost my appetite."

I abscond back to the boat to be alone and find Geddes has beat me there, plucking chords from a guitar.

"Sounds nice," I tell him.

"Do you play?"

"Yes. Although it's been a few years."

He passes me the guitar, which I take with some reluctance. Plucked notes die in the night, swallowed by the vast beachhead. But the chords ring for me, filling me with awful nostalgia. Clive is in the melody. He put his hand on my belly. *Should we share our lists?*

"Doctor Darrow?" I hear Ward.

I stop playing. "What is it?" I don't turn to face him.

"I didn't know you could play."

"What do you need?" I ask.

He puts up his palms. "Jeez. I'm just checking."

"On what?"

"On you. You don't seem well. Are you okay?"

It's a hell of a question. "Yes."

"Are you mad at me again?" Ward asks.

I sigh. "Not at you. I'm sorry I made you feel that way."

His eyes follow the guitar neck. "I think we'd all like to hear you play. Might liven things up a little. No one's talking."

I don't want to. I'm sick of being the adult—tired of being the doctor to a colony that really doesn't want me. I don't want to console these boys who could never understand the things that I understand—could never live the ages that I've lived. But I nod and follow him back to camp, guitar in hand, the mood as sour as when I left. Reece and Sabion won't look at one another.

I finger-pick a melody, their eyes following my fingers along the neck of the guitar. I strum a series of chords, a song so old to me, I can hardly remember if I made it up or if it was a song from the old world. Sabion and Reece say nothing, but I can see they are enraptured by the notes. Sabion asks, "Can you sing the words? Songs about what life used to be like before?"

The cobwebs in my brain clear as I reach for the few songs I remember. I clear my throat. "I can try." My voice is scratchy and rough, but I sing them a song:

When the day comes, when I'm a man
And my mother taught me
The best that she can
I'll buy me a briefcase
I'll buy me some shares
And get me a job in a city somewhere

Farewell to laughter
Goodbye to summers
So long to the daisies
I'm riding the metro
I'm paying the fare
Off to work in a building somewhere

When I finish, Geddes blinks away tears. "That's where people worked, right? In the tall buildings?" he asks.

"They dressed up in suits and went up into the tall buildings and worked all day," I say.

"What did they do in the buildings?" Geddes asks.

"Used computers and words to build the world that they wanted. And they made a lot of money doing it."

The boys nod along, but I know they only have vague ideas of what a computer even is. Ward says, "People had nice things then. Cars, computers, airplanes, cell phones. They could do anything they wanted, whenever they wanted. They must have been so free."

"Freedom is not always what you think it is," I tell him. "Some cages are just bigger than others."

"I still would've liked to live in the old world," Ward says.

"Not me," Sabion says. "I wouldn't like all the rules. I like to be free—be my own man."

And then they argue. They debate which era is best—the futuristic past or the apocalyptic present. I say nothing, knowing I can explain very little to them.

EIGHT

"ANYTHING?" I asked Marjorie, the communication manager of the Sierra Nevada bunker, crouched over the Comms array.

She bristled. "This is your third time here this week. We don't even have the system on right now. You know that. We must conserve power."

"I don't know that. I don't know anything. Do you know what I do all day?" I asked.

"I'm sorry that I don't have anything to tell you." She crossed her arms and leaned back in her chair, a long squeak agreeing with her refusal.

I clenched my fists, digging nails into my sweaty palms. "I listen to lungs and hit knee reflexes all day, wondering if my husband is dead."

"I understand," she said as bureaucratically as possible.

"I don't even know where they sent him. You must have some news from up there? Wars? Fighting? The Hila?"

"I'm sorry I don't have any information for you," she said as sterile as possible, unwilling to get entangled with me.

"Your family is down here, aren't they?"

She cleared her throat. "Yes."

"Mine isn't. I was pregnant, but then last week, I bled in between my legs and gave birth to my dead son."

The coldness melted from the woman's face.

"I'm alone," I continued. "I have no one. I need to know what has happened to my husband. I know he's probably dead. The only thing that's worse than him being dead is losing him and not knowing if he's gone or not. I'm cracking. I must know what kind of life sits before me before I go mad with uncertainty. Do you understand?"

"Yes. I'm sorry."

"Then please tell me. What did you know about US military deployments before we came down here?"

She looked down at the table as if ashamed. "They're gone."

"Who is gone? Which ones?"

She shook her head like I was not understanding the butt of a joke. "They're all gone."

"You mean..."

She said nothing else because there was nothing else to say to me. The world was suddenly just a concrete hole in the ground with anyone I had ever loved gone forever. A grief settled into my bones that never left me like an incurable cancer that would never kill me.

At dawn, I watch as Geddes and Ward prepare breakfast underneath the naked sky. We sit in chilled silence, spooning oatmeal and chewing dried fruit. Sabion and Reece appear to reach some sort of reconciliation as they plan the expedition, speaking to one another as if they were the sole decision-makers. Geddes watches them as he eats, resentment on his face as he chews fruit leather. In the dawn light, we see that the playground where we camped is choked on all sides by plant life. Several derelict cars stud what was once a grass field, windows broken by gnarled branches, their once brilliant paint coatings corroded by salt and time.

A branch cracks somewhere and we all stop packing, looking at one another. Just beyond camp, a grunt followed by shaking leaves makes my pulse jump. Sabion brandishes his rifle while Reece brings his finger to his lips. He uses non-verbal cues that bring Geddes and Sabion into formation, rifles poised. Controlling my breathing, I draw my Glock and follow them to the concrete wall from where we heard the noise. There's more shaking of leaves and then I hear a low humming. Sabion and Reece look at one another, perplexed by the noise. Reece indicates to Geddes to flank the sides of the wall where concrete blocks have crumbled. They inch slowly—a branch cracking under Geddes' boot.

The noise stops as my heart starts racing.

Whoever it is, they're waiting—watching.

Geddes climbs through a break in the wall. Silence as Reece and Sabion creep forward. We gaze at the wall, waiting, waiting—Sabion climbs up and over.

I jump as a shot is fired.

Reece yells something but I'm moving, climbing up the crumbling concrete and landing in dense foliage—a thicket of thorns and ferns. Nothing but green, scattered dawn light filters through the canopy.

"Sabion!" Reece yells. "Report!"

Silence. And then I hear, "Hold." Sabion is breaking through branches somewhere ahead.

"Do you have a visual?" Reece asks. "Who fired?"

"I did," Sabion says. "There was movement."

"Do you have a visual?"

"I didn't see anything," Geddes says from the forest.

I hate all of it. I wish I was back at the east wing watching people die in the hospital rather than watching them die by gunfire. But I creep forward and see Sabion crouched by a boulder, rifle raised. He's spotted something—movement a dozen yards away. I see it too, and there is more than one of them. I raise my Glock as I creep, knowing they can hear my every footstep. There's a dumpster wedged between two trees, which I climb, careful with my footing on the flimsy plastic.

"I have a visual," Sabion says.

"On what?" Reece asks as he slinks forward, negotiating the forest.

Sabion responds with one word. "Hostiles."

"Take the shot," Reece commands.

Slowing my breathing, I focus my aim on where the boys are converging. And then I lock my gaze with a set of brown eyes. "Don't fire!" I yell.

"Sabion, if you have a visual on hostiles, take the shot!"

"Do *not* shoot!" I say, leaping from the dumpster and running into a forest clearing.

"I am in command here!" Reece yells.

I find Sabion and put my hand on his rifle. "Non-hostile," I say. "Go and have a look at what you were about to obliterate."

The boy lowers his rifle, muscles shaky. He stands and swipes leaves from his view and squints. "What is it?"

The animal has its head low, a frenetic humming coming from its trembling lips. Beneath its belly, two calves stand, cowering below their mother. The others arrive, gaping at the beast.

"A giraffe?" Reece says, awe in his tone.

"Yes. They're still around from old-world zoos. I saw a rhino once in Berkley." I leave them gawking at the animal. "Sabion, next time you have a visual on a hostile, make sure you *actually* have a visual before firing."

With camp packed, we return to the pontoon, where Ward sits patiently at his post, guarding the boat. "Was that gunfire?"

"Giraffes," Geddes says with a wide grin. "And they're okay."

A smile cracks Ward's lips. "Can we go back?"

"No," Reece spits, climbing aboard. "We're shipping out. Now."

The sky is clear as we embark, gentle waves guiding us from the beach. Once the boys paddle us out, they deploy the main sail, which catches the south winds and carries us down the Bay. We pass under the San Mateo bridge. There are men up there—men I don't recognize. They watch us as we pass, rifles in their arms. Reece commands the boys to also brandish their weapons. It's a childish show of force as we glide beneath the men, their gazes never breaking from the boat.

"Raiders?" Ward asks.

I shake my head. "Raiders aren't usually so well-armed. They lack the community and infrastructure to have gear and weapons with good upkeep. Those men are from a colony. They don't look SF. They don't look like a trade caravan, either. Not sure what they're doing this close to ours."

"They're from Sacramento," Reece says.

"How do you know that?" I ask.

"I just do," he says without his typical arrogance. He may be basing his knowledge on actual colonial intelligence. And then I know what some of Mayor Hutch's meetings have been about. We'd always been on good terms with the Sacramento colony with open trading routes. Why was he worried about them? And why now?

The bridge vanishes behind us as we sail south.

We travel in silence for some time with Sabion at the tiller and on constant red alert with binoculars glued to his eyeballs. Geddes has occupied himself with a yo-yo while Reece perseverates over a tattered map. As we skirt the coast, Ward lingers at the edge of the pontoon. He crosses the deck and then returns to the same side, studying the water. And then again, he crosses the deck and looks in the water, a wrinkle parting his brow.

"What's wrong?" I ask.

He shakes his head. "No-nothing." But then he's crossing the deck again and, this time, sits at the edge of the pontoon, gangly legs dangling over as he peers ever closer at the waves.

I loom over his shoulder. "What are you looking at?"

"I thought..." But then he stands, giving himself that frenetic hug he does when he is sapped of self-confidence. "I thought I saw something."

"What?"

He notices Reece and Sabion looking at him, ready to pounce on anything he says. "It was nothing, just the waves playing tricks on me."

I move, blocking Reece's line of sight and ask in a low voice, "What did you see?"

"Shadows," he whispers.

"Shadows?"

He squints at the water. "Thought I saw shadows under there. But it was just shadows from the boat." He feigns a shrug, adjusts his cracked glasses, and finds his pack to rummage through.

I look over the edge.

Only frothy water churns below.

．　．　．

As we approach the southern delta of the Bay, I feel a stiff cross-wind as we're greeted by another storm. Reece and Sabion render themselves useless debating navigation while Geddes negotiates the turbid waves. Reece grips the edge of the pontoon, binoculars in one hand while shouting directions to Geddes so he doesn't crash us into a rocky shoreline. I peer through my binoculars and see not-so-good news—the tidal marsh has flooded large swathes of San Jose. Brackish water swells beyond the bounds of the main river that once quested through the heart of the city.

"Get control!" Reece yells at Geddes. The boys manage to weave us through the estuary, only to have us instantly swallowed up into the flooded streets of San Jose.

"The current is sweeping us in!" Geddes yells as I grip the edge of the boat from the turbulent water.

Roadway bridges that once spanned above the river are now buffeted by waves gushing over medians, swamping the concrete passages with river flow. Geddes navigates through the broken concrete of the bridges as the current draws us further into the city. Tilted streetlights litter the cityscape, providing new causeways for the unstoppable ivy dangling from every imaginable surface.

We float by skeletonized buildings, their innards now eviscerated of walls and flooring, showing only bald sky through empty windows. Water-logged furniture floats aimlessly in flooded lobbies, trapped and circling forever in their little lonesome whirlpools. Only iron struts remain of most buildings, bearing the boney beginnings for plant growth to fill the belly of the structures, ushering in a new-world economy of bugs and rodents. Parking garage levels have long since collapsed under the weight of abandoned vehicles, leaving mounds of cars and building detritus within the few remaining walls that stand.

"Where the hell are we supposed to moor?" Sabion asks,

which is a stupid question really because the obvious answer is absolutely nowhere. Unabated, the water rapids sweep us south toward downtown. We float under freeway overpasses with holes crumbling through, the rebar grinning at us from above. Curtains of ivy are draped from the overpasses, wrapping around concrete columns, their tips streaming in the waters beneath. The faded green of exit signs peek through the choking foliage, signaling the way home for a people that are no longer here. Like San Francisco and the rest of the Bay area, the people of San Jose evacuated during threats of imminent nuclear strikes that never came to the Bay area.

The flooding lessens as we distance ourselves from the Bay and we now understand that San Jose is suffering end-stage disease of metastatic sinkholes. The entire cityscape looks as if a giant came upon the city and occupied itself with a jackhammer. Gaping ravines occupy what were once thriving plazas or strip malls. Cars and trucks are scattered along streets where the earth has lifted and dropped, fracturing asphalt and edifices along the way. A vibrant mossy green is the pavement of the new world, coating and claiming the city back from the once civilized veneer of smoothed concrete.

"Oh, shit!" I say as my back slams to the deck. Several river torrents converge around the pontoon, rushing us down the flooded streets. The crew gives up their tenuous control over the boat and now uses paddles to bat away tree branches that threaten the mast. We dip into a momentary pool of turbid waters that spins us one-eighty and spits us out backwards and rushing once more into inner city rapids. Like I'm being jolted side to side on a roller coaster, water pummels us on all sides, swamping the deck.

"Ah!" Ward cries as he slips with water hydroplaning beneath his feet. With glasses askew on his face, he manages to get to one knee but flops to his belly as the pontoon slumps into a ravine carved in the middle of an intersection.

"Ward!" I yell as he's washed to the side of the deck, one hand gripping cargo netting. With Ward's legs dangling off the edge of the deck, Geddes slides on his belly with outstretched arms toward him. They clasp hands but Geddes quickly loses leverage on the living side of the boat, and his legs flop over the deck along with Ward's toward the dying side of the boat. The two dangle in the torrents, moments from being ripped off the deck. Reece and Sabion watch, frozen in inaction. I move, my hip screaming as I fall, and slam my chin on the deck. Spitting water blurs my vision as I reach out to grab an arm or a leg—anything to stop them from falling overboard. But my hand slaps on the empty deck.

"Doctor Darrow!" I hear Ward scream like he's calling for his mother.

"Where are you?" I yell, rubbing water from my eyes and then I spot the pair, barely clinging to the side of the boat. I stumble to reach them, but then Sabion shimmies over to them, anchoring his waist to the mast with a rope. Burly arms moving, Sabion brings the boys from the edge of the pontoon onto solid footing.

Just as I'm getting to my feet, I slam onto the deck again as the pontoon spins like a top. We twirl and twirl, bobbing from one torrent to the next, bouncing off building cornices that have crumbled to the ground. We white-knuckle it for the next few minutes, pinballing from a gated fence to toppled gas station ports and then an upside-down McDonald's M that fell from its perch. Somehow, the pontoon manages to avoid capsizing through the barrage.

Suddenly, the boat disappears from beneath my feet.

I'm airborne. I'm panic incarnate. I'm drowning—I'm already dead.

A thundering crash ripples through my spine, strikes my neck with whiplash, and crunches teeth over tongue. Sheets of water are pouring over me, choking the breath right out of me. My mouth fills with a medley of coppery blood and salty marsh. After coughing up briny water, I look up and see we've literally fallen off of a waterfall.

A sinkhole the size of a bowling alley has swallowed up half a city block, which has churned up piping, gas lines, and fiberoptic cables that reach through the chasm wall, scraping along the pontoon as we cascade down the muddy waterfall. It's not a sheer drop-off, but it's steep enough that all of us cling to anything we can find so we don't go tumbling into the oblivion of San Jose's sewer netherworld.

And we still don't capsize.

There are so many offshoots of water drainage from a thousand streams and a thousand pipes that I stop trying to understand the forces at play that have quickly turned our expedition into an abject catastrophe. I'm gasping for air, yelling out to the boys, and have my belly wrapped around the mast, which rattles against its bolts. A hand grabs hold of my boot, and I lift them toward me, guiding their arms to the salvation of the mast. Voices shout out of anger and fear and wild exhaustion.

Clefts of rock and truck wheels loom above us as the boat levels out and splashes down into a murky pool. We bob around like a cork for a moment as the bottom of the plunging waterfall knocks us away. The mist recedes as the water calms. Lying on my back, I see the sky has cleared as sunlight stokes wisps of steam from the soaked deck. Ragged and shivering, I get to my knees, pleased to discover I didn't suffer a paralyzing neck injury. I do a headcount.

Four boys—

"Jericho!" Ward screams.

—Minus one ferret.

"Jericho!" he wails, voice cracking while frantically searching his coat pockets. He cries the ferret's name again, throwing gear around, searching for the animal. His anguish goes unconsoled as the rest of the boys look around, completely dazed. Reece has lost the shirt off his back and gazes with a confused snarl at the towering walls of dirt that surround us at the bottom of a massive sinkhole. Sabion wears a befuddled expression of which I didn't think him capable. I would take a small measure of joy at the abrupt humbling of the competing alpha males if I wasn't worried about how absolutely screwed we are. It's sheer dumb luck that we're even alive and not corpses floating in the forgotten deluge of San Jose. Ward continues sobbing over the loss of his pet while the other boys are too dazed with rank trauma to mock him.

"Okay, Reece," I say, snapping my fingers at him. "How do we get out of this hole?"

We abandon the pontoon, pack whatever gear we can on our backs, and step off the pontoon. Swirling around my knees is the commercial flotsam of twisted metal and plastic shavings churned by the neo-apocalyptic flood system of San Jose. My neck throbs with pain, which joins the symphony of suffering from my hip. I quickly inspect the rest of the boys who, aside from abrasions, are void of injury. Waist-deep in brown water, we give a collective sigh when our feet touch something solid. We climb up the skeleton of an enormous airplane wing deeply wedged into the bottom of the sinkhole. Peering up, I see the crusted edge of crumbling asphalt wreathing the sinkhole. The chasm walls are about thirty feet deep with no obvious way up other than trying to skirt the side of the waterfall.

"How are we getting out?" Ward asks, fog in his glasses.

No one answers.

I touch the chasm wall and feel the fresh earth give way.

"We've got rope," I say. "This wall is soft enough to get a foothold in. Shallow enough that we could hike up with a well-anchored rope and hopefully not have the wall crumble on top of us. The first up can tie off the rope and we can all climb out of here. I've got the bum hip. Who's climbing?"

An embarrassed silence blooms between the boys.

"I'll go," Geddes offers.

"No, no," Sabion says, throwing his hands up as if offended by his suggestion. "Gimme that rope." He takes it from Ward and arches his back, sizing up the facade as if he's done this a thousand times before. After cinching the coiled rope to his belt, he rolls up his pant leg cuffs and climbs. He makes short work of the wall and heaves himself over the lip, disappearing from view. After a few moments, a knotted rope drops down the chasm. "Secure," Sabion declares.

I'm the last to climb up and feel the relief of having my boots on solid ground. An actual gasp escapes my lips when I look at my surroundings. San Jose is not just an abandoned city, it's a city reclaimed by primordial forces—water, wind, and green life. Seabirds are absolutely everywhere. They nest high in crumbling skyscrapers, swooping down into the sprawling waters that cover the city. Many buildings still stand, but there is no way to tell which still have structural integrity without searching them, no way to safely navigate the city—no way of reclaiming medical supplies.

"So, where's the hospital?" Reece asks.

I look at him for a moment. "The *hospital?*

He nods and then unfurls his stupid map.

"Look around you," I say. "There's no hospital anymore. The city is completely destroyed. This expedition is a total loss. Your dad's scouts aren't as thorough as he would have me believe," I say that last part with a bite of acid.

"Then how are we going to get pregnancy medical supplies?"

"*What?*" Sabion hisses. "That's why we came here? You knocked up Priscilla?"

Reece's face darkens. "Shut your mouth."

Before the boys can pummel each other again, they're interrupted by sobbing. Ward has started back at it again, and this time, he's mourning over his open-sketch diary. Charcoal etchings of Jericho the ferret litter the soaked pages. The boy shakes with grief, the sketchbook falling from his hands.

"Will someone shut that queer up!" Sabion barks. "I'll throw him back into that pit if he doesn't stop that crying, I swear. Gimme that—" He picks up the sketchbook and unceremoniously tosses it into the sinkhole. Ward watches in stunned silence as it falls, pages fluttering in the wind. And then he wails louder, a piercing din rolling out over the flooded city, startling some birds who fly off to another lake away from the human drama that has briefly interrupted their pleasant bird lives.

I no longer have the energy to berate Sabion—no vigor to console my medical student. I look at Reece, a very stern you-better-get-control-of-this-situation look painted on my face. He says nothing and he does nothing—a tacit approval of Sabion's cruelty.

"There he is!" Ward shouts.

We peer into the sinkhole, and sure enough, a long weasel-shaped animal is bobbing along the water, alive but struggling. "Someone needs to go down there," Ward pleads, clearly intimidated at the prospect of climbing back down. "He's going to die!"

"It's just a dumb rat," Sabion says, picking up his pack. "Let's head out."

"Move out!" Reece says.

Geddes drops his pack, takes off his shirt, and loops a rope around his waist. "You're not going back down there," Reece warns. But Geddes is already lowering himself into the sinkhole, collecting the weary ferret in his shirt. Back on top, he hands the animal to Ward, who returns a hug to the boy before nuzzling and fretting over Jericho. The creature is noticeably chipper after lapping water from Ward's palm and eating some rabbit jerky.

"Now we can go," I say with a nod to Geddes and pick up my pack. I head northward.

"Doctor Darrow, where are you *going*?" Reece calls.

"Home."

"But we have the expedition to complete."

"This is not an expedition anymore. It's a rescue mission."

NINE

THE DAY WAXES late as the sun sinks into a blood-orange horizon. The mood is sour as we travel north, back to the Bay and away from the underwater lost city of San Jose. I leap from one car hood to the next, my hip and neck complaining with each lunge. We skirt the edge of the city, away from the rapids of the inner city. Through binoculars, I find peripheral suburbs are largely intact with standing water in the streets rippling with the drizzling rain. The boys follow me in silence as we cross through soggy homes with foundations sunken and cross beams collapsed. It's clear that powerful winds sweep through on occasion as we step over felled trees, phone lines, and entire rafters unroofed from homes, splintered across the streets.

The boys trudge through the flooded streets, water to their knees, needlessly sweeping their rifles. Reece and Sabion finally fall in line behind me, temporarily relieving themselves of the burden of pretending to be in charge. I know it won't last long. As soon as they dry up and get food in their bellies, the power struggle will be back in full swing. The hierarchy is still intact, however, with Geddes behind Sabion and Ward trailing last with ferret in hand.

We find an office building built along a business park that looks like it once housed telemarketers and multi-level marketing schemes—businesses that my traveling companions wouldn't even begin to understand. I test the flooring under my boot, feeling the spongy spring of decay. Black mold arches its way up every exposed surface and tracks along couch upholstery. While most of the sheetrock has rotted away, cement and steel foundation remain intact. We creep, silent and armed, up a stairwell until we arrive at the third floor, which appears to have stable flooring. I stop when I hear a high-pitched sound behind a closed door. Sabion lifts his rifle to the door.

"Remember the giraffe?" I ask him.

He crinkles his nose. "What about it?"

"Don't fire until you actually have a visual—a visual on an actual threat. Do you understand me?"

"Don't tell me what I'm about." He brushes past me, kicks open the door, and aims at a rookery of seagulls that are already fleeing from the commotion. He grunts at the birds as if it is from his sheer intimidation they scatter and not animal reflex.

Reece points to the floor, indicating for Geddes and Ward to drop the supplies they've been hauling. "We'll camp here. There's enough ventilation for a small fire."

I say nothing and turn from the room.

"Doctor Darrow?" Ward calls.

"What?"

"Where are you going?"

"To find my own room," I say.

"Oh." He looks at the other boys with apprehension.

"Come on."

. . .

I'm startled awake in the middle of the night by shouting. Ward's prone figure lies on an office desk, where he sleeps soundly. I'm on my feet, Glock in hand, moving to the door. The office where the other boys set up camp is empty, a drowned fire stoking smoke through a hole in the ceiling. Once I realize the voices are coming from the street, I make my way down the stairwell and find Sabion ducked behind a concrete column in the lobby, Reece with his back against the wall, head turned in mid-conversation.

"Now, now," a man calls from the parking lot, voice issuing from behind tree and shrub debris that had been swept in from previous flooding. "No need to get riled up, boys."

"Why did we just find you in our stairwell?" Reece yells.

"Innocent mistake," he says. "We didn't know anyone was in the building."

"Bullshit," Sabion says. "Planning on slitting our throats in our sleep?" And then he and Geddes are on their bellies, inching their way out of the foyer and through the thick grasses of the building patio, trying to get eyes on the hostile group.

"Me and my men were only looking for a place to lay our weary heads," the man says, still hidden from our view.

"And this building, in all of San Jose, was the only place you looked to camp?" Reece asks.

"Place is flooded to biblical proportions, son—not uncommon for travelers to find the few remaining sound structures for respite," the man says. He speaks with the gruffness and ease of an older gentleman—wait.

I know the voice but it brings me no comfort. "Anders?" I yell.

Silence for a moment. "It seems you have me at a disadvantage," the man says.

"How long have you been following us?" I ask.

"I'd be more than happy to continue this conversation after I've had some introductions."

"Elspeth Darrow, SF," I say.

"Reece Hutch, Mayor Hutch's son," Reece also adds.

Anders laughs and shows himself along with his gray stubble and pot belly. I recognize that smug smile from a few months back when the man came with his trading caravans from Sacramento. He repeatedly tried to sell me spoiled medical supplies.

"Why have you been following us?" I ask.

He steps forward, hands beneath his poncho. Sabion emerges, rifle aimed at his chest. Anders nods to him and says, "Doctor Darrow, would you mind calling off your dogs?"

"She is not in command here," Reece says, hands on his hips. "I am, and I would like an explanation of why you were sneaking into our camp in the middle of the night."

"I've offered my explanation already. Elspeth, I haven't earned the disrespect of having to repeat myself. I now kindly ask that these boys lower their weapons."

"Show us your hands," Reece demands.

Several figures emerge from the darkness, rifles aimed squarely on us. Three, four, and then eight. They've been watching us the whole time. "Everyone, lower your weapons this instant," I demand.

After a solid minute of smoldering testosterone, both sides of men lower their weapons. Geddes and Sabion stand up from their cover in the tall grasses.

"Four," Anders comments on our party as if taking notes.

"What brings you down here?" I ask.

"Was going to ask you the same," Anders says.

"Salvage."

"Salvage of *what?*"

"Medical supplies."

"Find anything?"

I shake my head. "The whole city is a loss. We damn near drowned on our way in. Headed back home now."

"So... you didn't find anything?" Anders asks.

"Just told you the city is a loss, nothing out here."

"Didn't come down here looking for anything else?"

I glare at him. "No. Did you? Other than us, of course."

"Nothing," he says. "Like you said, San Jose is a loss. No reason for anyone to come poking around here anymore."

"That a warning?"

"A suggestion—"

A tree branch snaps—a loud pop of gunfire echoes in my ears.

Everyone takes cover. Confusion and indignation are knit over Reece's brow. "Who fired?"

"You fire on us, Elspeth?" Anders shouts.

Sabion looks down at his gun, marvel and guilt blooming on his face. "Did you fire?" I ask him, but I need no answer because I know what happened. "One of our boys fired over here," I yell out. "Thought the tree branch breaking was gunfire. It was an honest mistake—don't fire!"

Anders yells, "We've got a man down over here! What kind of amateur operation are you running?"

My breath quickens as I rush out into the parking lot, unarmed, toward the Sacramento group huddled around the injured. I elbow my way through and find a teenage boy in the dirt, blood gushing from his thigh. "Am I going to die?" he asks, his face a blank sheet of dismay.

"Someone give me a belt!" I yell, reaching my hand out. They look to Anders. "Now!" I demand before two belts are thrown at me. "Where is Ward?" I yell at Reece as I tie a belt around the boy's upper thigh. "Get him out here and tell him to bring my med bag." I inspect the wound—it's midline on the thigh with an exit wound at the back. I have no idea if it shattered bone and—even worse—if the bullet lacerated the femoral artery. The kid is toast if he's bleeding from a major vessel out here in wasteland San Jose.

Ward is at my side with my med bag, blinking sleep from his eyes. "Put in an IV," I tell him. "Hang a liter of normal saline." Ward's hands tremble over the boy's wrist, quivering as he repeatedly fails to tie a tourniquet. "You've done this dozens of times," I complain before pushing him aside. "He might bleed out. He needs fluid right now."

"I—" Ward shies away as Anders watches, condemnation written on his face.

My knees are wet with warmth—fresh blood pooling along the boy's leg. I cinch the belt tighter around his upper thigh and flick on the boy's wrist. I know I should ask what his name is—should comfort the boy as his vision fades. But I can't care like that anymore—not after twenty years of this. I can only move my hands, not my lips. A vein plumps, I place the IV, connect tubing, and get to my feet, squeezing on the bag of fluid to get it into his body as fast as possible.

Anders shuffles to my side. "What now?"

"Do you have med supplies?" I ask.

"We have a surg kit." He looks at his men who collectively extract a bundle from their supplies.

"Take this," I hand Anders the IV bag. More blood issues forth, pooling at our feet as my heart quickens. "Keep squeezing," I tell them as my mouth dries with panic. "Once it's empty, hang another bag and don't stop." I unfurl the surgery kit, the metal instruments clanking along the mossy ground. Now I know the bullet lacerated an artery, but I have no idea which artery and I can't know. If it's his femoral—he's dead. If it's a smaller artery, he's still probably dead.

Wordlessly, Ward now kneels above the boy, poised with an open bottle of sterile water ready to irrigate the wound. I'm both oddly proud and profoundly disappointed that this is the only initiative of which he is capable—pouring water into a wound.

"What else do we need?" I test Ward.

"Sterile towels. Lots of them. Need to keep the surgical wound dry so you can see." He produces the towels from his med bag.

I nod and bring a scalpel down to the edge of the wound and slice it open as the patient howls into the night, startling the armed men, who watch with morbid fascination. I ignore the boy's suffering, moving to sit over his knees to stop him from bucking as I dissect further through the fat tissue. Ward irrigates and dabs, irrigates and dabs, but he can't keep up. So, I probe with my finger, bluntly dissecting as the boy yelps into greater echelons of suffering.

"He's fine," I hear Sabion conclude from behind me. "Just a flesh wound."

I screw my face toward him. "Get out of my sight," I demand, acid in every word. The boy-man grins in mockery as if the mortal struggle at his feet exists for his bemusement.

Blindly, my finger staunches the bleeding but I have no idea where the lacerated artery is. "I have to expose the vessel from above and tie it off." With my finger still deep in the leg, I continue to open the wound from above with an awkward grip, creating jagged tears through the fat and muscle.

"What are you doing?" Anders asks, accusation dripping from his words. His men tense. One aims his rifle.

"Shut up and hang another bag of saline," I tell him.

Anders complies, but his men stay on edge.

More dissecting down as the patient sobs into the crook of his elbow. "Keep it dry," I tell Ward and finally discover the glistening artery pulsating under a shallow pool of blood. "Put your finger where mine is and do *not* move it." Ward holds pressure on the bleeding vessel, freeing my hands to create more space around the proximal part of the artery. Boots scuffle and I discover one of Anders' men has fainted from the gore, the back of his skull connecting quite beautifully with a felled stoplight. In some sort of comically cosmic twist of fate, I now have two trauma patients. "Check him!" I yell at Anders, gesturing to the fallen man without looking away from the gunshot wound. The man quickly comes to and sits on a curb, chugging water.

I try threading sutures behind the artery but the scant glow from Ward's flashlight bobbing up and down in his mouth doesn't exactly provide operating theater conditions. He sees me struggling and strains his neck to shine more light on the surgical field. Between the tourniquet and surgical towels soaking the field, I get a long enough window where I can actually see the artery and loop some suture behind it. One, two, three knots lay down and I tie it off. I hold my breath and gently pull Ward's hand away from the wound.

The bleeding stops.

Anders releases a spectator's whistle between his thin lips. "Fine work, Doc."

I brush strands of hair from my eyes and lick my lips, grimacing from the sweaty salt flavor in my mouth. "He may still die." I take quick measure of the pools of blood surrounding me. "He's lost probably a quarter of his blood volume. If he doesn't lose more, he may live—assuming he doesn't die of sepsis." I look to Ward, who produces a single vial of powdered antibiotic from Anders' med kit. "Mix it," I tell him. "That's the only dose, correct?"

"Yes. Will it be enough?" Ward asks.

"No." I pack the wound with gauze—the boy now snores, the agony has long since saturated his ability for executive function.

"So, now what?" Anders asks, the toe of his boot coming into my view.

I stand, my hip complaining with warnings of how the rest of the night will be for me. "Give another bag of saline," I tell Ward. "Bring him into the building. Sit with him. Watch him overnight."

"And now what?" Anders repeats, annoyed that I don't address him.

"You can pray, if that's something you do."

"I am a praying man, but I'm talking about us—our situation. What do we do now about this debacle here tonight?" The rest of his men stir, ready to resume the skirmish that Sabion started.

"Go to bed," I say, walking past him without ever making eye contact. I pass by Reece and Sabion, who have receded back to the building foyer, scheming their battle plans.

"You probably killed the boy," I tell Sabion, dabbing sweat from my forehead.

"*They* killed him," Reece answers for him. "The Sacs shouldn't have been following us this whole time." Sabion's gaze meets mine—sheer defiance burning in his eyes.

"Since when have we been calling them *Sacs*?"

Raw silence sits between us.

"Why do you think the old world was destroyed?" I ask.

"The Hilamen," Sabion answers. "They wiped us out."

"The Hilamen brought no weapons to our planet—made no attacks, no threats. We don't even know if they are sentient."

"Bullshit."

"The old world was destroyed because of what you just did."

"And what is that?" Sabion asks.

"Thinking with a gun."

. . .

I don't sleep, only gaze into the darkness. My fingers run nervously along the rosary I took from the school. Like a fool, I hold the wooden beads, click them along my fingernails, and thumb the wood grain. It's an eternity I'm cloaked in the darkness of the room, the weight of the rosary filling my soul—eating my thoughts and holding me there, fixed between the present misery and sour memories. I want to pull the damn thing apart, break the thread, cast the beads. But I see Clive smiling in an impossible past—a past that is a parallel dimension of who I was. He opens a box, the rosary coiled within tissue paper, the name *Gabriel* engraved along it.

The next morning, I find the boy—his pale profile emerges from the darkness as dawnlight filters through the building's foyer. Ward has stayed with him all night, the boy's rigid hand resting in his grasp. Ward looks at me, eyes fatigued from hours of spent tears. "He dead," my med student sputters, losing his grasp on basic language.

"The leg got infected, it went to his bloodstream, and he no doubt died of septic shock." I walk past him. "He couldn't have been more than fifteen."

The Sacramento men are camped outside. Two sentinels watch my approach and feign outrage as I blow past, my eyes pinned on Anders. The man hastily cuffs sticky syrup from his chin scruff as he sets a can of peaches on a log. I cross my arms as he produces a wood pipe carved into the shape of an erect penis. Merrily, he packs the ludicrous pipe with tobacco, strikes a match, and draws air through the weed. "Know where I got this pipe?" he asks.

"I don't care. Why were you following us?"

"The boy dead?"

"Yes. Are you going to answer my question?" I ask.

"There will be problems."

"There were already problems. You were following my scavenger party. I would like to know why."

He only grins, revealing a mouth full of decay.

"The body is in the foyer. Do not follow us." I leave him there, that horrendous grin frozen on his face.

"Not good, Doc. Not good."

TEN

WE SKIP breakfast and head north to the Bay shoreline, away from Anders' men and their impromptu funeral. Sabion and Reece appear completely unphased by the boy's death, rationalizations churning full steam beneath their skulls. Geddes offers no commentary and appears thoroughly shell-shocked from a night of listening to the whimper of a dying boy tumbling through the stairwell. Ward travels with an unusual confident stride, Jericho over his shoulder. He notices my gaze on him.

"I stayed with him," he says.

"You did," I say.

"The whole night. I didn't fall asleep once. I stayed with him." For the first time since I've known the boy, there is dignity in his voice.

"He deserved an usher like you to see him off. Not everyone gets it." I wince at my own words, knowing I can no longer do what Ward did—sit with the dying. Breaking my heart with them over and over has left nothing but scar behind. If I hold the hand of one more dying patient, I don't think it can heal back over again.

We travel under a freeway overpass, gray skies peering through the crumbling concrete. It leads us out of the swamp land in a straight shot, delivering us into a series of rolling hills interrupted by curved fields untouched by any building. Geddes squints at the isolated wilderness like an oasis among the flooded city. "Weird looking park," he says.

"It was a golf course," I say.

"What's that?" Geddes asks.

"A game people used to play."

"They just take up this much space for fun? Couldn't they just play dice?" Ward asks.

"They would hit little balls with metal sticks. Tried to get them into holes in the ground." All four of the boys look at me. I put up my hands. "I never played it, alright?"

"Into those huge holes there?" Ward points to a row of holes in the ground, all at least ten feet deep. "Doesn't seem like a hard game."

"No," I answer, creeping closer. "Not holes like that." I peer into the gaping hole. "Not sure what all these are." The mouths of the holes appear to have been created by a series of small, repetitive scratches layered over one another, each about two shoulder widths in diameter. I have no idea what tool dug the holes, but it wasn't a shovel. At the very bottom lies murky water choking my throat with the stench of brine and rotten eggs.

"Stinks. Keep moving," Reece commands, weaving in between the holes.

Soon, we're skirting the marshland of the southern tip of the Bay. The ocean waves lap gently through the grasses as fish scurry at our movements. We find a line of row boats abandoned along the beachhead. Most of the hulls have long since corroded, breached with rusted craters making an ideal nesting spot for the numerous rats that scurry across the sand at our approach. We discover a boat that appears seaworthy and, after tossing it into the waves, the thing stays afloat. After loading our gear and party in, we wait a full twenty minutes near the shore to make sure we don't end up at the bottom of the Bay, and then we leave. The sky clears as we row, dipping paddles the only sound among our sordid party.

"The hell is that?" Reece says, hand brought to brow. "And what is that rotten egg smell?"

At first, I have no idea what he's talking about, but then I see it —a smudge of black in the waves ahead. "Oil slick," I answer.

"That's no oil slick," Sabion argues. And then my knees bonk together as the boat turns toward the slick, the boy's curiosity getting the better of them.

"It's probably an old oil drum," I say with impatience. "At the bottom of the Bay. It recently ruptured and is leeching oil up—" And then the smell hits me and I finally see it more clearly. It's no oil slick. "Wait... that's a body."

"What happened to them?" Geddes asks as we near the floating corpse. "He's all covered in... what are those black beads?"

From head to toe, the body is black as tar—blacker—but covered in an interrupted, capsular texture that shimmers in the sunlight like a sheet of beaded jewelry. The arms and legs are diminutive mimics of human anatomy, and the hands and feet taper into thin tendrils of bulbous beads like a row of shiny beetles floating together.

My breath quickens with flashes flickering across my mind, making the past as fresh as the present. The pods are in the sky. My baby is kicking. My shoulder dampens from Clive's tears. I'm descending an elevator into a mineshaft to await the end of the world, steel struts endlessly flicking by. Panic prickles up my spine as wild speculation storms. A thousand questions immediately bubble up from almost twenty years of mystery, misery, and loneliness, but only one matters to me right now—*why did you come and take my husband away from me?*

"That's not human," I manage to tell the boys.

Ward backs from the edge of the boat. "So it's a... a..."

"It's a Hilaman," Reece says.

The Hilaman's limbs bump the hull of our boat as an awed silence descends on us. I have never seen one—the creatures that descended from the sky heralding the final age of madness. The creature's eyes are inky black bulbs the size of sand dollars. I have no idea if its eyes are open or closed because I'm not certain it even has eyelids. Its head has the shape of a tree stump but sprouts with beaded threads at the top like a mockery of human hair, bobbing along with the waves. Aside from the prodigious eyes, the face has no other discernible features—no identifiable orifices at all. Its torso has the physique of a telephone pole, almost the girth of a telephone booth, and it is taller than any human by at least two feet. Given its wide-set hind legs, I suppose it is bipedal, but I struggle to imagine how the thing stays on two feet with nothing but strands of beaded tissue for feet. As I watch the creature, I realize that it may not be dead at all. The boys notice my withdrawal from the edge of the boat.

"We burn it," Sabion says, dropping his pack. "Send that thing back to hell."

Reece puts his hand on Sabion's shoulder. "Stop." He turns to Geddes. "Poke it."

Geddes looks up at him. "*Poke* it? Are you kidding—"

"Take your oar and poke it."

"I'm not touching that thing," Geddes protests. "I say we leave it and get out of here."

Sabion swipes the paddle from Geddes and brings it down

with a hard *thwack* over the alien body. The arms flail toward the sky, making it seem like the thing has awoken from aquatic hibernation. But it simply rocks in the water like a fallen tree trunk, appearing very much to be dead.

"It's dead," Sabion declares. "Let's drag it to the beach and burn it."

I glance over the water, beyond the waves. Why is it here? How did it die, and how did it meet its demise at the south end of the Bay? How does a creature live without any orifices? My pathology brain is flickering to life as I consider all the implications of the alien body. Ancient but welcomed memories of pathology residency come crashing in. The smell of egg rolls and coffee at 3 a.m. haunts me as I remember staining one specimen slide after another, inspecting tissue samples for cancer margins. Despite my anxiety at seeing the creature, I'm also dying to look at its cells under a microscope. What kind of cornucopia of astrobiology would stare up at me through the lens? Will understanding how they tick tell me why they came? For the first time in years, a thrum of excitement blooms in my belly as all the unanswered questions about their arrival rise to the surface anew.

"We need to bring this to the colony," I announce.

Sabion erupts. "What!" He looks at Reece. "There is no way we're bringing one of these things back to the colony."

Reece sets his jaw. "You heard the doctor. We're taking the Hilaman back with us."

I'm just as surprised as Sabion—just as unsettled but for much different reasons. "What is your interest in the body?" I ask.

Reece hesitates in a way that makes me suspect he's about to lie. "You're a doctor. You want to study it—want to learn how they work, right?"

"Yes..."

"Know your enemy," he says, looking to Sabion who nods with

new understanding. The sudden amiability leaves me deeply suspicious that Hutch's instructions are behind Reece's motivations.

"The alien body is potentially dangerous. We can't just handle it with bare hands," I say. "It could have pathogens that are deadly to humans. We'll have to somehow bring it ashore, camp here while some of us return to SF for isolation supplies—"

But then Sabion jumps in and swims toward the body.

"No!" I yell, but the boy is already tying together the arms and legs and tying off the end of the rope to the boat.

"We should bring it back now," Reece says. "No time to wait."

I want to argue, but I can hardly even think about what supplies I have to safely handle the body. I have no hazmat suits and only a few functioning respirators. Before I can protest, we're paddling again, towing an alien behind us in the San Francisco Bay. Maybe I say nothing because I don't want to wait either.

We dock at the Marina District, the north end of the peninsula and away from the traffic of the wharf. Hutch meets us there, draped in a poncho with a rain hat shadowing his face. Droplets fleck on us like unrelenting spittle when we disembark. My hip squeals in protest as I slump my pack on a dock that's rotting from the inside out with feathered wood planks. The mayor's face is inscrutable as his gaze falls on the alien body bobbing in the water. I had been too angry to talk to him over the radio on our way back as Reece explained to him the cargo we carried back.

"Why didn't you know San Jose was flooded?" I ask him.

His face unpeels from its stoic uncertainty and an apologetic smile emerges. "We knew it started a few months back. Had no idea it had gotten so bad. Truly, I'm sorry for putting you and my boy in so much danger. The Sacs have been getting aggressive in those parts lately, stopping our scavenging parties from getting through to get reliable intel. Did you see any other Hilamen out there?"

"No. Just the one."

He levels his gaze at me. "No one can know. No one except the group standing here now. I will not allow panic to catch fire in the colony. Both you and I know what happened to the world when these things showed up in the first place."

For once, we agree. I don't like it. "I'll bring the body into the basement of the east wing. I'll be able to do an autopsy there but I may need new equipment."

"You tell me what you need. It's good to have you back."

His sporadic amiability does little to put me at ease.

We heave the Hilaman from the water, tendrils of black beads dangling from its limbs. It's heavy like an elk carcass. Donned in respirators, goggles, and gloves, it takes all the boys, myself, and Hutch to heave the thing onto the dock. We gaze at the alien body like we had just felled a second-generation oak. With a face void of any features other than oily black eyes, it's hard to imagine it was once a living creature. Seeing it here, the torrential memories explode again. They're on TV, floating in the sky—almost dancing in the wind like dandelion spores. My baby stirred within at twenty-eight weeks, bacon fried on the stove, and Clive had let a bowl of cereal spill down his lap as he stood from the couch to get a closer look at the screen. For a moment, I'm back there with him—his scent, his hand, the awful uncertainty of a new world ripening before us in real-time.

"What happened with the Sac boy?" Hutch asks after we load the body into a refurbished delivery truck.

I gesture to Sabion. "Ask him."

"It's a big problem, Elspeth," Hutch says.

"You don't need to tell me that the death of a child is a big problem."

"Talking about me?" Sabion asks from around the truck with an ugly scowl.

"You need to go into quarantine," I tell Sabion. "You were the only one who touched the Hilaman without protective gear when you jumped in the water and tied it up. Two weeks isolated in your apartment. Do you understand?"

"Yeah, yeah," he says.

"You don't understand," Hutch continues saying. "The Sacs will use the death of that boy as an excuse."

"An excuse for what?"

He bristles, clearly hesitant to get specific. "Aggression."

"Why do they want to be aggressive? We've been friendly with Sacramento since refounding."

Hutch grunts. "Times change. You should know that more than anyone."

"It's not always times that change—it's circumstances and motivations. Aggression can be manufactured."

He snorts. "Yes, and the Sacs could manufacture more aggression over the death of the boy."

"And why would they do that?"

He licks his lips. "You'd have to ask them. I only mean to defend our people."

"That all?"

"Yes," he says with wholesome haste as if no other motivation could have possibly nested inside his brain. "We are a bastion for the new world."

"Don't stump-speech me." And then I remember our past conversation—Hutch prohibiting me from going to San Jose in the first place. "Why didn't you want me to go? Is it really about the Hilamen migrating north?"

"Yes. I didn't want to put you and the boys in harm's way with recent sightings of those things. But with this development with Priscilla, I thought it a necessary risk. And now the whole trip—a total waste with terrible political fallout. Exactly what I was afraid of."

"So, it was political."

"Everything is."

"Even that?" I motion to the truck and its interstellar cargo.

"Especially that. Please, find out everything you can about that thing. How they work, how they live—how they die. Make it a priority."

I say nothing, unsettled that our priorities have aligned.

ELEVEN

NURSE MAX IS the first to greet me at the east wing hospital with notices of mayhem and gleeful exasperation. "Patient from Utah? Died. Old man with TB coughed up a gallon of blood and then died. Had another cirrhotic show up, but don't worry... she died. The autoclave? Broken. Generator has gone down twice and there is flooding in the basement."

Ward sets his pack at his feet. "And Jericho was lost while we were away."

Max looks at me. "Who?"

"His ferret," I say.

Max opens his mouth, too stunned by the banality to utter a single word.

"But then Geddes went back and saved him," Ward says.

"That's a relief," Max says.

"How's Mavis Ulrich?" I ask.

"Engineer from San Diego? She's alive. She's out of her mind, but alive."

We immediately proceed to rounds, where I'm once more

regaled by Nadine and Patience about the apparent clustering of astrological events that has doomed our attempt at providing patient care. Nadine had performed several bedside debridements of wounds, suturing, and intubations. Since I left, half the medical ward had died and been replaced with new patients that were just as sick—a type one diabetic in ketoacidosis breathing a thousand times a minute, a young woman with stroke-like symptoms and a white blood cell count of one hundred and fifty thousand—undoubtedly dying of leukemia. Traumatic limb amputations, crush injuries, and many, many stab wounds. A cacophony of groans and screams accompanies us around the patient wards as we make plans for every patient. We're mostly just rearranging the deck chairs as our ship of dying people sinks beneath the waves.

"You've got a couple of clinic patients to see, too," Max taunts and walks off.

"Get to the clinic," I tell Ward.

Ward's eyes go wide. "We just got back. I haven't even been back to my apartment yet."

"I'm just as exhausted as you. There are patients to see—patients that aren't dying. People that we can actually help. Go and see them—wait."

"What is it?"

My nostrils flare. "Go and bathe first. But come right back."

At the clinic, there are more than a dozen patients loitering around the waiting room. As soon as I'm spotted, a commotion erupts, each vying to be seen first. Priscilla is seated in the corner. I pawn Ward off on a man complaining of hemorrhoids and take Priscilla into a room.

"How far along now?" I ask as she takes a seat.

"Twenty-four weeks."

I expose her belly and feel along the uterus. "Been reading the book I gave you? Taking the vitamins?"

"Yes. How was the trip with Reece?"

I sigh. "San Jose is a loss."

"Meaning?"

"We weren't able to get new supplies." I produce a handheld doppler machine from a cupboard.

Her face pales. "Am I going to die?"

"Because we couldn't get supplies? No. But the birth will be painful because I won't be able to do an epidural." I lubricate the doppler and slide it along her belly, listening to the chaos of the doppler snowstorm, trying to triangulate the baby's heart tones. "There."

Her eyes crinkle, a smile emerges. "That's his heart?"

"You think it'll be a boy?" I ask.

"It's a feeling."

"Sounds like the baby is doing fine. Any vaginal bleeding?"

She shakes her head. "No. And it's ok if it's painful. It'll be worth it. How is Reece?"

"From the trip? He's fine."

"No. What is he like to you? Do you like him?"

I clear my throat. "Doesn't matter what I think."

"That's a no."

"If you love him, it doesn't matter what I say anyway. Reece is Reece. Sabion is Sabion. They are products of their age."

"What does any of that mean?" she asks, annoyed.

I rub my eyes and take a deep breath. "It doesn't mean anything."

"Are you okay, Doctor Darrow?"

I know that I'm not. I know that I'm deeply unequipped—both medically and psychologically—to be carrying the patient load that is constantly on my shoulders. But then I smile, thinking about the autopsy that awaits me in the basement and the answers to a twenty-year mystery that it contains. "I'm fine. Come and see me in a few weeks."

Ward catches my sleeve as I flee the clinic. "Where are you going?"

"Stay here."

"I kind of want to be there to learn."

"Stay. Here," I repeat. "Finish up seeing the clinic patients. Write notes on all of them for my review. I will see you tomorrow."

He narrows his eyes.

"I will *see you tomorrow*."

In the basement of the east wing, the Hilaman lays on three wooden tables lined end to end to accommodate its length. Never since my time as a physician in Neo SF have I performed an autopsy on a patient. No time, no reason. When people die in this new world, they take their mysterious cause of death with them, and I move on with my day. I do have some equipment, meager as it is, to actually perform a dissection. I even have a shit-box microscope lurking in the corner that I use to gram stain bodily fluid to see if patients have bacterial infections. But that's pretty much it.

After donning a respirator and gloves that go up to my elbows, I simply gaze at the thing for a moment. Each of the thousands of bead-like protrusions of its skin reflect the single naked light bulb hanging above. I'm still uncertain that it's dead. For all I know, I'm three seconds from an alien waking up from a thousand-year hibernation state, hungry, confused, and very angry, sparking a global war between humans and the Hila. But living things usually don't deposit themselves, exposed to the elements, in a large body of water to hibernate. So, I'm at least twenty percent sure it is dead.

And then I wait. Something about *do no harm* echoes in the back of my mind. So, I come back a day later and it hasn't moved. I stand there, soaking in the sight of this thing that shouldn't be here but somehow is. For the first time in eons, the thrill of something leaps inside me. Novelty, discovery, answers to the miserable questions festering in bile at the pit of my stomach for the last twenty years.

Its skin, colored an inky black, has no give beneath my fingertips—the texture almost chitinous like a beetle shell. I measure its girth, limb circumference, and length. It has the physique and proportions of Gumby. Somehow, its eyes have more black depth to them than the beaded skin. The two protrusions on the front sit like dollops of black meringue situated on its head. There are no orifices. No mouth where a mouth might be, and no anus where you might find one of those either. Every surface of the creature is one continuous plane of beaded tissue. Oh, except the back of the head, where I discover another set of eyes.

I sit down and take a deep breath.

What do I know about this thing? I know it did not evolve on Earth. I know it, or its progenitors, arrived in organic pods by the thousands and scattered across the planet wreaking havoc across human civilization by virtue of their sheer existence. I know they are reclusive to humans and I believe they form stable colonies based on rumors. I know that whatever biological processes they need to live are at least met in part by Earth's chemical, barometric, and climate composition. That means they must have at least something in common with human biology. What I do know is dwarfed by what I don't—what they eat, how they eat, what they metabolize, how they breathe (do they even need to breathe?), how they communicate, and even more unknown unknowns. I stop myself before I get too overwhelmed and stand once more, ignoring the most important question—why did this one die?

I swipe a scalpel from the table and bring the blade to the surface of its arm, hovering there for a moment. I can't possibly be the first to find one of these and do an autopsy. Somewhere on the planet, surely someone has stripped one of them down to their bare molecules and is halfway there to figuring them out. So, why am I so nervous? Is this wrong?

I cut.

But the blade glances off the skin, the edge still clean. Again, I bring the blade to the skin and draw my wrist down, but nothing gives. Not a single mark and my blade is now dull. After bending the scalpel blade on my third attempt, I find a fresh one and try again with the same result. Whatever the Hilaman's skin is made of, it's stronger than the sharpest blade I own. I don't know what else to do, so I thrust the tip of the scalpel in with a stabbing motion and the damn thing breaks from the handle, leaving the alien unscathed and me feeling pretty stupid. Probably best. I'm about to perform the Pandora Box of autopsies and the universe is giving me a clear sign to stop.

But I don't.

And I come back with a damn ax.

Mavis Ulrich stands at her window at midnight, cane in hand, silhouetted against the gas streetlights of the Civic Center Plaza below. Last time I spoke to the woman, she was in the throes of a fatalist fever dream about the nature of humankind—a sentiment I couldn't really deny.

"How's the leg?" I ask.

She cocks one eye at me. "You always visit your patients so late?"

"Usually only the ones who are dying and I think I can do something about it."

She glances down at her right leg, where more than half the calf had been resected from flesh-eating bacteria. "Thought I was out of the woods."

"You are. I'm here for a different reason."

"Do you have any weed?"

"No. But I can get you some. Our pharmacist keeps it stocked."

"What can I do for you?" she asks.

"You're a materials engineer."

She holds up a finger. "Ah. Now I remember. Want me to sign up for a colony rebuilding pet project? Going to build our way back to a new beginning?"

"Not exactly," I say.

"I remember feeling that way—when my group hatched from the bunkers and re-populated San Diego. I was just as drunk on that hope of rebuilding like anyone else." She scoffs. "But almost twenty years of disease, starvation, and sectarian fighting has a way of sucking that hope right out of you. All that rebuilding propaganda is just to encourage opposing colony defection to recruit into competing militias. LA and San Diego colonies have been fighting for the last two years now that commerce between the two is going flat from the drought and Mayor Gustavson is acting like a little Hitler. Can you tell me things are different in the Bay Area?"

"I thought I could, but recently..." I think of Anders stalking us through San Jose. Just a few years prior, we were doing joint salvaging missions with people from Sacramento. "We might be having the same issues here."

"Then I'm not going to build anything for any upstart warlord."

I cut my hand through the air, cutting her off. "That's not why I'm here."

"Then why are you here, standing in my room at midnight?"

I turn to the doorway. "Let me show you."

\

Mavis steadies herself on her cane, ratted robe loosening about the hips. With goggled eyes bugged wide as a cartoon character, she looks as unhinged as a patient from the psych ward. The illusion is complete as her robe unfolds about the chest, unwittingly exposing herself. I can't blame her. She is, after all, looking at a dead alien.

"Mavis. Your robe," I say.

"I've—this is the first time," she says. "I didn't know if they were actually real. There were rumors that a colony of them lived near San Diego but no one had seen one. How did you find it? Where do they live?"

"Found it in the Bay just a few days ago."

"They show up often around here?"

I shake my head. "Never. There are occasional sightings of them near Monterey. But they seem to be just as reclusive here as they are for you in San Diego."

"It's dead, right?" she says, taking half a step back.

"I believe so."

She finally covers herself up. "No wonder you made me wear a respirator." I explain how poorly my autopsy has been going as evidenced by the numerous bent scalpels lying next to the Hila-man. "Did you try using an *ax*?" She points to the ax on the floor, the heel of the blade fractured from the butt.

"Yes," I admit. "Didn't make a dent. I cannot cut into the body with any blade I have available to me." I motion to a table littered with bent knives, saws, and serrated edges of various sizes and craftsmanship.

"Now I see why you came running to me." She runs her gloved hand along the beaded skin of the Hilaman. "Are we sure this thing is even organic?"

"What, you think it's a robot?"

"I didn't say that. Living matter can have inorganic components. What do you think is carrying around all the oxygen in your blood right now, Doctor?"

"So, what do you think the skin is made of?" I ask.

"Many materials can be resistant to penetrating objects like your little scalpel and that ax. Most we use are artificial. Kevlar, carbon fiber, and various grades of steel are the strongest practical materials in use, although boron and carbon nanotubes had a lot of potential before everything went to shit."

"What naturally occurring materials could be this strong?"

She looks at the ceiling. "Diamond, obviously. Spider silk, silicon carbide. There's a mollusk whose teeth are pretty tough—made of goethite."

"And so what does this look like?"

"Well, it's got no bling and it doesn't look like a snail." She leans closer. "Cellulose fiber can get pretty strong, especially if it's reinforced with inorganics." She presses on the skin. "Hard. But it doesn't feel that dense. Almost like a polymer or polysaccharide. But I don't think those would be strong enough to withstand your serial killer starter kit over there."

"What kind of environment would create a creature this strong?"

"Killer pressures. Killer heat. Killer predation."

"How can we figure out what this thing is made of?"

She shrugs. "Do exactly what you're trying to do. Cut off a

chunk of it, take a peek under a microscope, and run it through chromatography for starters."

"Any suggestions on how to get a sample?" I ask.

"Get yourself a blade made of diamond."

The next morning after rounds, I make my way down to the wharf. I want to go straight there but begrudgingly take a detour down Turk Street to the old YMCA hotel. Three floors up and I knock on the door. Sabion opens with profound shock on his face at seeing me.

"How do you feel?" I ask.

"I'm fine," he says with a scowl.

"No signs of infection? No cough, fever, light-headedness?"

He crosses his arms. "No."

"You stay in this apartment for a total of fourteen days. Do not interact with anyone until we know you didn't pick up an infection from you-know-what." I turn from the door.

"I didn't kill that kid," he says as if it's a taunt.

I don't turn, just stare down the opposite hallway. "Your bullet certainly did."

"That's not fair."

"I agree. The boy didn't deserve to die."

"No. Blaming me. It was—they shouldn't have been following us. The Sacs put that boy in danger. That's what happens when you try sneaking up on a lion. You get bit."

"Fourteen days," I say, vacating the hallway.

A chilled wind sweeps the street as I amble my way down to the wharf. My hip feels better and my mood isn't so sour. Something about being on the frontier of astrobiology has a way of putting a kick in my step. Prasad greets me as I enter his shop. "No car batteries for me, I presume?" he asks.

I wince. "You were right about San Jose."

"I heard. Just glad you made it back safe. How's the east wing?"

"Half morgue, half hospice."

He snorts nervously.

"Sorry," I say. "Sometimes I forget non-medical people aren't used to the grim humor of working with death on a daily basis. But it's ok," I backpedal. "Although we really needed that re-stocking from San Jose. Have you heard of any good salvage caravans coming through?"

"Nothing. Everyone's hurting. Except Harlo's shop and their LA trade pipeline. Bastard's monopolizing things around here."

"I don't understand, why don't the LA caravans trade with everyone?" I ask.

"Closed deals. Their traders aren't showing up and opening their wares for everyone. It's all behind closed doors."

"They can't do that," I say. "There are laws in our colony charter—written up in the bunkers before the colony was even founded. Trading practices cannot be exclusive. You talk to the mayor about this?"

"Pfft. That man won't listen to me. He's a disgrace. I can't wait for the next election cycle and kick him out. I can think of dozens of people, children even, who could run this place better than him. I have no political experience and *I* could do a better job of it."

"How many tyrants have said the same? How do you know you wouldn't just fall into the same trappings of power?"

"Because," he says, "I don't actually want to be in charge. I'm just saying I would do a better job—doesn't mean I *want* to do the job. That's the difference."

"You got my vote."

He waves his hand, dismissing the speculation. "Anything else you need?"

"Yes, actually. Do you have a diamond knife?"

"Is that slang for something?"

"No. I'm looking for a blade that is made out of pure diamond."

He shakes his head. "Diamonds haven't exactly retained their value in the new market economy given the abundance of jewelry left behind. There just isn't that much use for shiny rocks anymore. I do have some reclaimed diamonds but not an entire blade made of diamond. Why would you ever need that?"

"Not important. Know where I could get one?"

"No—wait..." He looks at the ceiling for a moment. "You know Rafa?"

My heart sinks. "Rafa Montijo?"

"Yes. That man has all sorts of old-world equipment."

I rub my temples. "I know Rafa."

"Know where he lives now?"

"He left SF?" I ask.

"Kind of."

Reaching out to Rafa did cross my mind for a split nanosecond but I didn't relish the idea of seeking out my post-apocalyptic ex-boyfriend. We'd met in the bunkers but only got romantically entangled after SF re-colonization, even lived together for a few years with eight of his dogs—*eight*. We built up a little house on the corner of Polk and Bush, cramming it full of all the scavenged junk we thought we'd need but just collected dust. After a year, I realized I was living with a hoarder who was more interested in meditating into astral planes of existence with an African Congo Gray on each shoulder than spending time with me or raising a family.

"Please respect my spirituality," he told me a few days before we called it quits, looking out over the wharf.

"Your spirituality just takes you away from a colony that needs your mind. It takes you away from me," I said.

He shook his head. "I'm not needed here anymore. Things are changing and I don't think you see it."

"Rafa, you are a trained biochemist and a physicist with a penchant for knowing absolutely everything. Right now, you could tell me the thermal expansion coefficient of liquid iron off the top of your head while deriving Maxwell's electromagnetic proofs." What I didn't say was the rest of that thought... that his brain was a cornucopia of information and data, most utterly useless, and none very conducive to a healthy relationship with another person. "I need something more, I don't know, grounded in actually doing things for the future of this colony. Your spirituality just, I don't know..."

"What?"

"It's alienating."

He backed away from the railing of the pier. "I don't think I can give you what you want."

I left him after a few years of being together but still saw him occasionally at the wharf, offering one another brief and automated pleasantries.

"Coming through," I tell the guard at the border gate after leaving Prasad's shop.

"Do you have a work or salvage order?" the guard asks, a boy of seventeen with a semi-automatic weapon strapped across his chest who I delivered into this world.

"It's the mayor's business, Jameson."

He shifts his weight. "But do you have the paperwork?"

"No. Now open the gate."

The kid knows I've raised hell before and doesn't appear eager to start something with me. He peers over a clipboard, feigning important internal decision-making, and says, "Got to call it in."

I clap my hands. "Be quick about it."

He radios some other teenage superior and together they decide they need to talk to Reece. I hear his voice over the speaker. "Where are we heading today, Doctor?"

"Mayor's business."

"And that makes it my business."

I step around the guard, reach into the kiosk, and pull the lever to the gate. A rumble of gears churns over his protests as the gate lifts. I'm well aware that the gate cannot close until it has fully opened. I inspect my nails as the gate rises to my height and I step under. Reece's voice screams something over the radio as I walk outside the borders of SF, whistling with a kick in my step.

TWELVE

RAFA HAS CREATED an empire of barbed wires, electrified fencing, motion sensors, security cameras, and automated firearms, all of which are completely covered in bird shit. His compound at Alamo Square may as well be on Galapagos considering the amount of wildlife that occupies the area. A giraffe looks at me from behind the fence, takes a bite of leaf, then snorts me out of its mind. There are three humongous tortoises with their own little grotto built right into the street just bathing in the sun. Hosts of tropical birds roost in rookeries that have been erected throughout the property. The compound is ensconced in so many layers of chicken wire, I can only assume the man has covered his entire home in a Faraday cage—an aspiration he had spoken of often when we were together. Rafa has gone off the grid from a post-apocalyptic colony that is already very much off the grid. I'm not remotely surprised.

Loudspeaker static chirps at me, and then, "Hi."

"Hi, Rafa," I say.

"Nice to see you."

"May I come in to see you? *Can* I come in?" I don't see an actual entrance to the fortified fortress that sits opposite the square to The Painted Ladies.

"Oh, sure."

Something buzzes and an entrance materializes in the foliage as a camouflage gate opens inward.

Things get weirder.

There are statues everywhere, mostly by the artist Rodin. I have no idea how he had the time, gasoline, and energy to lug over a dozen of the hunks of rock from the Legion of Honor museum and plunk them down into his weird garden. Almost every statue is of a figure crying or in a tragic pose, and someone—Rafa I'm assuming—has painted over every single one of the priceless sculptures in vibrant splashes of neon paint and glitter. Frogs are legion around the statues, literal hordes, jumping and croaking like an Egyptian plague. "Ah!" I scream as the frogs are suddenly on me. I run through the garden toward the house while frantically batting them out of my hair. Another door opens and I'm inside, chest heaving to catch my breath and with nothing close to relief because I've no idea what new horrors now await me. But it's just Rafa, standing in a shaft of light, dark hair matted, beard frayed into tendrils.

"You couldn't have warned me about the frogs?" I ask.

Genuine surprise fills those small brown eyes. "Oh, I forgot about those."

"You forgot you had a million frogs living at the front of your house?" I suspect that isolation has been very bad for the man. All my fears about what my life would have been with him are instantly and retroactively confirmed. "I didn't know you had moved out of the colony."

"Couldn't handle the shackles."

"Are you well?"

"Is anyone?"

"No. Here." I drop my bag on the floor, producing a stetho-scope and a blood pressure cuff. He lets me do a brief physical and run his vitals. "Your blood pressure is ridiculous. Stop eating so much salt," I scold him.

He shrugs and rubs his chin scruff. "Should have had you visit sooner. I'm sorry." He flashes those baleful eyes at me and unceremoniously walks down the hallway. In the kitchen, he presides over a freshly brewed gourd of yerba mate. After motioning to a wicker chair, I sit and watch him take a sip through a metal straw, sifting the tea through the loose leaf. He offers me the gourd.

"You know I hate that stuff." Undaunted, he pins his eyes on me, lifting the tea. I give in and take a sip. It tastes like weird memories. I take another sip.

"So, you never adopted," he says at the risk of rekindling the blow-out fights we had when we were together. But there isn't any passion between us to burn the kindling.

"Turns out it wasn't just you standing in the way of starting a family," I say.

He sips as we share welcomed silence.

"I have a dead Hilaman in the basement of the east wing," I tell him.

He chokes on tea. "*What?*"

"And I can't cut into the thing."

"Why are you cutting into it?"

"Autopsy. And I *can't* cut into it. That's why I'm here," I say.

Delight washes over his face as he looks at the ceiling, bewitched with the engineering conundrum. "What have you tried?"

"Everything but diamond. Do you have any?"

He leaps from his chair, spilling tea over the table, and disappears into a basement. Something tells me he has a diamond blade.

It's literally just a circular saw with a normal-looking blade in there. "Did you expect it to sparkle?" Rafa asks, reading the disappointment on my face. The man had brought a battery of other saws, blades, hammers, tinsnips, and half a dozen other equipment I don't recognize all in preparation for alien butchery. After carefully laying out his equipment, he towers over the Hilaman. "You name it?"

"It's not a pet," I say.

"Looks like a Francine to me. Who's this?" he asks, gesturing to Mavis, who has retired to a corner of the room, a joint in between thumb and index finger.

"Mavis Ulrich. She's a material engineer," I say.

Mavis waves, takes a drag, and holds it.

He greets her with a bark of the diamond blade, whirring in his hands. "Where do we start?"

"A basic sample of the skin," I say. "We need to eventually get a sample of organs, too. I hope the entire inside isn't as strong as the skin or we're going to be having a hell of a time getting thin enough samples to put under a microscope with your enormous saw blade there. I guess start with what we would call the lower leg. Make a complete cut."

The blade spins to life once more as Rafa approaches the Hilaman. It makes contact with the lower leg but catches and sputters off. He stops, probably thinking the same thing I am—what do we do if diamond won't cut into it? Undaunted, he tries again, the blade whining as it tries to get purchase on the alien surface. The appendage quivers and then jumps on the table as the blade finally makes a ludicrously small cut into the surface of

134

the beaded skin. Rafa stops, probably gives me a satisfied smile beneath his mask, and keeps going with a rhythmic pulsing to the saw. At first, it appears that exactly zero progress is being made, but after two minutes of working, the blade sinks a few millimeters deep. Mavis stalks closer, watching as Rafa throws his entire weight onto the blade, rattling the Hilaman's leg on the table. Ten minutes pass by and we inspect the cut. It's getting deeper but probably only by a few more millimeters. Rafa inspects the diamond, eyes squinting behind goggles, and starts again.

We know the exact moment the blade cuts through the outer layer because a phantasmagoric flood of technicolor issues forth from the wound. Indigo liquid marbleizes with vibrant red—eddies of chartreuse swirl within orange whorls of dozens of shades. A chaotic surge of colorful body fluids weeps over the Hila skin, refracting radiant light in an almost psychedelic display.

"Whoa." Mavis looks at the joint in her hand.

"We're seeing it, too," I assure her.

Rafa looks at his blade, which is now coated in at least two dozen shades of vibrant colors. "I guess Francine bleeds rainbows," he says before continuing the cutting. Mavis and I back up as the colored fluid spits from the moving blade, painting the opposite wall like we are in the quarters of an artist, coating the walls in paint during fugue states of inspiration.

"Ugh," Mavis grunts. "The thing smells like rotten eggs."

After working the blade down to the other side of the leg, the colorful fluid has puddled beneath the corpse, many of the colors still very much insolvent, others mixing together to form a muddy brown. "Yah!" Rafa cries in weird triumph as he finally frees the leg, exposing the cross-section.

The severed limb continues to drain the colorful fluid. The seeping abates as I dab the specimen, soaking towels in the discharge. I get my first glimpse of the gross tissue and I'm shocked by what I see next—the same. There are no internal structures other than the same bead-like structures that coat the outside of the body. No bone, no muscle, no ligaments, no blood vessels. It's one homogenous tissue through and through, almost identical to the outside.

Rafa paws the inside tissue of the leg. "Not much here. Kind of spongy in the middle, not as hard as the skin, but it all looks the same. How does that work?"

"I have no idea," I say.

"Do you think it has organs?" Rafa asks.

"Again, I have no idea." The three of us stand in silence for a moment. "Keep cutting," I say before rushing to afternoon rounds.

After several days in the autopsy lab, we uncover many more questions and exactly no answers. Besides two sets of what I believe are eyes, the Hila indeed does not have any organs. None. We made dissections into the torso, thorax, and head stalk. It is all the same tissue we found inside the leg—not as hard as the exterior but the same beads linked together by some sort of slippery connective tissue. I'm able to pull on a thread of a bead and bring an entire string of the things out of the body, dangling them above the floor. I place some of these samples in water, not knowing if this is an appropriate medium. We found the body in water either because it was in the water when it died of something else or water itself is toxic to it. I haven't a clue. But then I remember Ward jumping at dark shadows in the water of the Bay. For all I know, there's a colony of the creatures living in their own version of alien Atlantis beneath our wharf.

Each bead we cut into contains an absolute cornucopia of color pigmentation that is completely obscured by the black outer layer. The pigments appear to represent the entire spectrum of visible light from what I can tell—and there are many shades that I'm certain I've never laid eyes on. Each bead we break open is like a sunrise and sunset over every ocean, worlds within worlds of colored beauty that I didn't know was possible. Often, the three of us watch in stunned silence as the colors leach out, twisting light with reflective particulates that dazzle us with the wonder of the world that created such beings. Certainly, the creatures are mobile given the four appendages, but it's only my human-centric brain to assume they're bipedal.

Using some of Rafa's thinner diamond blades, I throw some tissue in a dish and look at it under a microscope. I don't have any staining materials or a microtome, a specialized cutting tool for precision slices of tissue, to do a proper pathological review of the samples. I can, however, pop open a bead, take a crude smear of some alien cells, and throw them on a slide to look at under a microscope.

"Kind of looks like a plant," I say to Rafa and Mavis who watch over my shoulder. "Rigid cell walls, a mess of color every-where." I squint into the eyepiece again, tongue at the side of my mouth. "But I really don't know. Could be a synthetic polymer making up these cell walls for all I know."

"Do you have stains?" Rafa asks.

I shake my head. "I'm only prepared for gram staining here to see if a patient has a bacterial infection or not. That's pretty much it. I don't do any real pathology stuff anymore. Don't have the resources and I certainly don't have any treatment if I were to actually find out if someone has cancer or something. I haven't done a proper fixation and staining since before the wars. Besides, we don't even have a microtome to do the precision cutting of samples."

"Any reason to do a gram stain on the sample?" Rafa asks.

"Couldn't hurt, but I highly doubt the Hila cell wall is of the same thing as Earth bacterium—oh... duh."

"What?" he asks.

"Crystal violet—what I use to look at bacterial cell walls. It stains DNA."

"Ooh," Mavis says.

Delighted to be doing lab work once again, I go through the routine gram staining process, except without the discoloration because I wasn't really trying to differentiate bacteria here. I only want to see if the Hila tissue has anything in common with Earth life. I prepare the sample and splash in the crystal violet. Before looking through the eyepiece, it finally crashes in on me that I'm on the precipice of making one of the biggest discoveries in the history of humankind. Too bad humankind doesn't care anymore.

"Take a look," I tell Rafa. "See those little clusters of deep purple stain?"

He cups his eyes around the eyepieces. "Yeah?"

"Those are DNA nuclei. The Hilamen are DNA-based cellular life."

Later that day, I knock on Mayor Hutch's door and find only his assistant, who tells me he's gone to the colony border wall.

I find him there supervising drills of three dozen young men, each strapped with heavy packs and semi-automatic rifles, dashing through an obstacle consisting of abandoned cars and tires. He smiles at my approach.

"Why aren't LA traders open to everyone in SF?" I ask.

His smile turns to a very bummed-out frown. "There are no restrictions on trading of goods."

"And what about firearms? I hear Harlo has an exclusive contract with an LA arms dealer there. That true?"

"That is a colony-sanctioned contract."

I just look at him.

"It is a colony-sanctioned contract," he repeats as if this performative utterance is justification alone.

"Which means the colony, an allegedly democratic institution, has legally sanctioned a single company, Harlo and Sons, to have exclusive trading rights with a major firearm dealer, essentially giving them a monopoly over high-power weapons. Is that right?"

"Not exactly in those words," he says.

"In what words, then?"

He pauses.

"And how does this exclusive contract benefit the people who elected you twice to your office?" I ask.

"It's colony business."

"Yes, I know. I am asking as an SF colonial."

"How is the work in the basement?" he deflects.

He's lucky I didn't actually seek him out to talk about whatever crony arrangements he was making with Harlo. "I need to commission an expedition to UCSF medical center."

"What have you learned about the creature?"

"Its skin is tough as hell. I can only imagine the type of hostile planet that produced that kind of natural protection. No wonder they came to Earth."

"What do you mean by tough?" he asks.

"Took a diamond blade to cut into it, and even with that, it took a bit. Oh, and they are DNA-based. Either we share common intergalactic ancestry or DNA is a universal go-to structure to pass along genetic information."

"I see," he says, feigning intrigue over what is possibly the world's greatest discovery. "So, how did it die?"

"Why so interested?"

"Is it that unusual to you that I would like to know why an alien died on our planet?"

"I don't know what killed it," I say.

"But you at least know it wasn't by gunfire or a weapon of any type."

"Correct. No traumatic injury to it whatsoever."

"Good. Why go to UCSF?" he asks.

"I need more pathology supplies if I'm going to figure out the thing's biochemistry."

"Go, but with the stipulation—"

"I know, I know, Reece leads the party."

THIRTEEN

BACK AT THE east wing hospital, I find Ward sitting at the foot of a patient's bed, sketchbook in hand. The boy is drawing a flower with a bumblebee rooting through the petals for nectar. Through labored breathing, a patient dying of septic shock watches him with sunken eyes, Jericho the ferret sleeping between his legs.

"Where's your white coat?" I ask Ward.

He shrugs. "Left it in the office."

"How are patients going to know if you're the doctor or not?"

"They'll know because I'm right here trying to care for them," he says like a little shit.

"Come on." I turn to the office. "Lecture time."

I close the door behind him and hand him a piece of chalk. "Draw out the coagulation cascade."

He takes the chalk, stands at the board, and then hangs his head.

"You haven't been studying," I scold.

"I have some."

"Not enough."

"I've been here more than ever."

"What have you been doing for patients?" I don't mean to, but I look down at his sketchbook.

"I've been spending time with patients—people that are dying and have no one else with them like that boy in San Jose."

It's true that him showing up at the east wing every day is a vast improvement from hunting him down and rooting him out of his apartment. "You can't save any patients with drawings," I say.

"You literally just asked me to *draw* the coagulation cascade. How does that help?"

"Because a blood clotting disorder can happen at dozens of different points along that cascade and it's important to understand."

"But, is there anything we can even do about it? We can't even test for the majority of the things you have me reading about."

"We still run a lot of the same basic labs from before the wars. You need to understand the basic science and medicine to make the right decisions for patients. Hemophilia is a lab test, yes, but it also has signs like bleeding into a joint. If you don't understand that science, you'll never suspect the underlying disease, and you won't treat correctly."

"You don't stay with patients," he says with an acid I've never heard in his voice. "You just talk and try to treat them with therapies that hardly even exist anymore and move onto the next one. You barely talk to them—don't even get to know them—and then they get worse and die and you just keep moving."

I know the feelings of resentment he's having because I felt the same way as a medical student. Watching my old, cantankerous attending doctors became wholly out of touch with treating human beings and reducing them to a fleshy bag of chemistry and plumbing. I didn't know then what Ward doesn't know now—that a doctor can't emotionally connect with every single patient or their heart will explode from grief and futility.

"Anything else?" I ask him.

That scares him a little and I hear him take a hard swallow. But then he steels himself and asks, "How's it going in the basement?"

"Ah, you're mad I've been doing the Hila autopsy while I've stuck you in east wing work with Nadine and the nurses bossing you around. Right?"

He looks up at the ceiling. "Maybe a little."

"The Hila have DNA."

"Whoa, like humans?"

"Like all Earth life. Maybe life has the same template wherever you are in the universe. If you have pre-set values of gravity and stardust, you get a planet. Have the right witch's brew of amino acids and lipids, you get a cell. Have the correct terrain, climate, and ecosystems, you get a multicellular organism."

"Are they intelligent?"

I shake my head. "An autopsy can't tell me that. They don't seem to have brains, but that's not the only requisite for intelligence."

"Why did they come?" he asks.

"I know the answer to that even less."

A knock on the door interrupts us. "Doctor Darrow," Patience says from the doorway. "You've got a visitor."

In the foyer, my visitor is seated at a bench and looks up at my approach. "Geddes? The clinic is down that way if you're not feeling well. There's usually a wait, but a nurse will triage you up front and take your vitals." I turn.

"Doctor Darrow," he calls. "I'm not sick."

"Then what can I do for you?"

"I want to be a doctor," he says.

"Is that right?"

He nods.

"And why?" I ask.

"The way you worked on that boy in San Jose. The command and confidence. You stopped him from bleeding—all with just your hands. And you completely stopped a battle from breaking out just by caring about that boy. I've never seen anything like it."

I shrug. "He died anyway."

"Wasn't your fault and you at least tried. I want to do that." He pumps a fist in the air.

"Go and start emptying bedpans."

"No, no, I want to study medicine with you," he says.

"That is medicine. Two weeks of bedpans and learning with the nurses and then we'll talk."

"Is that what Ward had to do?"

"Yes. Anything else?"

He puts his arms akimbo and rubs his chin. "I guess not."

The next morning, I meet Reece and Sabion at the colony gates. I'm relieved to have Mavis and Rafa join me for the trek to UCSF hospital to keep the boys in line. Ward managed to convince me that he should come along using the same logic when he came to San Jose—he needs to know where potential salvaged medical supplies may be found. I had long since raided UCSF of its medications and perishable medical supplies, but there were scores of usable materials still stored there that could be useful, so I consented with a groan.

"Any symptoms?" I ask Sabion. He shakes his head. "Did you quarantine?"

He shakes his head. "I don't even know what that word means."

Cradling an automatic rifle, Reece spouts entirely unneeded instruction to the group before signaling for the west gate to open. "We'll be heading down Haight, hit Golden Gate, and up through Parnassus and the hospital," he says.

We've loaded two pick-ups with supplies enough to last a few days as well as a few generators so we can get lab equipment running. I visited the UCSF pathology lab a few years back and know everything is still intact. Reece drives one truck and Sabion the other, an arrangement that I immediately regret as Reece floors it through the corner of Market and Haight. A mischievous grin sweeps his face as he looks in the rearview mirror to see if Sabion is able to keep up with him.

"Slow down," I yell at him from the passenger seat, knuckling the door handle. Rafa is seated behind, but his complaints also go unanswered as Reece turns up a heavy metal ballad that's blasting through the speakers. I can only imagine the anxiety rising in the truck behind us as Ward and Mavis are likely yelling the same thing at Sabion.

Indifferent to our complaints, Reece continues to barrel down Haight as Sabion finally overtakes us to the left. I jostle in my seat as both trucks cruise side by side, wheels bumping over asphalt that hasn't been maintained since Uber drivers prowled these streets. Rafa's tattooed arm reaches forward, and his hand grips the back of Reece's neck. From the satisfying squeal that erupts from Reece, it's not a friendly gesture.

"Stop this vehicle," Rafa barks. Either due to Rafa's scary voice or the grip he continues on the boy, Reece brings the truck to a halt. "You will not be driving," Rafa informs him before opening the driver door from behind and thrusting Reece from the vehicle.

"You have no idea what I can do to you," Reece begins what sounds like a comic-book villain tirade.

"Get in the back and shut up. Damn near killed us, you idiot.

Look." Rafa points ahead down Haight where Sabion has stopped his truck. A sinkhole has enveloped a city block, half of the intersection replaced by a gaping hole. A rim of asphalt hangs around the edge looking as brittle as an eggshell. Reece broods in silence as Rafa starts the engine and takes a wide detour, gingerly going south through Buena Vista as Sabion follows.

Torrential memories crash in on me as we traverse old SF. The city outside the colony resembles some of its former glory aside from wild plant life reclaiming its foothold over every surface possible. There are the occasional blackened buildings from fires, felled telephone poles, and flooding, but I can still make out my favorite coffee shops and bookstores I visited when I was a resident. Looking through the window is like looking into a parallel future of a dark timeline that was never supposed to have happened.

Rafa takes us up Parnassus where the hospital towers over us. The buildings appear structurally sound under the darkened sky as a slug of fog looms overhead. Thousands of people once crossed this street, arriving for their early morning shifts or leaving from night calls. This morning, we are the only souls here. Our two trucks pull up to the circle driveway of the main entrance. The tatters of a blue awning above the airway flicker with a crosswind, the lettering sun bleached into oblivion. The facade of the building is a toothless face of shattered windows, rusted trails of water damage from burst pipes and backed-up sewage. Many scavengers and raiders have come and gone from the facility over the years.

Reece cranes his neck, taking in the building. "The doctor and I will infiltrate the vicinity and set up a perimeter. Sabion, you stay behind here and keep watch before we unload and set up camp within the hospital. Doctor, after you."

I make eye contact with Rafa to confirm our unspoken agreement—we'll both keep our eyes on the dangerous boys with automatic weapons. I remove my Glock from my hip, boots crunching on shattered glass as we move through the entryway. I hear complaints from behind and see Mavis following us.

"Stay with the vehicles," Reece tells her.

"No. It's boring out here." She hobbles forward with a cane in one hand and a handgun in the other. His face darkens. I enjoy irritating the boy as much as anyone else, but I'm also well aware of what the humiliated ego of a small person is capable of, so I offer Reece a frown of solidarity to keep the peace.

It's a routine abandoned and rotting building that is slowly being refurbished into a forest from the inside out. Reece and Mavis follow me as I know the exact way to the pathology department where I had spent many long hours of my past life. I lead them down several long hallways, flashlights sweeping across mostly clean floors that have been too dark to attract plant life. We arrive at the pathology department, and like a ghost from the future, I enter the lab where I used to churn out my daily existence. As I suspected, it's mostly intact. Whatever new-world scavengers were looking for, it clearly was not found amongst a bunch of industrial freezers, microscopes, incubators, and bioreactors. I find my nook, which should contain everything I need to really start analyzing alien tissue—a microtome for ultra-thin slicing of the tissue, an oven for drying, some paraffin wax for structure, and my babies... the staining solutions. I have no clue what kind of stains are going to bind to the Hila tissue, but given that I know the thing has DNA, I'll at least start with a basic H & E stain to root out any familiar-looking organelles and cell structures that are common with human cells.

Of course, the equipment doesn't work and I have no way to know if it will until we get the generators down to the basement and get power going—something that takes an entire day. Rafa, like some sort of electrical wizard, and Mavis, his engineering sorceress counterpart, patch together the lab and get power after many, many curse words and cigarette breaks. The two even split half a flask of something to celebrate after some lights flicker on and then immediately pop with bad bulbs everywhere. Ward and I make ourselves busy going back and forth by truck between the east wing to check in on patients, escorted by either Reece or Sabion for reasons only known to them. "For your protection," Reece tries to reassure, which provokes the opposite effect.

We finally get some power going to the equipment and it's all very sketchy, but some of the interfaces actually light up. Dust and particulates are absolutely everywhere, and it takes me another day with Ward to get the microscope and equipment even halfway worthy to actually do some science. I take Hila beads that I dissected from the inside of the specimen's leg—not from the outside of the body that is coated in the strongest substance on the planet. I go ahead and prepare the beads like I would a human sample.

"Ward, come and watch me," I say as I take a seat on a lab bench. "One aim in the field of pathology is to preserve the integrity of the tissue you are about to cut up and observe under a microscope. Fixation of the specimen helps preserve that structure of the tissue you have before it deteriorates." My Hila sample, however, has been rotting in the Bay and the basement of the east wing for who-knows-how-long and has likely undergone a lot of natural decay already, so chances are high that the entire endeavor is a crapshoot and I'll see nothing but necrotic tissue under the lens and learn very little. "When we first made the dissection in the east wing basement, I had no idea what fixative would work, so I put separated samples in formaldehyde, acetone, ethanol, and methanol and crossed my fingers that one of those would do the trick."

I produce these samples from our packs and begin infusing them with paraffin wax to give the cellular structures even more support for when I make the delicate cross-sectional slices across the Hila beads. And then I fire up the microtome, which looks like something an old-worlder optometrist would have in their office, only you wouldn't want to be sticking your head into it or you'll start making thin slices of your eyeball. I hold my breath as I take the slices off the fixed Hila bead samples, hoping the cellular structures will stay intact. I can at least see with my naked eye that the samples don't just fall apart from the blade. Once the slices are cut, I place them on slides and put them in an oven to dry out. Once dry, I stain the samples with hematoxylin and eosin—a very go-to dye for humans—hoping the Hila have similar cellular components that will bind to the dyes and pop out under the microscope.

I breathe slowly as I place the first sample under the lens. "It looks like someone shattered a rainbow." The first thing that comes to mind is one of those kaleidoscope toys I looked through when I was a child. Brilliant pigments litter the microscope field with trapezoidal and rhomboidal crystals refracting light in every known color. There are colors I've never seen before, which makes describing them in my lab notebook impossible. No one color is dominant in the streaks across the slide. I have absolutely no idea why the Hilamen are completely black on the outside but full of all the universe's colors on the inside, but I'm willing to bet that the color pigments are sequestered in cellular compartments, and by slicing through the cells, I've loosed the pigments throughout all the cells, making it difficult to see if my stains have actually bound to anything. So, it all seems futile, but then I dim the light, lessening the strength of the pigments and, slowly, the saturation of my stains start to come through. My heart quickens as the outlines of cellular structure emerge. The stains—the ones I use for human cells—are flagging the same types of proteins also found in an alien that presumably evolved on another planet far, far away.

Another enormous breakthrough that no one will care about.

Cell walls start to emerge, much like I saw during the autopsy. They aren't membranous like humans but rigid with right angles like plant cells. There's a sort of scaffolding crisscrossing the cells, likely buttressing the walls for structural support. A bunch of amorphous blobs come through on the stain and I have no idea what they are, but I know they are made of amino acids similar to human life or else they wouldn't stain. There are DNA nuclei but —I back away from the eyepiece.

"What?" Ward asks.

I look back. "There are two DNA nuclei in each cell. Wait... some have three."

"How would that work?" Mavis asks.

Rafa stands, tea gourd in hand. "It makes total sense."

"Competing DNA?" I ask him.

"No. It's a redundant system. These are space-faring creatures, no?"

"Ah," Mavis says. "It's a backup system to protect from solar radiation. Got one nucleus that's riddled with solar radiation? No worries, you got two more to keep that cell humming along and to fix genomic injury."

"Something tells me these things spend *a lot* of time in space," Rafa says.

"How long?" Ward asks.

"Enough time that evolutionary pressure would produce three nuclei in their cells."

"So, why did they come?" Ward asks me as if looking through the microscope has answered the question.

"Let's deduce, my friends." Rafa brings a finger to his lips. I fondly recall many monologues starting out like this when we were together. "We start with two questions—why would the Hila leave their planet and why would the Hila come to our planet? The answers to those two questions may not be as related as you might assume. First question... why did they leave their planet?"

Mavis answers. "Typical stuff. Their planet was dying, climate disaster, incoming asteroid, supernova sun, war, overpopulation, etcetera."

"And what about positive reasons for their species?" Rafa asks.

"You know. To boldly go," I say.

Rafa points at me. "And maybe they're already intergalactic and have already expanded from one planet. Maybe they inhabit multiple star systems and coming to Earth is just a quaint expedition."

"They could've left to mine resources," Mavis adds.

"I think that covers the main reasons they left. Now, why would they come to Earth?"

Mavis says, "Basic interstellar colonialism. Or to study humans for some godforsaken reason."

"Does it have to be so nefarious?" he asks.

"Yes," she answers.

"Maybe they would want to help us," Ward offers. "Trying to help us with our problems."

The three adults let that comment sink like a rock.

"Now that we've laid out some possibilities, let's make some assumptions," Rafa continues. "All creatures want to live. All creatures act in self-interest. Resources are finite. Space travel is enormously risky. A threat or resource constraint must exceed the risk of space travel."

"So, you think something threatened them?" I ask.

"They may have left their planet because of a threat. And since they have come and stayed, it can be assumed that they are likely not explorers. If they came here only for resource exploitation, they would probably be aggressive but they're not. They are exquisitely reclusive, suggesting their motivations on this planet have more to do with survival than conquering anything. And if that's true, the reason they left their planet may have nothing to do with the reason they came to Earth. Earth may have just been an available planet nearby that looked habitable to them."

"But why not communicate with us? Why just float in the sky for months watching us destroy ourselves?" Mavis asks. "And why didn't they retaliate when we bombed a bunch of the pods around the world?"

"Maybe because they didn't know how," Rafa says. "You've seen the body. They don't have a single orifice. I don't know how they're communicating, but I'm thinking it's not through soundwaves."

"So," I summarize, "you think they were threatened and Earth was the closest place?"

He gives a noncommittal shrug.

"You've talked about the things we know and what we don't know, but what about all the things we don't even know that we don't know?" I ask.

"It's a theory," Rafa says. "One of many. For all we know, they're here because they lost a bet. Maybe they ran out of milk. Maybe they're a bunch of religious fanatics who heard the Arecibo message and think we are a fulfillment of a prophecy."

"I'll put my money on that one," Mavis says, picking at her nails.

"You forgot to mention the other thing we know," Ward says. "At least one is dead, and we don't know why."

With that last comment, I get back to work at the microscope.

FOURTEEN

AFTER A FEW MORE DAYS IN the pathology lab, I don't learn much more about the Hilamen. I know they are weird, but their cells seem to obey the same biological laws as humans. They have DNA nuclei, up to three per cell, that produce RNA, which is fed into an amino acid factory (ribosomes in humans, but something much beefier-looking in the Hila) that produces proteins making a creature that is almost nothing like a human. I suspect they use some different amino acids than what are found in humans because when I degrade the proteins and try to sequence them through electrophoresis, there's a bunch of blank spots that scream *this is an alien amino acid that I can't see!* But I can't prove this without mass spectroscopy. There are many questions that will also remain unanswered without gas chromatography and electron microscopy. That's where Rafa comes into play.

"We're heading out," he says, hefting a bag.

"*We?*" I ask.

"I'm going with him," Mavis says. "It's going to be hard getting that electron microscope up and running alone."

"I will be escorting you to San Francisco State," Reece adds as if the matter is closed.

"No you won't," Rafa says.

"As colony leadership, I have authority to head the expedition."

"I don't live in your colony, and I don't care that your dad is the mayor," Rafa says.

Reece folds his arms. "You can't take our trucks."

"That works out perfectly because we'll be walking. Better way to not attract unwanted attention," Mavis says.

"You're going to be okay with the cane?" I ask Mavis.

She shrugs. "I hardly need it."

After Rafa and Mavis set out to uncover more secrets of the Hila, with Reece clearly intent on following them, Sabion drives Ward and I back to the colony. Geddes has been dutifully emptying bedpans since we last spoke and gives me a nod of reassurance that he's holding up his side of the bargain. The boy gets my hopes up about actually training another medical student who will stick around for more than a few days. I round on the wards and give several of the nursing staff a much-needed night off, taking several patients under my direct care. I show Ward and Geddes what it actually is that nurses do for patients but without the pomp of being a doctor. They are almost immediately exhausted from the work.

Before climbing the stairs to my sad little room, I find Hutch standing at the landing. "I just wanted to thank you," he says.

"For what?" I ask.

"For all the work you do here." He motions to the walls. "And teaching my boy so many valuable lessons. I know he can be a pill, but he learns a great deal from you."

"I'm sure he's told you all about those valuable lessons."

The mayor smiles and thumps his fist on the railing. "You are an asset to this colony, and you deserve better."

"My quarters are fine. I don't need anything else."

He chortles and says, "I wasn't talking about upgrading your apartment. If you wanted a mansion, you would've carved that out for yourself years ago. As part of my gratitude, I've allowed Geddes' training with you to count as part of his colony defense duty. I know you need all the help you can get here. I'm also thinking about giving you a position on my council."

"Why do you want me?" I ask.

"Because you are the smartest, most levelheaded person in this colony."

"Let me rephrase... why do you want me *now*?"

"I need people I can trust to do what's right, now more than ever," he says.

"Trust to do what's right or trust to do what's right for you?"

He purses his lips. "I'm the mayor of a fledgling colony. Those are the same thing."

"It depends entirely on whose interests you care about. Do you care about the colony, or do you care about running the colony?"

"Again, those can be the same thing," he says. "You care about the colony by running the east wing. I care about the colony by being mayor. I'm not some would-be despot. Forces will always conspire to take control. For a people to thrive, you must exert power or else external power will be thrust onto you."

"I'll think about taking a council position," I tell him, worried about how he'd react to a flat-out refusal. I suspect the man is in the consolidation phase of his rule and clearly sees me as an unknown but indispensable quantity. And I'm not entirely certain why he has a sudden interest in my expertise.

"Any more details about our friend in the basement?" he asks.

"Not much yet."

"I've placed guards down there. I only want you and select people seeing it. I've heard you've had a patient down there?"

"That's right," I say. "A materials engineer who helped with the autopsy."

"And Montijo?"

"Rafa is the smartest person in the colony. He will figure out more about the Hilamen than anyone else."

"The man is odd," he says.

"No argument there." I take a step upstairs.

"Just be careful."

I freeze on a step. "Of what?"

"Just be careful."

I actually sleep better than I have in years. Something about the abject awe of looking through a microscope at alien cells leaves me with a restful satisfaction I haven't experienced in years. My sleep is so deep that I have a dream in which I open my eyes inside my room. There's a wide San Franciscan vista I recognize from the Twin Peaks with its notorious three-legged radio tower looming nearby. A strong wind sweeps through the grasses and shrubbery, and for a moment, I think this is one of those feel-good dreams, but then I notice that the hills are littered in dozens and dozens of holes. Each hole has mounds of dirt surrounding the lip, displaced from prior digging and they look exactly like the holes that had been dug near the beachhead in San Jose.

There are dead Hilamen everywhere.

Probably a dozen. Some are in the holes, some lying aside the holes, others lay lifeless in the grasses. And like a TV going dead, the dream is over and I'm just sitting there in bed. "What was that?" I say to no one and drop my feet to the floor, not sure if I'm still dreaming. My hip informs me I'm awake as I move to the window where dawn light greets me. I turn on the light, look in the mirror, and grimace at the permanent frown lines that crest my lips. For the first time, I notice my brown hair is streaked with gray highlights. After knocking back a couple of ibuprofen, I shower and go down to the basement where Sabion guards the autopsy room. Ignoring the boy, I jangle my keys trying to get the door open.

"Working late or early?" he asks, looking at his watch.

"Early." I open the door.

"Figure out what killed it?"

"That is not information I will share with you."

"Sounds like you don't know," he says.

I ignore him.

"Kind of like how you didn't know how to save that kid in San Jose?" he tries to goad me.

"I see you're still in the denial phase."

"No one cares about your fancy talk."

I slam the door in his face. The Hilaman lays lifeless on the table, dismembered and gouged from dissection. I come mostly to stare and wonder. Wonder at how a creature can exist without organs or a circulatory system. I wonder what happened to its people and why it made a trek across space to turn our world upside down. I wonder why they are still here, why they are dying, and most of all... I wonder if there are more dead Hilaman laying around at the top of Twin Peaks. I'm also wondering if I'm going a bit crazy, which is fine as that seems overdue anyway.

"Come on," I tell Sabion as I leave. "Let's go. I need a truck."

"I'm on duty here," he says, motioning to the walls.

"Call Reece and tell him you're coming with me and to send someone else here."

"Why? And where?"

"Twin Peaks. Got to make sure nothing is there."

I leave Ward in charge of the clinic and Max and Nadine in charge of the wards, to everyone's dismay except my own. Everyone complains except for Geddes, who I allow to start shadowing Ward. Nadine takes me aside and gives me a veiled lecture about providing good continuity of care to our patients, words borrowed from a dead era of hospital corporate propaganda. The truth is, the woman is exhausted and getting a tiny taste of what my actual life has been like for almost the last two decades. "I can't always be here," I tell her. She pouts and I can't possibly emote about it.

Sabion and I ride in silence as we leave the colony in a pick-up until he asks, "Why does everyone care about what these aliens are doing?"

I bring sunglasses over my eyes and flip the sun visor down. "Before you were born, the idea that life could live somewhere beyond our planet captivated every single person. And then when they actually showed up in the skies? We all lost our minds. The Hila coming to Earth is the most significant event that has ever happened in human history."

"But why does that matter now?"

I realize the boy is being sincere. "It would be foolish to assume that whatever brought them here has just gone away."

"They came here to wipe out mankind. What else could we possibly need to know from them?"

"I'm just as pissed as anybody about them showing up," I say. "I had a life, a family, a job I loved. The Hila changed the world order from top to bottom, including my little attempt to be happy. You don't think I want to hate them, too? Believe me, I do."

"But you don't?"

"I didn't say that," I say. "I'm just trying to use the thinking part of my brain and not the doing part of my brain. The Hila don't know me and it's stupid of me to be resentful this long after. The fact is, there are specific reasons that people—or aliens—migrate. It's probably extremely important that we understand why they are here because the reason could deeply impact us as well. You want to think they came here just to wipe us out? Fine. But I want you to ask yourself two questions. Why do you believe that? And, who benefits because you believe that?"

His brow crinkles, clearly not following me. "I believe it because it's the truth."

"Truth is truth, not just someone else's own brand of truthiness."

"Truthiness?"

I wave my hand at him. "Never mind."

We spend the rest of the winding drive up the hill in silence as the radio tower comes into view. After parking, Sabion hops out of the truck and says, "My foot hurts."

"Okay."

"Why does it hurt?" he asks as if he is posing a question during a lecture.

"I thought you didn't care about my fancy talk." He just stands there like a dumb boulder until I tell him to take his shoes and socks off. His ankle is as swollen as a grapefruit. "What did you do?" I ask.

"Jumped."

"And how did you land? Thing looks sprained or broken. Ice it and stay off of it," I tell him, but he's already putting his shoes and socks back on and then limps toward the staircase carved into the side of the hill. Brandishing his rifle, he nods me onward. "Come into the clinic to get an X-ray when you get back," I say.

"Maybe," he says like he did me a favor by letting me look at his ankle.

A strong crosswind chills me, almost taking me off balance as I ascend the staircase up the hill, the gaping vista of San Francisco opening before us. I stop walking.

Sabion looks me up and down. "What?" And then he sees what I see.

Before us are gaping holes in the exact visual detail from my dream. There are numerous Hilaman bodies either laying in the grass or halfway out of the holes. All are motionless. And then the smell hits me, rank with rotten eggs.

Sabion raises his weapon, face snarling above his beard. "They've been right here the whole time? This close to us?"

Covering my nose, I kneel by one of the holes, the width of which has been dug enough to accommodate the stature of a Hilaman. The holes are in varying degrees of depth, and some are full of some sort of brown sludge. On closer inspection, I see a bunch of plant debris floating along with—

"Is that a spine?" Sabion asks.

Several vertebrae are still loosely associated by ligaments, frothing on the surface. "Yes. Antlers, too," I say, pointing. "Looks like deer remains. There's fur here from many other animals, too. Raccoons, rats—"

"What?"

I snap a branch from a dead tree and prod it forward into a hole and lift up animal hair. "I think that's bear fur. It's like they made a big animal stew in the dirt—ah!" I fall on my tailbone as the hole erupts with a geyser of decayed organic matter spewing toward the sky. I gag, blinded by the organic matter that splattered over my face. After retching and wiping my eyes clear, I see it before me.

A Hilaman.

It stands before us, oily and slick with animal fat dribbling over its black-beaded skin. It tries slithering toward us, its appendages whipping their beaded threads in fruitless motion, bulbous eyes turning wide on its head. Before I can tell Sabion to not open fire, he opens fire, scattering bullets across the ground that ricochet off the alien's near-indestructible skin. "Stop!" I yell but he keeps firing as I hear bullets whizzing by my face. I take cover behind a boulder until his magazine runs out. "Sabion, stop! Its skin is bulletproof!"

He stops firing and looks down at the Hilaman who has fallen at his feet, now motionless. He kicks it in the head and says, "Well, it died, didn't it?"

Beside the hole, the creature looks like a large lizard that has just emerged from a swamp. For the first time, I understand how they were named—it has a passing resemblance to an enormous Gila monster. "Just step back," I warn him, but the idiot takes out a hunting knife and tries to stab it. And then I'm in his face and slap the knife out of his hands. "Stop using your weapons! You have no idea what these creatures are doing here and how dangerous they are. Their skin is impenetrable to bullets and blades."

He glares at me, enraged. "Seems like something you could have told me before we came up and discovered an entire *nest* of the things."

"Judging by the fact that all its friends here are dead, I think this one has died too but it wasn't from you." I squint around, looking at the rest of the bodies, counting.

"From what then?" he asks, wiping his face with his shirt.

"I have no idea," I say, still holding back a gag.

"I count fourteen. Why would they come here and dig all these stupid holes?"

Reeking gasses escape one of the holes, belching fumes into

the air. "They don't just dig holes," I say, thinking. "They fill them with plants and animals and then get into them."

"So, they're filthy *and* stupid."

"No," I say, finally putting something together. "They're digesting."

"What?"

"They don't have organs. No stomach as a food reservoir, no intestinal tract to digest, no liver for processing—they don't even have blood vessels to distribute the nutrients to cells. But they do have cells that need nutrients. These holes must be like an exteriorized stomach. They probably secrete digestive juices into the hole, jump in, and somehow absorb."

"How'd they get all the animals in there?" Sabion asks.

"Obviously, they're very good at hunting. And if they can hunt and kill a bear, they can do the same to a human."

"What made you come up here looking for them?" Hutch asks a few hours later, two thumbs behind suspenders. He whistles as a dead Hilaman is hefted into the back of a pick-up by six men.

I deflect while crouching at a Hila hole. "None of those men are wearing protective infectious disease gear. You need to quarantine them after this."

"They'll be fine."

"You don't know that. The Hilamen could carry a pathogen that could wipe out the human race for all we know."

"It would have already happened, but yes, I will do as the good doctor says."

"I don't have room for all the bodies in the basement," I say.

He shakes his head. "No, these aren't going to the east wing. You keep trying to figure out what makes them tick with the body you already have. These are going elsewhere."

"Where?"

"We will bury them in an undisclosed location so that word doesn't get out that the Hilamen are on our doorstep. Panic will flood the colony," he says.

"We counted fourteen dead Hila here but twenty-five fully dug holes. Makes you think there were more here that didn't die."

A garbled radio interrupts our conversation from Sabion, who had returned to the colony. "Mayor, I just got word from the men you sent. They found more of them out by the old zoo. Holes and Hila up and down the beach. All dead."

Something happens in the mayor's face like a cross between anxiety and satisfaction. It's like he's not displeased but he's also considering a new burden. "Had no idea they'd moved up north so quickly. Why now?" he asks me.

"Why do people and animals migrate?" I ask.

"Weather changes, hunting, exhausting resources."

"There you go," I say. "However these things live—whatever was keeping them alive in Monterey—is probably getting used up there so they're on the move."

"So, what's killing them?"

"What kills any migrants—disease, starvation, or predation."

The mayor nods. "I have plenty of work ahead of me to clean up this mess and apparently I'm heading to the beach. I suggest you return to the east wing and figure out why these things are dying. I need answers."

FIFTEEN

BACK AT THE east wing the next day, I relieve Nadine and Max of their duties and go to round on the patient wards. Ward and Geddes meet me there. "Still happy you've made a switch to the east wing?" I ask Geddes.

"Yes. Thank you for having me."

"Better than being conscripted in the military?"

"I'd rather clean bedpans for a year than do guard duty at the colony gate. Also, I hate Reece and Sabion," he adds, which certainly tracks.

Ward tries hiding a smile about the addition of Geddes to the east wing. "Doctor Darrow, I've been showing him how to irrigate and dress a wound, how to do inventory, how to perform CPR, how to mix up antibiotics, and when to give it—he's a fast learner." The boy exudes pride from the unfamiliar role of giving feedback to a subordinate that isn't a ferret. And so, I let Ward lead rounds. He makes an absolute mess of it, confusing diagnoses and offering absurd treatment plans, but at least the kid is not moping around in his apartment splashing paint on a canvas. After rounds, I

164

stress-eat three donuts while recalling how difficult it is having medical students rooting around, trying to make themselves look busy.

After failing to nap, I radio Rafa to see where in the hell he and Mavis have been. They haven't checked in via radio and they're two days overdue from returning from the university.

His garbled voice picks up. He just says, "Yeah?" as if he's never communicated over radio in his entire life.

"There's a protocol for talking over CB," I scold him. "What if you have sensitive information to share?"

"Good point. I'll draw up an encryption system soon."

"Where are you?" I ask.

"On our way back. Coming through The Sunset."

"What took you so long?"

"We made a detour to the beach," he says.

"Why?"

"The ocean is very conducive to astral projecting, Elspeth."

"You took a detour to go and meditate at the beach?" He just sighs, disgusted with my abject ignorance about whatever it is he does when he drops acid and rockets his consciousness into the nether worlds of parareality. "Did you see anything else unusual at the beach?" I ask.

"Yes—"

I cut him off. "Don't say it. Anyone could be listening."

"We're being followed, too," he says.

"Reece?"

"No—well, yes, the kid is tailing us. Poorly. I let him catch up just to make sure he hasn't killed himself out here. But, no, there are men out here that spotted us on our way back up 19th. I think they're still following us."

"Are they from our colony?" I ask.

"Doubt it. Probably would've joined up with Reece."

"Just get back here as soon as you can."

"It's late. We'll camp one more night," he says.

"Fine. Oh... uh."

"What?"

I want to ask him about weird dreams that predict the future. Knowing Rafa, he's probably an expert, but it's perhaps a bad time over the unsecure radio. "Never mind," I say.

The next day, I make my way down to the wharf and give Prasad a visit at his shop, where I've learned he has fresh medical supplies. "Where'd they come from?" I ask, picking through surgical kits and yellowed IV tubing.

"Neo LA, actually. Big caravan came up overnight. I'm talking semi rigs."

"They brought that much salvage? You don't have a whole lot here."

"I thought the same thing. I don't think the trucks were full," he says.

"What are they transporting from here?" I ask. "SF doesn't have that much surplus to export all at once. We don't even have anything valuable enough that would be worth the gas running those trucks."

He leans forward over the shop counter. "You're asking all the right questions."

"Where are these trucks now?"

"Pier 27. Just sitting in a parking lot."

"Send all the med supplies to the east wing." I turn.

"Leaving so soon? Why not stay a bit? I can make coffee."

"Take you up next time," I say. "Send the purchase receipts for these supplies to the east wing. I'll approve them all."

"My pleasure."

I walk down to Pier 27 and see two semi-trucks parked with security guards stationed around the parking lot surrounding a warehouse. They stiffen at my approach. "What's with the trucks?" I ask.

They look at each other. "We don't know."

"I'll just have a look."

"Doctor Darrow..." the young man says, blocking my path. "We aren't supposed to let you pass."

"Let anyone pass or just let *me* pass?" I ask.

"Yes."

"To which?"

"Please, just move along," the other guard says behind aviator sunglasses.

I return to Prasad's shop and find him in the back room. "Prasad, can you do me a favor?"

"Anything," he says, hastily wiping his mouth as he looks up from a sandwich.

"You pass by Pier 27 quite a bit throughout the day, right?"

"That's how I know the semi-trucks were there in the first place."

"Mind keeping an extra eye on it? Try to figure out what all the fuss is about?" I ask.

"Was already planning on it."

Rafa and Mavis are at the east wing hospital when I get back from Prasad's shop, almost giddy. Rafa carefully removes a stack of paper from his pack and unfolds reams of data before me like he's unfurling lost scrolls.

"What did you find?" I ask.

"Some answers and many more questions," he says. "I ran

whole cell mass spec and gas chromatography to try to get a general metabolomic profile of the cells."

"And?"

"It's a lot of data that's going to take me a bit to parse out, but I can tell you a few things. Hila cells are power houses. They have five times the ribosomes of a human cell. Whatever proteins they're making, their cells are pumping them out with huge turnover. I think the pigmented crystals are made of lead oxide because that signal was off the charts. The crystals must be embedded with some sort of pigments that I haven't figured out. Two other things in abundance in the Hila cells are lithium and sulfur."

I tap my chin in thought. "High sulfur content is common with humans, but lithium?"

"Lithium is only trace amounts in humans. The Hila have one million times the amount we have and also much more sulfur as well. And it gets a lot weirder."

"How?" I ask.

"They have boatloads of yttrium."

"What is that?"

He unfurls a chart spooled on the wall, revealing the periodic table of elements, and slaps his hand at the element labeled Y. "An element. Was mined here on Earth. Used in ceramics, alloys for LED lights, YAG laser, radars, and microwaves, too. It's also found in moon rocks."

"Moon rocks?"

He nods.

"Why would a biological organism need yttrium?" I ask.

"No idea, but the possibilities are endless. It gets *even weirder*," Rafa continues. "The beach was littered with dead Hila. Probably two dozen holes they'd dug. Full of all sorts of junk. Trees and branches and brush—dead rodents. Some of the holes just had junk in them like TVs, aluminum siding, coffee table legs, stuffed animals. Just random crap you can find in any home and then they coat them with some sort of frothy substance they secrete."

"Weird," I say. "I thought they were digesting organic material and then absorbing them by getting into the holes. But, knowing they're just throwing random junk in there makes me rethink this."

"The holes are definitely how they absorb materials to function, which explains why they don't have mouths—there's no intestinal tract to take in food. They must be able to open their cells up to their outside environment to directly absorb. Maybe they expand the interstitial spaces between their beads or something."

"It's as good a theory as any," I say.

Rafa continues. "Clearly, they also have significant inorganic needs and that's why they're throwing in metals. As far as the other random junk in the holes, not sure what they're trying to get out of those materials, but it's probably some of these metals we're detecting in their cells."

"Do you think they have intelligence like us?"

Rafa sucks his teeth. "Can't imagine something like a cow achieving space travel."

"That's assuming someone else didn't just drop them off," I say.

"Anything is possible."

"How can they be intelligent and not even have a brain?"

Rafa shrugs. "My only explanation is emergence. Take a simple thing like an ant, multiply it by millions, and suddenly, you get a metropolis city way more complex than a single ant could ever imagine, yet it is still made only by ants."

"You think the Hila body is like a hive mind?"

He nods. "Yes. Their cells are spectacularly complex, but the entire Hila body is just a bag of these cells formed into beads with little differentiation. There must be an emergent intelligence from the cellular interaction that drives the logic and behavior of the individual Hilaman. Otherwise, I've no idea how the thing is supposed to interact or socialize with its environment in a way meaningful enough that it would be capable of space travel."

"Can we finally get to the weirdest part?" Mavis asks, appearing like she's going to gnaw her fingernails off. "Their skin!" She slaps a hand on the table, clearly gearing up to geek out. "I shaved a slice of their exterior beads and ran it through gas chromatography."

"And?" I ask.

"There was no signal that would explain its incredible strength, so I knew we were reaching the limit of detection."

"What did electron spec show?" I ask.

She pauses for dramatic effect and then says, "Carbon."

I shake my head in confusion. "So, is it cellulose-based or something? Wouldn't that show up on gas chromatography?"

She hinges her head back and releases an emphatic *ha!* and then produces a piece of paper, slamming it down onto the table. It's a picture of what looks exactly like a gray net made up of hexagons, all zoomed in and grainy. "I don't know what this is," I say.

"It's *graphene*."

"I don't know what that is," I repeat.

Mavis rolls her eyes at my apparent stupidity. "It is a single layer of carbon atoms bonded together in such a way that makes it extremely strong. It's two hundred times stronger than steel—one of the strongest materials on Earth. And beyond, apparently."

"Okay," I say.

She sighs, exasperated by my pea brain. "Graphene is a *semimetal*. It is extremely good at conducting electricity and heat.

Also, it absorbs all wavelengths of light—that's why the things are black."

"Then why are they full of so many color pigments? What is the point of producing all that color pigmentation if it just stays within the darkness of its cells?"

"We don't know," Rafa says.

"So," I say, "just bringing this all together... we have aliens that landed here twenty years ago, for some reason, who have barely been seen since. They are made of the strongest material we know of, they have four eyeballs but no organs—no circulatory system, no lungs, no neural tissue but may or may not be intelligent. They are DNA-based with triple the amount of DNA per cell than humans. They are full of rainbows for some reason, dig holes in the ground filled with junk, and secrete digestive enzymes to somehow absorb something that their body needs to live. And they are now dying in large numbers."

"That's the short of it," Mavis says.

"So, what's killing them? They seem to be dying in and around their digestive holes. Are they being poisoned?"

"Maybe, but you found the first one floating in the Bay," Rafa says. "They must be under the water, digging holes or floating around, trying to absorb raw organic material there, too."

"Did you hear anything like the Hilamen doing this around San Diego?" I ask Mavis.

She shakes her head. "Never heard of anything like it. I'd never seen one till we met Francine in your basement."

"Their metabolic needs aren't being met anymore," Rafa says. "Whatever it is they digest and absorb in the holes—it's not enough. So, they're migrating out, trying to dig their holes more and more away from their colony because they're desperate. Clearly, they aren't doing very well."

"It's a decent theory. So, who was following you?" I ask.

"Men," Mavis says. "They spotted us near the university and followed us along the beach."

"Raiders?" I ask.

"No," Rafa says. "They would've tried killing or robbing us. They were trying to be sneaky and peeled off after we moved through The Sunset."

"So, whoever they are, they also know about the dead Hila on the beach?" I ask.

Rafa nods.

"And they might know about the dead Hila at Twin Peaks by now as well," I say.

"Wait, Hila are up there, too?" Rafa asks.

"Yes. I found fourteen dead up there. Hutch dug them up and shipped them off."

"How'd you find them?" Mavis asks.

I swallow. "Um, I had a dream they were up there." I otherwise wouldn't have been so bold with my ridiculous confession, but I knew with Mavis and Rafa, I had found the right audience.

Shock floods the man's face. "Are you joking right now?"

"No," I say. They both stare at me for a moment. "Why?"

"I had a dream, too," Rafa says. "A very vivid dream about a bunch of dead Hila at the beach. We went, and sure enough, it was precisely like in my dream. Mavis had the same dream as me."

"What?" I look at her. "You both had an identical dream?"

She nods.

"We thought it was too weird for you to believe," Rafa says.

"You would've been right." I can tell he's a bit crestfallen that I, too, agnostic to his Rafa brand of meta-spirituality, also had a prophetic dream. "Group psychosis? Shared trauma or something?" I offer.

"Maybe," Mavis says. "But our dreams independently depicted something that was real. That's not delusion."

I pinch the bridge of my nose, thinking, and deduce exactly nothing. "I don't know what bond unites the three of us, but I do know one thing—something is guiding us toward the Hila for a reason."

"And what reason is that?" Rafa asks.

"To help."

"Why?" Mavis asks.

"I don't know, but it's something that is bigger than just the three of us."

SIXTEEN

ONCE UPON A TIME, I believed in God.

But once you lose your unborn child and husband and emerge from an underground bunker with a group of strangers to rebuild a world that was destroyed by overreaction, pessimism becomes gospel. Whether a divine being was still there permeating all existence while nodding supernal approval or condemnation doesn't really matter when you convert half a capital building into a hospital that mostly serves as a hospice. When hope crumbles to despair, faith is exposed as a fairy tale of the good times. Maybe at some point in my life, I could believe what Rafa was winking at with our dreams—cosmic connection. But if I have learned one lesson since the world broke, it's that the fundamental force that connects humanity is self-preservation with a connective tissue of bullshit and lore to prevent the whole charade from running off the rails. I'm also pretty sure I'm not a prophet and neither is Rafa the Oracle and Mavis the Stoner. But none of this changes the fact that I keep a rosary in my pocket with the name *Gabriel* etched into the wood that I thumb when I'm stressed.

. . .

The next day, my two medical students speak to each other briskly by the clinic. They hush at my approach. "What's going on?" I ask.

"We have a patient in the clinic," Ward says.

"And?"

"It's Sabion," Geddes says.

"Oh, his foot. I told him to come," I say.

"Doctor Darrow," Geddes says. "We do not want to treat him."

I narrow my eyes. "If you want to be a doctor, you cannot decide who is and who is not worthy of your care."

"But I hate him," Geddes says.

"That doesn't matter. Either you go in there right now and take an X-ray of his foot or you are done here. That's it."

"Which one of us?" Ward asks.

"Both of you. Right now." I blow past them and into the clinic, where I find Sabion unwrapping his ankle from bandage. "My medical students here will examine you and take an X-ray."

Sabion's lips curl with disgust at the sight of the boys. "You want me to be treated by a *traitor*?" He flicks his chin at Geddes. "This coward is trying to flee his conscription. I've been trying to convince the mayor to banish the bastard from the colony for dereliction of duty."

Geddes bristles. "I'm still in the colony defense. The mayor has allowed me to do some medical training with Doctor Darrow."

Sabion says nothing and starts wrapping his foot back up. "I'd rather be a cripple than have this chickenshit touch me." And then he hobbles out like a goblin.

I tell the boys to go and help out in the emergency bay as Mayor Hutch appears, beckoning me from the foyer.

"Have you given any more thought about joining my council?" he asks.

"I'm still considering it, yes."

He scrunches his lips in disappointment. "Please, follow me to my office."

I join him and find a bunch of men seated around his office, surrounding his oak desk with the seal of California burned across the top. He seats himself at the head of the desk and gestures at a single unoccupied chair in the middle of the room. I don't sit. "What can I do for you, Mayor?" I ask.

He gestures to the seat again but, after it's clear I'm not going to sit, he gives up. "We would like a formal report on your findings of the Hilamen." A man in the corner picks up a pencil, poised to record.

"What would you like to know?"

"Everything that you know."

I shrug. "That's not a lot. There's still data that we need to comb over to even begin to understand how they work."

"What are they made of?" Reece asks from the corner of the room.

"I don't know yet."

Hutch furrows his brow. "You know nothing? You've had days in a lab to get answers."

"You think scientific discovery happens in *days*?" I look around the room at dim, unforgiving faces. "It would take a team of scientists and anthropologists with perfectly functioning pre-war technology decades to figure out their biology, chemistry, physiology, and social structure. I've only been able to look at some of their tissue under a microscope."

"And what did you see?" Hutch asks.

"Why the sudden curiosity about the Hilamen now?"

His chair squeaks as he leans back, crossing his arms. "Intellectual curiosity."

"Fine. Their cellular metabolism is highly dependent on sulfur and lithium. They also have high levels of yttrium."

Hutch sighs with annoyance. "Why can they only be cut with a diamond blade?"

"I don't know," I lie.

"Is there any other way to destroy their bodies besides cutting into them with a diamond? Any sort of penetrating metal that you think could get through the material?"

"It's called their skin," I say.

"What is?" Hutch says.

"The 'material'. It's the skin of a living thing."

"They're dead. And do you know why they are dying?"

"I do not."

"When will you know?" he asks.

"I don't know that either." I'm suddenly aware that the conversation is a rehash of a conversation we've already had. Whatever Hutch is doing, it's a performance for his men. "Gentlemen," I say, mustering a respectful tone. "These things take time. I will provide you with crucial intelligence when I'm certain about what makes the Hilamen tick. I don't want to make rash assumptions about their biology that could end up being wrong. Men get killed in battle by acting on bad information. As leaders of this colony, you know that better than anyone." There were nods all around, their egos adequately stroked for the time being. Hutch gives me an unmistakable look that he knows exactly what I'm doing. "Anything else, Mr. Mayor?"

He offers me a thin smile. "That's all for now. Thank you, Doctor Darrow."

. . .

An hour later, Prasad waits for me at the patient wards. "I didn't know you were making your own deliveries. I thought you had your sons do that," I say.

"Supplies are out back at the loading dock. I was happy to come in person. Also wanted to talk to you..." He scans the area, asking for some privacy.

"What can I do for you?" I ask him after leading him to my office and closing the door.

He peers around the room like he's in an art museum. "So, this is where our greatest medical mind figures out all her medical mysteries."

"Not exactly."

"You found Rafa Montijo outside the colony at his compound?"

"Yes. He's been very helpful with what I needed."

"Hmm. Good," he says, over-polite. "You've known him for some time, right?"

"Is this what you came here to talk about?"

"No," he says, embarrassed. "I've been keeping an eye on those trucks at Pier 27 like you asked me to."

"You figure out what's in them?" I ask.

"No. But I saw some men watching them."

"Who?"

"I don't know. But there are these same couple of guys who walk by at different times of day. I followed one of them down the street and even saw him later in a building spying on the pier with binoculars."

"You didn't recognize them?" I ask.

"No. And they're not from SF—I know that."

"You know where these guys are hiding out?"

He nods. "I can show you right now. Probably five of them in an abandoned building right by Coit Tower."

"Can you meet me tonight?"

"Would love to."

I meet Prasad at the corner of Kearny and Filbert after midnight, the darkened Coit Tower looming above in the moonlight. He leads me through a back alley, has me hop a few fences, and weaves us through abandoned homes until we emerge on a rooftop. He brings a finger to his lips and points across the street to where a fire is lit on an adjacent rooftop across the street. A single man sits on the roof ledge, his silhouette outlined from the firelight. Aside from the man's stature, it's impossible to make out any more details even with binoculars.

"What now?" Prasad whispers.

"Let's wait and see who else shows up."

He produces a coffee thermos and sandwiches, which he doles out with somewhat of an embarrassed grin. "Are you hungry?" We sip and chew in silence, watching the lone figure on the rooftop. "What do you think you'd be doing right now if the Hilamen hadn't showed up?" he asks me.

I wince a little. "I've been through enough hypothetical conversations like this over the years that I learned they don't help —they only hurt."

"Sorry, it's probably pointless." He bows his head, making me feel like a huge ass.

"No, wait. I'm the one that should be sorry. What would you think you'd be doing right now?"

He chews slowly, considering his words. "I guess looking forward to retiring from an IT job. Maybe watching my boys graduate from college. I'd already lost my wife before the wars, so I know that she still wouldn't be around. Did you have much family?"

"I didn't know you had a wife before."

He throws up his hands. "It's done. In the past. What about you?"

"I had a husband. And we were expecting." I don't really want to say more, but something about Prasad's authentic curiosity disarms me. "There was this little catholic school on Pine where my aunt taught. That's where I wanted my son to go to school. Sometimes I still visit her classroom and imagine my little boy seated there in one of those little desks."

"I'm... sorry."

"And for me, it's not done. Losing them both was like a sliver under the skin. I could never take it out and it just scabbed over, hurting me over and over again." My pulse rises, regretting getting so vulnerable.

He's silent for a moment and then says, "Feels like we died and we're living in purgatory. Hard to believe it all happened."

"We're ghosts. We put on the masks of a new society, trying to build our way back to greatness. But we were never that great. The Hila showed us who we really are."

"And who are we?" he asks.

I gesture to the rotting city around us. "Selfish talking primates playing make-believe."

He offers a weak chuckle to break the awkward tension I've created. "Pretty grim."

"Just being realistic."

"An attitude like that might make it hard to get out of bed in the morning without a stiff drink."

"You're not wrong."

"So, why are we out here tonight?" he asks.

It's a fair question that I don't really know how to answer. "I normally don't care what men do," I say. "It's too predictable at this point to even pay attention. But I do want to find out what is in those trucks without drawing the mayor's attention. Those men over there," I say as four new figures appear on the rooftop, "also appear interested and probably have a good idea of what is in those trucks. I'd like to know what they know."

"What do you think is in them?"

I hush him and bring binoculars to my eyes, watching the new arrivals find seats around their fire. They eat and drink and gesture in conversation, but I'm too far to hear anything they're saying. A few of them roll cigarettes and bring out pipes and start lighting up. I then see the unmistakable shape of a novelty erect penis being loaded with leaf before being brought to a man's lips for smoking.

"Anders," I say.

"From Sacramento?" Prasad asks.

"The same."

"How do you know?"

"That's his stupid pipe, look." I brush crumbs from my jacket and move to the stairs.

"Where are you going?"

"To find out why he's here."

"Sure that's a good idea?" he asks.

"No."

Prasad follows me down the stairs and across the street. I peer up at the rooftop where I hear men laughing. I cup my hands and yell, "Anders!"

Dead silence.

"I know you're up there with that stupid pipe of yours. Come down and have a chat with me."

A forehead and a set of eyes emerge from the rooftop, peering down at us. "Who is that?"

"Elspeth Darrow."

"Fu—" he starts and then sighs. "How did you find me here?"

181

"Thank you for confirming that you are indeed trying to hide. Why don't you come down to chat about it? I have some questions."

"Is that Jack Hutch with you?"

"No, and he doesn't know I'm here," I say.

Long moments pass as the man deliberates about what to do with the curveball awaiting him below. "Go away," he decides.

"I can do that. The question you need to ask yourself is what happens after I leave here with my questions unanswered."

"Just wait, goddammit."

Minutes later, the man appears in the foyer of the building with three men behind him brandishing semi-automatic weapons. They're not exactly aiming the barrels at me when the door opens, but they sweep the streets around us and set up an adorable perimeter to show me who's in charge. Anders looks a mess with a beard that hasn't been trimmed since I saw him in San Jose and purpled half-moons under each eye.

"You've been traveling this entire time since San Jose?" I ask.

He grinds his lower jaw and spits tobacco on the pavement. "Why are you here?"

"As a citizen of Neo SF, I believe I have the right to ask you that question first. I'm certain Hutch did not give you leave to come inside our borders, so you're here illegally and with armed men. You can either put a bullet in me and Prasad here and throw us in the Bay or you can start talking before I bring an armed militia to your doorstep."

Prasad shuffles behind me. "I feel like there are more than those two options," he says. I grab Prasad's wrist and squeeze. Hard.

"This coming from the woman that killed one of my men in San Jose?" Anders asks in what mostly appears to be play-acting for his men.

I bristle. "That child was killed by another idiot child because you were spying on us in the middle of the night."

"Kind of like what you're doing right now?"

I cross my arms. "What are in the trucks?"

Genuine surprise washes over Anders' face. "Hmph. You really aren't with Hutch."

"What are in the semi-trucks?" I repeat.

"Why do you want to know?"

"I want to know what would make you violate colonial law to try to steal whatever is in those semis," I say.

"I'm not stealing anything."

"So, you haven't set up camp here with eyes on those trucks to know the moment they leave the colony to then rob them en route to wherever they're going?"

"No, ma'am," he says.

"Who's buying?"

"Buying what?"

"The contents of the trucks."

He picks at some paint chips in the doorway and says, "Information has a cost."

"Okay, here's the offer... I'll pay you with silence. You can flee here now without facing colonial charges of illegally entering a colony with armed men and the attempt to commit grand larceny. If I'm lying to you, you will be telling me information Hutch already knows, so there is nothing for you to lose at this point."

"You're too smart for your own good."

"What are in the trucks and who is buying?" I ask.

His eyes dance with excitement. "Strongest material known to man. Neo LA."

"LA colony? Mayor Carmichael is the buyer?"

He nods.

"And what is the material?" I ask.

"That's all I'm telling you, Elspeth." He shoos me away. "Now get out of my sight before I consider throwing you two in the Bay. You've ruined my night."

"What is the material being used for?" I ask.

He withdraws into the darkness of the foyer, but then turns, his face lit by the moon. "What else, Doctor? War."

SEVENTEEN

WARD DOESN'T SHOW up at the east wing the next day, so I cross the Civic Center Plaza and make my way to his apartment. After climbing the stairs, I knock at his weird door he painted with sets of shrinking colorful frames telescoping into nothing.

"You are missed in the east wing," I say after he opens the door.

He lets me in and then flops on a couch. "I know. Just can't today. Geddes can take over my duties."

"Geddes knows how to empty bedpans, record vitals, and measure urine. You're needed to run the clinic." I actually mean it. The boy had somehow become essential staff for the hospital.

He says nothing, face flat.

There are charcoal sketches littering the floor of a single scene —a patient lying on a desk in darkness. "What is going on with you?"

"It just feels pointless, sometimes—what we do."

"Shit," I whisper, which he obviously hears.

"What?"

"I've imprinted my cynicism on you. That's not supposed to happen for at least another couple of years."

"Why do you show up at the east wing every day? How do you stay motivated?" he asks.

I rub my forehead, gearing up to give him some rehashed platitudes so I can convince him to come and run the clinic today so I don't have to. But I just don't have the energy. In fact, I'd like to sit there right next to him on the couch and zonk out for the rest of the day, too.

And so I do.

We sit and stare for a bit until I pick up one of his drawings. "What is this drawing of?" I ask.

"The boy who died in San Jose."

"You have depression," I tell him, letting the drawing fall to the ground.

"Yeah."

"So do I," I say, running my hands through my unwashed hair. "It's crippling and consuming and awful and never goes away."

"What do you do about it?"

"Don't look for something to blame. I do that and it only makes it worse. You cope. Do anything other than what you're doing right now. Every day is a fight and every day after is a victory in a war that never ends. Helping people with medicine is good, even if it's just holding their hands as they die. I know it matters for that one person and that is reason enough to show up to the east wing. We don't need to cure everyone, and we can't. What we're doing is giving dignity to people so that maybe they don't experience the same despair we have. It's enough of a reason to get me out of bed every day."

He nods, considering my words. "I've been having weird dreams about the Hila," he says.

"Are you being serious?" I ask.

"Yes, why?"

"What are you dreaming about?"

He breathes deep. "Dead Hila. All around. Dead in holes. It's almost not even a dream. It's like I'm really there seeing it."

I sigh.

"What?" he asks.

"Why can't anything ever be simple?"

"What are you talking about?"

"I'm having the same dreams," I tell him.

"*What?*"

"Rafa and Mavis, too. Same dreams. And the dreams are showing real things. There are dead Hila out there right now exactly where you dreamed."

He stares at me. "Are you messing with me right now?"

"No. Someone is trying to tell us something."

"Are they telepathic?" he asks.

"I considered that. We should probably figure out what's going on and help them."

"How do we know that we should help them get better? We still don't even know why they came, and they've brought nothing but destruction to us."

"I've blamed the Hila many times over the years. I've been angry at them ever since they showed up. I still am. But you can't ask these questions for every sick patient that comes through the door, otherwise, you become a sort of doctor executioner. If you want to find a reason to not heal someone, you'll find one pretty damn quick. Medicine is about unconditional help. The Hila deserve that, I think," I say, wondering if I believe my own words. "At least I hope."

"Okay." He shrugs on a jacket. "Let's go and cope together."

.   .   .

"Thirty-two weeks," Priscilla tells me as she hops onto the exam table the next day.

"Any bloody discharge? Still feeling the baby move?" I ask.

"Everything is going great," she says. I feel the uterus and baby through her abdomen and am happy with the baby's position. The doppler spits static as I sweep it over her belly. She reads my face. "What is it?"

"Heart rate is just a little on the low end of normal," I say.

Her face crimps with concern. "What does that mean?"

"It's very likely normal—it's just where the baby's heart rate likes to live. But why don't we have you come in the next couple of days to take the heart rate?"

"Definitely. I want to do everything possible to make sure he's safe."

"How's the nausea?" I ask.

"Bad. But I don't care. And I'm keeping food down."

"How's your mood? Depression symptoms?"

She shrugs. "A little. Always a mix of excitement and worry."

"It's natural to be worried about the pregnancy."

"It's not just that. I worry about what I'm bringing the baby into. Reece is scaring me."

"Is he violent with you?" I ask.

She shakes her head. "No, no, he's as gentle as a lamb. It's the things he's saying about the Sacs trying to start trouble with us. Why do they hate us so much when we didn't do anything to them?"

"You think the colony of Sacramento hates us?"

"They have it out for us. I'm just so happy the good folks in LA are able to supply our militia with better guns. Reece thinks it's more than enough to keep us safe, but I still worry. You think the Sacs are going to attack us?"

"It's possible..." I say.

"And I hear the San Diegans are starting up trouble down south with LA. Talking about how they're the colony that's going to become the first real city for America to rebuild from. Reece says we need to side with LA and that the Sacs are trying to side with San Diego."

I wasn't expecting Hutch's propaganda to be spat out at me during an obstetrics exam but it's useful to see what kind of levers he's pulling. "So, there's conflict down south?"

"Both LA and San Diego have stopped trading to each other because they went crazy with tariffs. They're the biggest colonies in California, which makes them the biggest colonies in America, given that the east coast is a dead zone."

"So, who are we siding with?" I ask.

She shrugs. "Dunno. I think Hutch is smart trying to stay out of politics and just keep us fed, safe, and the free markets open to trade. I trust him."

"I certainly hope he makes the right decisions, too. Okay, we're all done," I say, getting up to leave. "Make sure to come in tomorrow for a quick doppler of the baby's heart."

"Yes, ma'am."

I have another dream that night. I open my eyes to my room and, like a vision before me, scores of dying Hila stir in their sad little digestive holes. In sequence, I see them in Monterey, San Jose, and a beach I recognize at Half Moon Bay. I blink and reach my hand out and know damn well that I'm not asleep.

"Who's there?"

The vision collapses and I'm alone in the darkness. But then, white light flickers back to life from across the room and a scene is projected there. I get out of bed and move closer as the scene plays from the corner of the room. I rub sleep from my eyes, trying to understand the images and I finally see.

It's a cat stalking a mouse.

"What is this?" I ask my empty room.

Like a looped video, I see a cat creeping along roof rafters, slowly hunting a mouse. I dash across the room to the light switch and flip it. Instantly, the vision is gone, and I'm standing in my room in the middle of the night, completely alone as if none of it happened at all.

"Cat hunting a mouse?" Rafa asks as I step into his house the next day. Ward and I had made our way to Rafa's compound, past the menagerie and frog plague at the front, and seated ourselves around his kitchen table. Mavis is at the sink peeling potatoes and humming to herself.

"Yeah," I answer and point at Ward. "Him, too."

"He's getting them, too? When did they start?" Rafa asks.

"The night after we all came back from UCSF after looking at the Hila under the microscope," he says.

"Same with us," I tell Ward. "It's clearly coordinated messaging. And I don't think they are dreams. The 'Cat and Mouse' message from last night happened from the corner of my room while I was standing and wide awake."

"They're not dreams," Mavis agrees as she turns on a burner, hot oil popping. "Has anyone else you know been receiving the messages?"

"Not that I know of," I answer. Everyone else shakes their heads.

"So, what do they mean?" Ward asks.

Mavis brings a freshly brewed gourd of tea to Rafa, who smiles at the rising steam. It's at that moment I realize the two are sleeping together. He takes a sip and says, "There are a few things we can deduce from the messages. Number one, there is a coordinated effort to communicate the same message to us. Why us? We seem to care about the Hila by our investigations into the cause of their demise. Someone—presumably the Hila—has started a campaign to show us where more of their dead and dying are located. They want us to know what is happening to them so that we can help them."

"Why would they communicate to us in this way?" Ward asks.

"You've seen their bodies. They don't have mouths. They don't have ears. They are not equipped for language and sound-wave communication in the same way that we are. They have four eyes studded around their heads. They are visual creatures and they're trying to tell us they're dying. Well, message received. The next question is how are they aware that we have been doing an autopsy and trying to figure out their biology?"

"They're watching us," Mavis answers, flipping hash browns in a griddle. "Closely."

"But how?" Ward asks.

"To speculate would take hours," Rafa answers. "Advanced technology, incredible penetrating eyesight from afar, ultrasound sonar location, infrared. We can't be sure. But they know what we're trying to do, and they want to imbue us with a sense of urgency." Rafa speaks with a vigor I have never known him to have. Mavis must be doing him some good. "They are able to surveil us—could be doing it right now. But they probably don't understand our verbal language. They may not even know that we use sound waves for communication. At any rate, I believe we can conclude they are an intelligent species capable of abstract thought based on this coordinated effort to reach out to another intelligent species."

"So, what's with the cat chasing a mouse?" I ask.

"They've communicated their most urgent matter first," Rafa says. "That they're dying and they need help. Once you believed an alien life understood that message, what is the next thing that you would want them to know?"

We share silence for a moment, thinking. "The reason," I say. "They want to give us an incentive to act."

"Bingo," Mavis says, bringing an enormous plate of hash browns to the table.

"And how do you incentivize someone?" Rafa asks.

"Stick or carrot," I answer with dread sinking into my stomach.

"And which of those does a cat hunting a mouse most likely fit?"

"Stick," I answer.

Rafa nods. "What is the most overwhelming message from depicting a cat hunting a mouse? Threat. Predation. Warning. Impending doom."

"But why use a cat and mouse as their message?" Ward asks.

"They are trying to communicate with us with visual imagery we understand," Rafa says. "There possibly isn't something more universal, across solar systems and galaxies, than a predator hunting its prey. It is unambiguous to any intelligent life anywhere. They've certainly seen cats and mice while they've been on Earth over the last twenty years, and they've chosen them to represent their message."

"So, bringing this together," Mavis says before stuffing a forkful of hash brown into her mouth. "The Hila are dying, they want us to help, or else..." She brings the fork across her neck horizontally.

"Or else what exactly?" Ward asks.

"A cat will get us," Mavis says with a weird wink.

"So, we are the mouse? And who's the cat?" I ask. "The Hila? Are they threatening us?"

"That would be an easy assumption to make, but I don't really see a dying species thinking an empty threat will get us to do anything," Rafa says. "Maybe we're the cat and they are the mouse and it's us that's killing them. A warning about something we need to do to stop from killing them? Maybe we're all collectively the mouse and there is a third-party threat that we don't know about. The Hila could be trying to appeal to a sense of solidarity with us against a common enemy."

"And what enemy is that? Another colony?" I ask.

"Maybe they'll help us fight off another aggressive colony if we help them. They do have some pretty killer protection with that graphene skin of theirs," Mavis says.

"I think Hutch is selling dead Hila bodies to LA," I say.

Potato falls from Mavis' mouth. "What? Why—oh my god. For their *skins*?"

"I believe so," I say.

"You think they're, what, repurposing their skins?" Mavis asks.

"I'm not surprised," Rafa says. "The potential uses for Hila skin are endless. The material is nearly indestructible, lightweight, elastic, impervious to projectiles, and—well, let me show you." He abruptly stands from the table and walks out of the kitchen, leaving us to traipse after him into the basement. One wall is completely lined with enough automatic weapons for a small army. The other side of his workshop is full of distillation equipment, volumetric flasks, powder vats, and ventilation hoods. On the table before him is the Hila leg that we had dissected away from our prior autopsy. Rafa flips on a propane blowtorch that he has suspended above the tissue and releases a jet of flame to blast the tissue. "There is no amount of heat I can hit the skin with that it cannot resist. It probably has heat resistance into the thousands Celsius."

"Probably above two thousand degrees Celsius," Mavis confirms. "It cannot melt."

He turns off the propane and flips a switch at the base of the table, which prompts an electrical hum through the basement. Tongues of electricity coruscate along the tissue, cracking and writhing along the surface. "It's also a perfect conductor of electricity at room temperature. The Hila have a coating of material that is basically designed for space travel and defense from many, many threats."

"And," Mavis says, "if someone were to wear a coat of armor made of Hila skin, they would be unkillable with current Earth technology."

"Sounds like the perfect material for an invading army," I say, cobbling together a picture of what Hutch has been up to. "How were things between LA and San Diego before you left San Diego?" I ask her.

"Southern drought was bringing lots of problems," Mavis says. "They kept fighting over access to different trade routes and threatening each other with tariffs. There was talk of a total embargo of LA before I left. You pair that with existing tensions between the mayors, Carmichael and Gustavson, who clearly have had their eye on becoming the neo-American capital, and a potential powder keg is ready to explode. I've seen that shit too many times. That's why I came up north. Plus, Gustavson is a psychopath with his own personal paramilitary group. He shut down elections through some emergent loophole clause in the colony charter and controls the entire colony economy."

"So, would LA and San Diego actually both go to war with each other?" Ward asks.

Mavis shrugs. "I don't know, and I don't really care. Just don't want to be around."

"For all we know, the recent advent of Hila dying is actually sparking more conflict and accelerating existing aggression," Rafa says. "We've only recently discovered the Hila are dying around here. Whatever is killing them off here may be killing them off at other colonies. There are certainly some old-worlder scientists like us in LA and San Diego who have also discovered the amazing properties of the Hila skin and have made their mayors aware of the potential use. Both colonies may be trying to dominate a new covert Hila skin market to get the upper hand. When something that has such tremendous economic potential that it tilts the axis of power, that's when people go to war. Been happening since the dawn of power."

"This is making sense," I say. "It's why Hutch has given us so much leeway to figure out how the Hila work. He knows LA and San Diego are trying to get their hands on Hila and they've probably offered large contracts to smaller colonies like SF and Sacramento to collect the Hila bodies like bounties. This explains why Hutch and Anders have been so territorial over San Jose—they've probably discovered Hila bodies there, too. Hutch has set up an arms arrangement with one of the local gunsmiths from LA. I know there's been a big influx of weapons into the colony militia. It's possible they haven't told him why they want the Hila and he wants us to figure it out. That's why he's been playing ball with us."

"Have you told him anything?" Mavis asks.

"As little as possible but enough to keep him satisfied."

"Hutch is getting paid in guns?" Ward asks.

"I think so, directly to Harlo. Hutch is undoubtedly taking a healthy cut for setting up the exclusive contract. The recent Sacramento aggression against us also explains some things."

"Proxy war," Rafa says. "Between us and Sacramento."

I nod. "Yes. Anders was up here, and I think it was him and his men following you. They saw what you saw on the beach and snuck into SF to see what Hutch was going to do with the Hila. Hutch loaded them onto a couple of semis for transport to LA and I suspect Anders was planning on hijacking the trade caravan. That is until I came along and spooked him."

"So, are the Hila trying to warn us about colonial war coming?" Ward asks. "Like it's in their interest and ours in the colonial conflict? Are we the cat?"

Mavis cracks open a beer from the corner of the room. "Men are most definitely the cat."

"Anyways," Rafa says. "Mavis and I are going to head up to the Twin Peaks Hila holes and take some soil samples. We'll need to make our way back to the university for gas analysis. If we can figure out what their metabolic byproducts are, we may be able to pinpoint a nutritional deficiency they're having."

"And then what?" I ask. "Supplement it?"

Rafa winks. "Bingo."

EIGHTEEN

A FEW DAYS LATER, I find half the shop owners from the wharf congregating at Civic Center Plaza, shouting the mayor's name. It's not organized enough to be a demonstration, but not unruly enough to be a mob. Either way, there is an angry group of merchants wanting to talk with Hutch at the same time and about the same thing.

Prasad is at the periphery. "What is this all about?" I ask.

"Total San Diego embargo."

"No way. We get nearly a third of supplies and foodstuffs from them. When did they drop the embargo?"

"Not *them*. Us."

I bug my eyes at him. "Hutch started the embargo? There is no way SF can survive with an embargo like that."

"Any idea why the man is interested in crashing our attempt at a market economy?" he asks.

An hour later, Hutch calls for a town hall where he stands at the podium, removes his wicker hat, and reveals a plume of comb-over hair that sticks straight up toward the ceiling. Like a sail on a ship, the white hair waffles side to side as Hutch lavishes his audience with praise about efforts to establish commerce in the Bay Area and lift all of Neo California from the brink of hunger and war. "Alright, now I'll get real with y'all," he says, dabbing sweat from his forehead. "You have nothing to worry about. Our colony is strong. We are the backbone of the great American recovery. The Sandies are the ones we need to worry about. They are acting belligerent to LA and the rest of this great state and her colonies. The Sandies want to steal our rights as neo-founders. You all know the laws and stewardship entrusted to all U.S. bunker citizens when we came back to recolonize. Every colony was to be a bastion of freedom, hope, and economic prosperity. The Sandies want to monopolize all for themselves. They wish to see themselves as the new capital and subject all the colonies to itself. Even their own citizens are rebelling as refugees are even today showing up at our doorstep. The time has come to stand up to them and refuse to cooperate. If they're going to bully us, our answer is an embargo."

"We get most of our refurbished parts for heavy machinery from San Diego," someone shouted, followed by another, "We won't be able to feed ourselves on SF agriculture alone!"

Hutch lifted his hands to calm the anxiety in the room. "I would never place this embargo without a plan. I have signed a trade agreement with LA Mayor Carmichael, which involves an exclusive trading route between us and them. We have received an infusion of arms to increase our militia. Both SF and LA will establish a well-guarded trade route between the two colonies, free of raiders and the influence of the Sandies. It is called the Free Trade and Protection Treaty of Northern California—the FTPT. Not only will the San Diegan embargo not be a problem for us, but the FTPT will also be a boon to our economy and prosperity.

It will open up a new age of advancement toward the once former glory of the United States of America."

"Will Sacramento be a part of the trade route?" someone asks.

"Only if they stand with us against tyranny," Hutch answers. The prior anxious whispers had died down into a pleased murmur. Hutch continues outlining his economic plan for the future as well as more vague threats that the Sandies pose on SF freedom. And then, the mayor places his hand over his heart and gives the pledge of allegiance, which I thought was laying it on a tad thick. He fails to mention San Diego has been a reliable trading partner and friend to SF since we all hatched from our bunkers twenty years ago, but no one seems to notice this omission. Also notable is the fact that Mayor Hutch has blasted the message from SF radio that we are the destined colony to form the new capital of America—the very thing he just accused the San Diegans of doing.

"Had no idea they were such a threat to us for the last twenty years," I say to him over the crowd as the meeting adjourns. The mayor locks eyes with me for a moment and then smiles. It's a smile not for me but for everyone else in the room to see.

Later that day, a man is wheeled up to the steps of the east wing. Some good Samaritan found him outside the colony walls, dumped him into a wheelbarrow, and pushed him three miles to my doorstep. We bring him up to our resuscitation bay, drill an IV into his shin bone, and start pumping him full of IV fluids. His blood pressure is precisely fifty over nothing. I feel for a pulse at his neck.

Nothing.

"Get on the chest!" I yell. "Ward, do chest compressions. Show Geddes how it's done." Ward gingerly places his hands on the patient's chest and pushes. "That wouldn't get the blood flowing for a mouse. Like this." I show him, pumping deep into the patient's sternum. "If you're not cracking ribs, you're not doing it hard enough."

After a few rounds of chest compressions, we can't get a pulse back. During a pause, we shear his clothing from his body and there's nothing—no bullet holes, no stab wounds. But then I feel around the back of his skull and bring blood back on my gloved hand. "Gunshot wound to the head," I announce. After a few more rounds of chest compressions, we still can't get a pulse back and I call it. The man falls motionless in the bed, eyes open with a dead gaze on the filthy curtains over the window.

"Raiders?" Patience asks.

I shake my head. "Raiders usually don't execute people like that. Wait—" I recognize the dead man from San Jose. He was in Anders' party.

"You know him?" Patience asks.

"Officially? No."

An hour later I'm summoned to Hutch's office. "Thank you for meeting with me on such short notice, Doctor Darrow." He motions for me to have a seat in front of his desk.

"What can I do for you, Mayor?" I ask.

"I have refugees in need of your medical expertise."

"And what kind of political or natural disaster has created these refugees?"

"They were deported from Neo San Diego for being political dissidents," he says.

I groan a little. "Those are some old and complicated words you're using there."

"Three arrived yesterday. One doesn't look well. I had her escorted to your clinic where she awaits you. Is that agreeable?"

"Yes," I say.

"Thank you, and please be delicate about her circumstances and why she arrived here. I ask that you not talk to her about her time in San Diego. Miss Horvat has been through a lot."

"I will go and see her now." I turn toward the door. "I've made a decision about your offer."

He raises his eyebrows. "And?"

"I will take a seat on the council."

He crosses his arms.

"Is the offer still good?" I ask.

"It is, but I have concerns."

"About what?"

He counts on his fingers. "Back talking, rebel rousing—"

"Would you like me to be your pawn or actually offer you critical thinking about how to run this colony and the challenges we now face with the Sandies?"

He puts up his hands and chuckles. "Never change, Elspeth. I'm happy to have you on board. Will I be getting any updates about your research on the Hilamen?"

"Yes. Very soon. Have there been any trade attacks you've heard of today outside the colony?"

He stiffens. "No. Why?"

"I have a man in the ER bay. Showed up in a wheelbarrow. Shot in the head. Once. From behind."

He jumps to his feet and rushes to the door. "Take me to him."

"He's dead."

"Take me to him."

I lead him down to the resuscitation bay and remove the blanket covering the man while studying the mayor's face. He clearly recognizes the dead man. "Who is he to you?" I ask.

He removes his glasses and squints at me. "You're truly part of my council now?"

"Yes."

"That is Matheus Weinart."

"Never heard of him," I say.

"He's a spy I planted in Sacramento."

I pinch the bridge of my nose and sigh. "You have *spies*?"

He brings one finger to his lips and nods. "And one has been executed. Just outside our walls." Hutch rifles through the dead man's discarded clothing and produces a piece of paper from a pants pocket. He unfolds it and reads.

"What does it say?" I ask.

He shows me the slip of paper. It's a hand-drawn penis urinating on a stick figure wearing a hat that says, 'Mayor Hutch.'

Late that afternoon, I meet the San Diegan refugee in our clinic. "Miss Horvat?" I say coming into the clinic room.

"Nika." She's a wiry young woman with a set of rotting teeth, inflamed gums, and a spattering of poorly-healed wounds across her skin that scream vitamin C deficiency. After a quick physical exam, I give her a bottle of multivitamins and instruct her to return in a week.

"How was the journey up here from San Diego?" I ask.

"Difficult and long."

"Why come at all?"

"Mayor Gustavson doesn't like me very much," she says.

"And why is that?"

She narrows her eyes at me. "It's complicated." She clutches the bottle of vitamins as if to get up and leave.

I hold up a hand. "I'm on Mayor Hutch's council. Whatever you say is safe with me."

"It wasn't even a big deal. I just wanted to study the Hila. My mother was a biologist before she died and always took me to the beach to do animal dissections on the washed-up animals."

"What were you studying about the Hila?" I ask.

"I don't really know much about them, I just think they're cool. Like, where did they come from and why are they here? No one seems to give a shit. A ton of movies and books during your time about this exact thing happening were made, and then, when it finally happened, it's just a big shrug from everyone. Know what I mean?"

"I do. Have you ever seen one?"

She shakes her head. "Never until I found one dead at Otay Lake outside San Diego. That's where they all say they have a colony there because of all those weird holes dug everywhere. A few weeks ago, I found one. It was dead."

"What did it look like?"

"Big black lizard-looking thing. Don't understand how we don't spot them all the time, looking the way they do."

"What did the mayor get so upset about?" I ask.

"I moved to Otay Lake. Set up camp there and wanted to spot more of them. Meet them. Talk to them. Share ideas and see what they're all about. Gustavson didn't like that very much. He'd have his cronies bring me back within the colony walls but I'd sneak out and go back. Found more of them dead. Something's wrong with them. I know nobody else cares, but I do. I never really cared about anything else in the colony until I started hanging out with dead aliens. I'm just a big weirdo."

I offer a smile of solidarity. "You're in company. I'm a weirdo like you. We've been finding their bodies here in the Bay Area as well. Something is wrong with them."

"That's what I heard—why I came up here."

"So, you're not really a refugee."

"What's a refugee?" she asks.

"In this case, a political prop."

"What?"

"Never mind. Is there anything else you learned about the Hila?" I ask.

"Not really. Gustavson's men dragged away the bodies. Don't know what they did with them."

"How long have you been visiting Otay Lake?"

"Couple of years," she says. "I knew plenty of Hila go back and forth from there because of so many new hole turnovers. But I still have never seen a living one. Don't understand how they could just sneak by without me ever seeing them. Pretty area, too. I could live there the rest of my life alone and I think I'd be fine with that. Was getting pretty good at hunting. And the northern lights above the hills there. Man, beautiful."

"Northern lights?" I ask.

"Yeah. Once a year for a few days."

I shake my head. "There aren't any northern lights in southern California."

"Sure, there are," she insists. "I've been going up there since I was a kid to watch. Lots of people go every year. Do you think your mayor here will have a problem with me snooping around where Hila have been spotted?"

"I would not count on that."

"Doctor Darrow, I need you," Ward says the next day as I'm irrigating a gaping wound down the back of a patient's hamstring.

"For what?"

"I need you to come to my house."

"Why?" I ask.

"Just meet me over there when there's nothing more urgent here."

An hour later, I curse the boy's name as my hip grinds cartilage to powder going up his staircase. I find him in his apartment just standing there looking at a painting of a cat stalking a mouse, mounted on an easel. It's also upside down.

"You painted their message?" I ask.

"Yep."

"This is why you wanted me to haul myself up your stairs? To look at your painting?"

"No," he says. "I finished it last night and put it on the easel. I wanted them to know that I got their message."

"And?"

"I put it on the easel and went to bed. Woke up and here it was. Only, it was upside down."

I touch the edge of the painting. "You didn't place it there upside down?"

"Nope. And not a soul has been in this apartment."

That very night, I lie in bed with my eyes closed but I don't sleep. I wait. I wait until light flickers in my room and then a new Hila vision plays before me. It's a night's sky displayed before me in perfect depiction as if I have a personal and miniature sky with twinkling starlight that hovers over my bed. The vision then switches to the same cat stalking a mouse. Instead of the cat watching the unaware mouse, the cat strikes, sinking its teeth into the rodent's neck. The vision then flips back to the starry night.

"Are you there?" I ask.

The vision collapses and I turn on a lamp on the nightstand. The room is empty.

"Are you there?" I repeat, this time reaching my open palms to the middle of the room.

The silence is interrupted by the floor creaking in the corner of the room. I stand, a cup of water in my hand, and cast the water across the room in an arc. Water hits something that isn't there, deflects, and for a millisecond, dribbles down a length of transparent beads.

And then there is nothing once more.

NINETEEN

"I THINK THEY'RE EVERYWHERE," I tell Rafa and Mavis, who are seated on Ward's couch. Ward sits at his easel, painting a starry night on canvas.

"Wait," Rafa tells Ward. "Your Aquaris is a little wonky. It doesn't taper so much in the middle."

Ward's jaw tenses as he makes the twentieth revision to the painting. "I'm getting these straight out of the constellations from the book you gave me."

"That's how I know you're not getting them quite right. Look." He motions to the textbook. "Your Pegasus is too close. We don't want to confuse them. Where is Venus?"

"I haven't done the planets yet." It's nice to see Ward annoyed for once and not doing the annoying, which is typically directed at me.

"They've probably been watching us the entire time they've been here," Rafa finally answers me. "In our streets, our markets— our bedrooms. Explains why they bleed rainbows."

"How so?" I ask.

"They're invisible," he says. "Well, at least when they're alive. When they're dead, they're black as tar. Invisibility is just a trick of light. It was clear from their four eyes that the Hila are creatures of optics. But I just had no idea to what extent. The kaleidoscope of pigmentation they have in their cells is how they do it. They get continuous feedback from their eyes about the electromagnetic spectrum that surrounds their bodies. This is somehow fed to their skin where the pigments are released from micro sequestration and then they mimic back the visual environment around them in a continuous fashion. As they walk, their skin is constantly receiving input and spitting out the visual output to make them completely invisible in the visible spectrum. Maybe in even infrared and UV. Hard to say without testing. They probably camouflage as an electric reflex without thinking about it. I mean, they would have to. They don't have a neural network robust enough to even process that kind of data."

"I bet the conductivity of their graphene skin acts as a nervous system but with way less resistance than a human nervous system," Mavis says. "So they can rapidly project their surrounding environment without missing a beat."

"Every one of their cells can probably create an action potential given all the lithium. Each cell is a battery," Rafa says.

"That explains why they don't have a visible nervous symptom on the gross exam," I add.

"It makes sense," Rafa says. "They don't even need a nervous system. Instead, they send electrical currents everywhere over their skin. The eyes provide the stimulus, an electrical impulse is sent, and each exterior cell broadcasts its pigmentation to perfectly mirror the surrounding environment. Boom—invisibility. These creatures have made hiding an art form."

"And apparently, they can also generate other images as well.

Like the messages they've been showing us at night," Ward says, not turning from the easel.

"Your Lacerta is just atrocious," Rafa points at another star constellation in Ward's painting. "But, yes, they also can apparently create visual imagery across their skin. It's probably how they communicate with one another. Big eyes to see and skin to broadcast what they want to say to one another. They're communicating with us the only way they know how but haven't wanted to actually reveal themselves to us. Again, the question you have to ask is what kind of evolutionary pressures created beings that are natural space-faring creatures, have nearly indestructible skin, and are also capable of invisibility?"

"Probably not evolutionary pressure that anything on Earth has ever had to deal with," Mavis says. She stands to inspect Ward's painting. "How are we supposed to know if this is the exact night sky they were trying to show us?" she asks Rafa.

"I recognized it," he says.

"Course you did." She smiles at him—the first smile I've ever seen on her skeletal face.

"It's a California sky," Rafa continues. "Just not quite sure what time of year, which is the exact reason they are showing us the constellations. They are trying to communicate time to us in one of the only universal ways they know—constellations and planet position. That's why our best bet is to just throw up the constellations we think we saw and get them to confirm to us. I wish they'd just show us what they wanted in real-time so we could take the guesswork out of this."

"What's to say they aren't here right now, watching us?" Ward asks, sticking his tongue out the side of his mouth as he works.

"They probably are." Rafa stands and flips open a notebook with a sketch he's done, showing a human and a Hilaman standing side by side. He shows it to all corners of the room. "I didn't know how else to tell them that we wanted to meet with them face to face."

"I couldn't think of a better way—" Mavis gasps.

A small night's sky unfurls right next to Ward's painting, twinkling with starlight as if someone put the sky in a terrarium. The Hila keeps the rest of its body invisible as the still image of constellations appears to float a few feet above the floor. Both Ward and Rafa frantically sketch the image as Rafa calls out the constellations he sees and their relationship with the seasonal sky. The night sky then disappears, followed by a cat pouncing on a mouse and sinking its teeth in its neck. A third image is shown—Hila dying in their digestive holes.

After a moment of stunned silence, Mavis translates, "Save us by a certain time or a big cat will come and eat us."

The images disappear.

"They've really just been in our homes, watching us for the last twenty years?" Ward asks with uneasy awe.

"I wonder what they think of us," I say. "Are they disappointed? Impressed? Are they just interstellar anthropologists? Any sense of what time they are referencing?" I ask Rafa.

The man is flipping through star charts until he lands on a page. He compares his and Ward's sketches to the book and then looks at us. "It's an October sky. Two months away."

I stand where the Hila was broadcasting the images and reach my hand out to empty space. The cool grasp of invisible beaded skin wraps around my fingers, plumping goosebumps up my arm. The reality that I'm holding hands with a living alien sinks in as I return its grasp. "We'll try," I say before the Hila releases its grip.

"I'm pleased to announce that Doctor Darrow has not only agreed to join our council but is also prepared to give an updated report on her research about the Hilamen." Hutch seats himself behind his desk and gestures for me to take the floor.

"Gentlemen," I say to a room consisting entirely of gentlemen. "The Hilamen are dying." I fire up an old projector, where I've drawn a crude map of the San Francisco Peninsula on transparent film. "Their bodies have been in the Bay near San Mateo, The Twin Peaks, the west SF beach, and just recently near Half Moon Bay." I bring up a photograph of Hila from my autopsy that prompts audible gasps from my audience. "They are extremely hearty creatures with nearly indestructible skin. They have no discernible organs, but they do have four eyes that are placed equal distances around the head stalk. We know very little about their culture or social structure, except that they are extremely reclusive, and they've only expanded outward because there is clearly a serious threat to them."

"And what is that threat?" Hutch asks.

"We don't know yet. Me and my colleagues are still trying to figure that out."

"Colleagues?" Handover, a prominent SF business owner asks. "What colleagues?" Ever since I'd refused to endorse his health tonics, the man never listened to a word I ever said, which was a shame because there is a large melanoma speckled across his left cheek that has grown since I last pestered him about coming to my clinic to get it removed.

"Rafa Montijo and Mavis Ulrich," I answer.

"You mean the psychotic hermit who built a zoo by the Painted Ladies?" Handover asks.

"Rafa has multiple degrees in physics and chemistry and may literally be one of the smartest men in the world right now," I say.

"Had," he says.

"Had what?" I ask.

"He *had* those degrees. Today, they mean nothing."

I turn to Hutch, gesturing to Handover, and ask, "Why is he here?"

"He sits on this council," Hutch says.

"And why does he sit on this council?"

"His businesses are the bedrock of the SF economy. He has earned a say."

"Because the man has profited off of selling tonics that do nothing other than give my patients rashes, he has a say in how this democratic institution conducts itself?"

Handover's glare to Hutch says everything... *why did you invite this woman here?*

"Doctor Darrow, please continue," Hutch says while Reece furiously takes the minutes.

"The Hilamen don't have stomachs—they don't even have mouths," I say. "They dig these holes." I slap down a photograph of a digestive hole. "They fill them with animal and plant matter as well as metals, secrete some sort of digestive enzymes into the holes, and then submerge themselves in the organic matter and likely absorb their nutrients through the skin. We believe they are expanding outward from their colony in Monterey because there are nutritional deficiencies in their diet that are killing them. They're throwing anything they can find in their holes to try to meet their metabolic demands. Clearly, it's not working and they're starting to die. These are desperate, starving creatures."

"So, they're not a threat anymore?" Reece asks almost like he's disappointed.

"No, and I don't think they ever have been. At least there is no evidence to suggest they've directly harmed any human."

"What is their diet lacking?" Hutch asks.

"We don't know. Yet."

"You can figure it out?"

"Yes," I say. "Rafa and Mavis are collecting samples as we

speak and are on their way tomorrow to the university to analyze. I suggest you send an armed entourage with them."

Hutch leans back in his chair. "And once you figure out what their diet is lacking, what do you propose we do about it?"

"Help them, of course," I say.

The council becomes very silent. Something unspoken happens where Hutch shares furtive eye contact with several members. They nod in a way that suggests they believe I can't see them, but I, of course, do because I'm looking right at them.

"How quickly do you think they're dying?" Hutch asks.

I shrug. "Impossible to know without research. Could be weeks of a nutritional deficiency, could be years. They probably have very robust cellular metabolism, and these are creatures that likely travel for a very long time in space on a limited diet. There's also another possibility of why they're dying that I haven't brought up yet."

"And what is that?" Hutch asks.

"Toxicity. There may be something in Earth's soil or our atmosphere that's killing them. That's the other theory we're considering."

"And you believe Montijo and Mavis will be able to figure out what's going on?"

"They might," I say.

"Very good. We would be pleased to send some men along with them to ensure they are able to continue their important work."

The meeting adjourns and I've never been more suspicious of Hutch's compliance.

"Reece Hutch is a slithery little snake," Rafa says a few days later as he drops his pack on the ground and collapses on the couch at his compound. "Couldn't shake that little shit the whole time—constantly looking over my shoulder as if he knows the first clue about gas chromatography."

"What did you find out and how much of it does Reece know?" I ask.

"We found out a lot and he knows very little. I also feel extremely stupid. Remember the smell during the autopsy?"

"Rotten eggs?"

He nods. "Hydrogen sulfide. It's clearly a waste product of their metabolism but I didn't really put it together that it could be a main driver of their cellular energy production. The soil samples of their digestive holes are absolutely full of hydrogen sulfide and completely devoid of elemental sulfur and sulfates. I looked at random soil sampling I took from our trip to the university, and there is baseline sulfur in our soil. The Hila are sucking up all the sulfur and spitting out hydrogen sulfide as the waste product."

"So, they're not getting enough sulfur?" I ask.

"Definitely not. They're also not getting enough nitrites and iron, other metabolic reducers that I think they definitely use to make cellular energy. These things don't care about oxygen to power their cells, and why would they? They basically live in space where diatomic oxygen may not be all that easy to transport. I bet if I could sample the pods they came riding in on, they would be chockfull of sulfates, nitrites, and iron."

"But then how have they survived here for twenty years?" I ask.

He shrugs. "I could only guess why it would just affect them now. Maybe they brought mountains of food with them from their journey and they've run out now. Or maybe they can tolerate the sulfur deficiency but for only so long before their health suffers. We're just groping in the dark here about their actual cellular metabolism. Things are much more complex in reality and I could be totally wrong. For all we know, they're being poisoned by something in the soil or animals they're consuming."

"So, what do we do?" I ask.

"That's the beauty. If I'm correct, the solution is laughably easy."

"And what is it?"

He spreads his open palms wide. "Plant fertilizer. Full of sulfur. I could make a blend with iron and nitrite."

"And then just what? Dump it in their holes?" I ask.

"Yep. Let's fill them up and see what grows."

TWENTY

"OF COURSE I can get you fertilizer," Prasad tells me a day later at his shop. "But you know I'm not the biggest distributor of fertilizer, right? Why not just head over to farming supply? They've got boatloads of the stuff."

"Because I don't want anyone else to know besides me and you," I say.

"Why would anyone care that you're purchasing fertilizer? Building a bomb?" His laugh quickly dies when he sees I don't smile.

"No. And I don't need very much. Just a few pounds."

"What's it for?" he asks.

"It's best if you don't know. For your own safety."

He laughs again, trying to shoo the weird tension out of the room. "Who am I in danger from? Anders?"

"The better question is who are you not in danger from?" I say. "There are vipers all around these days. Probably going to get worse."

"Just reassure me that this is all for something good."

I fold my arms. "I believe it is. I promise you that."

He nods like he won an argument. "I'll get you what you need by tomorrow. With discretion."

"Thank you." I turn to leave his shop.

"One stipulation," he calls, raising an eyebrow. "Let's go and get some coffee across the street. Look at the Bay."

"I've seen the Bay before," I say, genuinely surprised by the offer.

"It's just coffee."

I walk up to him and pat his cheek. "No, it's not."

"Doctor Darrow, what can I help you with?" Hutch says from behind the ajar door later that morning. I see eyeballs peeking at me from within his office.

"I'm here for the meeting," I say.

He shakes his head, unwilling to open the door more. "This isn't a meeting."

"Yes, it is. Every council member is in that room right now. You're sitting in chairs, generally congregating, and you're talking. That's a meeting." I elbow my way in and sit between Handover and Reece. Both appear quite annoyed at my presence. "Where were we?"

Hutch stands there for a moment as if the gears of politicking are churning behind those eyes. "Thank you for joining us, Doctor," he says, pivoting. "We were just getting updates from our men down south."

Hutch's scoutmaster, Zeke Plinth, continues to gaze at Hutch as if asking if it's really okay that he continues despite my presence. The mayor gives him a nod. "There's mustering happening. Mustering," Plinth declares this in a way that it's clear he's been looking forward to using the word. "Sandie Mayor Gustavson's got a militia in Bakersfield. About three hundred Sandies opposite LA's men there who number just about the same."

Hutch leans forward, his elbows resting on the table. "Have there been skirmishes?"

"No," Plinth says. "Tensions are high but no violence."

"We won't tolerate this type of aggression and illegal movement of armed men," Reece says.

Hutch holds a hand up to his son. "They technically haven't done anything illegal according to the colony charters. Aggressive, yes, but they aren't stupid. They're trying to draw us down there as a distraction. Zeke, did you get eyes on the coast leading up to Monterey?"

"Yes. There's activity of small groups of men. Scouts. Hard to know from where."

"We need to secure Monterey as soon as possible," Handover says like he's gearing up for a dormant argument.

"And why is that?" My question is directed at the mayor.

"We don't want the Sandies to take possession of another Hila colony," Hutch tells me. "They already have one near San Diego."

"And why would they want to do that?" I ask.

"I think you can figure that out."

"I'd like you to spell it out for me."

Hutch clears his throat. "Well, thanks to your fine work, this council now understands how powerful the Hila skins are and why LA and San Diego have been paying top dollar for recovered Hila bodies. I believe Mayor Gustavson and his Sandies want to use dead Hilamen's skin and repurpose it for commerce and war."

"And you and LA have no such interest in using the Hila skins in the same way?" I ask.

"No." He crosses his arms. "We only want to stop the Sandies from doing it. This is the source of the entire conflict. We don't know what San Diego intends, but we aim to stop them from having a monopoly on the strongest material the Earth has ever known. The Sacs have thrown in with the Sandies and we have sided with our LA brethren as their interests are also simply to stop the use of dead Hila for warfare. Does that square with your ethics, Doctor?"

"What do you intend with the Hila once you have control of the Monterey colony?" I ask.

"Protect the border."

"Anything else?"

"Is it acceptable if I haven't figured that out yet?" he says. "It's not every day a leader has to make decisions about the fate of an alien race that descended upon us and caused the unraveling of mankind."

"I suppose so," I say.

"And have you had any breakthroughs in how to save them?" Hutch asks.

"I'll have answers for you soon, but I'm hesitant."

"I assure you that me and this council haven't written off the Hila. If they are truly all dying, I desire the extinction of an entire alien race as little as you do. Now, I know you and I aren't always on the same page, and that's one of the reasons I invited you to sit on this council. I value and admire your skepticism and selfless motivations. If you figure out how to save them and we can do it without sacrificing the lives of the people of this colony, then maybe we can do some good for them."

"I have your word?" I ask.

"My word."

The next day, Ward is laying paint on a canvas in his apartment. He's depicted a series of Hila squirreled away in their digestive holes. Next to the holes, a few faceless humans have gathered and are leaning over a hole with a large sack in their grasp, pouring a sandy substance into the holes. "Think they'll get what we're trying to say about the fertilizer?" he asks me.

"Yes. They believe our little group is acting in good faith toward them, so I think they'll take this image as an offering of a solution."

"Think he's here right now, watching me paint?" Ward asks.

"Yes," I say.

"Should we give him a name then?"

"How do you know it's a he? How do you know they even have sexes?" I ask.

Ward shrugs. "Just helps to think of them kind of like humans. I get creeped out at night knowing they're just sitting there, probably watching me sleep. They've possibly been watching me my entire life."

I, too, hadn't been able to shake the immensely creepy feeling that an alien species has been watching me sleep at night, possibly for years. For all I know, they are an enormous threat to the colony and humans everywhere. But given that humans have been living with an indestructible, invisible species for almost twenty years without hearing a single peep from them makes me believe they don't have nefarious motivations. Whatever their reason for coming to Earth, it wasn't world domination. At least not yet.

"I guess they're kind of like angels," Ward says. "The way they just watch us without us seeing. Like angels in heaven, silently taking notes. Do you believe in angels?"

"Do you?" I ask.

"Yes. My mom is an angel, I think. Do you remember her well?"

"I knew her in the underground bunker. She was a lovely person. She was so happy when she found out she was pregnant with you."

Ward beams at my words. "Wish I could have met her. Just once. Just to tell her that I love her. Maybe I wouldn't have turned out this way."

"What way?" I ask.

"Me. Ward. Weird and broken."

I sigh. "There's something I've wanted to tell you for a very long time."

"What?"

I pause, regretting I'd brought anything up.

"What is it?" he asks again.

"I was going to adopt you," I say.

His shoulders stiffen.

"When I couldn't save her, I felt a guilt like you wouldn't believe. I wanted to take you in as my own, but I couldn't do it. I blamed Rafa at the time, but when we broke up, I still couldn't do it. I'm also weird and broken. I didn't have it in me to care for you that way. I'm sorry."

He sets down his paintbrush and presses his palms to his cheeks to wipe away tears.

"If you want to blame anyone for your brokenness, blame me. It's my fault," I say.

He lifts his face, wet and ugly. "I thought you were so smart," he says. "But you're just as stupid as me. You don't need to apologize. You didn't do anything wrong. It wasn't your fault she died. You didn't have all the fancy old-world equipment and hospitals to stop her from bleeding out. And you can't just adopt every orphaned child that comes through the east wing." He picks his brush back up, sniffling through tears.

"Then why are you crying?" I ask.

"I had no idea someone cared for me like that all these years."

I feel no relief of guilt at the boy's words. Years of remorse compounded by loss has long since burned my sense of relief to ash. "Since when did you get so mature?"

"The east wing does that to people." He steps away from the painting and sits on the sofa beside me where we wait for a Hila to appear. "Maybe he's not here—"

But then the Hila materializes before us, revealing its entire body. Tendrils of beads flare with iridescent light across the floor where they weave into its legs. Light pulses up the beads of its body, a spectrum of color more diverse than any earthly rainbow. Shadows spin around the room as the light washes over every surface, inducing me into an almost trance-like state. The light of all its beads converges into a scintillating opalescence, which is perhaps the most beautiful thing I've ever seen in my life. A scene appears before us depicting dying Hila at a beach head, the Golden Gate Bridge hovering in the distance behind fog.

"That's China Beach," I say.

I stand and reach out my hand. The Hila lifts its arm. Tendrils of beads extend from where a human hand would be, writhing like rogue snakes. My hand receives the tendrils, which spiral up my wrist and hold there, pulsing with light and a pleasant warmth. The worries of the world and men melt away for only an instant before I realize that the hope of an entire species that faces extinction rests on a half-baked idea and a bag of fertilizer. The Hila releases its grip, collects its light within itself, and vanishes.

"Let's call him Gabriel," I tell Ward, finally letting two decades of resentment melt away from me.

"Why?"

"You wanted an angel, didn't you?"

Two days later, Prasad has a few dozen pounds of fertilizer delivered to Rafa's compound, which we load into a pick-up before heading over to China Beach after midnight. Mavis drives while Rafa rides in the truck bed, crouched over the fertilizer, cradling an AR-15 and watching our tail. With a masked face and long hair whipping in the wind, it seems he's inviting more trouble than discouraging it. The engine of the truck roars down the narrow streets of the Richmond District and through the Presidio. We wind down the cliffside road and the beach emerges through the moonlit fog. I slam the truck door and remember when me and Clive came to the very beach after a six-month stint of his active duty. We ate pupusas and drank fruit smoothies only a few weeks before aliens appeared in the sky.

We find the Hila holes. Every single one of them has a dying Hila inside. Not dead yet as they stir at our approach. We unload the bags around a large barrel, where Rafa opens up the various grades of fertilizer. Consulting his notes, we help him measure out varying volumes of sulfur, nitrites, and iron concoctions that he believes will help optimize the Hila diet.

A branch snaps in the forest behind us.

Mavis and I move to investigate the sound while Rafa finishes stirring the fertilizer mixture. I approach the leading edge of the forest, rifle drawn. Our motley crew of alien saviors has a potentially growing list of enemies, including rival colonies and our very own mayor, who would hardly approve of our late-night shenanigans. We hear nothing but an owl hoot from a tree and return back to Rafa, who deems his witch's brew fit for alien consumption. As we start dumping buckets full of the fertilizer into the holes, I hear an annoyingly familiar voice behind us.

"Fancy meeting you here, Doctor Darrow." Anders stands there in the moonlight, a cigarette burning on his lip.

Mavis lifts her rifle. "Turn around and walk away." I lay my hand on her muzzle, lowering the weapon.

"What brings you out this evening?" Anders asks as his men emerge from the fog behind him.

"That's our business," I tell him. Rafa hasn't moved from his crouch at a Hila hole.

"Hutch's business?" Anders asks.

"No."

"I heard you were part of his council now."

"And where did you hear that?" I ask.

"Grapevine."

"From the grapes you have on our vine?" I ask.

He flicks his spent cigarette into the sand. "What?"

"Spies, Anders. Have you got spies with the mayor's council?"

"Why would I tell you that?" he asks.

"Because I don't work for the mayor."

"Just tell me what you're doing here with them." He motions to the Hila.

"It's an experiment," I say, turning to the barrel.

"What kind of experiment?"

"We're trying to figure out what's killing them."

"Why?" he asks.

"I'm a doctor. I generally try to figure out how to treat disease."

His boots crunch on broken glass as he crouches by a hole. "So, what's killing them?"

"We think it's a nutritional deficiency."

"Ha!" He slaps his thighs. "Not taking their vitamins, huh?"

"We're hoping it's as simple as that." I move to a bucket of fertilizer and dump it into a hole. "Can your men help unload the rest of our truck?"

Anders points at his chest. "You're talking to *me*?"

"Yes."

The man rubs the scruff on his chin as he considers pivoting from something that involved violence to providing aid. "You heard her, I guess," he tells his men, who swing their rifles to their backs and unload the rest of the fertilizer. Mavis and Rafa visibly unclench and go back to measuring out the fertilizer doses. I feel Anders' eyes on me as I take notes on a clipboard. He chuckles and says, "All of California is gearing up for war and all you're worried about is a bunch of dying space lizards."

"I can worry about multiple things at once," I say.

"Why do I tolerate you?"

"Because I don't lie to you."

He groans at me. "Don't know what I'm supposed to do about the fact that I know you've started up your own little Hila hospital during an arms race for their carcasses."

"Why did you kill Matheus Weinart?" I ask.

He plays dumb for a moment and then says, "I really didn't want to be inconvenienced knowing the rat's real name."

"Was he as much of an inconvenience as he was to me showing up in a wheelbarrow outside my hospital with a bullet hole in his head?"

He says nothing, only lights another cigarette.

"Did he really have to die?" I ask.

He clears his throat. "Warcraft is a bedeviling femme fatale," he says, closing one eye as he brings a flame to the cigarette tip. "There's always tension amongst men. It is in our nature. We try to stay ahead of the other because, if we don't, they'll act first. We let Hutch be the first to send out spies, so we had to be the first to punish a spy. It was a bit of an accident when I confronted him. I don't relish killing men, Doc, but actions have consequences, and your mayor needs to understand that. The current little neo-colony paradise we've been living in is coming to an end. There's too many of us that want control all at once. It's a powderkeg and the dying Hila have lit the fuse. I suppose that's why you do what you do. You're able to focus on the healing of individuals, which I admit, I do admire. Maybe you're even doing God's work, assuming he's still looking down on us. And I think that is actually why I tolerate you. There's no one like you, Doc. As for me, I'm cursed with the burden of men. And believe me when I say that it is a curse."

"It's not a curse," I say. "What you're doing doesn't have to happen. Men make the world they want, and this is the world you're choosing to make. You're not just along for the ride—you're driving the bus."

He blinks in the moonlight, cigarette burning, neither denying nor confirming.

TWENTY-ONE

NURSE PATIENCE APPROACHES me after our morning rounds in the east wing. "Sabion Jacobs wants you down in the clinic."

"As a patient?" I ask.

"He says he doesn't want to check in as a patient and will only talk to you."

I find Sabion loitering in the foyer, hands in pockets. "What do you need?" I ask.

He eyes me up and down as if unsure of even coming. "I'm sick."

"Is it your ankle again?"

"No. Something else. Can we go into your clinic? And I don't want to be seen by any of your medical students."

He follows me back to a room and I have him sit up on the exam table. "What kind of symptoms are you having?" I say, inching toward him on a rolling stool.

"I don't know," he says.

"You don't know?"

"My chest is heavy."

I listen to his heart and lungs and do a pupil exam—he stares vacantly over my shoulder the whole time. "Why are you here?"

"I told you. I'm sick."

I roll away from him. "If Reece sent you to do some secret inventory, feel free to go and check the back rooms. You don't need to play games with me. I don't have time for this nonsense."

His jaw tightens. "I don't feel well. Something is wrong."

"Then tell me what symptoms you're having. Chest tightness? For how long?"

"Forget it." He stands to leave but pauses at the door as if waiting for me to say something. But I don't, and he leaves without another word.

Over the next week, Rafa, Mavis, and I make nightly visits to China Beach, checking in on our Hila patients. "None have died but that doesn't mean the fertilizer is working," Rafa says. "Could just be regression to the mean. It's basically impossible for us to really know if the fertilizer is actually helping them. With this limited sample size, we have no idea if we're just detecting noise or signal. For all we know, the only reason they haven't died is that they just happen to be getting better, regressing back to a mean state of health, rather than our therapy doing anything."

"True," I say. "But what if the survival rate of these Hila is 100 percent?" I look into the darkness of the woods surrounding us, knowing full well Anders has eyes out there keeping tabs on us. "Wouldn't that tell us something?"

"It certainly wouldn't hurt, but we'd need more data and preferably a double-blinded placebo, randomized control trial."

"Don't think that's happening," I say.

"Not in our neo stone age. We may as well be throwing newt eye and bat wings in there and claim they work."

Mavis notices my gaze on the forest. "Anders probably already told Sacramento leadership what we're doing here," she says.

"He probably did," I say.

"And you're not worried?" she asks.

"Course I am. There's just nothing we can do about it. Hopefully, they'll tie themselves in knots about the little wild card we're doing here and slow their war machine down long enough for us to get fertilizer to the main colony in Monterey."

Rafa gazes at the stars.

"What're you looking at?" Mavis asks him.

"The dark forest," he says.

Mavis and I glance at each other, clueless.

"It's a theory about alien foreign policy," Rafa explains. "There are three basic tenets—all life desires survival amongst limited resources, you have no way of knowing if other alien life can or will destroy you given the chance, and therefore, the safest policy is to eradicate all other species when given the chance before they wipe you out first."

"So, basically old-world American foreign policy," Mavis says.

"The theory boils down to an analogy about the universe," Rafa continues. "That it's a dark forest where all life lurks, trying to remain hidden. As soon as a life form makes itself known, it is immediately destroyed by a more advanced civilization. From a pragmatic standpoint, it really is the safest bet, even if you discover a life form that has the intelligence of ants. You just get rid of them because ants evolve, and suddenly, they're aiming their ant cannons right back at you."

"Doesn't really explain the Hila showing up on Earth, does it?" I ask.

"Not really. I suppose they could be hiding here from something else. But nothing about them showing up here just to hide makes a lot of sense. They could've already killed us all, too. Even if it were slitting our throats one by one at night under their invisibility, they already could've wiped us out."

"But they haven't," I say.

"No." He looks over the moonlit bay. "They haven't."

"So, maybe the universe isn't as hostile as we believe?" I look at Mavis, doubting my own words.

"Let me know how that theory works out," she says.

The next night, after a painfully long day in the east wing, I climb the steps toward my apartment and find the darkness of my bedroom too inviting to turn the light on. After undressing, I walk across the room to collapse in bed but collide with something very heavy and fleshly in the middle of the room. Panicked, I back up to the wall, fumbling my hand over my dresser to find my Glock.

"I've got a gun pinned on you," I warn the intruder before flipping the light on.

It's Sabion.

His body hangs from a noose, gently swaying from where I bumped into him with a face as blue as a cornflower. He looks dead but I rush to the body anyway, giving his thighs a big bear hug before hoisting him upward.

"Help! Code blue!" I scream, hoping my words will reach someone in the east wing foyer just down the stairs. After a full minute of hollering, Nadine bursts into the room followed by Max, who makes quick work of the rope with a slash of a knife. Sabion collapses in my arms but I manage to keep his head from cracking open on the floor. I feel his neck for a pulse.

Nothing.

"Take over chest compressions!" I yell as more nurses show up. Max kneels at Sabion's side and pummels the boy, fingers and palms interlocked over his chest as they bob up and down in violent tandem. Nadine unzips a pack of emergency meds, spewing vials and syringes all over the floor, several of which crack and shatter underfoot. Ward peeks through the doorway. "Ward, get IV access," I yell at him. The boy's face floods with anxiety but he elbows his way through and wraps a tourniquet around Sabion's foot, flicking the veins and searching for a spot to strike. Meanwhile, a drill barks to life in Patience's hands as she lowers the bit to the patient's shin and looks at me. "Do it," I say before she unleashes the intraosseous drill, flecks of skin and bone churning in its wake. She draws back on the syringe, aspirating out yellow marrow. "A milligram of epinephrine through the intraosseous," I tell her, spotting a vial of the powdered medication under my bed. She finds it, reconstitutes the vial with saline, and flushes it through the bone. "Two minutes are up! Get some pads on his chest." I yell and feel for a pulse.

Nothing.

"Get back on the chest!" I yell. A line forms at Sabion's side to tag team the brutal and exhaustive work of pumping his heart for him by throttling his sternum and cracking his ribs.

"I got it!" Ward yells after placing an IV in the foot. He finally looks up at the patient and then backs up. "Is that Sabion?"

"Yes," I say. "Give another milligram of epinephrine through your IV."

"What is he doing in your room?" he asks.

"Just give the epi. I need airway equipment," I say to respiratory therapist, Tara, before elbowing my way to Sabion's head. His entire head is a swollen, soggy mess—water-logged corneas bulging beyond eyelids. I wrench the head back, hinge the jaw open, and slide a dull blade into the back of his throat. There's nothing but swollen tissue. No vocals cords. Just boggy flesh completely obstructing the way of putting a tube down. "Nadine, give me a needle and syringe full of saline." She slaps it in my hand as I feel Sabion's neck, where the rope has de-gloved a ring of flesh away, unleashing a wreath of blood. I feel my way down his windpipe, find his Adam's apple, and push my finger into a tiny springy ligament. Here, I press a needle in while pulling back on the syringe, nothing but the vacuum of the syringe sucking back at me. A millimeter at a time, I advance the needle until bubbles fill my syringe, indicating the needle tip is inside the trachea. "Wire!" I yell with my outstretched hand. "And stop chest compressions. I can't thread this thing with the jostling." Nadine places a wire as thin as a guitar string in my fingertips, which I thread through my needle tip and into the trachea. With wire in place, I take out the needle and then thread a tracheostomy tube over the wire. I dilate, dilate, dilate, punching a hole into the neck with quick movements of my wrist until the tracheostomy sits snugly into the trachea. I whip out the wire and hook up an oxygen bag and start pumping. "Tara, take over breathing," I say.

We're ten minutes into cardiac arrest—the last rhythm check went from zero electrical activity to something buzzing away in his heart muscle but not enough to actually create meaningful blood pressure to do things like make him alive. After we give another round of epinephrine and amiodarone, the familiar dread of futility echoes in my mind. I know how this ends because I've seen it a thousand times now, although never beside the bed I've slept in for the past twenty years. "Pulse check," I say. The compressions stop, the heart rhythm is there on the monitor, but the pulse...

Is there.

Beating like a hummingbird—but it's there.

"We have a pulse," I say. "Nadine, string up norepinephrine infusion, make sure fluids are open wide. Let's get him on a stretcher and over to the east wing. Ward, you're bagging the lungs."

"Lots of blood coming out of the lungs—frothy secretions too," Tara informs me, suctioning through the endotracheal tube. I'm not terribly surprised. Not only did we break his ribs with chest compressions, probably puncturing his lungs, but he also undoubtedly breathed against the noose wrapped around his trachea, which drew fluid into his little lungs sacs instead of air from above.

"Treat fever with acetaminophen," I tell Ward. "A fever will destroy whatever little chances he has at meaningful neurological recovery. Watch for sepsis—he easily could develop pneumonia. No sedation. Period. We have to see if he wakes up."

"You think he'll live?" he asks, motioning to the boy's ruddy face, features distorted by cartoonishly ghoulish swelling.

"No," I say.

After dropping Sabion off in the critical care unit, I take steps two at a time up to my apartment and find my sleeping quarters still strewn with the chaos of the resuscitation. I rummage through the paper packaging and medical equipment left behind, kicking away the clothes we sheared off of Sabion's body. And then I find it—a piece of paper with handwriting, partially covered with Sabion's sock.

His suicide note.

There is an upper portion written and then hastily scribbled over as to void what he had written, yet it is clearly still legible to me:

Do you think your little world exists without people like me?
Do you think you'd even have your east wing without men like me

~~protecting you? I am the Shield. The Defender. A patriot of Freedom. But you judge and hide—~~

Underneath are his revised words to me:

I killed the boy in San Jose. I am going to hell. Burn my body. No funeral.

TWENTY-TWO

THAT NIGHT, I disappear.

I leave the east wing without a word to anyone. My life was supposed to be simple—working in a lab, staining tissue, and calling surgeons in the operating room to tell them if the patient on the table had cancer. I was never supposed to *actually* do surgery. Or critical care. Or emergency care. Or anesthesia, or obstetrics. Or every other field of medicine I've taken on myself with which to inflict the people of Neo SF. The patients will certainly do no worse in the care of the nurses and Nadine. Ward still doesn't know much, but he at least knows the basics of trauma medicine and treating sepsis. He'll sink or swim and what difference does it even make? Patients live, patients die, and the world keeps spinning in its merciless orbit.

I leave the colony and hike up to Grandview Park—the same place I'd escaped to during residency before the Hila showed up and ruined everything. Renewed bitterness burns in me about their arrival as I hike through sheets of rain. It may have been men who scorched the planet in nuclear fallout, but the damn Hila showing up triggered the whole thing. I'd still be with Clive if they never showed up. Maybe my baby boy would've survived the pregnancy if I hadn't been stressed out of my mind in a government bunker wondering where my dead husband was. My boy would probably be in college now. Maybe have a fiancée—

"Stop it," I say to the wind.

If humans have to suffer, why not the Hila, too? Humans have been starving and dying of nutritional deficiencies for millennia. The Hila can do it now. Welcome to the show of misery and suffering starring humankind with a special guest—the Hilamen. Nothing but raw, existential anger pushes me up that mountain, contemplating all the moral injury I've burdened myself with trying to run a hospital that doesn't want to exist. Hutch and Anders can have their wars. The east wing can turn into hospice care and the Hila can try to make it on their own.

Doctor Darrow is retired.

I don't even have my Glock with me, halfway wishing raiders to rob me and leave me for dead. I have no gear, no food, no plan. I'm just a miserable soaking woman who wants to behold a beautiful view because it might be the last thing that stops her from careening off the edge of sanity. But when I arrive at the summit, all I see is a city blanketed in fog. From coast to bay, nothing but gray indifference hovers over the people beneath. I close my eyes and see Sabion, gazing back at me in the clinic, eyes pleading for help. All I could do was level accusations at the boy suggesting he was a murderous warmonger. I still feel the weight of his body swinging against me where I bumped into it in the dark. Just a dead boy who never had a chance to develop into something more. Nothing was his fault.

I rub my unborn child's rosary between my thumb and finger. I'd kept it all this time in a storage closet of a rotting catholic school where I'd hoped he would attend. It was a thread to a life that was now a dream. I'm incredulous that I was once a happy person—a hopeful person. That hope burned bright in me and fooled me into happiness. It was a joyful lie. When Ward found the rosary sitting there, it felt good in my hands again, like if I just kept rubbing it, the misery would recede into the background long enough to forget about it. What I forget is every time I dip my toes into that shallow pool of past hope, the reality crash afterwards is that much worse.

I cast the rosary to the wind.

I wake up on a metal bench, my hip reminding me that nothing has changed about anything except that I'm very cold and hungry. I feel tremendously stupid about leaving the east wing without telling anyone and hiking up to a peak to just sit there and rot. But the visage of Sabion's swollen face emerges, and I don't want to get up. When I sit up, my neck as stiff as the bench, my boot hits something on the ground.

It's a waffle.

Just a singular waffle, cold, on a porcelain plate.

I look around, finding myself alone and then reach my hand out to empty space. "Are you there?" A vision unfolds before me, depicting myself sitting at a table, eating a waffle. Given the high fidelity of my appearance and exact mannerisms, I know Gabriel has spent an unhealthy amount of time watching me. Also, I look terrible in the depiction but that is hardly the alien's fault. "Fine," I say, picking up the cold waffle, knowing the alien had probably swiped it off someone's breakfast table. Despite everything in that moment being very, very weird, the waffle tastes unbelievable. "Thank you," I tell the invisible Hila. "I get it. You don't want me to starve and die."

Gabriel reveals himself in a dull gray that matches the looming cloud cover. His black eyes scintillate, exposing lenses of deep blues and reds that slightly pulse in and out as if on stalks hidden within his head. "I just don't think I can help anymore," I tell him before he flashes the looped imagery of a cat stalking a mouse. The mouse skitters along rafters, unaware of the watchful eye of the cat in the shadows. Then Gabriel lifts one arm, shedding a small collection of beads from his hands, which float before me in spherical formation, about the size of a grapefruit. Gabriel vanishes but the collection of his beads still floats before me, bobbing against the wind. The beads then disperse around me and hiccup with bright light before they move again, this time in a synchronous spin with me in the direct center. Flashes of light scatter over the beads in an interrupted pattern both disorienting and dizzying. But then the circular bead complex spins at revolutions so fast that the hiccups of light become continuous with fluid images that jump into a perfect three-dimensional relief around me.

I'm immersed in a new world.

A holographic terrain of jagged mountains and wide gulfs materializes. And then there are unearthly creatures floating all over that look like someone attached the end of a Slinky toy to a Kleenex box and called it life. The creatures intermingle with flora that look like flat spaghetti noodles. Entire crags of mountain rock float above the surface, flush with animal and plant life that clearly have no earthly origin. Either this planet's ecosystem lives within a liquid atmosphere, a magnetized environment, or the gravity of the planet doesn't mind free-floating mountains traipsing about.

The scene changes to the Slinky-Kleenex creatures getting together and making what appears to be a civilization with burrowed housing littering rock faces, artificial lighting glowing purples and reds through a milky atmospheric medium, and spear-like vehicles flitting between mountain cities undergoing ballooning population growth. The floating mountains become honey-combed with Slinky-Kleenex life, busying themselves with whatever it is that Slinky-Kleenex people do, probably something pretty similar to what humans do. And then Gabriel zooms in on cities and shows me long, thin lines of malleable material that almost look like long train tracks, glowing white hot. Gabriel then shows me many such devices with similar pairing of tracks of various sizes throughout their dwellings. He then cuts to a radio tower, clearly human-made, on the side of a country road on Earth.

"What?" I ask, but then I get it.

He's making a parallel.

The Slinky-Kleenex aliens have some sort of technology similar to something on Earth that creates radio wave frequency. An aerial view zooms away from the SK aliens until I behold their entire planet like an astronaut staring down at it. It's a purplish, pretty thing with wisps of yellowish clouds like the whorls within a marble. Gabriel zooms out. And then zooms out much more, away from the alien sun, and then keeps going, the stars going from pinpoints to jagged rays of light as we accelerate away. We arrive in the dead of space in an apparent sea of nothingness. But then I see it—a decahedron vessel, clearly of intelligent design, the color of a pearl. Gabriel then cuts to another Earth radio tower and then back to the decahedron.

"Okay. The decahedron is also similar to something that transmits and receives radio waves," I say to myself, trying to keep up with what Gabriel is trying to show me. "And I take it that the decahedron thing wasn't made by the Kleenex box aliens? Someone else?"

Gabriel cuts back to the purple SK planet and then immediately shows a mouse. He flips back between these two images to hammer into my head—the Slinky-Kleenex aliens are like mice.

He then shows the decahedron vessel and cuts to the image of a cat. Back and forth, back and forth with the message—the space probe represents aliens that are predatory... like a cat.

A thread of anxiety pulls somewhere in me as he cuts back to the SK planet, which is there one moment and then annihilated with an explosion of energy that my tiny human brain cannot even begin to comprehend. Rock and debris churn through the vacuum of space around me as that thread of anxiety gets pulled into a full-blown panic attack. I close my eyes because I don't want to see what I know Gabriel is going to show me next.

Earth—cut to the image of the mouse.

And then the decahedral space probe—cut to the image of the cat, watching and waiting in the rafters.

"The Hila aren't the cat *or* the mouse," I tell Rafa that afternoon through the intercom at his compound, trying to catch my breath.

"Where have you been?" he asks.

"Just let me in." I find Rafa and Mavis at the kitchen table preparing tea. "Both of you, sit down." They see the terror on my face and obey. "We are in serious, serious trouble."

"Who?" Rafa asks.

"Not just the three of us," I say. "I mean *us*, us. Everyone. The entire planet. The cat and mouse have nothing to do with the stupid colony wars going on. Earth is the mouse, and a planet-destroying alien is the cat."

"How do you know this?" Rafa asks.

"Gabriel told me."

"Who is Gabriel?" Mavis asks.

"The Hila communicating with us," I say.

"You named it?" Rafa asks. "How do you know it's the same individual every time?"

"Who cares!" I yell at them. "Are you listening to what I'm saying? Gabriel showed me that there is an alien species that destroys other intelligent life when it detects their presence. Like in the dark forest theory you were talking about. He showed me how an intelligent alien species' planet was completely annihilated when detected by another predator alien race. The predator species has the capabilities of wiping out an entire planet in an instant." I relay to them the rest of everything I saw from Gabriel's vision. "*We* are the mouse. Us. Earth. And there is a predator alien race out there with their eyes in the sky. Watching."

"The cat," Mavis says, drawing in a breath.

"Yes. And they're coming for us."

We fall silent. Rafa just sits there, eyes glazed with intense thought and measurement. "That doesn't make any sense," he says. "If that were true, why would the Hila come to Earth? What's the point of him telling you all of this?"

"I don't know, but the next thing he showed me was the constellation from our October sky, and then he showed me thousands and thousands of Hila that live in Monterey. They're still there and they're dying. Many have already died. I don't know why they're here, but Gabriel's message is clear—you need to save us to save Earth. And there's a deadline in one month."

TWENTY-THREE

MAVIS AND RAFA smoke some marijuana while I just sit there and watch like they're the cool sophomores and I'm still a timid freshman. "Is now really the time to be doing this?" I ask.

Mavis scowls. "You expect us to raw dog the information you just brought to us? I can barely cope with the state of the world *as it is*, and now you're throwing in this nonsense that there's a predatory race of aliens that are going to destroy the planet in a month? What else would you propose we do?"

"How are the Hila at China Beach doing?" I ask.

"They're not dead. That's all we can say," Rafa answers after blowing smoke.

"None have died?"

He shakes his head. "But none have recovered enough to leave the holes."

"It's something," I say. "Maybe it's working."

"Even if it works," Mavis says. "How are we supposed to treat thousands of these things a hundred miles away in Monterey? Where would we even get enough fertilizer for all of them? And

242

transport? Not to mention that a turf war over dead Hila bodies is heating up between LA and San Diego at that exact spot."

"I don't know," I say, considering the obstacles, each as insurmountable as the next. "I don't know," I repeat, finding hollowness in the words. "But we should try something."

"Why?" Mavis asks with the same acid I hadn't heard in her voice since she was lain up in the east wing with flesh-eating bacteria chewing through her calf.

"I see," I say.

"What do you *see*?" she asks.

"When the Hila were poor, defenseless creatures, you had no problem trying to save them. Now that human survival is on the line, you don't care. Same reason you fled San Diego—you don't care what's happening there."

She takes a drag. "Why should I?" she says, bitterness in her words. Personal bitterness, too. I realize then that the woman doesn't like me and never has. I want to ask her if she's jealous of my and Rafa's history, but knowing that there are aliens lurking in the cosmos keen to obliterate our blue rock from existence makes the matter seem rather petty.

"Only you can come up with a reason for yourself," I tell her. "If you don't have one, I can't give you one."

"What's *your* reason?" she asks, Rafa fidgeting awkwardly at the increasingly heated exchange.

I don't want to admit that I'm only driven by outright fear. And not just fear of annihilation, but also the fear of the sudden intelligence of the stars. Up until Gabriel spilled his secret, the night's sky was just a fixture of nature, like looking into the woods —wild, sterile, and impersonal. But when I saw the SK planet vaporize to its raw constituents, it was like looking into the woods and seeing a tiger looking back at you, bringing a claw across its own neck as a threat. I now understand that the universe is intensely aware of who we are, where we are, and has nothing but intelligent contempt at our existence. It's a unique cosmic fear that I've never experienced and don't recommend.

"You can't even come up with a reason," she says at my hesitation. "It's just your raw survival instinct kicking in, nothing more. You're just having trouble translating primitive emotion into a logical reason. You're nothing more than a bag of flesh, biology, and evolutionary determinism. The facts are that men destroy themselves apparently at the same rate alien races destroy each other as well. Intelligent life is too dumb to live long. The history of this planet is just the history of the universe played out on a smaller scale. So, why should I get up and do anything about saving any of this? Being obliterated in an instant is starting to sound pretty good." She takes a drag and blows a puff of smoke, as casual as her regard for the human species.

Rafa puts up a hand of warning to me to disengage as if to say she'll calm down once I leave the premises. And so I do with great relief, knowing there is no answer good enough for someone whose cynicism has become gospel.

"Elspeth," I hear Hutch's voice as the colony gate opens for me an hour later. "I heard you'd come back."

"I needed to get away," I say, trying to scoot right past him. The problems I bring back to Neo SF are more than a man like Hutch is capable of undertaking. Number one, he wouldn't believe me, and number two, even if he did believe me, he'd manage to rationalize his way out of thinking the world ending somehow isn't his problem.

"Are you well?" he asks.

"Of course not."

"He's alive."

A knot of grief unties in my chest. "Sabion?" I ask.

He nods. "Your medical student stepped up in your absence and has done well in my estimation. Maybe he could be running the place soon." He swallows, his gaze revealing a fear I'd never seen in him.

"What's wrong?"

"Why do you think he did it?" he asks.

"Sabion? You can't make soldiers of boys without breaking them."

He wipes his brow, fingers tremulous, and then licks his lips. Rather than gearing up for a retort, he's silent. There is sadness in his eyes, but only for a moment, and then it's gone. "There's always a power vacuum to be filled," he says.

"Ah. There it is. The rationalization." I keep walking.

"You have no moral superiority here, Elspeth," I hear him spit from behind me.

I stop. "Didn't say I did."

"It doesn't matter what you say. It's how you act. You act like a saint, and you *are* a saint. Truly, and I don't deny that. In fact, I'll make sure there's a road or a statue made after you. You have sacrificed your entire life for that hospital. People have lived and people have died. You're probably the best person in this entire colony. But you've been given the protection and conditions to even exercise your sainthood. It takes men like myself, full of intrigue, scheming, and plotting to even give you an organized colony that doesn't just give way to barbarism and chaos. We are yin and yang, you and I. You exercise your goodness under the protection of my brutality. This is the way of men like me. We are not fit for peace. Never have been. It's a law of the universe. I create soldiers out of boys because I can see what is coming. It's the same thing that has come since the dawn of man. If we don't act first, we will be subjugated. I'm just playing the same awful game so we can even have something to call civilized society. So, no, you have no moral superiority here. Your goodness is built on men like me. You think me evil. That's fine. I'll be your villain if that's my cross to bear."

"How long have you been preparing that monologue for me?" I ask him. I realize that he and Mavis are more on the same page than either one would suspect. He's the smallest thing I've ever beheld in all the universe. And because of his smallness, the antipathy I've always had simmering on the back burner of my mind goes cold. "I don't think you're evil, Mayor. I think you're very sad. Like I am. You have been ever since you lost Grace. Grief and power are terrible bedfellows."

I leave him there, staring into the night, alone with his thoughts.

Sabion opens his eyes and goes into a coughing fit against the tracheostomy tube, phlegm rattling in his trachea. Max suctions out the trach, prompting another round of wild bucking from the young man.

"I'm sorry," I tell Sabion. His eyes swivel to me, gaze unrelenting. I'm relieved he can't talk with a tracheostomy in his neck, considering that he probably has not-so-nice things to tell me. I hold his hand. I don't like admitting it to myself, but Mavis' words shook me. I'm no stranger to the seduction of not giving a damn about anything. But discovering the impending global annihilation by a superior race gave me a bit of hustle. Mavis, on the other hand, had dug her nihilistic claws deeper into the despair of believing that since everything is so terrible, nothing must really matter. Her staggering cynicism has me questioning if I should even try to do anything about what I know. How much easier it would be if I just keep it a secret and never bring it up again. I could just move about this mortal realm until the predator race found us and then—*poof*—we could just blink out without even knowing what happened. What difference would it make if we eked out yet another cycle of flawed humanity? At least the suffering would end.

"You matter," I tell Sabion to cast away the alarming thoughts. I'm surprised that I also believe the words. Despite everything, we're still here. Sabion is still here. We fight, and bully—kill and scorn, but we're never destroyed. Maybe the stubborn audacity of human perseverance is the point of the whole thing. "You matter," I repeat, squeezing his hand. But he doesn't squeeze back.

"Heard you were back," I hear Ward say behind me. He kneels at Sabion's bed and empties urine from a bedside flask before bringing a stethoscope to his lungs, listening with his eyes closed. "He's neurologically intact," he tells me. "Moves everything, breathing without a ventilator. He's even been writing some things down." My medical student then inspects the circumferential wound around Sabion's neck and does a dressing change. "He's fevering, so I started antibiotics that we restocked from Prasad. He's probably getting pneumonia, but he's not in shock. I think he'll be okay. Geddes has been helping out a lot, too. I've put him on inventory and wound wash-out duty."

All I can think about is how Sabion had called Ward a queer before throwing the sketch of his ferret into a sinkhole in the depths of San Jose. The kindness of Ward's amnesia is a pretty good balm against the words of Mavis. I know that if I were to ask him why he helps Sabion in spite of how he was treated, Ward wouldn't quite know how to answer. "You've done well," I tell him.

"Are you doing okay?" he asks.

"No."

"Then let's go round on the rest of our patients."

. . .

Rafa shows up the next day at the east wing without Mavis. "They're better," he says.

"The Hila?" I ask.

He nods.

"Where are they?"

"Gone. They left their holes. All of them."

"It worked?" I ask.

"It's promising."

I put a finger to my lips and motion him up to my quarters and close the door. "How much fertilizer mix do we need to save the Monterey colony?"

"How many do you think are there?" he asks.

"It's hard to say. There must be thousands."

"More or less than five thousand?"

I tap my lip, thinking. "Less. But not by much."

He looks off to the ceiling, crunching numbers. "Probably need eight hundred fifty-pound bags for that many."

"That sounds like a lot."

"Me and Mavis may be able to salvage that with some more manpower, but it'll take time."

"Mavis?" I ask.

He rolls his eyes. "Ignore her rant. She'll help."

"You think there are that many bags of fertilizer to salvage in the city?"

"Maybe. May have to head north through Marin to look, too. Me and Mavis can go and scout. I need a good source of nitrite and iron, too, but that's easier to get."

"You think there's time to do that?" I ask. "We need to collect it and haul it to Monterey, dose it out to the Hila, and still have enough time until mid-October for them to recover."

"Why even ask the question? It must happen."

"But with so few of us..."

He reads my mind. "If you tell Hutch, it's over. He's a man fit for his current position of squabbling over crumbs of power. Not for saving the planet. Believe me, he will manage to make it about keeping himself in power while doing absolutely nothing to solve the problem."

"Damn it, I know you're right. Okay, I'll see what I can do about getting more fertilizer."

Prasad peeks his head from the back room as the bells of the closing door jingle behind me. "Doctor Darrow."

"I need more fertilizer," I say.

He holds up his palms like I'm sticking him up at gunpoint. "I think you tapped me out. But with the new secure trade route to LA, I can order you some and have it here in a few weeks."

"We don't have a few weeks."

"Who doesn't?" he asks.

I hesitate, wondering if I should place the astronomical mantle of awful knowledge on the man. "Everyone. There is nothing more important on the planet than getting me bags and bags full of fertilizer."

He laughs and then swallows when I don't mirror the joke back. "You're serious."

"Never been more serious asking for anything in my entire life. I must have fertilizer."

"How much?"

"Fifteen hundred fifty-pound bags," I say with a flat face.

His eyes go wide. "By when?"

"One week. Can you do it?"

"Maybe."

"Don't tell the mayor," I say.

"Wasn't planning on it."

That night, a knock at my bedroom door startles me from un-sleep. Rafa stands in the hallway light, a haunted tilt to his eyes. "I'm worried," he says.

"I know."

"The story doesn't add up."

"What story?" I ask.

"Gabriel's vision to you about the annihilated alien planet. They were destroyed because their radio waves were detected by the predator race. Earth has been broadcasting radio waves for over a hundred years."

"And?"

"The train has already left the station," he says. "The predator race has or will detect our radio waves depending on where they are. There is nothing we, or the Hila, can do about it. For all we know, they've already sent their doomsday missiles, or whatever they use. How does saving the Hila save Earth?"

"You think the Hila are lying to us?" I ask.

"Maybe they're just manipulating us to save them. Their behavior just doesn't make any sense otherwise. There's a reason they came to Earth and it's not just to help us. I just don't see how they could possibly prevent the attack on Earth. It's already done—written in the radio waves soaring through space. Sooner or later, the predator race will discover us and there's nothing the Hila can do about it."

"Then why would they come and colonize a doomed planet?"

He shrugs. "I have no idea and that's my point... the story doesn't add up. And have you thought about the colony in San Diego? Other colonies all over the planet? Are they dying, too?

What's the point in even saving the Monterey colony when the rest of the Hila are also dying?"

"Mavis has gotten to you," I say.

"It's not just Mavis. It's the reality of the situation." He stops, eyes wide with something close to skepticism but most consistent with despair.

"Your fears are based on your assumptions."

"Like what?" he asks with the offense of an academic.

"Radio waves deteriorate through space, right?"

"Yes."

"Meaning, perhaps the predator race has detected our non-random radio signal, but over the vast distances in space, they still can't triangulate where our tiny little planet is. They know we exist but can't find us. Is that possible?"

"Yes, actually, it is," he says like a snob.

"You're also operating under the assumption that the Hila think like humans," I say. "They do not. We can't even begin to guess their purpose and motivations. There are two things we chose to believe—there is a killer alien race out there that annihilates everything they detect, and that the Hila are exceptionally good at avoiding detection. In fact, it would seem the Hila have been evolutionarily engineered since the beginning of their biology to literally hide from anything. They may have evolved this way *because* of the predator race. It's not unreasonable to assume they've come here to hide as well. Does that square with your rules about our cutthroat universe?"

"It does," he says.

"Then let's assume that whatever the Hila are doing to hide from them is also helping all of us hide from them and so we should probably try saving them or we're done here."

"But what about our fertilizer problem? I was being too optimistic about getting that amount. With just us, it'll never happen. I wouldn't bet on us."

"I wouldn't bet on us either," I say as an idea bubbles in the back of my mind.

"What is that supposed to mean?"

"We should bet on something that we know will never fail."

"What's that?" he asks.

"The self-interest of men."

"Monterey is getting very popular," Zeke Plinth tells the mayor's council the next day. "Good news, we've located the Hila colony. Bad news, so have the Sandies. They're there, we're there, and a whole helluva lot of Hilamen are there."

"Are the Hilamen dead?" Hutch asks.

"No. We see them wriggling around in the foothills of the city. There are some on foot too, looking like a bunch of black-as-tar Bigfoots. And we've discovered a lot of their holes. Place is infested with them."

"Numbers?" Hutch asks.

"Sandie scouts? Maybe fifteen. Hila? Who knows. Thousands at least."

"Thousands?" Hutch asks, leaning forward. The body language is slight, but it's painted everywhere. The man is very interested at the prospect of thousands of dead Hila.

"Let's get down there," Reece says. "We must secure the Hila."

Hutch puts up a hand. "Reece, you're taking minutes. That's your role right now. I agree we must act in coordination with LA's men to secure Monterey from the exploits of the Sandies and Sacs and their alliance against us. Doctor Darrow, what's your report?"

I want to scream at them and spill Gabriel's beans,

252

completely shattering their infantile war games. I do not trust these men, but I do want the power they can wield. I realize the reason the Hila stay hidden—it's impossible to show your cards if nobody knows you have any to begin with. I've known all along why Hutch has placed me on his council—to control me. I'm too important to the colony to get rid of but not docile enough to believe his fairy tales. He wants me close. And I finally realize why I took his offer to sit on the council—I want him close, too.

"I have two pieces of bad news. It didn't work," I say. "The fertilizer. We tried it on about a dozen dying Hila at China Beach. They all died within a day of administering the fertilizer."

Handover erupts in laughter. "So, let me get this straight. You and Montijo get together thinking to save the damn things with *fertilizer*, and it ends up killing them instead?"

I bow my head in shame as a few of the other men join him in merriment.

"Knock it off," Hutch scolds. "Elspeth, I'm sorry to hear. I know it pains you to lose patients, even when they are extraterrestrial. I think you made a valiant effort to save them."

"Thank you," I say.

"I must admit, I'm a bit hurt that you didn't tell me about the presence of Hilamen at China Beach. Some of my men could have assisted you. The bodies are still there, I presume?"

"No. That's the other part of my bad news. The Hila we accidentally killed disappeared the next day."

"To where?" he asks with angered shock on his face.

"They were taken."

"By who?"

"Someone who is interested in the growing market of Hila hide," I say.

"Those bastard Sacs!" Handover slams his plump fist on the

table. "First, they murder poor Matheus, and now they're stealing property right from under our noses."

"Property?" I ask, looking at Hutch.

"The Hilamen are not property, gentlemen," Hutch says as if appeasing my Hila bleeding heart. "Doctor Darrow, would you mind writing up a full report of your research at China Beach, including what you gave to the Hila that led to their demise?"

"To the last detail," I say.

"It's only been half a day," Prasad tells me as I roll into his shop again that afternoon. "I haven't made much progress."

"I know, I know. Listen. I need another favor. Pier 27. Can you keep your eyes on it?"

"What am I looking for now?" he asks.

"Semi-trucks commissioned at the behest of the mayor."

"And what do you expect them to contain?"

"Fertilizer. About eight hundred fifty-pound bags."

"Think I'm ready to hear what this is all about?"

"No one is," I say.

"Perfect. I don't need any more time to prepare. Lay it on me."

And so I do.

TWENTY-FOUR

A WEEK PASSES with nightly visitations from Gabriel. He replays all the same information to me like an angel trying to hammer the importance of his divine message to a stubborn prophet. In addition to the SK aliens being obliterated from existence, he shows me a bevy of other alien lifeforms that also cast radio waves into space, piquing the interest of the space probe from the predator race. Soon after, all of their planets explode in surreal violence like I'm watching a doomsday sci-fi movie. He shows the threat with the dying Hila in Monterey and in the foothills of San Diego. The message is clear—both colonies are dying and both colonies are needed to somehow stop Earth from being discovered and exploded.

A chill sweeps up my spine, sitting in the sand at China Beach a day later. I wait an hour and finally hear Anders approach. He sits next to me in the sand with a tired grunt. "You took so long to show up, I was wondering if you had stopped spying on the beach."

"Why are you still here?" he asks.

"Came to check to see if the Hila would come back."

"You don't know where they went?" I ask.

"I assumed you'd taken their bodies."

"Bodies? They died?"

"I think so," I say. "You're telling me you didn't take the bodies back to San Diego or Sacramento?"

"No. My men came here about a week ago to check on them and they were just gone. You don't know anything about it?" he asks, skeptical.

"Hutch must've taken the bodies then."

"So, your miracle fertilizer didn't work."

"Not only did it not work... I think it killed them." I bow my head.

He snorts and then cuts it short, realizing the implications. Good. I want it to settle in his mind. "You've figured out how to kill the Hila," he says.

"Didn't mean to."

"Ah, Doc, don't feel too bad," he says, patting me on the shoulder. "Think how many people died from bad medical experiments before they figured out what works. You're just doing your best."

I find his words oddly comforting because I think he's actually being sincere. Although I suspect his main motive is to move me along as soon as possible and report back to Sacramento and San Diego leadership about a great new way to kill off the Hila faster than their slow starvation. "Thank you," I say. "Are you heading to Monterey soon to help secure the Hila there away from Hutch?"

"Not yet. They want me up here spying on you and Hutch."

"Makes sense."

"You tell him I'm up here yet?" he asks.

"Hutch? No."

"Why not?"

"Because I dislike him only slightly more than I dislike you."

He laughs and puts a cigarette between his lips. "I'm sure we're neck and neck."

I stand, brushing sand from me. "Good luck, Anders."

"With what? You want us and San Diego taking over?"

I shake my head. "It doesn't matter who takes control of Neo California. Might be the most insignificant war that has ever happened."

"Matters to me."

"I know. Good luck. And if I never see you again, thanks for not putting that bullet in me and leaving my body in a ditch."

"What aren't you telling me?" he asks.

"There are matters far more important than what's just sitting in front of you. Please remember that."

He cocks an eye at me. "Okay, Doc. Will do. But why not tell me what's going on?"

I place a hand on his shoulder, looking toward the Bay. "Because you're not ready to hear it yet."

Rafa brings a bag of fertilizer into Ward's apartment where he sketches it, with its exact branding and coloring, so Gabriel can understand it's the source of their salvation.

"There's just no way we can communicate with them the exact mixture of nitrites and iron that need to go into the sulfur," Rafa says. "We have no idea if they even understand chemistry or mathematics."

"They're an interstellar species," I say. "I think they know math."

"Yeah, well, a child can predict where a baseball is going to land and catch it without knowing a lick of calculus."

"What do you mean?" I ask.

"For all their advancement, it's all natural," he says. "Their invisibility is just an organic function. The pods they came floating in on were clearly organic as well, suggesting they grow them. I've begun to think their spacecraft are just a life cycle for them. For a species this adept with its use of light for communication, it had no reason to even develop a language, let alone a codified mathematical construct."

"If they at least know what we need, they might be able to find more of the fertilizer for us," I say.

"They're all sick," Mavis unhelpfully adds from a beanbag chair. "They can barely get out of their holes."

"About a dozen Hila at China Beach are now better, walking around somewhere," I say. "They could at least start. And what's the harm of at least trying to tell them what we need?"

"I still don't know how they're even supposed to stop another alien race from finding us," Mavis says, bringing up the point for the thousandth time.

"I think it's rather obvious," I say, preparing to share the most recent theory bouncing around in my head.

Rafa leans forward. "Is it?"

"You two are old enough to remember when astronomers were finding all those exoplanets, right?" I ask.

"What are those?" Ward asks.

"Planets that orbit suns within the Milky Way," Rafa answers. "Before the Hila came, astronomers would inspect far away suns to see if a tiny shadow cast by an orbiting planet could be seen. When they saw the dropout in light, they could pinpoint a planet that was there."

"There's the answer," I say. "The Hila, masters of light and shadow, have probably figured out a way of hiding the planet."

"Wait..." Rafa gazes off for a minute. "If they can project the same frequency of light as our own sun, it would hide the shadow of the Earth as it passes over the sun. If we are being observed by the predator race, they wouldn't know we're even there if they can't see us. They could hear our radio waves and know we're in the neighborhood, but they couldn't see us enough to pinpoint our exact location."

"How could they possibly project enough light?" I ask.

"I'm not sure," Rafa answers. "Assuming they don't have any spacecraft still in orbit, they'd be doing it from the ground. But projecting that much light from the ground would put on quite the light show down here."

"Wait a minute," I say, standing from my chair, heart pounding. "There is someone we need to talk to right now."

We find the San Diego refugee, Nika Horvat, near the farming district peeling potatoes. The girl looks remarkably better from our first encounter. "You've been taking those vitamins," I tell her.

She squints in the sunlight and finally recognizes me. "Yes. I'm feeling much better, too. What is this about?" She motions to my posse of would-be-Hila-saviors behind me, all eyeing her.

"Just a few questions about the Hila around San Diego," I say.

"What about them?"

"You know exactly where their colony is?"

"Yes," she says.

"You mentioned something about northern lights that happen near their colony once a year?"

She nods. "Yeah. Bunch of people come up from the colony and camp out to watch."

"What exactly does it look like?" Rafa asks, his voice going high.

She shrugs. "Bunch of colorful lights in the clouds. Green and blue, sometimes orange and red. The whole sky just kind of lights up."

"For how long?" I ask.

"About five days."

"When?" Rafa asks, anxiety rising in his voice. "What time of year does this happen?"

"October. Probably just a few weeks away."

Rafa lets out a little gasp, finds a chicken crate, and collapses on it with panicked astonishment knit across his face.

"What's wrong with him?" Nika asks.

"I know what's going on," Rafa says as a panic attack consumes him. "My god, I know what the Hila are doing."

"Thank you, everyone, for coming," I say to the group we cobbled together after Rafa's fit of certain doom next to a chicken coop.

He refused to say anything until going back to his compound to consult with a bunch of moldy journals and texts. The more he read and cross-referenced, the more he withdrew from normal human interactions until he became a haunted scientist, isolated from everyone by what he now understood. We spent a long night throwing half-baked schemes at the wall to see what stuck, which was nearly nothing. After I fell asleep in a hammock, he shook me awake and said, "Assemble a fellowship," which I found melodramatic and, at the same time, far too measly of a solution for what we faced.

I sent word through Ward for not only Prasad to join us but also Nika and Geddes. As much as I didn't want to burden more with the imminent threat of intergalactic annihilation, we simply needed more bodies to bring about our great plan of "Save the Laser Light Show," as Mavis put it. She was bundled in the back of the tiny classroom where we'd assembled, wound tight in a ball of surly comments. I'd had just about enough of her bullshit and didn't even want her there, but Rafa insisted that she copes through pessimism and that she was highly reliable—an observation I'm sure unsullied by the fact that they'd been sleeping together since nearly the moment they'd met. I'd prepped Geddes beforehand about what the meeting was about so that his young mind wasn't forever blown when Rafa started talking about the predator alien race stalking us from light years away, waiting for us to wave hello to them.

"We have about two weeks to save the Hila or Earth will be annihilated," Rafa says to our hastily formed fellowship, hand outstretched with chalk. "From what we understand, whoever the predator race is, they have technology that can remotely wipe out planets as soon as they discover precisely where they are. The predator race probably knows we exist because we've been broadcasting radio waves like a bunch of idiots for over a hundred years. But they cannot pinpoint our exact location. This is where the Hila come in. Based on their communications with myself and Doctor Darrow, it seems that the Hila have witnessed the destruction of many other alien races at the hands of the predators, and we can surmise that the Hila have come to Earth to prevent the same thing from happening here. It has become clear that the Hila also know the general place in the Milky Way where the predator race is located."

"How can you know this?" Prasad asks.

"Because once a year, at the same time every year, the Hila put on a light show." Rafa moves to the chalkboard where he has depicted the sun and Earth. "Let's say the predator race is located, or a probe of theirs, at a single point somewhere within the bubble of how far our radio waves have traveled for the last one hundred years." He marks a single X beyond the Earth and sun. "It's at this point that they are searching for us. However, given their distance, Earth itself is not bright enough to pinpoint. They probably rely on the dimming technique to identify tiny planets as they pass in front of the sun. When our planet passes over our sun, it casts a planet-shaped shadow to the predator race, which they detect as a momentary drop off of light from the sun. Given their relative fixed position to our solar system, our planet only crosses the light of the sun from their perspective once a year in our orbit. Some-time during October. And so, what do the Hila do during Octo-ber? They emit light into the sky that looks something to us like the Aurora Borealis phenomenon from all the atmospheric excite-ment going on. So, during this sensitive time, the emitted light very likely matches the exact frequency of our sun and masks our shadow as we pass by, essentially making the entire planet invis-ible to the predator race. The Hila have been doing this every year for the last twenty years ever since they landed."

"But how?" Ward asks.

"It's a sheer numbers game," Rafa says. "The Hila congregate in colonies. The two we are aware of are in Monterey and near San Diego. There are likely colonies all over the planet that also cast laser light at various times. Who knows, maybe the predator race has probes all over this galaxy and the Hila are all over the planet year-round. The cumulative effect of all these colonies casting laser light into space is a scattering diffraction of the light as it travels, creating a cloak of light by the time it hits the predator race's sensors."

"How do they create laser light?" Nika asks.

"Yttrium," Rafa answers. "It's a crystal I detected in their cellular structure. I've no idea how they do it, but their very bodies are creating the laser light. I think once every October, they assemble together and shoot the same laser frequency into the heavens, staving off doomsday for another year. The problem this year is that the Hila are dying. They've finally revealed to some of us that they are very much around, watching us and that they need help. There needs to be a critical mass of Hila bodies in both Monterey and San Diego in time for them to shine their laser cloaking. If not, we'll be detected and destroyed. Possibly immediately, depending on the technology of the predator race." He sets the chalk down and sits, out of breath.

Geddes raises his hand. "Why do these aliens want to destroy us?"

Rafa shrugs. "Scarcity, distrust, zero communication, and paranoia that we'll kill them first, given enough time for our technology to advance. It's the logical move for them to make."

"Nothing new," Mavis adds. "Been doing the same thing here since the dawn of men."

"That brings us to right here and right now," I say, trying to prevent Mavis from pontificating further. "We believe we've figured out how to save the Hila from a nutritional deficiency that's killing them. A fertilizer compound that Mavis and Rafa have refined seems to have turned them around in about a week. The problem is, we need to amass and deliver fertilizer to about five thousand Hila in Monterey." There are gasps around the room. "And to the colony in San Diego as well," I say, met by more sounds of astonishment. "All this with a colonial war happening with the powers that be very interested in keeping the Hila dead so they can use their highly resilient and valuable skins for profit."

"There is no way just the seven of us can pull this off," Nika says. "Why don't we tell more people about this?"

"Just hear us out," I tell her. "I've led Mayor Hutch to believe the exact opposite about the fertilizer—that it kills the Hila. I've also floated this idea to Anders—a Sacramento spy who works for

San Diego as well. I was hoping the arms race to capture as many dead Hila as possible would result in both groups—LA with SF and Sacramento with San Diego—to start stockpiling the fertilizer."

"And?" Geddes asks.

"Prasad, tell us what you discovered at Pier 27 yesterday," I say.

Prasad clears his throat. "A semi-truck came in from the Neo LA trade route. It was not hard to find out what it contained—over thirty-five thousand pounds of fertilizer."

I nod. "The precise amount I gave in a detailed report to Mayor Hutch. He has taken the bait and it is clear that his intentions are to dump the fertilizer into the Hila digestive holes at Monterey. He believes it will accelerate their death and help him get control of the region and out of the hands of the San Diegans. So, we already have the fertilizer we need. For the Monterey colony at least."

"What about San Diego?" asks Nika.

"I've no doubt my disinformation—that the fertilizer kills rather than actually saves the Hila—has made it down to Mayor Gustavson of San Diego. I would think he's already amassed the fertilizer necessary for both the San Diego colony and even shipping the same amount to Monterey to try to wipe out the Hila there too—a colony he also hopes to control and corner the burgeoning Hila skin market."

"So, you've only assumed they're doing the same in San Diego?" Ward asks.

"Yes. And it's a safe assumption and honestly the only strategy we have. There is no other way of amassing that much fertilizer in such a small amount of time. An arms race funded by state power is the only way to get this to work."

"So, can't we just sit back and let them do the work?" Ward asks.

"Not exactly," Rafa answers. "The dying Hila also needs a mixture of iron and nitrites. Mayor Hutch has those details in the report Elspeth provided him. But San Diego doesn't. We need a team to go to San Diego to ensure that our plan is working and to add the additive to the Hila holes there. We also need a team of us to Monterey to ensure the Hila are getting the fertilizer there as well. We need everyone in this room. Any problems?" They say nothing, which does little to dispel the anxiety in the room. "Me, Elspeth, and Ward will go to Monterey. Mavis, Geddes, and Nika will take an expedition to San Diego."

Geddes looks at me, stunned. "I thought you needed me at the hospital. Aren't I doing well there?"

"Yes," I say. "And it's exactly because of how well you're able to learn and adapt that I need you to go to San Diego. I've traveled with you and know you're smarter than other men your age. Remember when you moored the boat against Reece's orders during the storm? That's the kind of critical thinking we need right now. You keep cool, can take commands, and know when to speak up. Above all else, I trust you to do what is right."

"Like saving Jericho," Ward adds.

"Exactly," I say with a nod to Ward. "Mavis knows San Diego and she'll be able to identify where the fertilizer is kept. Nika knows where the Hila colony is. It must be the three of you."

"I-I just came up from there," Nika says. "It's a five-hundred-mile journey south."

"I know, but there is no other option," I say. "Rafa has a vehicle that you'll take away from the trading route to avoid detection. We'll communicate on a minor frequency using only coded language, which Rafa has already created. Can you do it?"

"What other option is there?" Geddes says.

"None. And you?" I ask Mavis. "Are you up for this?"

Mavis stands, propping herself up on a cane, a familiar crazed exhaustion in her eyes. "Despite what you think you know about me, I don't want Earth to explode and I certainly don't want it to be my fault if it does."

"What about me, Elspeth?" Prasad asks. "I want to help."

"We need you here as a backup person in the colony who knows what's going on. From raiders to wargames to dysentery, we have no idea what may go wrong out there, and we need a point person close to home. Are we all up for this?"

Disorganized nods drop like sad bells around the room.

"Good," I say. "Get some sleep. We leave in two days."

TWENTY-FIVE

"I NEED to go to Half Moon Bay," I tell Hutch after a council meeting the next day.

"Why?"

"Scavenge expedition. Running low on critical medical supplies."

"How long do you need?" he asks.

"Four days."

"Are you sure this is the best time?"

"It's never a good time, but we need the supplies. Besides, I'm not adding much to the council at the moment. You've got your advisors."

He shakes his head. "I can't spare you any men with things heating up in Monterey."

"I know. I'm going with Rafa Montijo and Ward. We'll travel light and be fast."

He brings a finger to his lip. "I'll be departing for Monterey in two days with my war band to support the LA forces there when they arrive. There may be violence. I was hoping you'd join us."

"Join you for the violence?" I ask.

"As our field medic."

"You already have several among your men trained in basic field medicine."

"They have a fraction of the knowledge and skills you have," he says.

"I'll tell you what, after I'm done at Half Moon Bay, I'll send Rafa back here with the medical supplies and me and Ward will join you at Monterey to help."

He chews his lip, considering. "That could work. You feel safe traveling alone with Ward?"

"We'll be fine," I say.

He nods. "Your trip is approved. Only communicate by radio if there is an emergency or if the plan has changed. We need the enemy to know as little information as possible."

"Agreed."

In my room, I pack my gear, thinking over the plan. It's a patch job, thrown together based on limited information and far too many assumptions but it's the best we can muster. I sincerely hope the Hila have more of a backup plan than counting on me and a fellowship of depressed, exhausted, and nearly suicidal individuals. I'm also unsettled by Hutch in new ways. The animosity between him and I during our last conversation had vanished. The reserved dislike that he keeps behind a bitten tongue evaporated. Maybe it's the scolding I layered on top of him for the past few years of his mayorship. Perhaps I finally broke him, but I worry there is something else and I don't have time to ruminate.

A knock on my door stirs me. "Prasad?"

He looks from side to side before stepping in. "The truck with fertilizer is still there. They haven't moved it yet to Monterey."

I close the door. "That's okay. It's only about a two-hour drive. Hutch and LA probably don't want to alert the San Diegans about their plans by bringing in the truck. They want to secure the Hila first. I may have to wait in Monterey for a few days more than expected."

"Are you sure you don't want me coming with you?" he asks.

"I told you, we need a point person here for when things inevitably go wrong."

"I know that. I'm just..."

"What?"

"I worry about you," he says.

"I'll be fine," I say as sterile as possible. "We'll be fine if we all do our part." I don't really believe my own words, but every moment needs an optimist, and I lost the coin toss for this conversation.

"This problem. Just seems so *big*." His eyes go wide. "But I'm glad you're here to lead us."

"I'm not leading anyone. I just don't want to sit back and watch the world burn."

"I just could never do what you do."

"And what is that?" I ask.

"Build people. Inspire them. Lead them."

I take a deep breath. It's late and I'm getting tired of the man's attempts to get a last-minute lay with me. "Prasad, leading is just doing what matters in the exact moment it is needed. Anyone can do it, most choose not to. You could lead people just fine. It's a choice."

He shakes his head. "But no one would listen to me the way they listen to you."

"People listen when you have their attention," I say. "There are many ways to get people's attention. Most are bad."

"Just... good luck."

"Thank you."

He offers one of his reserved smiles, confirming to me that he is a kind man without too much guile. I'm grateful for men like Prasad who've become as rare as antibiotics. He's not exactly a bad-looking man, and if I lived in a different parallel reality, I'd entertain getting to know him more. "If you get in trouble, I will come," he says before disappearing down the hallway.

Mavis, Nika, and Geddes leave early in the morning, packing up a small pick-up with extra gasoline for the return trip from San Diego. Mavis peers at Rafa and I from behind the wheel of a truck and clears her throat. "Don't worry about us," she reassures. "We'll find the payload in San Diego. I know all the right players down there who'd know where the bastard, Gustavson, has it stockpiled, *if* he has it stockpiled." I nod, not feeling particularly reassured. Mavis' earlier words echo in my mind when she was recovering from the staph infection—*rumors turn to reality, reality turns to surreality and like that... human beings turn to animals.*

"She's okay," Rafa tells me as they drive off.

"Rafa, one thing I've learned during my slow and painful days on this planet is that once people hit adulthood, they generally don't change, and if they do, it's over the course of uncertain decades and it's usually for the worse. I'm not sure who the real Mavis is—an end-stage cynic or reformed pessimist—and I partic-ularly don't want to find out while she's in San Diego trying to save the world for the rest of us."

"She'll get the job done," he says.

"You've only known her for a couple of months. How can you be so sure?"

"Ready to go tonight?" he asks, ignoring my question.

I nod. "6 p.m. sharp."

Ward and I finish our evening rounds with Nadine and the nurses, giving backup treatment plans for when things go wrong while we're gone on our fake scavenging mission to Half Moon Bay. I return to my quarters, heft my pack over my shoulder when Nurse Patience bursts into my room.

"Pregnant and bleeding," she says. "Let's go."

"Shit."

I follow Patience into a clinic room and find Priscilla breathing fast and clutching her belly in pain. "Get fetal heart tones," I tell Patience, who puts a doppler probe over the girl's belly searching for a heartbeat.

The young, soon-to-be-mother, wears a mask of fear. "It's too early, isn't it?" she asks.

"A little," I tell her. "You're at thirty-five weeks. I've delivered earlier and they do just fine. How much bleeding have you had—" I'm answered by a rush of blood that widens around the sheet beneath her. "Whoa, whoa, Patience, go and prep the OR. We've got to deliver right now. Go and get Nadine."

I place an IV, hang a bag of wide-open fluid, and get Priscilla, who groans while rubbing her belly in a wheelchair. My heart pounds in my ears as I roll her to the operating room where Nadine awaits at the head of the bed. I see relief wash her face after she sees the patient already has an IV placed. The pharmacist has a spinal tray already set up for me to get Priscilla numbed up for a C-section. "No, not enough time," I say. "We have to knock her out and put in a breathing tube right now. Get the mask." We move Priscilla over to the operating bed, her face a sheet of white terror. Nadine strokes her hair as a gesture of comfort before bringing a mask over her mouth and nose, flowing with one hundred percent oxygen. The girl descends into a panic attack, choking on her own breath and crushing my hand in her grasp. I push phenobarbital followed by a reconstituted paralytic medication that Nadine compounded herself. The girl goes limp as a puppet before I wrench her neck back, force her mouth open, and advance a dull metal blade into the back of her throat, exposing glistening vocal cords. I thread the breathing tube through and hook up the ventilator. Nadine bleeds in a volatile anesthetic gas through the tube to keep her asleep while I immediately move to operate.

Patience slaps on a fetal doppler and I hear the baby's heart rate—it's dangerously low. "Gloves and gown," I shout, which are brought to me. I splash iodine all over Priscilla's belly and bring sterile drapes up to her head, which Nadine tapes off. "Blade." It slaps in my hand and I make a straight, horizontal incision across the belly, the fat giving way to the deeper connective tissue beneath. I bluntly dissect the tissue away with my finger, probing down for the surface of the uterus.

There.

Carefully, I cut away the rest of the connective tissue, exposing the surface of the uterus, blood dripping off the bed onto the floor. I press the scalpel into the uterus as the muscle parts beneath the blade. Clear fluid erupts under the pressure and bursts over the surgical field. I widen the margins of the open amniotic sac with my finger and feel the baby's limbs. After getting leverage beneath its body, I pull the baby up and out, spilling blood and amniotic fluid absolutely everywhere.

The baby is blue and not moving.

I cut the umbilical cord and pass off the baby—a girl—to Max, who whisks her away for resuscitation. With the tang of afterbirth in the air, I reach my hands inside the uterus and try to get around the placenta, slowly peeling it from the uterine wall. Once it's freed up, I gently tug on the umbilical cord and feel the placenta start to give but then break away from the uterus.

"Shit!" I say.

"What is it?" Nadine peeks over the drapes.

"Retained placenta." I drag fragmented placenta from the uterus, which is bad—retained placenta makes it difficult for the uterus to naturally clamp down to stop bleeding. I sweep the uterine lining again and again, bringing up clumps of red tissue as the room fills with the coppery sour smell of blood and placenta.

"You got oxytocin going?" I ask Nadine. "The uterus is boggy as hell."

"I started the moment you took the baby out. Fluids are also wide open."

A sheath of sweat and anxiety tighten around me like a noose as more blood pools up from the uterus. *Not again. Not like Ward's mother.*

"Max, how's baby?" I ask without looking at him.

He says nothing for a moment, which is the worst possible answer. "I'm doing chest compressions," he says with a calmness that only comes with decades of experience.

"Give epinephrine," I say.

"Already have."

I press my fist into Priscilla's uterus to try to staunch the bleeding, which helps for a minute. I hold it there and come out only to see more bloodletting. "Get the balloon," I tell Patience. I place the long noodle-like deflated balloon into the uterus and push the plunger on an attached syringe, which inflates the balloon against the bleeding wall.

The bleeding stops.

"Nadine, vitals?" I ask.

"She's probably lost half her blood volume. Heart rate through the roof—shit!"

"What?" I squint at the vital monitor and see the electrical heart tracing go wild with ventricular tachycardia. Her blood pressure is gone. "Chest compressions—get pads on the chest!" Patience tears down the surgical drapes, exposing Priscilla's pallid skin, and slaps defibrillator pads over her chest and back. I leave the uterine balloon in place and start pumping on the girl's chest. "One hundred and fifty joules!" I tell Patience and step away from the surgical bed. "All clear." Her body jolts with a brief current of electricity before Patience gets back on the chest. "Nadine, amiodarone and lidocaine." She pushes the antiarrhythmic medications. After two minutes more of chest compressions, Patience stops and we watch the vitals as I place a finger on the girl's neck—there's a pulse. "We got her back."

I move back to the uterus and find blood pooling back, seeping around the pressurized balloon. I drag away the clotted blood and feel around the balloon—it's still holding in there tight. This tells me things are very, very wrong. Despite high back pressure on her uterus to prevent bleeding, her blood still can't clot and it's seeping out everywhere. All the clotting factors have been thrown off from the delivery and giving a bunch of fluid into her veins instead of blood transfusions.

"I'm taking the uterus," I say, widening the margins of the surgical wound. "If I can't stop it from bleeding, I'll just take the damn thing out." I suction, suction, suction around the uterus and start feeling along, trying to find the uterine arteries to clamp off before resection. Having only performed a handful of emergent hysterectomies, I'm just groping in the dark. I start clamping shit—ligaments, arteries—who knows? I slice a blade through both fallopian tubes and cut the uterus free from the cervix, bringing the entire organ out of the body. My feet give way underneath from the pooled blood and I fall to the floor, the uterus still in my grasp. Getting to my knees, I wrench my neck up and see sheets of blood flowing from the surgical wound. The blood flows like a deluge, ebbs, and then ceases like someone turned off the faucet of Priscilla's life.

And then the baby cries.

TWENTY-SIX

THE NEXT DAY, I'm arrested at dawn.

Reece stands in the doorway of my room, pregnant with misplaced wrath. He puts handcuffs around my wrists and leads me down to my own autopsy room, now bereft of a dead alien.

"What are the charges?" I ask.

"Sedition," he says, gaze burning into mine.

"What authority do you have to in prison me? 'Mayor's son' isn't an official position in the colony charter."

His face darkens and then he delivers a firm slap across my face. "Do you remember when you slapped me in front of your staff?" he asks.

Despite the sting, I refuse to flinch. "You've arrested me because I slapped you?"

"No—no, that's not what this is about."

"Ah, I see, you're just making clear your abuse of power. You've arrested me with no formal authority and now struck me as petty revenge simply because I can no longer defend myself."

"No, that's—" he snorts in frustration and strikes me again.

This time with a closed fist. "That should stop that mouth from running." He takes a few, erratic breaths like he's just gotten ahead of himself.

"How do you feel right now?"

"Don't—" he cuts himself off, appearing like he's about to cry.

"Do you feel how you thought you'd feel when you imagined this moment?" I ask. "Is it everything you dreamed?"

"You killed them," he says. "First my mom, and then my bride."

"No. I didn't."

"What am I supposed to do now?" His fists tighten at his side. "With a baby girl?"

"For starters, raise her not to strike defenseless women who you have locked up."

"It's not like that."

I lean forward, working my jaw up and down. "Tell me how it is then."

"You've wronged the colony," he says.

"You and the mayor are *not* the colony."

"That's not—Dad will explain it to you." He averts his gaze from me.

"Reece, if you can't explain it yourself, then you're not thinking for yourself."

He meets my eyes again, eyes hooded in shame.

"These expectations hanging over you—to fight for freedom, govern men, and raise a generation to defend against the evil Sandies or Hila. It's been fed to you to make you act like this. Do you understand that? You can't even say in your own words what I have done wrong."

He shakes his head. "You're just trying to undermine the colony. This is why you're guilty of sedition. You're against the colony and everything it stands for."

"And what does the colony stand for?" I ask.

"Free trade," he offers.

"Then why did your father shut down trading with half of Neo California?"

He says nothing to that and moves to the door.

"Let's forget about how you assaulted me just now," I say. "It's forgiven—it's already over. You do not have to do the things you're doing right now. There is something far more important than you or me going on. The survival of everyone depends on it. You must free me and you must do it right now."

"You've taken everything from me," he says, chin quivering. "And now I'm going to take everything away from you."

"Even if that means we all suffer for it?" I ask.

"Life is already suffering," he says before leaving, slamming and bolting the door behind.

My autopsy room is bare except for a cot, a table with a water jug, and a bucket in the corner. The door is unbolted once more and Hutch enters. "Where's the baby?" I ask, my lip bleeding.

He's surprised by the question, obviously prepared to discuss other things like his justification for kidnapping me. "In the east wing," he answers.

"I need to see her."

"You'll have access to your hospital while confined," he says.

"Oh, good, I can finally complete my lifelong dream of being a slave doctor."

"You've been arrested for sedition and conspiracy," he says, taking the tone of an arraignment.

"Timed precisely for when you don't need me anymore."

"Elspeth..." He crosses his arms. "I know."

"What are the conspiracy charges?" I ask.

"Conspiring to subvert the geopolitical standing of Neo SF

and its partnership with Neo LA and expose us to our enemies. I know everything you've been planning."

"Not everything. If you did, you wouldn't have me locked up."

"You mean the predator alien race coming to destroy us?" he asks, making my heart plummet.

I shuffle to the cot, sit, and stare at the floor, too overwhelmed with how much I underestimated the man's treachery. "You've bugged my room. Recorded my conversations."

He nods. "Wish I'd done it sooner, otherwise, I wouldn't have wasted so much time and resources gathering all that useless fertilizer."

"You're just going to let them die then?" I ask.

"Consider this a gift. You don't need to worry about anything but your hospital anymore."

"You finally lock me up because I couldn't save Priscilla?"

He shrugs.

"Probably helped tip the scales, I bet. Good timing for your plans to lock me away."

"I do sometimes wonder what you've been doing at that hospital all these years," he says, voice infused with dormant anger as he rubs his wedding band. "It's had its uses, I suppose, keeping you busy and out of my hair most of the time. Your age of medicine is dead, though. You can't even deliver a baby without killing the mother. The world has changed from what we knew before. You keep trying to drag us back to the modern past, and I'm trying to take us to the frontier of the future. You can't force people and society to be the way you want them to be. You must go with the winds of change and just make sure you're ahead of the storm, not behind it."

"There will be no future if you do not get that fertilizer to the Hila in Monterey," I say.

"Referring to your drug trips with your stoner friends?" he

says with a mirthless laugh. "The alien race coming to annihilate the planet?" He smirks with a condescension he's been waiting a long time to reveal. I finally know how much contempt the man has had for me all along. "Don't worry your head about that anymore. Everything will be fine."

"Listen very carefully to me. The Hila came here to protect us from a very powerful race that destroys every living species they detect. Once a year, the Hila in Monterey emit a signal that cloaks our planet from the predator race's sensors. They are too sick, with many dying, to transmit that signal. If you do not get that fertilizer into their holes in Monterey, they will probably all die and we will be detected and destroyed."

"I don't doubt that you believe that, but there is a glaring plot hole with your story."

"It's not a story," I say.

"Altruism is an illusion. The Hila wouldn't come here just to help us. They are getting something from us. Whether they are stealing, leeching, distracting, or waiting for the rest of their kind to flood our world. There is only one rule of the universe and the Hilamen abide by it just like anyone else—they compete for survival in a universe of scarcity. Whether it's your own fairy tale you've made up or the Hila have some sort of mind control over you, I don't really care. I will let whatever threat they pose to us die with them."

I lay down on the cot and stare at the ceiling. "You're just like the rest of them."

"The rest of who?"

"All the men before you."

"I don't claim to be anything new, Elspeth."

"Did you know Grace wanted me to marry you after she died?" I ask.

"What are you talking about?"

I nod. "She told me you were a good man but just needed a woman around to keep you in check. She was right. Not about you being a good man. Compulsory good behavior is no virtue. But she was right in her fears about what you'd become alone and in power."

He bristles at the mention of his late wife. "I will not be manipulated. You'll be sequestered until we've secured the Hila in Monterey and then we'll have a trial. Don't worry, I'll make sure you get a light sentence. Probably house arrest in the east wing."

"So, not too different from the last twenty years."

During his campaign of revenge humiliation, Reece brings me up to the east wing an hour later—in handcuffs—and walks with us as we discuss treatment plans with each patient. The absurdity that this is where I'll be, treating patients who are all going to die anyway in a cosmic blast along with everyone else, settles in. It's even more ironic that Ward has finally learned to lead rounds with impressive command. He knows every patient, every treatment plan, and discusses them all off the top of his head without looking at notes. Throwing him into patient care alone with the nurses was the best possible education I ever offered.

Max and Patience wear grim faces and nobody wants to bring up Priscilla's death only twelve hours ago. Her baby is doing well, although with a little more jaundice than usual. "What's her name?" I ask Reece, who stands by the wall, hand resting at his waist positioned over his gun holster.

"I don't know," he says with a scowl.

"You're her father."

He scoffs. "Maybe if you didn't let Priscilla die, the baby would have a name by now. Because of you, the baby will end up as soft in the head as Ward here because you couldn't save his mother either."

Patience cradles the baby as it begins to cry, bringing a bottle to its suck. "Get this asshole out of here," she says quite loudly, motioning to Reece.

"I'd be careful what you say," Reece says to her. "You never know who'll be running this place soon."

We arrive at Sabion's bed, who is clearly stunned at seeing my handcuffs. He looks from me and then to Reece and lets out a big, slobbery sigh from his tracheostomy tube. Ward promptly suctions mucus from the tube and adjusts pillows behind his back.

"Well, well, well," Reece says, taking in the sight of Sabion. "So, this is what happens when men go soft. Sitting in bed with queers and nurses at your beck and call while you can't even take a breath on your own." He laughs like he has an agreeable audience and remains oblivious that he's actually quite sociopathic. Shocker that an unfettered, power-hungry brat has the emotional intelligence of a scarecrow. Sabion averts his gaze from Reece's mockery and waves us away.

I give Ward, Nadine, and the nurses a few more backup plans for our patients if any of them crash overnight, and then Reece escorts me back to my little dungeon, where Hutch waits for me.

"Where is Prasad?" he asks with urgency.

"Is this my life now? Back-to-back Hutch and son controlling my entire existence?" I ask.

His face darkens in new and unsettling ways. The nature of my relationship with him has fundamentally changed from friendly foe to expendable liability. "Where is Prasad?" he repeats.

"I don't know. What happened?"

"Are you trying to say you didn't plan this?"

"Plan what?" I ask.

He studies my face, trying to figure me out. "Nice try." He opens the door. "I'll be leaving for Monterey tomorrow to protect our freedom. Work in your hospital or rot here in this room until I return. Makes no difference to me or my colony."

Of course, I don't sleep. After an hour of negotiating with the guard outside the room, I even started to think I was going crazy threatening the young man with the destruction of the planet if he didn't let me out. I learn once again—the more severe the imminent danger people face, the easier they completely write it off. It's the smaller threats like a stubbed toe or a bar fight about which human beings are designed to perseverate, not intergalactic warfare.

Lying on the hard cot, I wonder if Gabriel will come and free me. Does he even understand the concept of humans placing other humans in captivity? Does he know I don't want to be here? As the hours pass into the night, I remember what I'd forgotten— the Hila may have DNA but they are fundamentally different from humans. They don't have brains and likely operate from a collective hive mind of their cellular beads that communicate through electrical signals that flash across their skin. They also prefer to be invisible from human life. The responsibility of saving them crushes me when I consider how many years of evolutionary instinct they had to ignore to reveal themselves to me. Now rotting in a jail, my flimsy plans easily foiled—I've squandered their trust. If Gabriel knew what was good for him, he'd just abandon me and look for help elsewhere.

I spiral further into depression as Priscilla takes center stage in a slideshow of rampaging grief. She's followed by Ward's mother, who bled out after delivery in the exact same way. I learned nothing as a physician in seventeen years to prevent another young mother from dying? How many patients have died before my eyes? How many children have I orphaned? How many spouses have I sent to an early grave? And outside of my little east wing, all I do is complain and scold a mayor who actually understands the time in which we now live. I bring teenage boys to suicide because of the guilt I hang around their necks just for being products of their time. Lying there in that cot, at the crossroads of self-loathing and self-flagellation, I learn the lesson far too late that you cannot punish people for being who you think they are. They either retaliate against you or fulfill your prophecies.

I sit up from bed, startled by a sound in the hallway.

It's a slobbery chugging sound interrupted by ragged coughing —a guttural echo like a monster stepping out of a child's nightmare. Muffled speech outside the door erupts as I inch closer and then—*thwack!* I jump after the door quakes with a deep thud as my pulse races. The choking, slobbering sound gets louder. The deadbolt unlocks and the guard spills through the door and topples at my feet, unconscious, with blood swelling at his lips.

Sabion stands in the doorway above him, fists poised.

With chest heaving, breath sputtering through the tracheostomy, he steps through and meets my gaze. His haunted eyes flicker across my face, searching me for something. I believe this is the moment I die. The wrath of this disillusioned youth finally taken out on me before he finishes off his suicide.

Instead, he falls into me, wraps his arms around me, and sobs through the tube in his neck. I return his embrace and freely weep with him.

TWENTY-SEVEN

"GET PACKED," I tell Ward less than an hour later.

"Bah!" He jumps with surprise as Sabion and I emerge from the shadows in the hallway outside his apartment door. "Did Hutch let you out?" Ward asks.

"No. Sabion freed me," I say, motioning to the boy looming in the shadows.

"You're supposed to be in bed," he tells Sabion, brow furrowing with concern as he lets us into his apartment. "You've still got pneumonia."

"Ward," I say. "Do you recall our mission to Monterey?"

"Of course. I just—after you got arrested, I didn't know what else to do other than just show up at the east wing and keep working."

"What happened with Prasad?"

"I heard he stole the semi-truck full of fertilizer from the pier and drove off with it."

"That beautiful man," I say. "No doubt where he went with it.

285

We're going to get Rafa and we're leaving this very night to Monterey. Now get packed."

"That's going to be hard."

"Why?" I ask.

"Rafa is holed up in his compound, surrounded by Hutch's men. They've been trying to arrest him for the last two days but they're too terrified to storm it with all those frogs and animals around, so they're trying to wait him out."

I laugh.

"What?" Ward asks.

"There is absolutely no way Rafa is still there."

"What do you mean?" he asks.

"He's slipped them. Probably already on his way to Monterey. We need a radio to find out where he is and get out of the colony. Now."

"Hutch has increased security—has the whole place locked down."

I motion to his stack of easels and bucket of dirty paint-brushes. "Are you telling me you don't have a secret way out, getting all these art supplies from outside the colony over the years?"

"Duh! Of course, I know exactly how to get out. There's a rusted-out hole in one of the storage containers of the colony wall near the farms. It's a narrow path out, but I've been using it for years. I'm worried about him though," he nods to Sabion. "He should be back at the east wing.

"I'm worried, too," I say. "But we need him and he's not safe there anymore. Reece will know that he broke me out. You need to get to the hospital, gather up antibiotics for him and trach care supplies. We need a surgical field kit, too."

"What do you think will happen in Monterey?"

"Hopefully, anything other than the end of the world."

. . .

Sabion and I meet Ward along the colony border wall where Van Ness meets Cedar Street. Max and Patience are there, and both give me an unexpected three-way bear hug. They've brought more supplies than we can possibly carry. After we have a brief meal together of dried venison and coffee, the nurses insist on joining us.

"With Ward and I gone, you need to stay at the east wing," I tell them.

"If the world ends, what difference does the east wing make?" Max asks.

"I'd rather not have people suffer and die needlessly even if they would've died anyway with all the rest of us. Besides, I don't think more people are going to help our cause. We need to move swiftly and start getting fertilizer to the Hila as soon as possible with the least amount of attention." The nurses, my nurses, I've known for nearly twenty years, accept my words and hold me tight as tears escape from all of our salty, stubborn souls.

Sabion, Ward, and I bid them farewell and slip through the border wall, moving swiftly down Geary Boulevard while murders of crows watch us from rooftops. Sabion wheezes through the tracheostomy but improves after I drop the cuff that previously blocked air movement from his mouth. I could remove the tube altogether, but I don't have the time and surgical tools to make sure the hole in his neck is repaired properly and I don't want him getting a skin infection on our journey south.

"Here." I hold a Beretta handgun out to him. He recoils. "Never mind, it's okay," I say, putting the gun back in my pack.

We cut through the forest canopy of Golden Gate Park where gnarled roots have crumbled the asphalt and sidewalks. With the entire woods shrouded in luminous fog, I feel like I'm being swallowed whole by a haunted forest straight out of a fantasy book. We traverse murmuring streambeds and streets choked by grasses, ferns, and juvenile eucalyptus trees. Disoriented and overwhelmed by the growth, we finally find an animal trail and follow it south through the park until my legs are suddenly soaked up to my thighs. We had accidentally walked right into a bog. Drenched to the waist, we continue on the trail, Ward leading the front with a rifle pointed forward. We come to a clearing and I hear rustling ahead.

Ward stops.

He crouches and turns to us, one finger to his lips. With a pounding heart, I look over his shoulder and see it—a mountain lion devouring a goat. The beast's fur is black with blood as it looks up from its kill, eyes narrowing on us. Fortunately, it has little concern for us as it begins stripping more tendon from bone. We creep along the periphery of the clearing, leaving the animal behind. We make it to what I believe used to be Stow Lake and make camp underneath a Japanese gazebo whose roof is still intact. I get on the radio, dial to Rafa's frequency, and get out the notebook he created with a host of coded language to communicate over the open waves.

"CQ, this is Saint Monica, is this frequency busy?" I'm answered by static. "CQ, this is Saint Monica, is this frequency busy?"

Still nothing. I repeat the line a few more times and, finally, a voice crackles over. "Saint Monica, this is Siddhartha, over."

"It's Rafa," I tell the boys. "Where are you?"

"Go to Morse," Rafa says.

For the next ten minutes, we write down Rafa's encrypted Morse code that he repeats five times. I don't understand a single word of it, but Rafa insisted we communicate only by Morse code that is nonsense to anyone listening and can only be decoded from the encryption key he provided. It takes half an hour to decode his message, but we learn that he is just a little way down the peninsula coast, near Pescadero, with a vehicle and supplies. We meet halfway at Half Moon Bay, where he's waiting for us with worry on his face. I hug the man, taking in his familiar musk and all the tortured yet not unwelcome memories they stir within me. I still love him in the way that I love the ocean—with awe but from a safe distance.

"What's wrong?" I ask him.

"Mavis is gone," he says.

"What do you mean *gone?*"

"Nika and Geddes woke up from camp on their way south and she was gone."

"No explanation? She hasn't even tried to contact you?"

"No," he says with a measure of hurt in his voice. "Nothing."

I groan. "I knew she would do something like this. Why did you convince me to let her lead them south? She's not fit for this—can't get past her anger." I stop when tears cusp the man's eyes. "So, what are Nika and Geddes doing now?"

"They've made it past LA and are on their way to San Diego. Be there in a day."

"At least Nika knows her way around San Diego and can lead them to the Hila colony. But this whole plan is already falling apart. There's no guarantee whatsoever that San Diego even has the fertilizer stockpiled and will deliver it to the Hila colony."

Ward and Sabion set up camp in amiable silence. Sabion hammers in tent stakes while Ward gets a fire going. Ward produces something from his pocket—a mouse—and feeds it a bit of bread. "Where did you get that?" I ask him.

He stashes the mouse back in his pocket. "Sabion found it injured and brought her my way. Been helping her get back on her feet again."

"Where's Jericho?" I ask.

He points to Sabion. "In Sabion's pack, eating. He's been watching after him for a bit."

"Have you heard from Prasad?" I ask Rafa, distracted by the irony of Sabion now caring for Ward's ferret.

"He radioed this morning," Rafa says. "He's in Monterey. With the fertilizer."

"How is that possible?"

Rafa slaps his thigh. "That crazy fool broke into the pier and drove that damn semi-truck out of the colony, plowing through the colony gate. He just rolled into Monterey last night with the payload."

"Is he okay?" I ask.

"He got shot in the shoulder but he's alive. Obviously, he can't unload the fertilizer in the holes by himself, but he's got it hidden away and has spotted the SF and San Diego war bands who are forming there, says things are getting heated but he's managing to stay out of sight."

"So, the plan hasn't changed?" I ask.

"We head to Monterey as soon as possible, mix the fertilizer, and get it to the Hila."

"All while not being seen, imprisoned, or killed by a pissing match between Hutch and Gustavson."

"That's the short of it. Our options are certain death or uncertain death."

We head out early the next morning, Rafa at the wheel of the truck. The highway is a ramshackle mess of uprooted asphalt covered in vegetation, but enough traffic from wanderers, nomads, and raiders has kept even tire grooves, which we can follow and move along at a decent enough clip. Sabion keeps his eyes glued to binoculars watching for scouts or anyone at all. No humans we run into at the moment will be friendly. And they certainly aren't when two men wander into our rest camp, guns brandished while they root through our bags. A matured craze had settled into their eyes that only comes from years of despair, hunger, and general debasement of humanity. Fortunately, Sabion was away from camp, collecting kindling. The large boy emerged from the shadows, tracheostomy gurgling, which gave the intruders a much-needed fright. Sabion made quick work of them with nothing but his meaty fists and rope. Once hog-tied, I gave them stern warnings about certain death if they followed us before freeing them back into the terrible wild.

What would normally be a few hour's journey in a car to Monterey ends up taking two days. We arrive after midnight near Monterey Bay but stay outside the city proper and make camp. "No fires," I tell the boys as they set up tents. I crawl into the back of the truck camper and find Rafa poring over pages of calculations he's been scribbling on the last few days.

"I think we only have a few days. Four at the most," he tells me. "It took the Hila at China Beach a week to improve and leave their holes. The Hila at Monterey will probably need that same period of convalescence to be able to initiate their cloaking for the planet."

"And what will that actually look like?" I ask.

"I have no idea. I've done some rough math and I don't even fully understand how a mere couple thousand Hila will be able to generate enough laser light to provide cloaking. My math shows they'd need to cover dozens of square miles but there is no way even a few thousand Hila could do that."

"Could our theory be wrong?"

He nods. "Of course it could. But I don't know how else all these things fit together. Also—" he cuts himself off.

"What?"

"Nothing."

"Tell me," I say.

He bites his lip. "I had a vision quest."

"Okay..."

"I feel like this is how it's supposed to go."

"How what's supposed to go?"

"This." He broadly gestures. "Where we're at, what we're doing, the difficulty we're facing and the Hila dying. It all squares together."

"Squares with what?" I ask.

He hesitates like he feels major prejudice coming his way. "Just—never mind."

"You think there's some cosmic plan?"

He winces. "Let's just drop it. You never understood the way I see things."

"Does Mavis?"

"Mavis doesn't even understand herself," he says.

"I'm just a realist who doesn't believe in your form of spirituality," I bite back.

"You think you're a realist, but you're not. Now, Hutch... he's a realist. He understands that he must act or he will be acted upon. You act in the face of terrible odds again and again and again. How many patients do you try to save knowing damn well they will die anyway? A realist would let them go. A realist wouldn't be running a post-apocalyptic hospital. You're no realist."

"And how many patients in the east wing actually make it out alive?" I ask.

"Plenty. And that's not the point."

"Then what is the point?"

He narrows his eyes on me. "The fact that you try at all. I hate to burst your cynical bubble, but you're probably the most hopeful person in all of Neo SF."

"Hmm."

"What?"

"You're not the first to tell me that," I say, remembering the old man in the bunker almost twenty years back telling me the same.

"Despite what you say," he says. "Despite how pissed off you are at losing your prior life, every act you've done in the colony is driven by nothing more or less than hope. Many of your patients die, yes. But many live and that makes all the difference. If you were truly as pessimistic as you like to pretend, they all would die. I'm not surprised the Hila came to you first. You are exactly what they need. You and me. A lot of science, a little math, a big helping of hope, and a dash of luck."

"Things don't work out just because you have a pretty narrative to wrap around it."

"Let me have my pretty narrative," he says. "It's a fairy tale that keeps me going. I need it."

"It's not like what you're saying. Running the east wing just fills the gaping hole with enough distraction that I don't need to face reality. I'm not hopeful... I'm just sad. And I live in a world I don't fit in anymore—and I don't know what else to do."

He holds my hand, knowing there are no real words to comfort such loneliness. "I love who you are, always have. I also know for a certainty now that you have absolutely no idea what hope actually is. You're here now and it's why I believe we have the best chance possible of saving this tragic place."

I squeeze his hand. "You got any of that nasty tea?"

"I was just about to brew a cup."

TWENTY-EIGHT

AT THE END of his mad dash out of Neo SF, Prasad had brought the semi-truck full of fertilizer to a suburban neighborhood just north of Monterey and parked it in the driveway of a single-story home. We find him within the abandoned home leaning against a tipped refrigerator, sweat clinging to his face. His shoulder is still soiled in dried blood where he was shot on his getaway from Neo SF. I hug him and smell the sickly-sweet odor of someone who is halfway toward starvation. "When's the last time you ate?" I ask.

"I wasn't able to bring supplies," he says. "I was just so mad. I saw the truck there at the pier, and they were getting ready to move it. So, I jumped the fence, tossed the guard out of the driver's seat, and drove like hell out of there and didn't stop till I got here."

I squeeze his hand and bring water to his lips. Ward shears off the man's jacket and shirt, exposing a shoulder wound weeping with pus. We irrigate the mess while Prasad looks on in anguished silence. "The good news is, the bullet went through and through," I tell Ward. "Bad news is, he has sepsis."

After delivering IV fluids and antibiotics, he feels well enough to get venison stew into him. "You think my boys are okay? Hutch wouldn't hurt them, would he?" Prasad asks before sipping broth on a spoon.

"No," I say. "I don't think he would. He's not that kind of tyrant."

"We've got to get the fertilizer to the Hila," Prasad says, getting up as if to do that very thing.

"You are sick as hell," Ward tells him. "You're not doing anything but staying behind at camp to get better."

The back of the semi-truck slams open where Rafa undoes the latch. He walks in between the stacked fertilizer, taking inventory. "Hutch followed your directions perfectly," he yells back at us. "Got the exact amount we calculated we would need. Boys, come and help." Over the next hour, Sabion and Ward help Rafa with his brew, concocting together the same formula that healed the Hila at China Beach. "We'll dump half a bucket into each Hila and about a cup of my supplement brew."

"Where are the Hila?" Prasad asks, sweat beading on his upper lip.

"That's what's on the agenda for tomorrow morning," Rafa says. "Reconnaissance."

The next morning, I'm relieved to find Prasad still breathing with his fever abated. Ward sits beside him, keeping the man warm and comfortable. "Did you even sleep?" I ask Ward.

"I get naps here and there. I'm fine."

"You're fine until you pass out. We can take shifts overnight checking Prasad's vitals. Don't let me sleep through the night again like that."

"Sabion helped, too." Ward gestures to the campfire where

Sabion warms his hands over the flames, Jericho, the ferret, in his lap. I listen to Sabion's lungs and inspect his tracheostomy site.

"Are you feeling well?" I ask him.

Sabion nods.

"I think the pneumonia is better," I say. "When we get back to the colony, I'll take that tube out of your throat."

He gestures toward Monterey with urgency in his movements.

"We'll get going soon," I reassure him. "Ward, you stay behind with Prasad and the truck. The first thing you do if you see someone is radio us immediately."

Our priority is finding the Hila and the opposing militias that intend to squabble over them while they slowly die. Fortunately, they're all probably in the same place. We don't want to risk being seen in a vehicle or wasting gasoline, so Sabion, Rafa, and I set out on foot. We weave through derelict neighborhoods full of trash heaps, collapsed homes, felled power lines, and strip malls long since torched and ransacked of anything of value. We move uneasily, treading what is certainly a common traveling route among raiders and other ne'er-do-wells that we'd rather not encounter. We move in efficient silence other than the gurgling from Sabion's tracheostomy cutting the air over the crashing waves of the beach. It takes a good thirty minutes using Rafa's decryption key, but we learn that Nika and Geddes have arrived in San Diego but they haven't identified or heard of any fertilizer stockpiling down there. Mavis is still an apparent ghost.

"Everything we do here is pointless unless they have a payload down there, too," I tell Rafa.

"They'll head to the mountains where Nika knows the Hila have had a colony for years. I'll bet you ten thousand dollars Mayor Gustavson has a militia there too and they are already underway filling those holes up with fertilizer. Your misinformation to Anders will have worked. Have faith," he says.

We continue south, our route hugging the highway but through dense shrubbery and wildflowers crowned by looming cypress trees that we hope hides our approach from scouts. We pass miles of the same terrain, resting for a brief meal of dried bananas and nuts. Sabion hacks up a bucket of phlegm and half a lung, spoiling my predictions about his pneumonia improving. I spray saline through the tracheostomy, freeing up even more mucus from down below. After giving him another dose of antibiotics, we move.

We approach what looks like yet another burned-out strip mall, only—

It's full of people.

I squint at the parking lot and see something akin to a pre-war Saturday farmer's market outfitted with tents and wares with aromas of spiced foods and a general mingling of bodies. Someone has erected an enormous wood structure that resembles a rocket ship, and given the amount of wood bundled beneath the thing, the intent is to set it on fire. "Looks like..."

"Burning man," Rafa finishes for me.

Sabion gives us a quizzical look.

"Old-world festival," I tell him. "It was weird then and it is weird today, too." A young woman with a cart full of melons pushes past us. "Excuse me," I ask her, "what is all this?"

"First annual Festival of Light! Where are y'all coming from?" She crinkles her nose like one of those happy people.

I'm too stupefied to respond right away, so Rafa asks, "What is the festival for?"

"The northern lights," she answers. "It's been snowballing for a few years now. I was here last year—my friend, Cat, brought me when she came the year before from Sacramento. Word's been spreading and this festival thing just kind of popped up over the last few days as more people started showing up. So, a bunch of us got together last night around the campfire and decided to make this year the first official festival."

"Aren't you all worried about being out here unprotected? Raiders are all up and down these parts," I ask.

"Pish! Like those folks over there?" She points to some men laughing while kicking back beer. "They rolled in here this morning trying to rob the whole lot of us. We just gave 'em a beer and told them to string up a hammock and relax. And guess what? They did. That's how things work here. It's just a little bubble of friendly paradise among all the bickering. People can be themselves and enjoy the heavenly show."

"So, you've seen the lights?" I ask.

"Uh-huh. Last year was my first time, and wow, what an experience. The entire sky lights up with blues and greens, even some reddish pink colors lower on the horizon."

"How long does it last?" Rafa asks.

"Usually about five days. Gets sweltering hot during the lights. There's even a group that strips everything and becomes a part-time nudist colony," she says, a bit scandalized. "I won't be doing any of that but, hey, no judgment. People come here to do what they want. Whether that's burning a big wooden spaceship or just having a good time."

"When do the lights usually begin?" Rafa asks her with anxiety rising in his voice.

"They say it's never an exact day but it's usually around the eighteenth."

"Three days," he says.

"Yep! Why don't y'all come and join the festivities?"

Mute, we follow the girl to a circle of friendly travelers who greet us with wine and popcorn. We lean along a pick-up truck more stunned than anything else. Tension blooms in my chest as they dance and joke in merriment, unwittingly celebrating the possible end of the world. And then something cool touches my wrist but nothing is there. My vision then hiccups with flashes of a cat pouncing on a mouse. Over and over again, it pounces and tears its prey to gory ribbons.

"We need to get out of here," Rafa says. "Hutch may have spies here who could identify us in a second."

"Gabriel," I say. "He's here. There's not much time. I—" And then Gabriel shows me the Monterey Hila colony. Scores of their holes riddle long fields of marshland and long grasses set between lines of mature trees. Despite its overgrowth, it's an artificial layout of flora that I'd recognize anywhere. "Golf course," I say. "The Hila are at an old golf course."

We follow highway signs to the nearest golf course in Monterey called Del Monte. The old clubhouse is a sad, dilapidated thing that collapsed on itself and then became entombed in marsh grasses. As we creep through the soggy marshland, I worry we're not at the right golf course, but then I hear the sound of engines chugging in the distance. With our backs crouched beneath the head of the marsh, we push forward to the sounds and scents of men—tobacco, gasoline, and raw sewage. Men laugh and holler over the growl of chainsaws and revving truck engines. Our view still obscured by the marsh, we inch forward and finally see them —Hila holes.

The San Diego militia has cleared the marsh away, exposing hundreds of Hila holes scattered through the boggy ground. Sandbags hug the encampment as fortification against Hutch's militia and LA reinforcements, who are probably clearing their own plot of Hila holes themselves not too far away. The aliens are alive in their holes, beaded skin black as tar shining in the noon sun. They shift erratically within, appendages whipping about and stirring uproarious laughter from the men. They stomp on the Hila appendages or fire off shots that glance off their impenetrable skin. At one hole, four men have managed to bind a Hila up with rope attached to a truck winch. The truck's tires spin wildly in the mud, fishtailing the vehicle as it poorly gains purchase to wrench the Hila from its hole. The Hila writhes, flipping mud and digestive juices through the air. The men reel with laughter, throwing beer cans at the alien as it sinks back into its hole.

"These are some stubborn intergalactic lizards we got here," I hear the unmistakable voice of Anders. "Looks like we've got to keep playing the waiting game, boys. We're not taking these things alive." He sips on a canteen, appearing exhausted with massive bags under his eyes. He ambles off to a five-point tent housing a table, where other men sit. Through binoculars, I see who I can only assume to be the San Diegan mayor, Gustavson, decked in army fatigues. A scowl crosses his face as he gestures wildly about something. He looks to the sky as distant shots are heard from the other side of the golf course, where I can only assume Hutch and his men are engaging in the mirror-image lunacy of the San Diego encampment.

I feel a tug on my sleeve. Worry crosses Sabion's face as he gestures for us to leave. The boy has only grown in wisdom since the first day I met him.

Ward presides over a boiling pot of stew, a stirring spoon in one hand, pet mouse in the other. Prasad rests on a sleeping bag, trembling with fever as the infection roars back. I change his dressing, find the wound clean, and give him another dose of antibiotics. He pats my hand. "Everything will be okay." I purse my lips, searching for a response between utter despair and false hope. I don't find it. "Whatever happens," he says, "I'm happy for the life

I've had. I've got two boys at home who love me. I ran a business that helped people. And I got to know Doctor Elspeth Darrow and see all the amazing things one woman can accomplish."

I envy Prasad. Someone who I assumed led a rather simple life was telling me that it is within simplicity that he finds meaning. I could never be content letting the world happen to me. No, I had to consider every possibility and maximize all efforts in the terrible likelihood something good would trickle out. I was the type of person who set up thousands of monkeys on typewriters hoping, against all odds, they'd randomly author a Shakespearean sonnet. Prasad, on the other hand, simply sat at a single typewriter and wrote his own singular story and made damn sure it had a happy ending. And there we were, at the precipice of the end of the world—Prasad waxing joyful and me, ensuring a peptic ulcer completed its full erosion through my gut.

I pull my hand away from him, sick with self-loathing.

"I'm sorry," Prasad says. "What did I say?"

"It's not anything you said," I tell him. "It's a *me* problem. And it doesn't matter anymore."

"I have bad news," Rafa interrupts us.

"What is it?" I ask.

"I got off the radio with Nika. There's no fertilizer stockpiled anywhere in San Diego. The Hila are surrounded by Gustavson's men, and they're waiting them out to die just like they're doing here in Monterey. They must've figured out that the fertilizer doesn't kill them."

I say nothing and rise to my feet, looking up to the moon.

"Elspeth, did you hear me?" Rafa interrupts.

"Of course I heard you," I say. "Anders must have a spy in Hutch's council. They all found out the fertilizer doesn't kill the Hila when Hutch bugged my room. That's why no one stockpiled it in San Diego."

"So, what now?" Prasad asks.

"The plan has failed," I say. I sit back down and feel something that I've fought for a long time. Something I could never find since I descended to the bunkers with a pregnant belly and my husband fighting a doomed war somewhere.

Relief.

TWENTY-NINE

I LOOK AT RAFA. "You said yourself that the San Diego Hila colony is needed to complete Earth's laser cloak. All the Hila are going to die down there so there's no point in us doing anything else down here."

"Are you hearing yourself?" Rafa asks.

"Yes."

"Everything I've come up with are just my theories. Do you have any idea how many unknowns and variables there may be out there that I haven't accounted for? We need to get the fertilizer to the Hila here. Now. The Hila are a species genetically evolved to survive catastrophic conditions. They've probably been around for millions of years to have achieved what they can do. They may have backup plans, contingencies. Optical physics is literally a bodily function for them. We haven't a clue what they're capable of."

"I'm just so... tired," I say, giving into the seduction of forfeit. It just finally felt so comfortable to stretch my legs in.

"This isn't you talking, Elspeth, it's despair. Snap out of it," Rafa says.

Ward speaks up. "We've had patients that we thought—knew —were going to die who pulled through and then they lived to leave the hospital."

"Yes, but—"

"Then you can't give up now," Ward says. "It's the same thing."

"But how are we even supposed to deliver all that fertilizer to the Hila with Hutch and those militias literally standing guard over them?" I ask. "We go in there, we're just going to get killed anyway."

Rafa stands. "I don't know. But we must try. All of us have to go, even Prasad."

"Prasad is on death's door." I lower my voice, motioning to the sleeping man.

"We're *all* on death's door," Rafa says. "We need every person we can get. I'd go down and recruit people at the festival, but Hutch's spies would just catch us there. There has to be a way for this to work."

"Your cosmic blind faith isn't going to get us out of this. For a scientist, you really can be an idiot sometimes," I say, intending to hurt him. I don't even really know why.

Rafa gears up, ready to finally let me have it, but an engine ignition roars to life behind us. It's the semi-truck, brimming with fertilizer, Sabion at the wheel. The boy leans out of the driver window and stares daggers at me. I believe I shot him the same cold look on a number of occasions on our doomed voyage to San Jose. He flicks his head, gesturing for us to go.

I hold up my hands. "Okay, okay. Let's go and get ourselves killed."

Sabion revs the engine.

"And I guess we're leaving right now," I say.

It's past midnight as we drive the semi-truck along the north side of the golf course. We have a vague idea of where the SF and San Diego encampments are and take a wide berth from them, hoping they haven't surrounded every Hila hole. All crammed in the truck cabin together, an eerie silence settles over us. No one wants to talk about the task at hand and idle chitchat rings too hollow. So, Sabion drives with Rafa giving guidance as he surveys the golf course with binoculars. "Pull over here," he says.

We leave Ward and Prasad in the truck and quest out into the golf course, searching for dying aliens. Most of the golf course is a bog with shallow pools of water jigsawed with a micro archipelago of moss and grass. The pearl-white light of the full moon flits across the water as we search, finding nothing but frogs and belching gasses. Soaked to our knees, we trudge through, hot panic bathing my nerves and I can't stop thinking, *This world is going to end. This is the way the world ends. True, not with a whimper, but with a cosmic bang that only a handful of people will ever know about.*

Muddy water slaps my face, I can't breathe. I can't see. This can't be my life. I should be visiting my son at college. I should be planting orchids on our rooftop garden with Clive. I should die of a gentle stroke at the age of eighty-two after visiting my grandchildren. Not here. Not in a parallel future of—

I sink into the mud, my shins grind on rock as my face plunges into the water. Gasping, I come up and grope for a holding, getting purchase on more rock. But then the rocks move. I wipe dirt away and feel the smooth surface of the beaded skin of a Hila beneath the water. And then it rises, its head breaching the surface of the water. Its gyrating eyes fall on me. Motionless, we hold there, taking in one another.

"Why?" I yell at it. "Why would you come? Just to die with us?"

It says nothing, only gazes at me.

"Why did you come?" I stupidly ask again.

But it recedes back under the water.

Rafa slogs through the mud behind me. "Did you find some?"

"Yes," I say, looking at my muddy palms. "Let's get to work."

Equipped with backpacks and buckets, the five of us spread through the bog, finding one Hila hole after another, and start dumping fertilizer. Prasad slings a bag over his good shoulder and manages to distribute almost as fast as the rest of us. Sabion works like an animal, shedding the fertilizer quickly until his bag empties and then running back to the truck to refill. He easily does twice the work as the rest of us. After working well into the night, dawn light breaks on the horizon.

"How many have we fertilized?" I ask Rafa.

"Maybe four hundred."

"Out of five thousand?"

"Yes," he says.

"Any plan on how we're going to fertilize the encampments?" I ask.

"Yes," he says grimly.

"Just say it."

"We continue as much as we find here, very carefully during the day so we aren't seen. Tonight, we will... infiltrate the encampments."

"Do you plan on killing?" I ask.

He nods. "There's no other choice. We must get into the

camps as quietly as possible and that will involve killing the night guards and as many of the men in their sleep as possible."

"No," I say. "Just—no. There must be another way."

"Would you rather we just go knock on the door and ask to come in? This is the time to act. You know that better than anyone else. We keep pushing forward even without knowing how we will succeed. There's nothing else anymore—"

We are suddenly flooded in white light, a horn blaring.

"Stop what you're doing!" a voice commands through a megaphone. "Doctor Darrow, please ask your fellow spies and traitors to lower their weapons. No one needs to be harmed."

Before we can scatter, the men are already on us, several rifle muzzles converging. After they wrangle up Sabion, Ward, and Prasad with us, Reece appears from beyond the floodlights, pleased as sour punch. "Bind them," he commands his men as he eyes me. "You could have had everything you wanted," he says. "Your hospital to run as long as you wanted. Your med student, too. But you had to drag everyone into your crazed fantasy of saving a bunch of lizards stupider than anything on Earth. The dumb things don't even defend themselves. They just rot in their disgusting holes. Why do you care so much about them?"

As my feet and wrists are bound, I say nothing.

"After everything you've done, you don't have anything to say for yourself? Anyone else?" he asks the rest. "Want to say why you follow this mad doctor who killed my fiancée and mother?"

No one speaks.

Reece rounds on Sabion. "This is what you've become? You used to be a man of honor. We butted heads, but it was good for us. You helped make me the man I am today. How could this happen to you?"

Sabion answers nothing.

"You disgust me," Reece says. "Get him out of here."

We're rounded up into the back of a pick-up truck and share furtive glances until Prasad mouths, *"What now?"* Our knees knock together as the truck backs out of the swamp grass and finds a dirt road. And then Sabion is standing and lunging at one of the guards and cracks his forehead into the side of the man's skull. By the way the guard's body slackens, I know the man is knocked out cold. Spiraling from the momentum of the attack, Sabion tumbles from the truck bed and vanishes from view. "Stop the truck!" someone yells. They collect Sabion from the side of the road, blood cascading down his lips and saturating his shirt. After adding zip ties to hands and feet, they slap a piece of duct tape over his mouth and throw him back in the truck bed like a sack of potatoes.

The morning sun finally breaks over us as we wheel past the barbed wire fencing surrounding the Neo SF camp. Just like their San Diego and Sacramento rivals, Hutch and his men have made short work of clearing the marsh to expose the Hila holes. Tire tread has gouged the ground all over the marsh where Hutch has tried to expel the living Hila from their holes just as the San Diegans attempted nearby. But there are Hila in every hole, having resisted the attempts of prying them out to an early death.

"We're all going to die if you don't let us save the Hila," Ward tells the guards, who laugh in his face.

"She'd be proud of you, Ward," I say.

"Who?" he asks.

"You asked me if your mother would be proud of her son who is scared shitless all the time. You're not scared now, and I don't think you ever were. It's them who wanted you to believe you were scared." I motion to the men watching guard over us. "To make you silent. To make you not matter. I know she'd be proud. As proud as I am of you now. You've grown into the exact type of man that we need right now."

Sabion rolls at our feet. Despite the zip ties around his wrists, he reaches two fingers out to Ward's pant leg and manages to pinch the fabric in a show of solidarity. Ward reaches down his bound wrists and locks his index finger with Sabion for a moment.

"Sabion," I say. "Thank you for saving me, even after all the guilt I heaped onto you. You killed that boy, yes, but you were only doing what our colony had engineered you to do. You are not your past actions. You are who you are right now—a person sacrificing everything for everyone else." I stop talking when I realize I've started prematurely eulogizing our brave little band.

We arrive at a nest of tents where I see Hutch lounging in a camp chair, wicker hat shielding his eyes from the encroaching sun. Our eyes meet and his face crimps with disappointment. He approaches the truck bed, wagging his finger at me. "I knew you'd finally show up down here. Been sending out patrols twice daily just to watch for you. Hop on out of there."

"We need food," I tell him after we're released from the trick.

"Of course you all can eat," he says. "I'm not a monster. Join me at the tents."

Seated at a picnic table, hot stew and stale bread are brought to us before our hands are unbound. We eat in silence as Reece and Hutch watch us. "Doctor Darrow, as soon as you're done, will you join me in my tent?" Hutch asks. I immediately stand and follow him around a tent flap. He motions to a vacant folding chair, which I'd like to decline as a sign of protest, but I clumsily collapse into it from sheer exhaustion, my hip screaming. "Did you see any Sacs out there? Any Sandie militia?" he asks.

"No. It was just us where Reece arrested us."

"Good," he says, a vacancy filling his eyes.

"What's wrong?"

"Nothing is technically wrong." He swallows.

"Then why do you look like you're going to vomit?"

He licks his lips with hesitation. "Mayor Carmichael has informed me this morning that he will not be arriving from LA with his militia."

"Are you afraid of what you're doing here on your own?" I ask.

"Not afraid, no. Just uncertain about how to proceed."

"What does your war council tell you?"

His eyes roll. "The council is a joke. No one knows what they're talking about. Most wouldn't even come down to join me on the front line, and none of us have actually waged war or directed any sort of battle. Everyone was all bravado, but now they're tight-lipped and nervous with the enemy at our doorstep."

"You worked in advertising before the fall, correct?" I ask.

"Yes."

"That's why you're sitting here right now as Mayor of Neo SF. When you ran for mayor, you emerged from the population embodying the collective anxieties and moral panic of a people who had no idea who they wanted to be in an era that hadn't written its own history yet. You know how to connect with people to make them vote for and trust you. But now that you've balled up that trust and turned it into a little war engine, you're just as scared as the teenagers you have out there, rifles in their arms, fighting for a cause that you barely understand yourself."

He sets his jaw. "Something had to be done. We couldn't just let them walk up here and take the Hila bodies."

"You don't think they're here for the exact same reason?" I ask. "Maybe if you hadn't set up your trade embargo against them and been blasting the airwaves for the last couple of years about making SF the new capital, they wouldn't have felt so threatened. No one is innocent here and everyone is to blame. None of this matters now. What matters is if you're ready to kill and ready to have your men be killed for you. That's what you're struggling with right now, isn't it?"

He offers a little grin. "Always knew how to cut through the bullshit, didn't you, Elspeth?"

I lean forward, elbows on knees. "I'd like to cut a little deeper. What you're doing right now, grappling with your own ethics, is the highest degree of bullshit."

He leans back in his chair, mouth tightening at my words.

"If you're worried that you may have to cross an ethical line soon, I'm here to tell you that your ethics are an illusion, Mayor. You've become an evil piece of shit. Grace is rolling in her grave right now."

He cracks his neck.

"Don't bring me inside this tent and act like you've arrived at a moral crossroads. You've slowly boiled your poor little moral frog and it's been dead for a while now. You've fabricated all this your-self by all the terrible micro-decisions you've made to arrive at this point. I'm not here to relieve you of anything. You've created this mess and I want you to stew in it. You'll get men and probably even yourself killed, and you've doomed the entire planet because of the same little game of chess that scores of idiotic men like you have played for centuries."

He stands.

"But," I say, putting my hand on his forearm. "You're not beyond redemption. Everything you've overheard me and my group speak of is true. There is a predator race that will destroy our planet but cannot find us because the Hila hide our presence in space from them. I believe it is the entire reason the Hila came in the first place. If you stop this war and load the Hila holes full of the fertilizer, you have the chance for the biggest one-eighty in history. You can go from the man who ignored the end of the world to the man who saved the entire planet. A dead footnote to a living messiah. Which sounds better to you?"

He keeps his arm under my hand as we share silence for a

moment, and then says, "A few years before the wars, I had my elderly mother move in with me and Grace. She was a stubborn woman, something she passed onto me, but agreed to live with us as her mind went. One day, she put a plastic bowl directly on the stove to boil water and turned the damn thing on. We lost the kitchen to fire and barely saved our home. I know the signs of dementia and I know when it's time that someone is no longer safe on their own. But don't worry. I'll make sure you're taken care of when we get back to the colony after this business is over." He pats my hand and leaves me alone in the tent.

THIRTY

ON SUNDAY, the following morning, Hutch's men shore up the perimeter around the Hila with freshly arrived sandbags. They had dug trenches throughout the night and hammered in the last of the spiked stakes into the ground like they're preparing for a medieval siege cavalry. After a cold breakfast, a keg is tapped and the men drink. "Only one cup each, boys," Hutch tells them during a speech. "You need your wits and bravery sharper than ever this morning. Our scouts have confirmed our suspicions that the enemy may be preparing to meet us this day." He continues his little speech, borrowing heavily from the Gettysburg address, and then finishes with, "They may take our lives, but they may never take our freedom." He sits back beneath the cool shade of the tent next to where he has me and the rest of my fellowship bound to a picnic table under the watchful eye of an armed guard.

"Braveheart?" I ask Hutch.

"Hmm?"

"You stole that line from the movie Braveheart."

"Don't know what you're talking about," he says while checking his watch.

And then a literal bugle sounds somewhere in the distance, which gets the men all riled up. Hutch suits up in a flak jacket and brings an ammunition bandolier over his torso. In another life, he looks ready to do some yard work with a leaf blower slung over his shoulder rather than the M-16 he gingerly cradles. Reece shouts orders over a radio and men scatter throughout the encampment, most flopping into trenches or simply hiding behind trees. There are no technical formations of any kind happening.

"What now?" I whisper to Rafa.

"Was going to ask you the same thing."

"How does all this fit into your cosmic plan of everything working out?"

"You sound like Mavis," he says.

"Dammit, you're right." I sigh with depression so cutting and eternal that I'm almost looking forward to no longer existing. Our conversation is cut short by an explosion followed by a few pops of gunfire. From our front-row seats to the dimwitted battle, the SF encampment is still secure.

"Enemy spotted!" someone says with binoculars above us where a small observation post has been built into a tree. Reece climbs a rope ladder up the tree and peers through a pair of binoculars. "I see automatic weapons and riot gear. Lots of reinforced trucks. Bet they're going to use them as cover as they advance."

Hutch walks along the line of tents, speaking into a megaphone. "We have the advantage of being on the defense. Only shoot if they try to invade our encampment. This is probably all just a show to goad us out. Do not return fire if shot upon. Await my word, and my word only, to open fire."

For the next twenty minutes, the entire encampment is silent as the Sacramento and San Diego militias advance. Like clockwork, blasts and gunfire erupt every thirty seconds, none hitting our camp. Finally, around twenty trucks and Humvees can be seen across the marsh. Dozens of men line the back of pick-up trucks with several dozen more on foot looking like a homegrown paramilitary outfit. The preppers and extremists of the pre-Hila era have finally come home to roost, and they appear absolutely thrilled. Colonial peace has been grating on them for far too long. The advancing militia settles itself about a hundred feet away from the encampment and set up their own barriers of sandbags. As they begin digging their own trenches, Reece yells at Hutch, "We're just going to let them set up right here at our door stop? We need to attack." There is a chorus of agreement among the men at the tent.

"Shut your *mouth*," Hutch snaps at his son. "You are not in command here. You are a soldier, and you are to take orders. This is not the time for your opinions. Do you understand me?" Reece reddens and then scowls at the public humiliation in front of the other boys.

"Someone's walking up," I tell Hutch.

Mayor Gustavson of San Diego appears in front of his line, alone and unarmed. "Mayor Hutch," he calls through a megaphone. "Parley."

"Let him pass!" Hutch calls out.

Decked in military dress, including golden epaulets draped over his shoulders, Gustavson removes his helmet and walks past the SF line, wisps of hair reaching toward the heavens like his skull has grown wings. His face is as broad and as featureless as a frying pan and just as inscrutable. Walking with lazy confidence, his eyes flicker over the encampment, taking inventory of his enemy. He approaches the tents without fanfare and seats himself at a folding table where Hutch is waiting. Two tumblers are set out, which Hutch fills with a decanter. He hands one to

Gustavson, who downs the drink and nods in appreciation. "I found your spies," Gustavson says, looking at the empty tumbler in his hand.

Hutch poorly masks his surprise by taking a sip of scotch. And then he tells the most obvious lie ever detected in the universe. "What spies?"

"I didn't come here to bullshit with you."

"Why are you here then?"

Gustavson sets the tumbler down. "To tell you to go home. You have no claim in Monterey and you shouldn't be here. This is an unneeded conflict and you're going to get men killed for no reason."

"I have just as much claim here as you do," Hutch says. "I'll leave as soon as you guarantee that the Hilamen here will not fall into your possession."

Gustavson brushes a fly out of his face and says, "We will be transporting all the Hila here to San Diego. You are outnumbered and outmatched. Go home and tell Carmichael to come and fight his own wars without sending his lap dog from San Francisco."

"Outmatched? Outnumbered? My scouts have eyes. We are on equal military footing."

"You'd be a fool to think your scouts see everything. I assure you, Jack, I have the means to destroy every one of your men while suffering minimal losses," he says with no pomp as if he is merely stating a fact. "Don't test it."

"I won't let you have the Hila," Hutch says.

"I already have thousands of them secured near San Diego. I know you know this. I won't allow LA to get their hands on the bodies here. Carmichael wants to make himself king of California with you as his little princeling. You are being played. Played and used by Carmichael—who couldn't even show up himself to face me. Do you know why? He expects you to fail here." He points his finger into the table. "He's leading his own militia to San Diego right now. He thinks he has distracted me with you and that he will seize the Hila there. What he doesn't know is that I am already well-prepared for him down there. What I'm doing is fighting colonial tyranny by guarding the Hila assets from a man who wants to bring all of California under a martial law dictatorship. Now, I don't know the exact arrangements between you and Carmichael, but I'm not an unreasonable man. I want to see men killed today as little as you do."

"What are you suggesting?" Hutch asks with new intrigue.

Gustavson rests his elbows on the table. "A peace treaty between San Diego and San Francisco. One that involves dissolving your alliance with Carmichael and the colony of Neo Los Angeles. The rest of the details we can certainly hammer out, which will likely leave you and your colony in a far superior economic advantage than you are currently in. Your embargo? That, of course, will be lifted. In exchange, I will make Neo SF the only northern trading hub of Hila-fabricated technology."

Hutch's eyebrows raise. "What kind of technology?"

"Mostly military, but the potential is endless with Hila materials, which my scientists have started to figure out. Either way, the future is bright and yours will be even brighter when you are the sole distributor of Hila tech in the north."

Hutch rubs the back of his neck. "It's an interesting proposition. Carmichael will not like it."

"Come on," Gustavson says, slapping him on the shoulder. "I'll work that out with Carmichael. All you need to do is say yes." On cue, the man pulls out prepared documents. "You can have all the time you need to review the details of the contract." He places the papers in front of Hutch and circles around the tent, peering into the open marsh and then wheels around to me. "Who is this?"

"Doctor Elspeth Darrow," Hutch says, leafing through the documents.

"Ah, the Hila cultist," he says with bemusement. "It was clever," he tells me. "Your ploy to get us to unwittingly save the Hila with fertilizer. I had it stockpiled and ready to go until we found out what you were really planning. Those two teenagers you sent down to us are safe, by the way. I'll have them serve a small prison sentence for espionage and sedition and then have them conscripted into my militia. They are, after all, just two indoctrinated children. You bear most of the blame." He turns to Hutch. "I would advise you to not take hysterical women into your war council. I can see why your war effort here has been so poorly executed—"

Something large flashes across my vision and then I see a body lunge at Gustavson, tackling him to the dirt. Fists rain down on the mayor of San Diego, beating in rapid succession as he cries for help. As blood flings onto the canvas walls with every blow, I realize the man is actually being stabbed to death. The assailant rocks furiously atop him, long hair bouncing with each downward thrust. The man has easily been stabbed twenty times before Hutch's men pull the attacker off who rolls into the dirt. Despite a thick sheath of filth over their face, I can see who it is.

"*Mavis!*" I cry. She briefly meets my gaze, flashing her teeth, before being summarily bound and pinned to the ground.

"Free Doctor Darrow!" Hutch demands, fretting over Gustavson, whose brawny skin has taken on a ghostly pale. I'm freed from the table and hurry over to Gustavson, who is not only littered with lacerations along his chest and torso but also has a jagged slash running along the front of his neck. I witness the last few beats of his heart as blood weeps from his neck and then tapers off.

"He's dead," I say, closing the man's eyelids.

Hutch claps. "Well, bring him back! We can't have him dying here."

I put up my hands. "There is nothing I can do."

"No, no, no," Hutch says in disbelief as Reece comes barreling through.

Reece sees me, hands bloodied, next to the body of Gustavson and draws his rifle on me. "Don't move!"

"Put your damn gun down, you idiot!" Hutch yells. "We're in big trouble."

"How did this—" And then Reece sees Mavis flailing her limbs under the weight of three men. "*Her?* How did she even get into camp?"

"It doesn't matter now. Gustavson is dead and his army out there will never believe we didn't have him killed." Hutch sinks onto a stool and buries his face in his palms. "He was about to offer us a way out of this mess."

"Dad!" Reece yells. "What do we do?"

Hutch doesn't answer but moves to the table and pours himself a tall glass of scotch. He throws it back and then looks at me.

"You think I'm going to help you?" I ask.

"Neo SF lives hang in the balance of what we do next," Hutch says. "I think you in the least care about preventing a war, especially since it is one of your own who just murdered the man in front of us! How do I know she didn't do it under your orders?"

"I'm just a sad woman with dementia, remember?"

His hands shake around the tumbler. "Your advice would still be appreciated. You still care about the loss of life that is going to happen today, don't you?"

"You want my advice? Surrender and help me get fertilizer to the Hila. There. No one dies," I say.

He rubs his chin in thought as if he's actually considering my

319

proposal. Then he shakes it off and says to Reece, "Get rid of the body. We'll say we had a meeting discussing a treaty and that he left through the back of the marsh. Look, I'll even sign the treaty he brought." He hastily clicks a ballpoint pen and signs the paper. "We'll say he went out for a cigarette after and went missing. They'll go searching for him, find his body, and assume raiders got him."

"You think that will work?" Reece asks.

"Not sure, but it will buy us time."

"Time for what?"

The mayor chews his lip in contemplation.

"Time to get the upper hand? Withdraw?" Reece asks.

"He doesn't know," I say. "Never has."

"I wasn't lying," Mavis tells me. "I really did try." She looks to Rafa, who has no words for her. "I wanted to believe in all this." She motions with her bloodied hands to our failed fellowship, tied together to a picnic table like forgotten balloons during a birthday party. "But there was just no way."

"We all knew what we were up against," I tell her. "Why couldn't you have at least tried with us? Or at least come back to SF without sending those poor teenagers to be imprisoned in San Diego?"

"Gustavson is dead," she says, voice thick with satisfaction. "He's *dead*."

"Yes, we all just saw you murder him. So, now what?" I ask.

She bows her head to the ground and takes a deep breath.

"Nothing, right? Exactly what you wanted," I berate her. "You just want to release yourself into the void of nothingness but couldn't do that knowing that a tyrant was still alive and walking around. But now that you killed him, you'll go to your grave with a smile on your face. That's what this was all about—you. What you did here today, spilling your wrath all over everyone, was one of the highest acts of selfishness I've ever witnessed." Mavis says nothing, which is fine because I have nothing else to say to the woman. I look from Sabion and Ward and meet my eyes with Rafa's. He, too, bows his head in resignation.

The SF camp stirs with anxious futility as men check and recheck munitions and perimeter security. Hutch and Reece have their eyes glued on binoculars as they watch the enemy's reaction after they sent a runner for a request to parley once more. A lone figure walks across the marsh and appears at the edge of camp.

Anders.

"Deputy Mayor of Neo Sacramento," Anders corrects after someone introduces him as 'a guy from the other side.' He looks over at me and then to Hutch. "Why is Doctor Darrow tied up?" he asks.

"That's Neo SF business," Hutch says.

Anders' eyes roll in their sockets, searching the tent. "Where is Gustavson?"

"We were going to ask you the same thing," Hutch says. "The man stepped out for a smoke and never returned. You're telling me he didn't return to your camp?"

Anders folds his arms, eyes sweeping the ground, and then makes a small divot in the dirt with his boot where something that may have been blood was recently spilled. "What kind of bullshit is going on here?"

"You tell me," Hutch says. "We agreed on a treaty and then the man vanished. The treaty sits right there, signed by both of us."

Anders looks at me. "What's going on here, Doc?"

"Gustavson is dead," I say.

Hutch slams his hands on the table. "Dammit, Elspeth!"

"But Hutch didn't order it," I explain. "He was murdered by her," I motion to Mavis. "Working on her own accord."

Anders grunts in annoyance like he's just discovered a painful hangnail. "That's unfortunate." He then sees Sabion. "Isn't that the one who killed the kid in my crew down in San Jose?"

"Yes," I say.

"Why is he tied up with you?"

"You are looking at Earth's last defense," I tell him. "This small group of prisoners are the only thing between life and total annihilation."

He continues to gaze at our group, utterly perplexed by my words. "You lied to me," he says.

"Once. I'm not lying to you now."

"I don't have time for this," he says and turns to Hutch. "So, what now?"

"We honor the treaty," Hutch says.

Anders cocks an eye at him. "The treaty you signed with a dead man?"

"Well, who's in power in San Diego now that Gustavson is dead?" Hutch asks.

"I don't know. Me?" Anders says, bringing a palm to his chest.

"*You?*" I say. "You represent Sacramento."

Anders shrugs. "Sure. But I'm here now and suddenly command a large portion of both the San Diego and Sacramento militia. I think that means I'm in charge and I will be making the decisions."

"The colony charters state the deputy Mayor of San Diego would take command until an emergent election," I say. "Not you."

Anders looks around the tent, feigning that he's in search of something. "Nope. We're not in a colony at the moment. This might as well be the moon. And I'm here right now with two militias that will do what I say. That means I'm in charge. But no need to fret, Mayor," he says to Hutch. "I'll honor the treaty."

"Do you see?" I say to Mavis. "Do you see how quickly one tyrant is changed out for another?"

The men celebrate with a round of scotch and cigars. Anders slaps Hutch on the back and says, "I'll have some men come to retrieve the body and we'll just stick to the story that raiders got 'em. Easier to explain than all this other business." He motions to Mavis. They shake hands and Anders leaves, his eyes catching mine for a moment. I see regret in his face at my predicament and then he mouths something to me, almost too quick to read on his lips—"*Stay down.*"

THIRTY-ONE

I DUCK my head as a concussive wave moves through the dirt.

Hutch looks to Reece and asks, "What was that?"

Before his son can answer, another deafening blast pounds our ears. The men dive behind sandbags, Reece shouting on the radio to return fire. Hutch peeks his head up and peers through binoculars. "It's Anders. That *snake*! We had a treaty!" New and curious explosions interrupt his anger—a volley of grenades thrown into the encampment. Concussive waves boom through the soil, earth is churned, and men are violently displaced. I huddle beneath our picnic table, scooting in with my friends. A hand closes over mine. Prasad. I squeeze back and put my hand on Ward's shoulder, who is frozen in fear, pet mouse writhing frantically in his grasp.

"Fire!" Hutch says and then his men rally, gathering courage from one another as they fire indiscriminately. A few sharpshooters fire from the trees above us, skipping bullets off of enemy helmets. A decent firefight ensues after the initial assault, now that most men have found comfortable places for cover. It takes a good ten minutes for both sides to realize they're getting nowhere. A voice breaks through the din as the shooting ceases from the other side.

"Mayor Hutch!" Anders bellows from a megaphone. "Time to surrender."

"Traitor!" Reece yells back, sounding more like a petulant teen than ever.

Hutch rips the megaphone from Reece's hands. "I don't negotiate with men who don't keep their word!" Hutch yells.

"No way would I have left that tent alive without agreeing to your bullshit treaty," Anders says. "Leave now and surrender the Hila or every one of your men will die here today. That I can guarantee you."

Hutch lowers his megaphone and whispers something in Reece's ear, who nods in response and crawls away from the tent. Hutch and Anders then proceed with a shouting match full of equal parts vitriol, colony propaganda, and old-fashioned name-calling. It's only when a Gatling gun rolls out of a trailer that I realize Hutch has been stalling the entire time. After Reece and his men position it behind a wall of sandbags, he looks to his father, who gives a nod. The sandbags are promptly thrown aside and the Gatling gun unleashed on their enemy. For a single moment of everyone's lives, all that exists is that mounted cannon with its tripod feet digging into the spongy soil, muzzle sweeping the battlefield. Bullets and puffs of smoke belch from the war machine as we wait in terrible awe to see what kind of destruction is wrought on the other side.

The firing finally ceases, unmasking an incredible ringing in my ears. Anders' men are either dead in the marsh or well hidden behind their trucks. Hutch gets back on the megaphone and says, "I now give *you* the option to leave and surrender the Hila. There doesn't need to be any more bloodshed today."

And then a figure emerges near the line of vehicles, cloaked from head to toe in black. But by the way sunlight is bouncing off the person's clothing, they look like they are soaking wet. The person approaches alone, the rest of the militia left behind.

Rafa squints, scrutinizing the figure. "It's—it's a Hilaman!"

At first, I think Rafa's right, but as the figure approaches, there's something off. They are the height of a man, not a much taller Hila. The arms and legs are all the proportions of a human and it's walking exactly how a man would walk—in fact, exactly how Anders' walks. "That's not a Hila," I say, rage burning in my chest. As Anders arrives at the border of the SF encampment, I wonder how many diamond blades it took to cut and custom tailor a Hila skin for a man. Every inch of Anders' skin is covered in cascading layers of Hila skin. The Hila beads snugly wrap around the torso and thigh with layers of fringe covering the upper arms and neck. The head is a helmet of Hila beads with tiny openings at the eyes, mouth, and nose where a translucent shield has been mounted, presumably bulletproof.

"The bastards actually did it," Rafa whispers.

"Hutch!" Anders calls out from beneath the Hila beads. "Time's up!" Nine other men, all wearing the indestructible armor of the Hila skin, emerge from behind Anders and line up alongside him. "This is your last chance to surrender," Anders says. "After this, me and my men will single-handedly destroy your militia."

Hutch drops binoculars from his eyes and turns his back to Anders, slumping to the floor behind a column of sandbags. Reece, troubled by his father's despondent gaze on the dirt, says, "I thought they hadn't fabricated the Hila skins yet."

"Obviously the intelligence from LA was wrong," Hutch snaps.

"So, what do we do?" Reece says, breathing in a quick panic.

With new resolve, Hutch says, "We fight."

"Are you—are you sure?" Reece says, panic twisting in his face.

"Yes," Hutch says.

Reece gazes out over the battlefield. "Dad, I don't know if I'm ready for this. You know those ten men over there are outfitted in indestructible armor. They are about to come in here and tear us apart."

"They're still just men," Hutch argues. "Men can be killed. Let's throw Molotov cocktails—"

"Hutch!" Anders yells. "Raise the white flag. Come on now."

And then Reece vomits all over his own boots.

"Suck it up! Be a man!" Hutch hisses at his son, getting to his feet long enough for a distant shot to ring out and knock him to the ground, his hand clamping on his neck. He gasps for air, eyes wheeling and searching until they fall on me. "Elspeth!" he yells through ragged breaths. "Help me!" Reece kneels beside his father, who shoves him off. "Get Doctor Darrow over here." Reece stumbles over to me and, through shaky hands, cuts my bands.

"I need my medical student," I tell him before Reece frees Ward.

I kneel beside Hutch, who grabs my hand and painfully crunches my knuckles together. "Don't let me die," he begs.

"Let the fascist bleed!" Mavis yells.

"Shut your mouth," I tell her without turning from my patient. Hutch brings my palm near his bloodied neck where he's holding pressure with his other hand. Gingerly, I scoot his hand away and replace it with my palm, firmly applying pressure. Ward is next to me, unfurling a surgical kit that Reece had brought from our confiscated supplies. Ward lays towels down surrounding the gunshot wound and stacks generous gauze and irrigation saline along Hutch's chest.

"He's not coughing up blood and I don't hear any gurgling or

wheezing, so I don't think the trachea has been violated," I tell
Ward who produces a scalpel, clamps, and sutures. "When I
release pressure—"

"I irrigate and dab, irrigate and dab while we search for the
bleeding source," he says.

I nod and release pressure from Hutch's neck as I duck from
another volley of gunfire. Blood floods, immediately soaking the
towels.

"I'm going to die," Hutch says between plaintive cries.

"You might," I tell him as I apply pressure again.

"I'm sorry," he says.

"Save your guilt," I tell him. "That's for you to suffer, not
anyone else." I release pressure again and Ward irrigates the
wound, exposing the bullet hole, which has penetrated the far-
right side of his neck. I bring the bevel of my scalpel into the clean
wound and part the skin upward, exposing the gore of pulverized
muscle. Hutch howls as I dig my finger in along the bullet's trajec-
tory. I release and inspect with a flashlight and see nothing but
oozing blood.

Oozing. Not pulsating.

"I think the carotid artery is clean," I yell at Ward as shots are
fired all around us. No one actually commands the battle anymore
as Reece has taken to sobbing in a corner of the tent. "But there is
vessel laceration somewhere. Could be the internal jugular," I say
to Ward, who dries the wound in gauze once more while I extend
it further. "Retractor." Ward slaps the instrument in my hand and
I fit it snugly along a muscle belly and pull it aside, exposing the
deeper vessels. While cinching off the muscle and skin, I bluntly
dissect my finger down while Hutch gyrates in pain. "Stop
moving."

"Look," I tell Ward, moving my head out of the way so he can
see. "All the major vessels are intact and the bleeding has stopped.

Which means—" Gunfire erupts around us once more as Reece watches us. "Which means..." I release the retractor and blood floods the surgical wound once more. "The bleeding must be more superficial." With nimble fingers, I move along the tissue planes, continuously dabbing and drying the wound as I search. "Got it. The bullet lacerated the more superficial external jugular vein. See?" I dissect around the edge of the vein and clamp it and then peel back more skin. "Suture." I bury the suture needle around the open vein, thread it a few times, and then tie it off. The bleeding is dramatically better but still oozes.

"Where's the rest of the bleeding coming from?" Ward asks.

"I'm scared," Hutch says, his eyes on the ceiling of the tent. "I didn't mean for it to be like this. I tried, Elspeth. I tried to do good. Do you believe me? Tell me you believe me, *please*."

"I believe you thought you were doing good. I also believe you failed miserably." I look at Ward. "The rest of the bleeding is coming from the bullet. It's embedded in the muscle and I can't get to it right now. Might cut something I don't want to cut without him under some sort of anesthesia—"

Something explodes.

I peek up behind the sandbags and see Anders at the edge of the encampment, just standing there while the entire SF militia empties bullets on him and his Hila skin compatriots, all of whom are completely unscathed. Anders catches a grenade, fumbles with it through Hila skinned gloves, but manages to lob it back near three SF men who get cover behind a rock only moments before it explodes.

"Pack the wound," I tell Ward, motioning to Hutch.

And then I leap over the sandbag barrier, my hip grinding in protest.

"Elspeth!" I hear Rafa and Prasad yell. "Where are you going?"

I say nothing.

And I walk.

"Doctor Darrow, please come in." The old man of the bunker waved me into a room that smelled of rot. He laid in a bed appearing skeletal, purple veins snaking along his temple. "I'm dying," he told me before I could ask what was wrong.

"Why haven't you let me come and treat you?" I asked.

He lifted his withered arms to me. "There's nothing to treat. I'm almost ninety years old."

"I could have helped you."

"And that's why I called for you right here and right now," he said. "That optimism will be needed, but not in the way you think. You're still in the hope stage of life. But that hope will become brittle and shatter."

"Well, that doesn't sound good."

"The shards of glass will be little painful seeds inside of you. They'll ripen and mature into something new."

"Into what?" I asked.

"Hope is the vine on which virtue grows and ripens into action, moving on its own accord. You need to pick up the pieces of tragedy and meld it into action."

"What are you, a prophet? You can't predict the future."

He squeezed my hand. "Listen to what I'm telling you."

"Okay, I'm sorry. What kind of action are you talking about?" I asked.

"Any action that is for someone other than yourself. The bar is low, my dear, very low. I know you are the type of person capable of doing something for someone else with almost no self-interest.

Any act for another person, as small as it seems, can move nations. I know. I've seen it."

I squeezed his hand. "Okay," I said, believing that I was appeasing an old man in the delirious throes of a dying body. "I'll sit here with you."

"Thank you. I don't deserve that because I'm an evil man. Like most men are. When you resettle San Francisco, watch for men like me. We believe our own lies. We say we're joking when we're actually testing the boundaries. We support families with our words while we dismantle them with our guns. We say we're protecting when all we're doing is hoarding power. Watch for me."

"And what do I do when I find you?" I asked.

"That's the secret no one ever figures out. But I know the answer. Took my whole life, but I know..."

"What is it?"

"Don't fight men like me—that's what we want you to do. That continues the cycle and the feedback loop."

"What then?" I asked.

"Draw out the last ember of humanity that still burns inside of me..."

"And?"

"Give it breath."

———

Stepping over bodies and fire-scorched earth, I have no plan—
Only death.

I have no fate—only grief.

As bullets scream by me, I realize my wrath has no power and that the world is simpler to navigate when you have enemies. Enemies are easy to understand, but the morally gray is incomprehensible. So, we reduce, retrofit, and oversimplify that which we cannot comprehend until it is packaged as a tidy enemy, deserving of rebranded justice. But now, with all anger expired, I'm only a messenger. I will either die or deliver my words. Hutch, the California colonies, Ward, the boy who died in San Jose, Sabion, the old man of the bunker, myself—are all the same. We are imperfection incarnate —trying to be more and failing, most with disastrous impact.

As I weave through the SF encampment, Anders notices my approach and puts up a hand. "Elspeth, I told you to stay down!" he shouts through a megaphone. "One more step and you'll be shot," he warns.

But I walk.

"Stop!" he yells.

But I march at him.

A Hila-clad soldier next to him fires at me—

But I feel nothing.

I keep walking at them, unarmed. The soldier fires again. I feel nothing and my gaze doesn't break from Anders'. He shakes his head at me in pity. "It didn't have to be this way, Doc," he shouts. "I always thought you were a good person. Just happened to be on the wrong side. You've brought this on yourself." More shots are fired at me, but I keep my approach. I may already be dead, leaving my bullet-riddled body behind me in the dirt as my spirit marches on.

And then I'm consumed in fire.

Bullets rain on me in one great conflagration. I kneel to the ground, arms overhead like my flesh and bone will halt the curtain of lead and copper punching through me.

The firing stops.

I look at my hands. My legs.

I'm whole. Unscathed.

The line of Hila soldiers gawk at me like they're watching a shooting star. They inspect their weapons and then gaze back at me, eyes wondrous beneath the Hila beads. "What is happening?" one of them asks Anders, who has no answer for them.

I keep marching, stepping over explosive craters and bullet shell casings. The entire battlefield is quiet as all eyes fall on me. I weave through spiked plinths of wood and barbed wire bordering the encampment and come out onto the open marsh. Anders is there, arms slack, rifle dangling from his loose grasp. I lock my eyes with him.

"There's something I need to ask you," I say to him.

"How are you doing this?" he asks.

"Do you like who you are?" I ask him.

He stiffens at my question and angles his rifle back on me.

"You can change," I tell him.

He doesn't move, doesn't blink.

"You. Anders," I continue. "The man you are right now. You can change. You can be different from what you've done. Do you believe me?"

His eyes narrow on me. "You tell me how you're doing this right now."

"Answer my question," I say.

"I don't know what to believe right now."

"Remove the Hila skin," I say.

Anders chews at the side of his mouth, stalling. "Mason, bind her," he says to the Hila-clad man on his left. The soldier swings his rifle off his shoulder and produces zip ties from his belt. Gingerly, he approaches me... one step... two steps, hands outstretched toward me—a crack of white-hot light zaps the air, leaving ozone in its wake. The man crumples to the ground. All the men step back. "Check him," Anders commands another man but the soldier doesn't move. Instead, he takes off his Hila-beaded helmet. "What are you *doing?*" Anders asks him.

The young man strips off the Hila armor. "Listening to the woman who takes bullets like raindrops and drops men with lightning. I don't know who she is, but I think God does."

I level my eyes at Anders and make my gambit. "This battle is over. Remove the Hila skin." I kneel at the unconscious man, remove his helmet, and check the pulse. He's alive.

As Anders watches the rest of his men obey my words, he removes his helmet and scowls. "How do you manage to outmatch me every time you come into my life?" One by one, the rest of the Hila armor comes off each man and then are stacked neatly in two piles on the ground.

I walk past them toward the rest of Anders' militia. Bullets flare and glance off me in futile sparks. Another barrage sprays over me but none penetrate the invisible barrier of living Hila that now accompany me. Gabriel and those we saved at China Beach go before and after me, hiding in plain sight, protecting me and, at the same time, disarming all men with the most potent weapon that can exist on a battlefield—confusion. I approach a San Diegan soldier who maintains his rifle muzzle on me. His finger twitches on the trigger as if he wants to fire but is afraid of what will happen when I continue to miraculously not die from his bullets. I place a finger on the muzzle and push the weapon toward the ground.

"It's over," I tell him. "Come, follow me." I turn from him and the militia and walk away from them, away from the SF encampment. The man doesn't move. "Don't be afraid and follow me," I yell out to everyone now. But no one moves. And I keep walking, my feet sloshing loudly in the marsh as all eyes watch to see what I will do. I disappear from their view behind a line of trees and keep marching until I find the semi-truck we drove down from SF, brimming with Hila fertilizer. After unlatching the lock and heaving the door up, I lift a bag of the stuff onto my shoulder and turn.

I've been followed.

At least a dozen soldiers watch me in silence. Rafa, Prasad, Ward, and Sabion are at the head of men and walk up the truck ramp, hefting their own bags of fertilizer. "Each man with a bag; let's go," I tell them. The soldiers—some from the SF camp, some from the San Diegans—amble up the ramp and lift a bag for themselves. Rafa begins doling out instructions as more men trickle in. I see Anders at the periphery, watching me. As twilight descends over the next two hours, fertilizer is brought to the mouth of every Hila hole and poured in along with Rafa's mineral concoction.

"I'm going to figure out how you did this," Anders tells me, wiping sweat from his brow.

"Tell your men to take the rest of the fertilizer," I say. "And deliver it to your encampment. We're going to try to save every last one of these visitors and save ourselves at the same time."

Anders sighs, watching his men dutifully following my instructions and completely ignoring him. "Fine," he says, spitting tobacco in the mud.

Hours pass into dawn. Mist burns off the marsh from the rising sun as the last Hila hole we can find is filled with fertilizer. There is an unspoken and inexplicable solidarity in the work as the men look proudly across the marsh. Reece and Hutch are nowhere to be found.

"I think we found them all," Anders tells me.

"No, you haven't," I say.

"We've scoured the area," one of Anders' men says. "Where else do you want us to go?"

I look to the southern sky. "Leave now to San Diego and do the same thing there that we did here. We must save as many dying Hila as possible. And free the young man and woman I sent there."

Anders bristles. "San Diego. Now?"

"Yes," I say. "We don't have much time. But before you leave, put your Hila skin armor in their holes and provide a brief ceremony for them and make an oath that you will never wear them again."

"Yes, ma'am," one of Anders' men says. Anders glares at me, lights a cigarette, and follows his men.

"Why did they finally listen?" Ward asks as we clean our hands at a jug of water. Sabion flushes his tracheostomy with water and blows out muddy sediment. Rafa sits cross-legged in the dirt, a serenity washing through his countenance.

"They're scared," I tell Ward as I redress Prasad's shoulder wound.

Prasad nods and says. "And they think you're a saint or something. Performed a powerful miracle right on the battlefield." He winces as I probe his wound.

"I think we figured out the only way to actually fight the bullshit of men," I say.

"How's that?" Ward asks.

"With the truth—cloaked in power and myth."

Thousands of Hila die.

After inspecting the Hila holes over the next day, we see that nearly thirty percent of them did not get the fertilizer in time. They sit lifeless in their holes while the rest of their kin have apparently healed enough to vanish from sight. We learn from Anders that even more have died in San Diego.

"Have enough survived?" I ask Rafa as he inspects a hole.

"I don't know."

"And are the ones who survived healthy enough to produce the cloaking light emissions?"

"I also do not know," he says.

I sit on an overturned bucket, my hip grinding in its angry socket. "We did all we could. There's nothing more now." I'm blindsided by ugly sobbing that I fail to stifle into the crook of my arm.

Prasad notices and kneels at my feet. "Cry now," he says. "Once you're done, there is one more important thing we need to do."

"What?"

"Attend the first annual Festival of Light."

THIRTY-TWO

WHAT BEGAN as a fledgling gathering has swelled into a festival growing so large, it spills over to the beaches of northern Monterey Bay. Thousands of bodies mingle and weave through improvised kiosks brimming with wares and markets full of produce, nuts, oils, and herbs. Concerts of stringed instruments stud the beach, where I hear haunting tones of baroque one moment and the next a medley of nineties grunge. Vocalists meld their harmonies into a single body, enchanting everyone within earshot. I'm enlivened by the aromas of cooked game, spiced cakes, and fried dough stoking long-lost memories of a time where living in the present was all that there was. The people of the festival have been ground down from the anxiety of survival and the worry of hunger into a sort of classless jubilance at the Festival of Light. They shout, they sing, and they cry. They run into the ocean, hurry through the press of bodies, or drink themselves stupid from the rooftops. I find scores of jugglers, magicians, prophets, glassblowers, farmers, and tattoo artists. Occasional spats and drunken fisticuffs erupt, but the festival is completely void of gun violence and totally absent of the menace of raiding. Not once in my post-apocalyptic years have I witnessed such a concord of people and never a gathering of such proportion outside the safety of colony walls.

Ward can't stop talking about every novelty he lays his eyes on. Sabion appears equally absorbed by the festival, eyes wide and darting across the diversity of people. Rafa has already befriended a woman from the Tijuana border who studies the Hila all over Mexico. The two chat incessantly while Prasad walks alongside me quietly, taking in the festivities. Mavis trails behind us, miserably quiet. We didn't know what to do with her and she didn't know what to do with herself, so she just followed us out from the Hila colony. Our silence was enough consent for her to stay with us.

The wooden spaceship we saw earlier has inspired an even larger spaceship to be erected on the beach, at least five stories tall. Thousands of people descend on the massive construction, piling scavenged wood around the base. Looking down the length of the beach, there are at least three or four similar structures constructed of everything from furniture, car bumpers, street signs, and rebar. There's no one directing, no one planning—just spontaneous construction like Neolithic people building complex monuments without the arbitrary authority of state power. We hear talk about lighting all the pyres along the beach as soon as the heavenly light show begins, expected this very evening. I stifle the worry in my chest, fearing and knowing that there aren't enough Hila alive to cloak the planet and to save us all.

We arrive at the edge of a massive impromptu dance on the beach ringed by various bands of musicians. It's unclear to which concert the people are dancing and also concerning to no one. We line along the edge of the dance floor, squinting in the sunlight, watching the dancing.

"Wait..." Ward says, lifting a finger. "Is that *Reece?*"

"Where?" I say and then I see a flash of his red hair in the crowd. He sees us, looks like he sees a ghost, and vanishes into the crowd.

But then a young girl yanks Ward's hand into the circle, making us forget Reece was ever there. The two move with the disinhibition of very bad dancers who don't care who is watching. Sabion crosses his arms, eyes bobbing over the dancers. He hunches his back, hiding his tracheostomy tube and neck scarring down beneath his collar.

"Here," I tell him. I deflate the pilot balloon of the tracheostomy and remove it from the hole in his neck, prompting a coughing fit. The tube is absolutely filthy. "I don't think you even need it anymore." I button his collar up, hiding the hole and scarring of his neck, and nudge him out onto the dance floor where he finds a partner, a young man who he'd been eyeing. As I admire their dancing, new hope for them and the world they will grow into take root inside of me for the first time since the end of the world. But I fear that there will be no future at all.

And then I hear something.

It sounds like rain, only, the sky is cloudless. It's so imperceptible that I think it's in my head, but then I see confused faces screw up toward the heavens. It intensifies like sheets of rain are lapping over us. The masses of people quiet down to a whisper until someone shouts from a rooftop and points south toward Monterey.

"Come on," I say to my people before weaving through the throng toward the nearest building. We hike up a stairwell, arrive on the fourth floor, and find the roof exit. A few onlookers are perched at the edge of the rooftop, their eyes glued on something in the distance.

340

"What is *that?*" Prasad asks.

I don't know how to answer because I have no idea what I'm looking at. It looks like a flood of black tar winding through the city streets, cresting along buildings and cascading toward the shore. But the tar is not really tar because, as the mass moves, it leaves no residue behind. And it's not really flowing, it's *crawling.* Looking through binoculars, there's a shiny, scintillating texture to the mass. "Those are Hila beads," I say.

"Disembodied," Rafa confirms through binoculars. "It's like the Hila bodies have broken down into their bead parts. They've gone from corporeal to fluid but still made of the same constituent beads."

"Does Gabriel still exist there?" Ward asks, mirroring my concern. The beads continue to move through the streets, the leading edge covering the city, the receding edge leaving the city mostly untouched behind.

"Don't know if that even matters anymore," Rafa says as the beads finally make it to the beach. And then, as quickly as they flooded the city, the billions of beads crawl over the beach, sifting harmlessly between the legs of thousands of spectators, and disappear into the ocean as if they were never there. We stand in silence, as stunned as every person below us watching.

"Rafa, what is happening?" I ask.

"Are they leaving?" Prasad asks.

"I have no idea," Rafa answers, lowering the binoculars. He sits cross-legged on the rooftop and gazes at the pebbly surface in contemplation.

"Have you come here in previous years to watch the lights?" I ask a bystander who sits on the edge of the building, cigarette trembling in her hand.

"This is my fifth year," she says. "I started coming when it was just a dozen of us."

"And have you ever seen this before?" I ask.

"You mean the black sea that came from nowhere and just walked into the ocean? No. First time."

We all stew in miserable confusion, which seems universal as the festivities have come to a complete halt along the beach. After realizing we have nothing better to do, we set up camp on the rooftop and pass around tea and munch on dried parsnips. Others join us, regaling us of their travels to the festival. I nod politely, wholly uninterested in what they have to say as I contemplate the end of my mortality, perched on a rooftop with bitter roots in my mouth.

"Fog," someone says, pointing to the ocean.

Whorls of water vapor wafts over the ocean as the air clings to my lungs. Over the next hour, we're dripping in humidity. As we strip off layers, Rafa sits with a notepad in his hand, pen between lips, thinking. A commotion at the beach draws our attention as we see swimmers flopping out of the ocean in a hurry. After hearing complaints of the water suddenly turning as hot as a jacuzzi, I bring binoculars to my eyes and watch as steam continues to rise into the atmosphere.

"Oh my god," Rafa says, watching through binoculars. "It's a whale." I see the enormous underbelly of the animal bob to the surface, followed by several other whales. Sea lions and a great multitude of fish also rise to the surface, none of them moving. And then great bubbles belch along the entire surface of the Bay as far as we can see, agitating scores of underwater detritus that have surfaced. "And now the ocean is boiling," Rafa says amidst cries along the beach. The fear in his face mirrors my own—that the Hila never came here to save us. They are here for nefarious reasons, just like every other creature in the universe, and that we are about to die at their hand.

As visibility plummets, my heart hammers in my chest. I can

barely make out my hand in front of my face as we are walled off with fog that saturates everything we see. We huddle together on the rooftop, feeling for one another as if we're blind. A fire is started, which just scatters light throughout the fog, feeding the air with a haunting glow that stokes more fear rather than dispelling it. After the fire is extinguished, we sit with one another, speaking little because there is little to say. As night descends, we hear weeping and screaming—great howlings borne from confusion and despair. No moonlight, no flashlight, no firelight penetrates the fog. In moments of despair, my mind circles back to my unborn child, to my husband who should have been mine. But my circle of grief now includes those around me who I love as dearly as I've ever loved anyone.

The black pitch becomes so oppressive, I forget where my body ends and my soul begins, or if either even exist anymore. I become inanimate, my flesh turning to the stone of the earth— motionless and indifferent. There is no fear anymore, no hunger or concern. As we sit at the edge of the world, I'm pacified by the doom. It is not serene—it is not painful. It is simply nothing.

And it is more than I could ever ask for.

Dawn light creeps into my eyelids. As I awaken, I can see our sad little rooftop camp. The boys are asleep, Ward's back curled against Sabion's legs. Rafa and Prasad snore loudly while Mavis, already awoken, gazes out to the west. The ocean, no longer boiling, moves with the same morning tide that has ruled the shore for an eon. There is a thin strip of blue sky at the horizon, but the rest of the sky looks as if an enormous cotton swab has gotten stuck up there. The morning sun peeks just beneath the mass of water vapor that spans almost the entirety of the heavens, casting an upside-down sunset of flaming red across the underside of the cloud mass. The clang of cookware and chitchat of a farmer's market break along the beach as the masses emerge from the nightmares of the foggy night.

And then there is light.

There is nothing *but* light.

I've never experienced the color yellow until my gaze fell upon the Pacific Ocean at that moment. The murky blue now glows golden. The waves crash and roll as if made of yellow light edged with flaming red. I don't know if it looks more like heaven or hell, and I wouldn't be surprised if we were in either place. The firmament is a blanket of crimson as if the cloud cover has been soaked in blood. And then, on apocalyptic cue, the heavens swirl with vortices and eddies, rippling throughout the sky as the puny humans drop to their knees, anticipating the ax of a great and terrible god to cleave their souls from their indolent lives.

No gods come.

But the sky continues its hellfire.

"It's the predator race, isn't it?" Ward asks.

I don't have anything close to an answer. And then an hour passes and nothing changes. The vista all around us is a rainbow consisting of the light brown sandy beach, yellow ocean, a thin strip of blue sky on the horizon, and the torrential mass of vermillion clouds, turbulent across the sky. Mostly out of boredom, the tension eases and people get back to acting like people because, despite the apparent end of the world happening above our heads, humans still need to eat, gossip, cough, and find a place to pee. It's like we all just got off a weird carnival horror ride and are milling about looking for funnel cake, but the ride is still running in the background.

Our radio crackles with a voice. "Doctor Darrow?"

I lift the receiver to my mouth. "Anders?"

"We're pretty spooked down here," he says with a humility I've never heard in him.

"What's going on?"

"Uh, the Book of Revelations."

"I know what you mean," I say.

"The Hila turned into a damned black flood of locusts and emptied into the San Diego Bay and—"

"I know the rest. The same thing is happening here."

"What does it mean?" he asks.

Rafa finally stands and slaps his notebook on the rooftop. "Remember when we tried lighting a fire last night?"

"Yeah," we all answer.

"It made visibility worse, right? That's because all the air particulates scattered the light." He pauses, waiting for our excitement to mirror his own.

"Rafa, if you have something to say, now is not the time to be coy. What in the hell is going on?" I say.

"The Hila didn't have enough numbers for their typical light emissions to cloak the planet. So, they broke into their constituent parts to expose their beads to as much surface area as possible, ran into the ocean, boiled it to release a gazillion tons of water vapor into the air, and now they're collectively shooting a laser from the bottom of the ocean, through the dense clouds, scattering the cloaking light to envelope Earth's shadow as it passes in front of the sun so the predator race probe can't see us." He finishes, having said the whole thing in one breath. "If they hadn't shot the light through water vapor, the cloak would have probably been too narrow and we would have been detected and destroyed."

"So, we're not doomed?" I ask.

"Not at the moment."

"So, what do we do now? Just wait and see?" Ward asks.

"I'll tell you what we do now," Rafa says and then yells out to the crowds below. "We party!" He's answered by welcomed cheers, which quickly gets the music going. The rooftops empty and the host of humanity floods the beaches. Music blares and stove tops simmer as kegs are tapped and drinks start flowing. They celebrate for the highest reason creatures have to celebrate— they're not yet dead. For that one afternoon, thousands embrace the elusive peace of the present where worries for the future don't exist yet and the regrets of the past no longer matter.

But I stay on that rooftop, unable to find their jubilation.

"What's wrong?" Prasad asks me.

"Why can't I be down there with them?"

"What do you mean?" he asks.

"What's wrong with me?"

"Nothing's wrong with you."

I close my eyes. "Yes... there is."

"What do you mean?"

"So many things," I say. I don't tell him the truth. That grief has taken up rent in my heart and has been there ever since I lost my baby in the bunker and found out my husband wasn't coming back. I let it shatter me. I thought by helping everyone, running a hospital and caring for patients, that it would heal me over. But ignoring trauma doesn't heal, it only conceals, even for twenty years. And I'm more lost than I've ever been. I crouch and pick up my pack, heading to the rooftop door. I want to flee the alien landscape of suffocating happiness.

"Where are you going?" Prasad asks.

"Back to the only place that helped me forget that I'm broken."

I drive north, alone and along the beach highway. Almost, I stop to sit and watch the waves beneath the alien sky but I'm afraid I'll stay there forever. So, I drive, my breath like a metronome, anchoring me to the present. I stop at the side of the road where I find the unmistakable red pick-up of Mayor Hutch. When I see a trail of smoke trailing from the truck, I fear the man has killed himself in an accident, but then I see a small campfire with two men huddled there.

Hutch turns at my approach, wincing at the pain in his neck. "I thought that was you," he says, gazing back at the fire crackling with a roasting chicken dangling over the flames.

Across from him sits his head scoutmaster, Zeke Plinth, gnawing a chicken leg. Plinth shakes the bone at me. "Should lock her up again for treason," he says before devouring another bite.

Without a word, I kneel at the mayor's side and remove a dirty rag he has at his neck. The wound is surprisingly clean. "You'll live," I tell him. "But I'll need to take another look at the wound in the operating room when we get back." He only nods and gazes at the red sunset. I sit on a rock next to the two men and bring my hands together in my lap. "Jack, where's your son?" I ask Hutch.

Hutch doesn't look at me and says, "He left."

"Where?" I ask. "And why?" The mayor's face is red, either from drinking or grief. Probably both.

"The battle broke him," Plinth says. "The boy couldn't handle the stress. Went down to the beach to dance with the heathens."

"This coming from the coward who magically showed up late for the entire battle?" Hutch asks Plinth. He then gestures to the sky. "Did you break the world, Elspeth?"

"Can't break what's already broken," I say and stand, the chicken meat aroma flaring hunger pangs. Without protest from the men, I take some meat from the fire pit and eat in silence with them. With my belly full, I lay a sleeping bag down next to the fire and gaze up at the swollen sky, light draining into the horizon as my eyelids become heavy.

In the middle of the night, the warmth of glowing Hila beads in my palm awakens me. Gabriel is there, back in corporeal form, standing beside me. The soft embers from the fire dance light across his black beads before he flickers bright across his body, which coalesces into a refined image.

It's me.

A much younger me. Probably only a few months after hatching from the bunkers. I'm doing chest compressions on a young man in the east wing. The images flicker once more to me on a different day, putting in a breathing tube. The light hiccups once more of me, a little older, placing a cast on a broken arm of an elderly gentleman. Another hiccup, another me, putting in an IV, talking to a patient or washing out a wound. And then Gabriel shows me seated next to a patient with a breathing tube. My team of east wing nurses and I are working on keeping the patient alive, but then movement slows, and the nurses leave us alone. I let go of the ventilator bag and seat myself next to the patient—an older woman with dark hair that I don't remember at all. Some poor soul who never made it. I take the patient's hand in mine and wait with her until the vitals go flat and she dies. The vision ends and Gabriel's warm grasp wraps around my hand once more.

And then he's gone.

Hutch stirs in his sleep and awakens. "Did you see something?" he asks.

"No. But they did."

"What do you mean?"

"Just go back to sleep," I say, closing my eyes once more.

THIRTY-THREE

THREE MONTHS LATER, I'm crouched at a patient's bed in the east wing, my needle hovering over a patient's vein.

"Doctor Darrow?" I hear behind me.

I flinch, blowing the patient's IV. "Dammit, Sabion," I say. "Don't creep up on me like that. What is it?"

"The patient admitted yesterday with heart failure. She looks bad," he says in a hoarse voice.

"Bad how?"

"Come and see."

We move briskly along the ward beds and stop where a crowd of nurses are huddled around a patient, collective anxiety growing by the second. The patient arrived yesterday, short of breath and with ankles ballooned like marshmallows. She grips the bed sheets, breathing heavily and complaining of crushing chest pain.

Ward steps through the crowd of nurses. "Someone get an EKG in here," he says. Nurse Patience rolls in the EKG machine and places electrical leads to the patient's chest like she's hooking up to jump-start a car battery. The electrical activity of the patient's heart prints out from the machine. Patience rips the print off and hands it to Ward while I watch from the corner.

"She's having ST segment elevations," Ward says. "Get some oxygen on her and have her crunch an aspirin. Nadine, what do we have for pain control?"

"All we have in stock right now is heroin."

"Give it."

And then the patient's heart tracing on the monitor goes saw-toothed and her breathing degenerates into gasping. "V tach!" Ward yells. "Get some pads on her." The nurses slap defibrillator pads on the patient's chest. "She still has a blood pressure, so let's hold off on chest compressions or defibrillation, but be ready. Push some lidocaine if we have it."

"I just had some new powder compounded last week," Nadine says as she reconstitutes the medication. "Nice having trading lanes opened back up." She gives the medication and the patient goes back into a stable heart rhythm. She is also noticeably more comfortable with heroin now flooding her veins.

I place my hand on Ward's shoulder and whisper in his ear. He nods and then unfolds a chair next to the patient's bed, seats himself beside her, and takes her hand. "Florence, what would you be doing right now if you weren't in the hospital?" he asks.

"Gardening," she says with eyes closed.

"What kind of crops?"

"Not produce—no, no, no. Life isn't just about survival. I have a little spot with mostly peonies—my favorite. Been showing my grandson how to grow them. I'd be doing that right now."

"Where is your grandson now?" he asks.

She motions to the family waiting area.

"Can we have him brought in?" Ward asks the nurses, who promptly lead a young man to the patient's bed. "Florence," Ward says to the patient. "You're going to die."

"I know."

"You've suffered a very large heart attack. There is nothing more we can do about it and any further efforts to save your life will just make you suffer."

"When will it happen?" she asks.

"In minutes to hours."

She nods as her grandson collapses into the bed, head buried in her lap, sobs dampened by the bed sheets.

"We will keep you comfortable with pain medications and I will personally ensure that you do not suffer," Ward says.

"Thank you," she says.

"Can we bring you a peony from your garden?"

"I would like that very much."

"Would you like any music?" he asks.

"Zeppelin."

"Good choice."

"That right there," I whisper to Sabion, my newest medical student, "is how you practice medicine. I only wish I had learned it at the same age that Ward has."

"Elspeth?" I hear from the doorway. Mayor Hutch stands there, wicker hat in hand.

"What can I do for you, Mayor?"

"Can we speak in my office?" he asks.

"After you."

I follow Hutch up to his office where he sits at his desk, the Seal of California spanning the wood beneath the glass top. He runs his hand over the surface, looking at his own reflection.

"Going to miss that desk?" I ask.

"Would be lying if I said I won't."

"I'd be lying if I said I was going to miss you sitting there. You've been a god-awful mayor and I'm thrilled to see you go."

"I wanted to thank you for saving my life," he says, ignoring the insults.

"My pleasure." I move to the doorway. "Is that why you brought me up here?"

"How would you like to receive payment?"

"Payment for saving your life?"

He nods.

I sigh at the man and pinch the bridge of my nose. "Not everything is a quid pro quo."

"Even still, I insist," he says.

"You don't owe me anything," I say. "Please, for once, just accept that someone can do something for someone without expecting anything in return."

He licks his lips. "I'd be happy to render my services available to you for the incoming administration. I could act as a consultant or even a business liaison. I have considerable ties."

I bring my palm to my forehead, flabbergasted by the man. "You have the uncanny ability to hear only what you want to hear. And I have nothing to do with the mayor-elect and I will never sit on the council again."

He leans back in his creaky chair. "You had nothing to do with Prasad getting elected?"

I shake my head. "He was elected by the people of Neo SF. He's in—you're out."

"And you don't think your light show in Monterey completely changed the game?" he asks. "All the returning SF soldiers believe you were sent by God. And everyone knows Prasad was traveling with you when you returned from Monterey. You act aloof but you're smart enough to know you're now the most powerful person in this colony. The people know a vote for Prasad is a vote for Saint Elspeth. You single-handedly changed the political landscape."

"You're afraid I'm going to throw you imprison, aren't you?" I ask.

"Yes."

"Unlike you, I don't just put people imprison who I don't like."

He brings his index fingers together and says, "As a professional courtesy, I wanted to let you know I will be announcing my candidacy during the next election cycle. Someone needs to protect this colony from the threats outside our walls and I have no faith in your man, Prasad."

"You know you can't do that," I say. "Colony charter dictates a two-term mayoral limit."

"It did," he says as a smile creeps up his face.

"What did you do?" I ask, dread rising in my belly.

He taps his fingers along the desk. "The charter has been ratified to expand the term limits."

"When?" I ask. "And how?"

"Yesterday. I won't bore you with the details, but I want to assure you it is now set in stone by the judiciary review committee."

"A committee that you spent the last two years packing?" I say.

"I don't know what you mean," he says, lifting a mug of coffee to his lips.

I shake my head once again, underestimating the treachery of the man. I get up to leave, reaching new levels of disgust.

"After all we've been through, you've got nothing else to say to me, Elspeth? I protected your hospital all these years."

"Okay, I've got an offer for you," I say, turning back to him. "A question. And if you can answer it, I'll make sure you sit on Prasad's council. Hell, I'll even endorse you when you run for office again."

"Are you serious?" His eyes dance with new possibilities.

"Very."

"What's the question?" he asks.

"Right now," I say, pointing my finger into his desk, "this very moment, I want you to tell me where your baby granddaughter is."

He harrumphs and thumps his fist on the desk. "What kind of question is that?"

"The only question that could possibly matter."

He throws his hands up in surrender. "What do I look like, a nursemaid?"

"Do you know if Reece has any interest in raising his child?"

He shakes his head. "I doubt that very much. I received a letter from him yesterday. The idiot boy has joined some anarchist commune in Oregon." He sighs. "I have no idea where I went wrong with him."

"I do." I turn to leave. "Good luck with your political scheming, but I do think you should pick up another hobby, Mayor. You'll live longer. Maybe gardening?"

"Too boring."

I walk out of his office and yell down the hallway. "Come and see me in about a month. I'll need to check your prostate."

Rafa radios over to me that he needs to talk in person. When I arrive at his compound, I'm greeted by an ostrich. "Where do you keep getting these animals?" I ask after passing through his secret-grotto-frog-plague entrance.

"They just come to me."

"After you find them and feed them. Why did you need me to come running over here?"

He leads me into his basement lair, where he's been working with an anthropologist from Mexico, Consuela Jacinto, a woman who has lived on the Baja peninsula since the Hila first showed up. She looms before a sprawled map of North and South America where dozens of thumb tacks litter its surface.

"Are these all their colonies?" I ask.

"Yes," Rafa says. "Some are confirmed, most are theoretical. There are probably nearly thirty Hila colonies in North and South America where annual laser emissions occur. Consuela has helped me work out the rest of the math and we believe over a hundred sites are needed around the globe to maximize emission overlap and provide continuous cloaking as Earth revolves around the sun. This estimate is predicated on the assumption that there is more than one predator race deep space probes looking for Earth."

"Do you think that if any one colony dies off, it could expose Earth?" I ask.

"The Hila seem to think so," Consuela says. "We certainly don't want to find out. The predator race very likely knows there is intelligent life in our neighborhood. A single dip of light in front of our sun and they may strike. Each colony must be protected with ensured nutrition going forward."

"I agree there. What do you propose?"

"A global Hila foundation with open communication," Rafa answers. "We've recently been in contact with a group in China."

"China? We've never heard of survivors in that part of the world. Most of it was bombed."

"Just because you haven't heard from them, doesn't mean they're not there," Consuela says.

"There's a group there doing Hila gene sequencing," Rafa says.

"You're kidding me. What have they found?" I ask.

"Despite being a DNA-based organism, it doesn't look like they have any genetic ancestry with humans."

"The Earth-origin theory is basically debunked at this point," Consuela adds. "There are new and troubling theories about why the Hila are here." She shares a glance with Rafa.

"Like what?" I ask.

"The explanations are legion," Mavis says, emerging from upstairs.

"What are *you* doing here?" I ask Mavis. "You're supposed to be on house arrest. Rafa, why did you let her come over here?"

"We need people," he says.

"Don't worry," Mavis says. "I'll get back to pretend jail soon."

I shake my head. "That pretend jail was the only thing keeping you from Hutch and a public hanging."

"Which wouldn't have even been an issue if you'd just let the son of a bitch bleed to death," Mavis says.

"Don't start this with me again. You need to stay home until Prasad gets the judiciary reformed where you will have a proper trial. You're not just going to get away with murdering someone in front of everyone."

"Regardless," Rafa interrupts. "We need to be aware that the Hila may not be the selfless saviors that we think they are."

"Then tell me why they are here," I say.

"I believe they are not truly terrestrial creatures," Consuela says. "They never have been. These are creatures whose genesis and evolution occurred in space—maybe even asteroidal. Everything about their biology and physiology suggests this is the case. However, they clearly require organic and inorganic material to live, neither of which exactly exist in abundance in space. It is still possible that they are entirely synthetic organisms, manufactured somewhere, and don't even have sentience. At any rate, they clearly have terrestrial stages of their life cycle. For a species like this to survive so long, they also developed the natural ability to evade enemies that can act on an interstellar scale. We currently have a mutually beneficial relationship with the Hila wherein they hide our planet from predators and we ensure their nutritional survival. This works well. For the time being."

"What are you trying to say?" I ask.

Consuela continues, "It's become clear that they must make the occasional planetary pit stop, say every few hundred or thousand years to regenerate and gather materials. These pit stops likely last for many years. And even more, they may come in stages —an initial invasion, which then secures an environment foothold, which clears the path for more of their kind to follow. It's possible we are still in the initial stages and there are more to come. The symbiotic relationship we share with them may turn into something else."

"What?"

"Parasitic," Mavis says.

"You really think that's what's going on?" I ask.

"Why else would they just appear for all the world to see and wait for us to annihilate one another out of total panic?" Mavis says. "They orchestrated their landing in every major world power who had nuclear power and bet on us destroying one another in a mad panic to rid the world of the invaders. They played us against one another and it killed off almost the entire human race, readying the planet for their colonization."

"And it's a reasonable conclusion," Consuela continues, "that the Hila consume all resources on a planet before they go interstellar again, a stage that probably lasts centuries or even millions of years. They forage and consume and probably destroy their host planet in the process. For all we know, someone else made them and sent them here to harvest the planet. But we have the benefit of having studied their biochemistry. We are already at a considerable advantage if more Hila were to show up..."

I groan.

"What? Rafa says.

"It's only been a few months since the Hila literally saved the planet and you're talking about biological warfare against them? How does this make you any different from Hutch and the other warlord mayors who wanted to slaughter them?"

"Please don't make false equivalencies," Consuela says with irritation rising in her voice. "We just need to consider all possibilities," she says with a non-zero amount of condescension. "The most logical is that they are here for non-altruistic reasons."

"You can't possibly see any other motivation why they might be here?" I ask.

The three look at one another as if I've said something quite dumb. "Of course we can," Rafa says. "But this is the most logical conclusion to make and the safest for us given that the stakes are so high."

"Logic based on about ten thousand assumptions," I say. "You're using human logic to try to figure out non-human creatures. You're applying zero-sum game logic against creatures that have not given us any reason to believe they think the same way. Don't you see anything wrong with that? And how does this fit in with your cosmic faith about the universe?" I ask Rafa.

He doesn't have an answer for me.

"Next time you want to base a plan on some lazy faith-in-the-cosmos you cobbled together from tripping out on a beach somewhere, please let me know."

"I can see you're angry right now," Rafa says like he's talking to a five-year-old.

I get to my feet. "I'm retiring."

"Retiring from what?" he asks.

"The hospital. All of this." I wave my hands at them. "The politicking, the war games—the ridiculous sainthood. All of it. Go and set up your Hila foundation. Try to keep everyone alive, including the Hila. I can't do this anymore. And *you*," I say, pointing to Mavis. "Go back to jail and stop scheming with these two."

"But we need you," Rafa says. "The Hila chose you to communicate with the most. They trust you. You're a vital piece of intelligence."

"I haven't heard from Gabriel since Monterey. You'll manage without me."

"What *else* are you going to do?" Mavis asks, clearly intending it as an insult.

"I have things I need to work on."

"Something more important than the survival of our planet?" Consuela asks.

I think of the peaceful death of the patient just a few hours before. She was ready for the end in a way I've never been. I turn from them and walk to the doorway. "Surviving is not living, and I've been surviving for far too long."

THIRTY-FOUR

LATER THAT AFTERNOON, I enter the east wing where most of my staff are milling about in the foyer. Max, Patience, Nadine, and Tara, along with my burgeoning class of medical students, Ward, Sabion, and Geddes. "Good, you're all here," I tell them. "I've got an announcement to make."

"Oh," Ward says. "We kind of had an announcement for you."

I eye him. "I think I'll go first."

"Um..." He looks at everyone else as if trying to improvise on some sort of premeditated plan.

"I'm retiring," I basically shout at them.

"*What?*" Max says.

"I love you all." I'm embarrassed to say it in front of them all but figure that if I sugar-coat it as much as possible, they'll let me go with less of a fight. "You're the most honorable people I've ever worked with. But I'm done. Ward, you can handle it from here. Train anyone else who comes along and wants to help. You'll do fine."

Everyone looks at one another in stunned silence.

"I can't keep doing this my entire life. Don't you understand that?" I ask them.

"We do, we do," Max says. "There is just a surprise we were going to show you and this kind of changes things..."

"What surprise?"

"Uh..." Sabion looks at Ward.

"What surprise?" I ask again.

"What's done is done. Let's just go and show her," Ward says before spinning around and marching off. The crowd follows with me in tow where they huddle around an old classroom. The crowd parts for me where Sabion and Ward wait at the classroom door, expectantly.

"What's the surprise?" I ask.

Ward nods to the wall outside the classroom where a sign has been placed, fashioned from slate stone and etched with the words:

Doctor Darrow School of Medicine

"You founded a medical school?" I say to Ward and then I look to Sabion. "In my name?" And then I stare daggers at Max and Patience. "Without telling me?" Finally, I wheel around and narrow my eyes on Nadine and Tara. "And you thought this would be a great surprise for me?"

No one says anything for a moment and then Ward says, "We already filled the first class." He looks at the closed door.

"Bullshit," I say and turn the knob to see two dozen students looking up at me, stupid silly grins on their faces like they're ready to throw a surprise birthday party. Nika Horvat is in the front row. I slam the door on them. "I'm retiring," I say.

"Okay," Ward says.

"I'm done."

"You said that," Geddes says.

I bow my head, take a breath, and then open the classroom door. "Two hours of class, five days a week," I tell the students. "And then five hours of clinical exposure a day. You will do the reading or you'll be expelled. Is that understood? I'm too old and tired for bullshit from any of you. Are we clear?" They all sit up straight, confused smiles melting off their faces. I can almost smell the regret. "Open your notebooks. First class starts right now. Topic: Hila nutrition. Let's go."

I pick up a piece of chalk.

The next morning, I shrug on a jacket and make my way down to the Embarcadero, the January sky remarkably clear. The markets stir with shutters opening and the clopping of horse hooves dragging wagons full of the morning's produce. My moving presence causes a rippling of whispers through the market. Some are scandalized at the heretical Hila cult leader while others admire the woman who created a new social movement at Monterey Beach during the Festival of Lights. Not only am I none of these things, but the real reason for the light festival and the Hila remain largely unclear despite the multiple publications that I'd circulated about the purpose of our visitors. Some simply don't understand the words, some wildly misinterpret, and others overthink it, believing I'm making a fictional critique about colony politics. Even in the plainest language I can muster, I've utterly failed to convince the public about the reality of Earth's extremely precarious existence.

A tall, hooded figure watches my approach on the sidewalk as I near the wharf. The person moves aside for me and then says, "Doctor Darrow," from beneath the hood. It's a whisper, but I know the voice.

"Anders?" I say, lifting the hood from his head. He grabs my forearm and leads me into an alleyway. "How did you get into the colony? Hutch has a warrant for your arrest."

He finally lifts the hood. A few months' growth of a gray beard graces his face. "I figured out how you did it," he says, lifting a folded pamphlet. "It drove me crazy, but I figured it out. You're no *saint*. You had the Hila walking around you so the bullets couldn't hurt you." He opens the pamphlet and says, "You don't come right out and say it in your explanation of the Hila, but I put it together. They can completely cloak themselves, right? Go totally invisible?" He stares at me with either anger or sadness, I have no idea.

"Yes," I say with growing anxiety.

"This whole time they've just been... watching us?"

"Yes."

His breath staggers. "They could've just slit our throats in our sleep and we never would have known." He gazes at the brick wall for a moment and then locks eyes with me. "This whole time they've been watching me? They know everything I've done?"

"Maybe..." I say.

"They may know what *all* of us have been doing since they got here?"

"It's hard to know how much they've been watching us, but I know they've been observing me ever since I came out of the bunkers."

"And after seeing what we do to each other, they *still* want to save us from some other predator race?"

"Yes. They do."

He laughs. "Glad they were watching you, Doc. They probably would've let this place burn if it wasn't for you. I've been having these weird dreams about them."

I slowly nod. "Tell me about it."

"Just dreams about them dying in their holes. And then there's this cat and mouse. I don't know, it's strange. I've never had repeating dreams like that. It's scrambling my brain," he says, touching his temple.

"Interesting."

He takes a deep breath and pulls something from his jacket. I panic for a moment, believing the man wants to finally put the bullet in my head we had so much fun joking about. But it's not a gun in his hand, it's an asthma inhaler. "Here," he says.

"What's this?"

"From the boy. The one who died in San Jose. His name was Levi. He had terrible asthma. I packed a few extra inhalers for him that he never had to use after... what happened. I figure you could use them at your hospital to help someone else. I have a few more in my pack." He pauses for a moment, swallowing. "Levi didn't even want to come on the expedition. Me and his dad talked him into it—"

I take the inhaler. "Thank you."

He sniffs. "I want to help."

"Help with what?"

"With your hospital. Help the Hilamen out. I can get you medical supplies. Fertilizer. Whatever you ask."

"Why?" I ask.

"Why have you worked in your hospital all these years?"

"It's complicated. The hospital helps me cope with my problems."

He shrugs. "If that's a good enough answer for you, it's good enough for me. Look, I've done some bad in my life. I'm just walking in a fog. I need something..."

"I don't know if you'll find anything with me," I say. "Your life won't suddenly change."

"I know that, Doc. I just need to try," he says, eyes pleading.

"Okay." I nod. "You can come and try with me."

. . .

The bell on Prasad's shop door rings as I step in. I find Prasad sitting at his counter, reading an old manual written twenty years ago in the bunkers. "Mr. Mayor Elect," I say. "Did you have anything to do with a commission for engraving a sign for a new medical school?"

Prasad looks up from the book, arm still in a sling. "Medical school? I have no idea what you're talking about."

I roll my eyes. "A heads-up would have been nice. I announced my retirement moments before teaching my first class."

He stifles a laugh. "I thought your retirement plan was keeling over onto a patient during rounds."

I shake my head. "I'll teach but I'm done with the rest. My best years are gone. I cannot keep showing up there doing the same thing until I die."

"I support you," he says.

"And I'm not going to be on your mayoral council."

"I support that, too."

"I—thank you. But I do have one favor to ask when you take office."

"What's that?" he asks.

"Pardon Anders."

"The man who waged war on our colony?" he asks.

"Yeah, that guy."

"Okay."

"Just like that?" I ask.

"Just like that. I've learned to not question you."

"Thank you," I say. "Everyone else has been complaining so much to me, I expected the same from you."

"I'm saddened that supporting your decisions surprises you more than a boiling ocean."

"It's been a difficult pair of decades for me," I say, leaning over

365

his counter.

"Sounds like your best years are actually ahead of you then."

"Only if I do things different," I say.

"Different how?"

"Still deciding that." I look out his shop window at the ocean waves undulating across the Bay. "Gabriel visited me the night after the light emission. He showed me with my patients over the last twenty years in the east wing. He—or the Hila collective—had been watching me the whole time."

"Hmm."

"Why would he show me that?" I turn and ask him. "Most people, including Rafa's braintrust, think they're here because of the zero-sum calculus of the universe. Mavis says they're imperialists. When they got here, my husband thought they came because they were afraid of something. But they don't seem afraid to me. In fact, I don't think I've ever observed a creature so fearless in all my life. What do you think?"

"My opinion doesn't mean much," he says through a timid smile.

"It means something to me," I almost whisper, meeting his gaze.

"They're *here*, aren't they?"

"Meaning what?"

He sits on his stool. "My mother was a schoolteacher and woke up very early in the morning to teach. My father was a self-employed lawyer who could have woken up any time he wished. Instead, for twenty years, he woke up every morning to drive my mother to her school while she applied makeup in the car to save her time. He sacrificed his time and energy to be with her for that one moment for over twenty years. He was *there*. And more importantly, he was there when he didn't have to be."

"So, they have some sort of duty to rescue other intelligent life?" I ask.

"My father wasn't just duty-bound. The Hila came here themselves. When those terrible men at Monterey tried to tear them from their holes, what did the Hila do?"

I say nothing, thinking the question rhetorical.

"What did they *do*?" he repeats.

"Nothing. The Hila didn't do anything."

"They did *nothing*. They came here themselves, asked nothing of us, saved us from destruction, and offered no resistance to our violence. They do nothing to us and ask nothing of us. There is only one explanation for why a creature would have that kind of patience and suffering."

"Which is?"

"Servitude," he says.

"Servitude to whom?"

"That is the right question to be asking. They are either doing the bidding of something more powerful or..." he trails off with embarrassment.

"Or what?"

"They serve us because... they love us." He winces as if expecting immediate mockery.

I'm quiet for a moment, thinking about his words. "Is that what you believe?"

He runs his hands through his dark hair and laughs. "Depends on the kind of day I'm having. But for me, it's the explanation that is the loveliest to believe. It takes the dreariness of the universe and turns it into a belief that is joyful to my soul. And with that joy, inspiration and actions follow and those things *are* real to me, even if my belief is not. Does that make any sense?"

"It does, actually."

"Gabriel doesn't know how to talk. He doesn't know written

language. He came and showed you with all of your patients in the past to communicate something to you."

"What do you think he was trying to say?" I ask.

"He's sharing his people's mutual values with you. I think he—they—are trying to tell you that they see you. By showing you one of the highest acts of selflessness—caring for the sick and dying. They saw it in you all these years, which is why they trusted you to help them. And now they're mirroring it back and communicating across millions of years of evolution to say one thing... we see you, we know you, and we are the same as you. Rafa talks about how the universe is just one big dark forest where competition, scarcity, and greed are the rule of law. But what about the soil of that dark forest?"

"What soil?" I ask.

"The entire existence of that dark forest is dependent on the ecosystem of the soil itself—an open collective of nutrients, minerals, water, air, and structural support for anything to grow. The soil is a communal cycle of life, growth, and death where all partake and all contribute. It's the hunters in the forest above that see the illusion of scarcity. But the hunters are blind. The Hila aren't the hunters in the trees, waiting to pounce on their enemy. They are the ground beneath the hunter's feet—benign, unseen, forgotten, and yet supporting the entire forest, including the hunters themselves. The Hila are the soil of Earth. And so are you. And now, under your tutelage, so is Ward and hopefully many more."

I say nothing and look down at my hands.

"I'm sorry, I'm lecturing and have offended you," he says.

"No, I'm not offended," I say, looking back at him. "It's a beautiful metaphor. I just don't know what to believe."

"Who do you *want* to believe?" he asks.

"I want to believe like you do," I say, with something pretty and frail blooming in my heart.

"Belief is a choice. And what we choose to believe is what colors our reality. Choose wisely, Saint Elspeth."

"Do *not* call me that," I say. And then I smile. And then I laugh for the first time in twenty years.

"I didn't ask what you're going to do after retirement," he says, breaking the silence.

I lean back from the counter, clearing my throat. "I have plans."

"I would love to hear about them someday when you are ready to share."

"Why don't I tell you about it over coffee? We can look at the Bay," I say.

"But you've already seen the Bay."

I open the door. "I might enjoy looking at it with someone else for a change."

I sit at a bay window, watching people walk across Civic Center Plaza. Two couples chat and share stew at a communal fire pit. A group of women pull a cart full of cabbage on their way to the wharf. Three children re-draw hopscotch lines, readying for a game. Two men smoke cigarettes on a bench and throw sunflower seeds at crows. None of them have any idea of the millions of years of alien evolution that protects their little lives from being obliterated into the cosmos. None of them think of the never-ending loop of humanity between peaceful unrest and violent contentment. As many centuries as humankind wheels around, we always end up in the same spot. Whether we all deserve another go at it or not, the Hila seem to believe we are worth it. Because they trust me, I will trust them. And because they believe in us, I will believe in them.

"Doctor Darrow?" Patience says from the doorway, a bundle in the crook of her arm. "She just finished feeding. I see more Priscilla than Reece," she says. I look into the infant's brown eyes and see an entire universe there. There are worlds of possibilities within her—another round of the cycle of men. But it can be a new cycle in which belief breeds trust, which sparks action. "Have you picked out a name?" Patience asks. "We've been calling her baby Hutch—"

"Her name is Charity," I say, bringing my baby into my arms. "Charity Darrow."

REVIEWS MATTER!

Books can't go anywhere without reviews. If you enjoyed *Saint Elspeth*, please leave a review on Amazon, Goodreads or wherever you spend time on social media. I read a ton of fiction and non-fiction and make sure to leave a review for every book. I read every review written for my books and respond to reader feedback. Feel free to follow me on Goodreads or Twitter. Thank you!

ACKNOWLEDGMENTS

Most elements of this book fell into my brain one day while I was taking a jog through Golden Gate park so my gratitude first goes to the amazing and beautiful city of San Francisco. Thank you to University of California San Francisco where I not only did some of my own medical training but for letting my characters walk through your post apocalyptic hallways.

There were some strong influences to this book, one of the most obvious is Liu Cixin's phenomenal *The Dark Forest*. I was genuinely creeped out about the implications of alien life in the galaxy after reading that book because it very well could be true. In a way *Saint Elspeth* is my answer, my coping mechanism, to the pessimism of that series. Another big influence was Andy Weir's *Hail Mary*. The astrobiology of that book rocked my world and I wanted to do something similar. I dreamed up a lot of the post-apocalyptic imagery while playing the video game *Last of Us* 2. So, that amazing game deserves some credit.

During my research for this book, the planet cloaking idea came directly from a paper by David M. Kipping (David M.

Kipping, Alex Teachey, A cloaking device for transiting planets, *Monthly Notices of the Royal Astronomical Society*, Volume 459, Issue 2, 21 June 2016, Pages 1233–1241) which I suggest you look at if you have the time. I did quite a bit of outsourcing for ideas particularly about alien astrobiology, pathology and biochemistry from polls and videos on Twitter and Tiktok and got tons of ideas back so I'm hugely grateful for everyone that helped in my social media community. In particular was some advice from a pathologist friend on Tiktok @corpusmedicus. My good friend and former band mate Brian Shelby (who used to wake me up on early Saturday mornings to write lyrics to heavy metal ballads) helped with some material engineer questions. My friend DC Allen has been supporting me ever since I was writing bad zombie novels. Thank you to my beta readers: Nikke B, Amanda R, Dimitra, Mason Monteith, Bree, Monica M, Sarah Mae W, J. Flowers and Danny Decillis. Thanks again to my editor Laura Wilkinson.

Thank you to my wife who has supported my writing since day one and knows how important it is to me. Her suggestion about bringing a rosary into a scene completely changed the direction and tone of the entire project while I was writing. Thank you to my daughter for being the greatest source of joy in my life. Lastly, thank you to every single person who has ever read one of my books. Time is so precious and it means everything to me that you'd commit brain power and time to one of my little stories. Cheers.

REFRACTION EXCERPT

Check out Wick Welker's stand alone sci fi hit ***Refraction***.
Available now in ebook, paperback and audiobook!

WICK WELKER

REFRACTION

PROLOGUE

THE TERRAFORMING of Mars brought harmony to the atmosphere, but not to the inhabitants of the planet. A decade after geosynchronous orbiting mirrors evaporated carbon dioxide and water vapor into the atmosphere, discord raged among the rival colonies. The communities were nestled along the Telephus Mountains, creating territorial disputes, trade wars, and old-fashioned frontier violence. After several years of strife, a council sought to unify the people of Mars into something more noble than themselves:

A utopia.

Each colony elected a representative to attend the first grand council of Mars. The twelve delegates met at a single spot in the Martian wilderness as a symbol of their goals—to forge an unsullied society on fertile ground, liberated from humanity's past mistakes of poverty, starvation, and war. Forming a semi-circle around an enormous bonfire, they sat cross-legged in the rust-colored soil.

The council argued.

Tempers flared, accusations flew, and motivations were questioned. They mutually suspected collusion, spreading distrust like a wildfire. After days of fruitless bickering, the council was on the brink of disbanding. They prepared to return to their colonies and ease back into their prejudices about one another.

On the final evening of the council, an old man appeared from the horizon.

He knew things about the council members. He knew... *everything* about them. He addressed them openly, uncovering their suspicions. He exposed that there *was* collusion—back door agreements between council members. He revealed the truth about the council, that every member intended to take advantage of their neighboring colony. The dream of establishing a utopia on Mars was a pretense for self-interest.

Trust evaporated.

The council was destroyed.

And the old man was never seen again.

The next morning, however, the former council members reconvened in an impromptu assembly. With their secrets exposed, they found they were free to speak—no longer hindered by their suspicions. The truth that the man wielded had thrust them back on equal footing.

They drafted a new government in half a day.

The original colonists concluded their first successful assembly and commissioned a tapestry to be woven. It depicted Mars woven in bright red over the black of space. Earth—in the past and relegated to history—was a small circle in dark blue. The council agreed on a mantra and stitched it into the tapestry:

Live on, Our Hope of the Risen Red.

The city of New Athens was born.

CHAPTER 1: SEPTEMBER 1ST, 1986

BEFORE TIMOTHY STRAUS could save the worlds, he first needed to teach his class. The auditorium at the Georgetown physics department filled quickly. Students cut their chatter and stuffed their bags under chairs. Straus glanced at the front row curiously—the seats had been left empty. Before he could complain about the vacancies, several burly students stuffed themselves into the flimsy seats.

Straus eyed them skeptically. "Does the football team reserve seats now?"

A square-faced student shrugged. "We just like being up front. You're a... really good teacher." His fellow teammates nodded in unison.

He gave them a sidelong look. "That's new."

Straus looked over the auditorium, arms crossed, shaking his head. He tapped his watch and said, "Time is knowledge." He scribbled equations on the chalkboard. "Who recognizes this formula?"

A hand shot up from the back. Straus continued to write as

though he'd forgotten about the question. "Dr. Straus?" the student yelled.

Straus whipped around, strands of black hair falling in his eyes. He pointed at the student. "Yes?"

"Is it a Hamiltonian Wave Function?"

"No," Straus said, pleased that his trap had been sprung. "But I can see why you may have thought that. It does *look* like the Hamiltonian but there is one slight deviation that makes this wave function take on a completely new behavior. Does anyone see it?" He grinned, anticipating they would mirror his enthusiasm.

They stared back, eyes glazed with disinterest.

"No one?" He waited—only a muffled cough in reply. "You see this line integral right here?" He pointed at a symbol. "This single alteration here, if it existed in nature, would completely alter our reality." He let this last part hang in the air. "If that one variation changed, all of our atoms—every single particle that makes up our universe—would *pause* in their natural decay."

The audience was unmoved.

"The elements would never cease to exist but time would still progress. If time progresses without nuclear decay, it means that the matter would travel outside of time. Time would become an irrelevant variable." He lifted a hand with a flourish and looked back at the auditorium.

Someone said, "Pretty neat." A squeal of laughter erupted and then died.

"Yes, yes," Straus surrendered. "Looks like we don't have anyone here interested in *real* physics. Let's get to your homework."

The students pulled out enormous calculators as Straus provided solutions prompting many confused faces. A girl raised her hand and waved it. "Dr. Straus?" she finally chirped.

He looked out over his glasses. "Yes?"

"Can we go over question twelve? A lot of us aren't under-standing—"

"Of course—" His words cut off as a bolt of pain clapped through his head. He grabbed the edge of the table to steady himself. "I—" His mouth went dry.

Please, not now!

A chorus of voices swelled within him.

The voices scrambled together, pushing out the rest of the auditorium, the students—the world. The seams of reality split wide open, ushering a hurricane of voices flooding from a thou-sand worlds at once. The voices washed through him, pushing him to the ground.

As if rehearsed, the front row football team rushed to Straus as he faltered over the lab table. They clung to his limp hands as he sank to the floor.

And then it was over.

Lucidity returned.

He stood and straightened his tie. "I'm fine. I'm just having a very bad headache. You can take your seats, gentlemen." He adjusted his skewed glasses.

The football team gave one another furtive glances. "Are you sure? That was... was that a seizure?"

"No. Everyone, I think we'll cut class a few minutes short today. I'll see you on Wednesday." After a pregnant pause, there was a mad dash for the doors. As students streamed out of the lecture hall, Straus saw the rotund chairman of the physics depart-ment coming down the steps.

"Dr. Van Wert," Straus addressed him mechanically, collecting papers into his briefcase.

"Tim..." Van Wert furrowed his eyebrows.

"Yes?"

"Do you have anything to say about what just happened?"

"Did you ask the football team to sit in the front row today?"

Van Wert feigned surprise and then sighed, "It was just a precaution."

"An unneeded one. It was just a headache."

"Are you sure it wasn't... the other thing?"

"No, I haven't had those—that—in a while."

"It looked a lot like the same problems you were having a few months ago. I only asked those students to sit there to prevent you from falling. And I'm glad that I did."

"I don't have those issues anymore. I've been on some new meds that have worked perfectly." Straus winced at having brought up his medications.

He patted Straus on the shoulder. "I wanted to talk to you about something else..."

Straus looked at the clock. "I'd love to talk but I'm due back in my lab."

Van Wert continued, "I've been observing some of your classes. I'm worried about how you've been... running things."

"It was *just* a migraine," Straus said, frustration growing.

"No, I'm not talking about your... episode just now. It's your mate- rial. You've been teaching things that are way above these students' heads. Half the things you put up there, I don't even understand."

"I just like to have a little fun with them. It's important to show that you can get creative with physics."

"Matter traveling through time? I know you're teaching quantum mechanics but you've got to at least stick to the books. These are undergraduate physics students who can barely even grasp the basics."

Straus shrugged. "It all makes sense mathematically. The math is perfect, check it yourself."

"I can't. I have no idea about half the stuff you're talking about up there. No one does, it's all conceptual... speculation."

"Really, I can show you the math..." He picked up a piece of chalk as if ready for another lecture.

Van Wert put up his hands with a chuckle. "I'm sure you can. But please, stick to the curriculum and pay attention to student questions."

Straus nodded, "I understand. Anything else?"

Van Wert looked at him, hesitating. "I heard about your grant running out soon."

Straus chased a worried look from his face. "I'm optimistic I can renew it with a few tweaks—"

"If your projects were more stable, you might get more sustainable funding. But you're always onto some new pet project before you finish the previous one. A year ago, you were working with a free radical engine and now you're onto this Casimir thing?"

"Casimir Drive," he corrected. "And it's not just a pet project. It's something else—something big. I think it's something that could change the world."

Van Wert stifled a grin and patted Straus on the shoulder. "Of course, Tim. Of course. I would advise you to at least try sticking with this project for more than just a year."

"That won't be a problem. The Casimir Drive is the biggest thing I've ever worked on. It will define my career and, hopefully, much more. It will connect all people together over the planet and maybe even beyond our solar system." Van Wert offered a weak smile that Straus assumed he reserved for himself and perhaps his five-year-old niece.

Without another word, Straus picked up his briefcase while Van Wert watched him exit the classroom. Straus weaved through mazes of lab benches and into the catacombs of the physics department. After a few flights through dank stairwells, he came to his

laboratory door. Sliding his badge, he entered and found his graduate student, Duke, bent over a row of black grids that spanned
the length of the lab. It looked like someone had gutted a dozen
metal filing cabinets and placed them on their backs.

"How did it go?" Straus asked, looking over the grid.

"Bad. The whole thing is heating up." Duke reached for a
wrench. "Not surprised."

"No idea where all this extra heat is coming from," Duke said,
stretching his arms to the ceiling. The back of his shirt clung with
sweat.

"I don't see it when we run the numbers." Straus sat down and
flipped through a notebook. "Doesn't add up. We shouldn't be
generating this much heat. We'll need to get money to transfer the
whole lab to the super-cooled rooms."

"Great, we probably won't get those funds until after I
graduate."

"Assuming we can renew the grant—" Straus saw an unfamiliar girl hovering around the doorway.

Duke stood. "Dr. Straus, this is Chou Jia. She just had her
inter- view for one of our graduate spots. I thought I would show
her around the lab."

"Very good." Straus, still halfway across the lab, shot his arm
out at her unceremoniously. "It's nice to meet you, Chou Jia."

"Oh!" the girl said, surprised at Straus trying to shake her
hand from across the room. She dashed to him and took his hand.

"What makes you interested in the lab?"

"Well," she said, settling her nerves. "I think you have the best
labs on the east coast. Georgetown will definitely be my top
choice. What's that?" She pointed to the rows of black grids.

"Duke, our trap has been sprung. She wants to know about the
Drive. Are you familiar with the Casimir effect?" he asked her.

She bit her lip. "Vaguely."

"The Casimir effect is a phenomenon that occurs when you place two neutrally charged plates extremely close together, which creates negative energy in the space between them. Basically, energy out of a vacuum. What we're doing here," he motioned to the rows of grids, "is exploiting the negative energy produced between subatomic fluctuations."

"Uh-huh."

"There are more quantum fluctuations happening on the outside of the plates than in between the plates, so there is a tremendous amount more of quantum bubbling going on outside of the plates, which pushes them together, creating energy... seemingly out of nothing. We've designed a grid system of plates that are one atom thick and with a space of only one atom wide—extremely small spaces. The smaller the space, the greater negative energy comes out of it. We believe by stacking the atomic plates together, you can create an enormous amount of energy in a very tiny space."

"And what will that do?"

"Ever see Star Trek?"

Duke rolled his eyes as if tired of his overused explanation.

"Of course," Chou Jia said.

"I predict that focusing that amount of energy into such a small space would effectively *bend space*. Like a warp drive."

"Really?"

Straus simply nodded.

"I've never heard of the Casimir effect doing *that*," she said.

"No one has... *yet*. Assuming our funding doesn't run out..." he sighed, souring the mood.

"Dr. Straus," Duke said, "we're trying to get her to *come* to this school, not chase her away..."

"Thanks so much for showing me all of this," she said, sidestep- ping the awkward silence. "I would absolutely love to come here." She stepped over a stack of fallen papers and textbooks. "Thanks for showing me the lab, Dr. Straus. I hope to come back soon."

Straus only nodded and walked away. He sat at a rickety wooden table and poured himself a cup of coffee, letting out a slow breath.

"Do you think we'll be able to finish the Drive?" Duke poured a cup as well.

"I do, yes. I'm optimistic."

"But you're *always* optimistic. You see a half-full glass when there's only a drop left."

"Is that wrong?"

Duke shrugged. "Guess it depends on what you can do with that last final drop."

"Sometimes the final drop is more important than the whole cup," he said, slurping the last of his coffee.

CHAPTER 2: SEPTEMBER 1ST, 1986

TIME IS RUNNING OUT.

Straus picked up a sandwich from a campus deli, his mind muddled. A familiar anxiety churned within, punctuated by panic. It was a panic not about his research. It was a deep-rooted and unspecified paranoia that gnawed at the back of his mind, telling him... something—that time was running out?

Time for what?

He pulled into the parking garage of his apartment building and stared at the cinder blocks through the windshield, waiting for the voices to come—to urge, to incite, to cover his face in a cold sweat. He wanted to get the torrent of voices out of his head before entering his home. "Huh," he said to the empty car. He realized the voices were only from men. It surprised him that he had never thought of it before. He also faced the growing realization that the voices were getting worse.

He walked through the apartment door and saw his wife, Jo, sitting on the couch, breastfeeding. She looked up at him with a concerned frown she reserved only for her husband. "What're you doing home so early? It's not even lunch."

"I wasn't feeling well, had a... bad headache during class."

"Oh..." She switched the baby over her shoulder as it burped. "Just a headache?"

"Yep." He yanked a chair from the kitchen table, sat down, and unwrapped his sandwich.

She sidled up, sitting next to him with the baby in her lap. "We had a good day together—went out to the park. Did you see that it rained a little in the morning?"

"I was teaching."

"Why are you in a bad mood?"

"I'm sorry, hun. Worried about the Drive. Not sure if my grant will get renewed." He took a bite of his sandwich. "I *need* to get the Drive done. Something feels wrong. We have to finish it and finish it soon."

"Want to say hi to James?" She placed the baby into his lap.

He brought James up to his chest, looking into his eyes. The baby looked back with a wide smile. "How's my boy? What great wonders has he accomplished today?" The baby giggled and hopped on his father's lap.

"Why don't you go over and relax in front of the TV for a bit?" Jo offered.

Straus punched the button on the television and lay on the couch as a commercial for laundry detergent flashed across the screen. He suddenly sat up, staring at the screen. "Unbelievable."

Jo walked into the room. "What's wrong?"

"The Russians shot down a commercial airliner from the States," he said, gesturing to the screen.

"What're you talking about?" She pointed at the TV. There was only cascading laundry powder flashing over the screen. A split second later, it flickered with an emergency broadcast banner showing images of smoldering wreckage spewing smoke. "How did you see the news before—"

"Hang on." He turned up the volume.

A newscaster's voice came, "...not certain at the moment what the exact provocation was. We are confirming now that flight 007 from Anchorage to Seoul, South Korea has crashed and it is believed to be a deliberate attack from the Soviet Union on the aircraft. All 269 passengers on the plane are feared dead, including congressman, Lawrence McDonald."

Straus shook his head. "Those poor people. The Soviets will just keep provoking us—stockpiling nukes—and the U.S. will just keep toppling one communist regime after another, killing thousands of innocent lives. Will it ever change?"

"Things change," Jo said, bouncing the baby. "Sometimes it just takes time and the right kind of people."

"That's enough for one day. There's only so much of this world I can take." He switched off the TV set.

Noon turned to evening as Straus napped. He didn't dream but his mind wasn't empty. A rattling of distant voices bubbled up in his mind as he felt himself floating. An infinite horizon lay before him, one seamless ribbon of black. He was floating alone, in space, swathed by starlight. A cloud of silver gas burst around him, swirling with lightning and thunder. A chorus of voices rained down. Each raindrop was a shout or whisper that erupted in his ears. He tried flapping through the fog but was stalled by weightlessness. The voices stirred inside of him and chanted, *he is coming, he is coming, he is coming!* They crescendoed further, *HE IS COMING!*

He snapped awake and realized that the voices had assimilated from a sizzling sound in the kitchen. He looked over the couch and saw Jo moving a frying pan back and forth over the stove. He watched her hair sway in the pleasant way it did when she cooked.

"I'm sorry," he said, coming into the kitchen.

"For what?"

"Being grumpy earlier. It's hard for me sometimes." He touched the back of her apron and rested his forehead on her shoulder.

"It would be hard for anyone. Do you think the new medication is working better?"

"Too soon to tell. I accidentally told Jack Van Wert at work that I'm on meds."

"It's okay. He should know that schizophrenia isn't anyone's fault. It's just something you get, like pneumonia. You don't have any control over it."

He cringed.

"What?"

"I'm still not convinced it's schizophrenia."

"Tim, you hear voices. *Voices*. Auditory hallucinations are a hallmark of schizophrenia."

"I know. But there's more to it than just the voices. I—" he hesitated.

"What?"

"I don't always feel like... *me*. There's something on top of me or under me but it doesn't have anything to do with the *actual* me. And besides, the medications clearly aren't making the voices go away. If anything, they're stronger."

"Should I schedule an appointment to see the doctor tomorrow?"

"That's fine—oh, hey!" He ran out of the kitchen.

"What?" she called from behind.

"The comet that's been on the news... it's supposed to be the brightest tonight. It only comes around once every twenty years."

"Oh." She went back to the kitchen.

Straus ducked out onto their porch overlooking the George-town campus. Swinging his telescope from under the awning, he peered up into the night's sky and saw it—a smudge of blue smeared across the sky. He followed the blue trail as it moved, ignoring the chanting voices bubbling in his mind.

ABOUT THE AUTHOR

Wick Welker writes in multiple genres including medicine, post-apocalyptic and science fiction. He is also a medical doctor who practices critical care medicine and anesthesiology. He is supported by an amazing cat, an incredible wife and an adorable baby girl.

f facebook.com/wickwelker

𝕏 twitter.com/wickwelker

a amazon.com/Wick-Welker/e/B00J21FNRI%3Fref=dbs_a_mng_rwt_scns_share

Printed in the USA
CPSIA information can be obtained
at www.ICGtesting.com
LVHW092025111023
760850LV00001B/1/J